WHAT FAMOUS DEAD GUYS ARE SAYING ABOUT *TIMESLIDER* BY CHEROKEE STEIN ROSS

"If you only read one time-traveler, talking-cat, vampire novel this year, make it *Timeslider* by Cherokee Stein Ross!"

> *Edward III, by the Grace of God King of England, Duke of Aquitaine, Count of Ponthieu, Earl of Chester*

"The Timeslider Cat is awesome! Of course, I really like cats."

> *Akhenaten, once known as Amenhotep IV, Pharaoh of Upper and Lower Egypt, the Living Spirit of Aten*

"I laughed, I cried, and then I laughed again! But I still do not like cats. Josephine, however, does."

> *Napoleon Bonaparte, By the Grace of God and the Constitutions of the Republic Emperor of the French, King of Italy, Protector of the Confederation of the Rhine and the Grand Duchy of Frankfurt, Mediator of the Helvetic Confederation*

"An entertaining tale, one of great profit and moral instruction. And the Timeslider Cat is totally kick-ass!"

> *Benjamin Franklin, patriot, printer, statesman, scientist*

Timeslider

The First Timeslider Cat Novel

CHEROKEE STEIN ROSS

Bishop Lane Media LLC

Author's Website:
www.cherokeesteinross.com

Published in the United States by
Bishop Lane Media LLC
www.bishoplanemedia.com

for my browneyed girls

CONTENTS

Through memory we travel against time, through forgetfulness we follow its course.

Joseph Joubert

The past is never dead. It's not even past.

Faulkner.

PART ONE

Meeting The Doctor

CHAPTER ONE

I've always liked the view from here—from a seat on a low branch in the trees running up the slope from the College. Especially on these clear, late spring nights. My eyes narrow as I scan the still buildings of the campus down the slope. White moonlight broken with black shadows. The night air is full of honeysuckle and the thrumming of insects. I can hear the tiny stirrings of mice at the grassy base of the ancient oak below me—tempting. I can sense the owls watching on limbs of trees higher than mine. But I'm not leaving this perch, not now. I'll concede the mice to those owls this time. I curl my tail around my haunches, and close my eyes as I briefly wash a paw.

Yes, of course: I am a cat. Small and half-grown—a kitten, if you will. Tiger-striped fur, short-haired, with a white belly and white socks. Pretty ordinary markings, really; if I were to list myself in my mental catalogue of natural phenomena, I admit it would be a prosaic entry. Something like: "*CAT – COMMON – STRIPED.*" But a valid entry, nonetheless. Fully consistent with scientific method. Because I am a scientist, and I take pride in viewing the entire world as a scientist, even myself. And the first responsibility of a good scientist is taxonomy, is it not? Classification. What is the thing—whatever it is? How would you describe it? How would you list its features? How would you relate it to other things, similar or different? I'm a scientist, and that's the way I deal with the world. But, even so, I'm conscious of a tiny voice in the back of my mind that regrets my scientific classification would be so ordinary. A cat's pride, after all, might still desire to be a little more unique. A little less ordinary than a mere, tiger-striped tabby.

But I suppose that being a mere unremarkable cat is to my advantage in my present circumstances. It's better for me to remain unnoticed, invisible. Because, in fact, I am more than just a mere cat. I'm a very special cat indeed. For one thing, I am over 6,000 years old. With an array of special talents. Telepathy, for instance—well, you understand about the telepathy, since although I make no sound you can hear my every word in your mind. (Quite unlike your own cat, I am sure.) A capacious intelligence, a prodigious memory—I have learned and remember more than you will ever dream of knowing in ten of your lifetimes. As for the rest, my other skills and talents—well, let's just leave it that I am a very special cat. I may explain more to you later. Or I may not. I mean no disrespect, but I just don't know that I should tell too much to you. We've only just met.

But despite being a cat I am, as I said, a scientist, and I find humans to be of infinite interest. And look at this place—as a venue to study humans, it's perfect. The place is called Forshay College, a small women's college in the American South, close above the South Carolina border, only about thirty-five miles west of Charlotte. On very clear nights, if I scamper up the slope of Forshay Mountain above the campus and leap into the highest branches there, I can even see the tiny glowworm of the city skyscrapers gleaming beyond the meanders of the Catawba River. Sometimes I gaze at that skyline for much of the night—it reminds me of the great cities I have lived in, and makes it seem like those city streetscapes aren't so far away. But back here in Forshay, the great advantage is the College's isolation. It's a population set aside in woodsy foothills where the land begins to rise into the Blue Ridge, away from the noise and highways leading to Atlanta and Washington. Here, a scientist like me has a properly controlled, integrated sample for observation. It's so much easier to understand humans if you limit the experiment.

In one way or another I have lived with humans for centuries, millennia. People flow through my sweep of time like water through a riverbed; they make their brief appearances, they make some lovely noise, and then they're gone. But in all those various times in all those various ages I have always attached myself to one human in particular, one special one. And that's why I am on this perch tonight, on this low limb in this oak tree—because the Visiting Faculty houses are ranged along the slope going down from here, and this limb is within easy kitten-leaping distance to the windowsill of the first house on the row, where my owner Renata lives.

I say "owner" but of course she's not literally that. She doesn't own me any more than I own her. She does leave a dish of cat food every day for me on the stained linoleum floor of the tiny alleyway in her house that the College audaciously claims constitutes a kitchen. And that is much appreciated on days when the mice are scarce. But *owning* me—no. If pressed, I would say maybe that we're friends, confrères, buddies, even if I don't think she has ever quite realized exactly who—*what*—I am. I can hear her thinking, just as I can hear any human thinking. But can she hear me? I don't know. I don't think so.

Still, I look out for her, protect her. If you saw her, you would think she looks like the type of human that other humans so often seem to take advantage of: a pretty, young female, on her own, trying hard. It's the other

3

reason I'm still waiting on this tree limb outside her window in the warm moonlight, listening. Because I saw the human who went into her house with her an hour ago.

He's a human who would fall into the classification of "Bully." I know that humans use all sorts of classification systems for other humans—classes based on age, colors of hair or hide, or weight, or decimal places in bank accounts, or geography of their ancestors' birth, all that. Or standard human-scientific biological classification—how does it go? Domain, kingdom, phylum, class, order, family, genus, species? But *homo sapiens sapiens* just means human being— how does that help to explain anything? All such human classification systems seem like random nonsense to me. I use my own classification scheme for humans, and after 6,000 years I find my categories far more useful. Human systems are based on misunderstandings, and they change from place to place and time to time. My classifications are *functional,* and make far more sense. In my system some humans are Feeders, some are Protectors, some are Helpers, some are Agree-ers. And some are Bullies.

My observation of humans over the centuries has revealed to me that, while most humans seem to have many different threads woven into their make-ups, one thread always seems to predominate. And this one, the visitor whom the students call Mr. Cuthbert but Renata calls Trace—he's a Bully, pure and simple. He's the Assistant Director of the College's Department of Buildings and Grounds. That sounds as if it should be a position of some discretion and responsibility, but you would need to know a couple things. First, the only *other* person in the Department of Buildings and Grounds is the actual Director—a small, rodentlike man named Tug Martin, who seems neither to ever leave his office nor to ever hang up his telephone. And second, since Trace Cuthbert constitutes the entire balance of the departmental staff, his being Assistant Director doesn't carry with it any duties that involve actually *directing* anyone. Rather, as best

4

I can determine from my observations, Trace Cuthbert's duties consist entirely of mowing the splendid green lawns that spread like velvet across the Forshay campus, beneath the canopy of its massive oaks. Usually, with his shirt off. And with a sheen of suntan oil gleaming on his (admittedly) well-proportioned torso. That expanse of sleek, bronzed muscles between Trace's black goatee and the waistband of his jeans doesn't escape the notice of the undergraduate girls. Bully though he might be, wherever Trace Cuthbert is working on a hot day always just happens to become the popular place for the Forshay students to sit outdoors and complete their reading.

In any event, my prior studies with other groups of humans have led me to think that there is a natural bias among humans in favor of Bullies. Certainly all the Legionary commanders I knew on the Roman frontiers were Bullies, including both of my owners who became Emperors. And the *gran seigniors* during my life in 15th century France—cruel, vicious Bullies to a man. But this society seems different. Surely many Bullies rise to the top here. All the American politicians would fit into that category, as well as most business executives and NASCAR drivers. But a cat can see perfectly well that in this society many Bullies don't rise high—they become instead, in the local vernacular, "losers"—and one keeps an eye out for them. Particularly if one's owner would be classified in a category that is very incompatible. And here my classification of Renata becomes relevant, because I am confident that Renata would be properly classified not only as a Helper, but as a *Teacher*—the very highest subcategory of Helper, and one into which, incidentally, only a very few of the humans who call themselves "teachers" would actually fall. But a true Teacher getting romantically involved with an underachieving Bully? No. My scientific conscience would not countenance that.

And then of course, then there's the incompatibility inherent in Renata's other classification, a very unique and rare classification. Renata is a vampire.

OK, OK—you don't have to say it; I know what you're thinking: *Vampires again! We're all sick of vampires!* Look, I'm not trying to jump on any vampire bandwagon. In fact, I don't even understand what it is about human culture at this moment in the postindustrial world that has created your present fascination with vampires. That's a question you mortal humans should be asking yourselves, not a cat. And believe me, I'm not interested in all the adolescent, sex-saturated, sparkly, bosom-heaving nonsense that seems to dominate the current vampire meme. Don't get me wrong, I don't have any problem with vampire fantasy stories as entertainment. Sexy vampires can be fun!—I understand that. But I'm a scientist. When I relate facts, I do it rigorously. And the vampires I've known are the real thing—they're not your little sister's vampires. I feel a scientific obligation to impart accurate data, and the writers and filmmakers who have been doing all those vampire stories recently are just all over the place with their facts. For one thing you just can't trust them to get vampire physiology straight. You'll hate me for saying this, but they've got the vampire reproductive system all wrong.

Sorry, I didn't mean to rant. I just don't want you to get the wrong idea about my intentions. When I speak of vampires I'm not speaking as an entertainer, or trying to give some artistic impression. Or, perhaps you think that when I speak about vampires, I'm speaking figuratively— that my references to vampires are instances of metaphor, or hyperbole, or some other subtle figure of speech, as that nice, black-skinned Mr. Pearson might term it. (I learn so much sleeping under his desk during his freshman English comp lectures.) But no—when I say Renata is a vampire I mean it quite literally. It is a simple, biological descriptor. I know you've been conditioned to regard vampires as fabulous creatures, fantastic, supernatural. But it's easy to misperceive the natural for the supernatural. After all, the difference between natural and supernatural is only a matter of the adequacy of data. A very wise human once said that a sufficiently advanced technology is indistinguishable from magic. Well, as it is with technology, so it is with the supernatural. Once a supposedly supernatural phenomenon is explained, understood, categorized—poof!, it's no longer supernatural, is it? The magic disappears, and it becomes just part of the ordinary, observable, natural world. Vampires are just like any other classification of humans— they *are*, after all, humans, albeit dead ones—and I have known several during my long acquaintance with people.

But I've learned that Renata is very special as a vampire, much as I am a very special cat. For one thing, she hides her vampirism, and blends in among the rest of humanity as if she were just another ordinary mortal person. She lives in her Visiting Faculty housing, drives her beat-up old car around Forshay village, prepares her notes, delivers her lectures, meets with her students. Lives her life unobtrusively, going about her workday, and all the while her special condition resides there, just below the surface.

But even more unusual than that is Renata's mind. When I listen to Renata's mind what I hear is different from every other vampire mind I have ever listened to. As a rule vampires' minds are dull things. They have a fixed and staring quality, like the eye of a corpse. The vampire's mind is a simple reflection of what it perceives around it, registering only its present moment, recalling nothing of its past, anticipating nothing of its future. Vampire minds lack the complexity, the music of mortal minds. Despite—maybe because of—their immortality, vampires have boring minds—limpid, flat, immobile.

Renata's mind is different, though. When I listen to her mind, behind the flat tread of the vampire mind I hear a kind of roiling background noise, similar to the mind of a mortal human: a compound of fear and gladness, resentment and expectation, love and hate. The music of emotion—that is the essential character of the mortal mind, and Renata's vampire mind seems to share it, though in a curiously stunted way. It is as if vestigial echoes of the emotions that bathed her mind during her mortal life keep trying to rise to the surface, but remain just out of her mind's grasp. I have often wondered if it was this quality of her mind—its strain of mortal music— that has led her to her current life of fellow-travelling with mortal humans. I don't know. Through our years together she has never confided in me about her secret life as a vampire. I doubt she has any idea that her cat knows her secret. I am absolutely certain that Trace Cuthbert doesn't know.

I hear a breeze rustling the leaves above me—is that an owl's call? No, I hear other noises, ones that make my cat's eyes go wide and bring me softly to my feet. I listen again before testing the branch, first one white paw, then the other. Yes, the sound is unmistakable. The humans are mating. I have to move.

I leap from the tree limb to the windowsill silently. The window is only barely open, but a small cat can squeeze through remarkably tiny spaces. I am through; I drop to the floor in the darkened kitchen, and scamper like an optical illusion along the shadowed baseboards. My food dish is nearby, but there's no time to check it now— I'll come back soon. Through the dark hallway, slipping into the bedroom through the wide-open door. I can hear the breathing, the loud banging of bedframe against wall. The odd vocalizations that humans make at these times— surely that's worth a research monograph of its own some day. But I haven't come for scientific observation this time. I'm here to break this scene up. I spot a chair just opposite the left side of the bed; a quick, silent leap onto it brings me eye level to where, one further jump away, the blankets have fallen away and exposed a pair of big and extremely white male buttocks, working away. The contrast with Trace's suntanned skin beyond his tan line makes them seem incandescent. I think to myself what I have thought a hundred times before, observing humans in this posture: How ridiculous.

My jump from the chair was perfectly timed. I caught the left buttock in mid-thrust and dug my claws in. I scratched with my rear paws a few times before scampering over the right cheek as well, and then launching myself up Trace's back as he reared out of the bed in pain and surprise, screaming and grabbing his butt. But I was already up the curtains, down the wall and rocketing out the door.

CHAPTER TWO

"Son of a *bitch!*" Trace Cuthbert was on his feet and hurling his heavy shoe out the door after me, before Renata could react. But little cats are quick, and I easily dodged the shoe as it caromed down the dark hallway. I then turned and skittered silently along the dark baseboard again, slipping unseen back into the bedroom.

"Jesus! Did you see that?" Trace was waving his arms, shouting. "Did you see what that fucking cat did?" He peered awkwardly over his shoulder, trying to see the welts rising where my claw-marks scratched his skin. I thought he was making quite a fuss over it—after all, I am only a small cat. Granted, there is the surprise factor, but really.

But what was more concerning to me was the look coming over Renata's face, a look I knew well. I saw her now sitting up in the bed, clearly illuminated in the moonlight from the window. The softness had left her expression, and her mouth and eyebrows were setting into an adamantine immobility starkly different from her usual sweet smile. Her eyes hardened into a fixed and penetrating stare, the irises glittering in the moonlight as if replaced with chips of shattered glass. It was unmistakable: the thanadoxicil must have been wearing off, because here was Renata's vampirism, rising to the surface.

"Fuckin' cat," Trace muttered, looking for his other shoe. He reached down to the floor for it, putting his head low by the side of the bed. And although I froze immediately as he bent down, I knew that he had spotted me, not four feet away. A sudden fear seized me. I knew that I had slipped up: a momentary inattention, looking at Renata when I should have been careful to stay out of Trace's line of sight. Trace grabbed the shoe by its laces and, as he swung it back behind his shoulder, I knew that this was going to be bad news. Not for me. For him.

"Leave the cat alone!"

Renata's voice resonated in a way that should have been impossible for such a small woman. It sounded unnatural, as if it had originated from a deep, stony well, somewhere several feet off to the side of her—hollow, ringing, portentous. She was out of the bed, walking slowly toward Trace, the small, black-nippled breasts over her ribcage and the points of her hipbones casting dark shadows on her pallid skin in the moonlight. *"Leave the cat alone!"*

I tried to signal a message, a warning, to Trace as he stood towering over Renata in the dark room, but he didn't get it. Bullies are like that. They're basically pretty thick.

"Are you kidding?" he bellowed. "Fuckin' critter just scratched *the shit* out of my back, man! I've *had* it with that little piece of…"

He didn't finish that sentence because his face crashed into the wall. Eight feet he had flown through the air, his errant left arm sweeping a cascade of cosmetic bottles off Renata's dresser. His forehead had left a nice dent in the plaster, and as he turned over onto his back on the floor I saw that the abrasion the wall had made above his left eye was beginning to redden. Beginning to *bleed*. Renata was slowly approaching him from across the room. This, I knew, was getting out of hand.

There was no way I could help him directly. He was a big specimen—undeniably handsome, I'll give that much to Renata's animal tastes—but at over two hundred semi-conscious pounds a small tiger-striped kitten was not going to provide any physical assistance. All I had immediately at hand were my needlelike claws, which I had already demonstrated could get Trace's attention. I'd have to try the same once more. As Trace groggily struggled to his hands and knees, I sprang onto his back again, clawed in, and leaped up to the light switch on the wall. The pain snapped him back and onto his feet, so that he missed most of the force of the next blow Renata delivered before the sudden light blinded her, and sent her creeping back toward the bathroom. Still, the force was enough to propel him sliding, headfirst, down the hallway and spring the doorlatch on the front door. I heard him grab his first shoe (he still gripped the other by its laces) and stagger out the broken door. The light in the bedroom went off as I slipped out the front door and followed Trace partway down the sidewalk, toward the main campus. I didn't know how hurt he was. Renata already had enough trouble with the College without Trace Cuthbert turning up dead outside her doorway, naked and holding his shoes in his hands.

But Trace managed to walk heavily away in the dark. I followed him for a few paces. When I had satisfied myself that Trace was whole enough to make it back to his car in the main parking lot I stopped, and returned to my tree limb to watch. I saw a pair of headlights switch on and a car turn slowly—very slowly, like a car driven by a man with an excruciatingly sore head—and go out of the campus lot. The car drove slowly back down Ridge Street to Main, and crept its way out of Forshay village.

But then, as I watched Trace's car making its painful progress away, I spied another, quicker movement in the corner of my eye. It was only for a moment, but it seemed as if a woman, all gleaming white, had stood in the black and white shadows of the campus before fleeing into the foliage verging the lawns. But it must have been a trick of the moonlight—I looked again, and instead the movement I saw was a dark, solitary figure darting from the South Dorm on the other side of Main Street. I watched as the figure ran from the shadows of the oak trees by the dorm entrance to a long, low car idling on Main Street in front of the dark movie theater, its headlights off. The figure reached the car and, as it pulled the car door open and hurriedly climbed in, I saw a dark ponytail switch from side to side from under a baseball cap. The long car struggled as it drove off, its exhaust system hoarse and complaining as it accelerated slowly out of the village. I watched for a few moments longer, wondering at the curious coincidence of the simultaneous, furtive escapes of Trace and the other figure. The figure with the ponytail was clearly a student illicitly sneaking off campus. The curfew rules at Forshay College—for junior faculty as well as undergraduates—were strict, in closer keeping with the mores of the 1940's than the 21st century. Had she seen Trace leaving Renata's house? But I dismissed the worry. Whoever she was, she would hardly admit to violating the student curfew just so she could inform on Trace Cuthbert driving his car slowly away from the campus, naked and holding a hand on his bleeding scalp. There seemed to be no risk. I hopped down the tree once more and slipped back into the darkness of Renata's house.

When I found Renata she was in the bathroom, sitting on the edge of the tub. She had already prepared the first injection of thanadoxicil and was intently slipping the silvery hypodermic into the flesh between her toes. Vampire skin carries puncture marks in ways that other human skin doesn't—big, discolored purply splotches that could disfigure an arm or leg, calling attention to themselves and defeating Renata's efforts to pass unnoticed. Renata had experimented with injections everywhere—scalp, fingernails, pelvis. Between the toes seemed to be the best compromise between discomfort and concealment. The dose was already taking its effect. She had had it prepared; she must have known the last treatment was ready to wear off. She prepared the second hypodermic and laid it on a tray by the sink, next to the smooth, dark mahogany box the supply of thanadoxicil always arrived in. She would take that dose another four hours hence. I came in and paraded by her other foot, rubbing on her ankle.

"Kikki!" Her voice was back to normal, her English carrying just the edge of the French accent she had never completely lost. "Are you all right?" She reached down to stroke my back; I arched my spine in pleasure as she reached the base of my tail. "Well, I wonder what we'll say to Trace Cuthbert tomorrow. I can't believe he did that," she said, shaking her head slowly. She looked away, distracted, still massaging the medicine into the flesh of her toes. "I can't believe *I* did that," she said softly.

CHAPTER THREE

"Kikki!"

It was early—*very* early, not yet 6:00 a.m., and still before sunrise. In the blue morning light Renata's voice came bright and clear, as if the strangeness of the night before were a mere imagining. Renata was at the hall table near the front door, fussing with her keys and white scarf and the big ring, red with an enameled white star, that she always wore on her left index finger. She picked up a handful of misdirected mail that had dropped through the slot in the front door yesterday. Catalogues, advertisers, bills, various miscellaneous personal mail that didn't go to the college mailboxes, and all addressed to a Miss Kjerstin Thorstad, who Renata had been told was both the prior occupant of her house and her immediate predecessor as Visiting Lecturer in the Forshay history department. Renata knew that Kjerstin Thorstad had moved on to the University of Gothenburg in Sweden, but had apparently never told the post office about the change of address. Even a year later, a steady flow of Kjerstin Thorstad's mail dropped regularly through the mail slot. Renata lifted her broad canvas bag onto the table and pushed the mail in— she could have it forwarded later. She held open the canvas bag for me to slip into as well and I climbed in, finding my footing among her pens and lecture notes and the student essays that she had stayed up late grading as she had waited for the second dose of thanadoxicil to finally take hold. I poked my whiskered face out the top as she shouldered the bag, slipped on a pair of large round sunglasses, and briskly started walking down the slope toward the village.

Forshay College was, according to its promotional pamphlets, the "Pre-Eminent Women's College of the Upper South" (though I think that Salem College up in Winston might take issue with that claim). It was unquestionably a pretty place, its campus ringing the small Piedmont village of Forshay in the North Carolina hills, and the college students and faculty mingling with the local townspeople. BMW's and Audi's driven by wealthy faculty or the occasional spoiled upperclassman shared the slanted parking spaces on Main Street with ancient Ford pickups that dated from an era when the Beatles were hot new act. The faculty housing Renata lived in ran up a dead end side street, up the slope leading to the mountain ridge; the campus proper and Forshay village lay in the valley below, along a small rushing stream that everyone called The River. The willow oaks along the green in the middle of the village were huge, more than a century old, with twisted roots that looked like giant feet beneath gray robes, the fine halo of leaves above like green mist in the distant morning air. It was mid-May and finals were approaching—it was too early for the students to be out. We did not meet any as we reached the village and hurried along to the row of stores on the far side of the green to the Sisters' Store. Coffee. Even vampires need coffee in the morning.

"Hey Renata, doll," Beth said as we swung in the old glass door. Beth and Lucy were the owners of the store, and one of them was always behind the counter at first light. Middle-aged, gray-haired, courteous to everyone—

by scientific classification they were classic Feeders. All the townspeople knew they were a lesbian couple from New York who had bought out the old River General Store twenty years ago or more, and had redone it as a coffee shop-cum-restaurant-cum-touristy gift shop. But, village sensibilities having been what they were in those days, the women had prudently at first told the townspeople that they were sisters. And so all these years later they were still always referred to as The Sisters— except by a handful of elderly Forshayans who insisted on calling them "Miss Lucy" and "Miss Beth." The old folks' sense of polite forms of address was not mitigated by anything, not even by Beth's New York accent or Lucy's tattoos. Even so, the incongruity of being called "Miss Beth" by some formidable local dowager still tickled Beth's East Village sense of humor.

But the refurbished store quickly became a hit with both the town and the college people. The Sisters hadn't changed much in the store, to outward appearances. The windows still carried the faded lettering of antique advertisements for carriage wheels and buggies. The walls were still of the same weathered plank they had always been, and a variety of rusting farm implements, mule collars, and gas station calendars six decades expired were still nailed to the venerable walls. To the Sisters, the historicity of the artifacts was fundamental to the store's charm. But, small-town sensibilities notwithstanding, everyone in Forshay liked the big-city idea that the Sisters had imported of really, really good coffee—and the local Forshayans especially liked the fact that the coffee was fresh and ready by 5:30 in the morning.

"Morning," Renata answered. She waited as a pair of farm workers in overalls and faded t-shirts paid for their morning coffee. I glanced from my perch in the canvas bag—cinnamon house blend, I saw. The farm workers were Latinos—Mexican or Central American, each with a long, aquiline face and a thatch of black hair. They murmured quietly between themselves in a language I couldn't catch—it wasn't Spanish, though—as they carefully rolled the bills of their change back into their money rolls. The growing season in the Piedmont was already in full flower, and crews of migrant workers were unobtrusively filling the fields in the valley below the ridge as they did every year at this time. The pair smiled shyly as they turned and found Renata behind them at the counter. Renata had not removed her sunglasses.

"Buenos," one said, nodding politely to Renata as he took the coffee and an English toffee scone in his calloused hands, and walked away toward a dusty green truck parked outside.

"Usual?" Beth asked Renata. "Large Columbian, two sweetener, lots of cream?"

"Why don't you give me what our friends had," Renata answered, motioning toward the truck. "That scone looked good."

"Ah, hungry this morning I see." Beth grabbed one of the scones from the glass case and put it on a thick plate. Coffee appeared next on the counter, steam billowing out of the tall mug.

"And, some extra cream," Beth said, laugh lines creasing her eyes as she poured a generous puddle of cream onto another saucer. "Come on, Kikki, pets are welcome at dawn. The Health department's nowhere to be seen this early."

Renata put the saucer of cream on the old pavingstones of the floor by a wobbly table near the window to the street—the old River General Store, I have heard, used to be a blacksmith in ancient days, and the stone floor had never been covered over. Beth came over and sat down with Renata, glancing at the sheaf of papers in the bag. Beth was short and stocky, and she smoothed a blunt-fingered hand over her helmet of short, steel-gray hair. I liked Beth—Feeder as she was, she assumed an air of aggressive protectiveness in favor of anyone within the ambit of her affection. That included me as well as Renata. If I were ever in a fight, I should like to have Beth on my side.

"How's that article coming, the one you were working on for that historical quarterly in Atlanta?" she asked. "Any progress?"

Renata made a face. "Ugh. Let's not talk about it."

"Sorry," Beth said. "Didn't mean to needle you. It's just that you seemed to be doing great with it last week."

Renata sighed. "Oh, that's OK. I don't mean to be grouchy. But I really do need to get it together, or they're going to cancel my contract for next year."

"You mean, that turd Claude Preen? He could do that?"

"Absolutely. He's the Chairman of the History Department. If fact, I think he's looking forward to it."

"So that's the deal? Either you publish an article by the end of the year or you're out?"

"Not in so many words, but effectively, yes—'publish or perish'." Renata gave a quick peep over her sunglasses. "And I am perilously close to perishing."

Beth stood up, a look of determination in her eyes as she wiped her hands on her apron. "Not going to happen," she said, "not if we can do anything about it. Didn't Lucy look at your first draft—what, a month ago? She said it was really good. And she really knows. She's got her masters in history from NYU, you know. And she could've got her Ph.D too if she hadn't, you know..."

"Got swept off her feet by the love of her life?" Renata asked.

Beth smiled, abashed. "Yeah," she admitted. Her formidable confidence seemed suddenly softened by the thought of her partner. "You know, I've told Lucy a hundred times we could go back if she really wanted to finish her degree. But she doesn't want to—she says she likes it here, she likes the store. It's more simple." Beth paused, crossing her arms reflectively. "She grew up in

North Carolina, you know—Gaston county, just east of here. Ran away to New York when she was seventeen—couldn't abide high school. And besides, I think that was before she realized she was gay. I mean, *really* realized it. And so then, ten years in New York—ten years of hairstyles, tattoos, piercings. When I met her, I sure didn't notice anything North Carolina about her anymore. But I guess she never forgot. Somehow she heard about this store and, well, here we are." Beth paused again, perhaps thinking of Lucy asleep in the rooms above the store—if Beth was in the store early, Lucy would be on the late shift. "Besides," Beth said, "she says she could always do the work on her doctorate at the College here, if she wanted to."

"Ah, then we'd both be beholden to Preen," Renata said, smiling, "and that's not something I'd wish upon my enemies, much less my dear friends."

Beth laughed and walked back to the coffee counter, where a trickle of customers—now including some college people—was beginning to flow in. I finished my cream, silently leaped onto the table and sat, quietly cleaning my paws and watching Forshay village awaken through the ancient, foggy windows. I listened to the thoughts flowing through the minds of Renata and Beth—over my shoulder, as it were—as I looked through the windows. Beth's thoughts sailed smoothly along a happy swell of warmth, the recollection of her early days with Lucy. Renata's mind labored. She was going over her class notes for her 9:00 a.m. section of Europe Since The Renaissance, before she finished grading the stack of student essays. Her vampire mind re-absorbed the information that she was to teach, information that her sluggish memory struggled to retain despite having re-learned it a dozen times. The end of World War I was today—in her lecture, I mean. The withdrawal of Russia from the fighting after the 1917 Revolution. The arrival of the Americans. The Treaty of Versailles. National self-determination. The settlements among the powers: France with Germany, Italy with Austria, Turkey with Greece.

At that last thought, I heard Renata's mind suddenly lurch unexpectedly, an involuntary spasm like a child kicking in the womb. It startled me—where did *that* come from? It puzzled me. It felt as if there was something buried in Renata's mind, and it was trying to assert itself. Could it be some kind of deep memory lurking there? I was tempted to dismiss the idea; vampire minds don't have the capacity for that kind of memory. The moment passed so quickly, though, that it hardly registered—certainly Renata did not seem to notice it. But it intrigued me. I settled back to watching the village outside the store window, and filed the episode away—yet another piece of data attesting to my vampire owner's uniqueness.

The College and village outside the window of the Sisters' Store was quickening; bleary-eyed girls walked with backpacks from the dorms across the green toward the classroom buildings, professors were arriving in their cars from their smart homes in tony mountain subdivisions nearby. It has always surprised me how charming humans are in the morning. There is a quietness, a docility that pervades human society as the humans shake off the effects of sleep. It does not seem to matter whether they are in an idyllic college town, in a metropolitan center, in a war zone—there is a sweetness about humans at this time of day. They're just adorable.

Renata checked her watch and began scooping her papers back into her canvas bag. I skittered back into the bag just as she picked it up, and shouted, "Bye, Beth!" over her shoulder. I poked my head out again as we hurried across the green to the history classrooms.

The history department was housed in the Everett Building, which also contained the student union, the infirmary, the cafeterias, the Fed Ex drop-off and the administration offices. It was the buzzing heart of the campus. A steady flow of students and faculty entered the main door and into a main corridor, which halfway down the building's length intersected another corridor at the perpendicular. The staircases to the upper floors rose from the intersection. It was the perfect center of all human traffic of the College; one way or the other almost everyone would need to pass that point at some time during any given day. And there, vigilant as a stone guardian sitting before a Chinese temple, sat Margaret, erect at her desk and sternly watching the faces stream past her.

Margaret Viper was technically only the secretary to the Dean of Students, but in fact she was much more. She knew more about what happened at Forshay College than anyone—more than the deans, more than the faculty, certainly more than the President. In the days before e-mail and online document management, all student and faculty mail had been delivered by means of a rack of hanging folders to the side of her desk, and every student and every professor of necessity made a daily stop to see Margaret. Those days were gone, of course, as were the mail folders, but packages, Fed Ex boxes, flower bouquets, engraved invitations—anything that was a physical communication still passed through her hands. She was supposed to put a slip of paper into the locked mailboxes next to the Student Union downstairs to tell a recipient to retrieve a package or note she was holding for them, but she rarely did. Anyone who was expecting anything knew without being told that Margaret would have it. Her respect for everybody's privacy was scrupulous—no breath of suspicion ever fell that Margaret would ever improperly *read* anyone else's mail—but she nonetheless somehow gleaned enough intelligence to know, with impressive accuracy, what was contained in each parcel, what news lay in each envelope, what was going on in each life. She had a dour and frosty demeanor, reputedly honed back when the rules about the girls' uniforms were even more strict than the curfew rules. Her eagle eyes still seemed to measure the passing hemlines and necklines disapprovingly. The uniforms were gone now, but Margaret remained an intimidating obstacle that each person at Forshay College had to negotiate in her daily life. And, despite her odd (and strangely appropriate) surname, she never acquired a nickname derivative of "viper". No one ever called her "The Snake Lady," no one ever called her desk "The Viper's Nest." Every year, of course, some enterprising freshmen would try, thinking themselves very original and witty. But the nicknames they attempted to hang on Margaret never stuck. It was as if, eventually, everyone concluded that there was nothing scarier to call Margaret than just Margaret.

Over the course of the academic year, I had made an art of avoiding Margaret. I knew without asking what Margaret's view would be on cats parading through the halls of the Everett Building. On my peregrinations through the campus, even when those took me through Everett, I have always given Margaret's desk a wide berth. No sense antagonizing her—and besides, for a small cat like myself, remaining unseen in such a large and busy place is fairly easy. And yet, any time I traversed the building the thought of Margaret sitting a few yards away never failed to provide a small jolt of anxiety. Somehow I always felt that she knew I was there anyway, the way you can feel the eyes of an unseen watcher. Over the whole year, Margaret still hadn't caught me in Everett; on days when I rode into class in Renata's canvas bag, I made a point of burrowing down deep among the papers and hiding as we passed Margaret's desk, my mind trying ignore the feeling that somehow Margaret's penetrating gaze could still see me as we passed. Margaret makes me nervous.

Renata's classroom for her lecture that morning was on the second floor. As she moved hurriedly through the corridor, now filling with girls rushing to morning classes, she made a quick nod and smile toward Margaret's desk before starting up the stairs. She made two steps, no more, before Margaret's voice hailed her.

"Miss Beaumanoir! Something for you here!" The miracle of Margaret's voice was not its volume, for she never spoke loud; it was its penetration. Imperative but hardly above a conversational tone, it cut through the ambient hubbub demanding to be heard. Renata stopped short and turned around. She crept back down the stairs, as timid before Margaret as any of the girls.

"Yes, Margaret? How are you this morning?" Renata ventured.

Margaret paused pointedly, as if slightly disappointed. "You know, it's really not done to wear sunglasses indoors, Miss Beaumanoir. Especially at nine in the morning."

Renata obediently slid the glasses off her face and folded them into a case in the canvas bag. Margaret wasn't even watching; she was reaching into the bottom drawer of her desk and continuing to speak, as if she needn't even look to see if Renata were complying with her direction to remove the offending sunglasses. "Professor Preen asked me to ask you to stop by his office immediately after your morning class. And no, he did not say what it was about. And here," she said, extending her hand. "This came for you." She gave a sniff. "I must say I wouldn't have expected you to be receiving perfumed letters at your age."

Renata was looking at the envelope in her hand, and it was clear she recognized it. It was heavy cream stationary, with a black border and a cursive, deeply embossed *"VCA"* lettered on the flap. No return address or other identification. And yes, it was perfumed. The Vampire Council of America always drenched their letters in perfume. If they didn't, the smell of death that would have clung to the paper would have been off-putting at best— and at worst, could have prompted the involvement of public health authorities. For a while the Vampire Council used "Eternity," by Calvin Klein. They thought that was funny as hell.

"Miss Beaumanoir, is everything all right?"

Margaret was peering closely at Renata—more precisely, at Renata's eyes. They were a mess. No wonder she had stuck with the sunglasses all morning. Bloodshot, slightly swollen, faint bluish circles like old bruises underneath, she looked for all the world as if she had spent the night with a whiskey bottle. It was the thanadoxicil, of course, or, to be exact, having let the thanadoxicil wear off in the first place. I didn't expect Renata to tell Margaret that she was feeling poorly because she is a vampire and her vampirism had resurfaced the night before. However, she put Margaret off more deftly than I thought she was up to this morning.

"Yes, fine," she said. She held up the envelope. "I just fear this may be bad news." Renata slipped the letter (which of course looked exactly like a death announcement—another piece of Vampire Council humor) into her bag and moved to head back up the stairs. "Thank you so much for your concern, Margaret." Nicely done, girl, I thought.

Margaret of course insisted on the last word. "I hope it was not anyone close, dear," she said, full of reptilian empathy. "Our condolences, in any case." *Our.* As if she spoke on behalf of the entire College. As if the main thing were not whatever death in the family Margaret imagined Renata to have suffered, but instead Margaret's splendid, superior sympathy about it. A Bully. Classic Bully behavior.

Suddenly a voice, unbidden, sounded in my mind as clear as a bell.

Oh, a Bully, am I?

The words startled me. When Renata had shoved the Vampire Council letter into her bag—deep into her bag, almost involuntarily trying to bury it, it seemed—I had popped my head and one mittened paw out the top to make way. Now Margaret was glaring at me, and I found myself fixed by her stare. At the moment she seemed very much deserving of the surname Viper. But how was she talking to me? Could it be possible that she knew what I was? Could it be possible that I had misjudged what she was?

"Miss Beaumanoir, is that a cat in your bag?"

Renata froze. "Sorry? A cat?"

"Yes. A cat. In. Your. Bag." Margaret's finger pointed repeatedly, emphasizing each word. For the second time in twelve hours I, who scrupulously try to remain among the unseen, felt myself uncomfortably in the spotlight. "I'm sorry, Miss Beaumanoir, but you know that the rules are strict about pets in the College buildings. And teachers must be all the more scrupulous, as you set an example for our girls. Now, you must take it out."

"Yes, Margaret, of course," Renata gushed. "As soon as class is over!" Renata gathered herself and hustled off up the stairs at a run.

"No, Miss Beaumanoir, *now!*"

"Sorry, can't be late for class! Thank you again, Margaret!"

I think she put the bag under her arm with my head poking out the back on purpose, so my kitten face and whiskers would bob tauntingly at Margaret as she bounded off up the stairs. A group of girls heading up behind us had spotted me, all making the *"awww!"* sounds human females universally seem to reserve for kittens. Because of the new noise I wasn't sure if Margaret's final remark was one she actually vocalized—under her breath, perhaps, but intentionally audible—or whether she had spoken it to me directly into my mind.

"Impossible!

CHAPTER FOUR

I don't usually stay while Renata teaches her classes. It's not that I don't enjoy them. Some class days I slip away from my comfortable nest in her canvas bag, and slink about the classroom observing the students. The students are all women, of course—or, to be truthful, girls. They're still adolescents, despite what they think of themselves. And I know what they think of themselves; I can hear all their interior voices. They don't notice a little cat loping around the seminar rooms, pausing to wash a paw. Most of the students are not focused on Renata's lesson. They are on their computers, but not taking notes. They are IM'ing their friends, surfing the Internet, checking out the latest blogs, videos, comic strips. But Renata's history lectures themselves—the students don't seem to pay them any more attention than I do. It's not that I don't find them interesting, because I do—I love history, which after all is just another aspect of my scientific fascination with the human species. It's just that I have heard it all before—or else, I have lived it. And it's hard to stay interested in a course you could teach yourself.

So after a while, I tend to slip away and wander. Everett is the oldest building of the College, or parts of it are anyway, dating from the Reconstruction era after the Civil War. Samuel Everett was one of those do-gooding Northerners who endowed schools and institutes across the South at that time. His money built the original central part of the building to provide a place for freed slaves and Unionist back-country whites to send their children to, and learn the lessons of the new Constitutional order. Mercifully perhaps, he did not live to see the school as it became a decade later—a segregated, all-white bastion of stubborn Southern womanhood. However, the enthusiasm with which those succeeding generations added onto old Samuel Everett's original bricks has left the building with a maze of cracks, joints, and passageways where the old pieces do not quite perfectly line up with the new. For the humans, this is mainly an issue of drafts, rain leaks and bad air conditioning. But it makes a perfect ground for a small cat to sneak unseen from room to room.

Renata was desperately trying to interest her charges that morning in the aftermath of World War I. With the exam period looming she had to get them at least to the Great Depression and the rise of Fascism before she could stop. I silently leaped up to the opening where a steam pipe emerged from the wall and joined a radiator.

"So not only did the end of the war redraw the boundaries of what had been the German and Austro-Hungarian Empires, but it also redrew the map of— where? It was another empire… Anyone? Does the Treaty of Sèvres ring a bell? It's in a region that's been in the news lately…"

I glanced over my shoulder at the depressing scene before slipping into the passage of the steam pipe. I felt sorry for both Renata and her students—they were facing another solid hour of this. Well, not me. I'd heard it all before.

The steam pipe tunnel led first to another classroom next door, which was dark and not in use, and then along

28

to some science rooms. A chemistry lab was in progress there: lab coats, hair nets, Bunsen burners on the lab benches. Strange smells in the air. One of the chemistry teachers was inscribing an intricate molecular diagram on a chalkboard, as the girls watched with dull expressions behind their safety goggles. Who knew if they were learning anything, but it all looked very impressive. In the chemistry lab, by climbing onto the top of a glassware cabinet in the corner, I could get access to a ledge that ran along the top of the corridor walls in the old part of the second floor—which was the more elegant part of the building, with the more spacious rooms and the more picturesque views of the sweeping lawns of the quadrangle. Naturally, these had been appropriated by College administration and department heads. Old-fashioned tilting glass panels topped the office doors, just at the height of the ledge. For a cat with a curious streak about the exercise of power at Forshay College, it was a perfect arrangement. I could wander about the ledge like the Eye of God, peering into the offices of authority, overhearing its unguarded speech. Scientific curiosity—or perhaps it was really just unabashed nosiness. In any case, after a while I have found that I have almost as much information about people's secrets as Margaret.

First stop that morning was the President's office, but she wasn't in. Probably out of town fund-raising, as usual. Diane Hutchinson was as well-liked as any other recent President of the College, possibly because she was never around. I had nothing against her, though she gave me the impression of being less a real person than an emblem, an elegant blonde hood ornament with impeccably coiffed hair. Her office was beautiful, filled with magnificently carved Low Country furniture. I could tell the value of much of it just by looking; many of the antique pieces were authentic and museum-quality. But that was the problem—the office looked like a museum. It was a backdrop for color photographs for the brochures, a stage set for ceremonial occasions. And it was far, far too tidy. Nobody's actual working office looked like that. Well, maybe I could help a little on that score. I lit onto the President's desk blotter, pawed down a little cup of pens and pencils so they scattered about the desktop, and shuffled a few of the papers around. I just wanted to make it look as if such a beautiful piece of furniture were the site of some actual expenditure of mental energy. But the effect was disappointing. Leadership is hard enough to demonstrate when it is actually present—how much harder it is to simulate when it is absent. I leaped back up to the wall ledge and crept back out the window panel.

Down the corridor, the department offices were on the shadowed side of the building this time of day. The corridor was quiet below me; no students ventured here unless they were summoned to meet with their professors, and all too often that was not a happy occasion. I continued down the ledge in the shadows until I got to the history department offices. The door to the history offices was on the other side of the hall. I checked to make sure that the corridor was deserted, and then I carefully jumped down from the ledge on one side and used a handy steam pipe to climb up onto the ledge opposite. I slipped through the glass panel, across the wall of an anteroom where a secretary was supposed to be on duty but wasn't, and crept through the similar glass panel above an interior door to a private office, this one with the name "Claude DeB. Preen, Chairman" stenciled on the frosted door glass.

He was on the phone, his chair swiveled around to allow him to survey the view of the campus that unfurled magnificently from his window. It was a view worthy of a powerful man—a statesman, a CEO, a law firm senior partner. But what about the History Chairman at the Pre-Eminent Women's College of the Upper South? Claude Preen seemed to gaze at the view out his window as if to convince himself that he indeed belonged in exalted company. He was a Bully if I have ever seen one, but of a dangerous kind—not a Bully with great power, but worse, a Bully with just a little power.

"No, I've the read the first draft, and it's completely unsuitable," he said. I could only see the back of his head, his black-and-gray hair thickly spread and cut short in a dignified, professional style. He bent his arm over his head, hunching the phone in his shoulder and stretching his arm as he spoke. Blue shirt, white French cuff. Did he wear a diamond in his cufflink? I couldn't tell from my perch on the ledge, but I wouldn't be surprised. I knew that he custom-ordered bespoke suits when he made College-funded trips to New York or London. How much was the College paying this guy?

"Yes…yes, of course, I realize that," he continued. "I know…I know that Forshay always *stretches* to find qualified women professors, especially in departments that have predominantly male faculties. Yes, I… Yes, I… Yes, I *understand* the mission…"

Whoever he was talking to wasn't letting him finish many of his thoughts. Whoever it was, that immediately endeared them to me.

Preen grabbed the initiative back. "Look, I've asked her to come see me this morning. I plan to talk to her very frankly. I understand your interest, Diane, but I am not going to recommend renewing her contract unless something very definite changes. And so far I don't see it. I just don't see it." The arm uncurled, he straightened up. "There's just something wrong about her, I know it. I can't put my finger on it, but I know it. And I trust my instincts."

He listened now for several long seconds. I realized that he was talking to President Hutchinson, and they were discussing Renata. It did not sound particularly good—but was the President sticking up for Renata? Was I wrong about her? Was she showing some leadership after all? Or was it just a matter of quotas, making sure that wealthy alumnae donors wouldn't be upset by any skewed male-female ratios among the faculty at the next fund-raising dinner?

He finished the call and swiveled back around to hang up the phone. Silent as a shadow, I skittered along the ledge to a vantage above the window, placing me now behind his desk with a fine view of the papers on it. I could see in the center a manuscript copy of Renata's article, the one she had described to Beth that morning. She must have finished it—or else just submitted it as it was. I had read the article, or at least the last version she had left on the table a week before. It was actually quite competent. One or two conclusions she reaches—well, I would have proposed that she follow some different lines of research, and see if her conclusions would come out differently. Of course, Renata wouldn't have thought of discussing her article with her cat. Pity. But surely the article was a strong enough piece of scholarship to please any reasonably impartial department chair. Preen was sitting quietly, staring blankly at his desk. I tried to listen to Preen's thoughts as he sat, fingering the article—reading his mind, I guess you would call it. I couldn't get a grasp of anything illuminating. But something was wrong, something was quite wrong about Renata's article. I focused again, listening to Preen's thoughts some more, trying to get a handle on whatever it was. But no, nothing, no clarity in the confusion of thoughtstreams—other than random irruptions of thoughts that made it very evident to me that here is a man who should not be teaching at a women's college at all.

I should perhaps explain a little about this whole business of listening to people's thoughts—it is one of the talents that I mentioned, and I do indeed possess it, but I don't want you to get the wrong idea. It's easy for me to *hear* what is going on in the mind of a person near me. But it's hard—often impossible—to make much sense of it. I call much of the traffic of a human mind "thoughtstreams," because that's what they seem to be as I listen to them—an onrushing cascade of brain signals that are unorganized, unfiltered, unmoored to anything but their own internal chatter. It's only when the conscious mind takes a hand and imposes a logic on this stream of data, *formulates a thought*, in other words, that hearing someone's mind conveys any useful information. You would be surprised how infrequently people actually formulate thoughts. (Actually, with some people, perhaps you wouldn't be.)

No use staying—I crept back along the ledge and out of the office into the corridor. It was still dim and shadowy, completely empty. For no other reason than to prove that I could, I climbed down from the overhead ledge and sat in the middle of the hallway. I bent down to clean my hindquarters—just to defy one and all. Just to show Margaret—that I could sit here in the middle of the corridor, performing the most mundane of feline activities, out in the open. With no fear.

But after a time, even that got boring. There is something unsatisfactory about acts of defiance done with no audience. So I sauntered down the hallway again, leaped back up onto the ledge, and followed another passageway—this one behind a false wall that was put up at some point to block off an arched doorway. Of course, for a small cat, the doorway was still there, just behind a gap in the wallboard inside the second floor coat closet. A few steps was all it took to get to the other side of the building, and the seminar room where I knew Denis Pearson would be teaching his English class.

This was a classroom that I could walk straight into—through the door, which Mr. Pearson always kept open during class, as if he were freely inviting all passers-by to come in and participate. I peered in; he was speaking and all eyes were riveted on him. This was not the struggle for attention that poor Renata had—Mr. Pearson had the gift of a performer, and not a head turned to see me as I sauntered through the open door, tail high as a flag, and settled under Mr. Pearson's desk. He spotted me, of course—he always did. This was his freshman composition class, and he was supposed to be teaching the girls how to write. Not how to write better, but how to write *at all*. I do not know how some of these girls had managed to get through their high schools and into a fairly selective college like Forshay, having seen some of their work. Mr. Pearson would have needed more than the year allotted to him to cover the prescribed curriculum. And yet, I loved to visit his class precisely because he never followed a curriculum. His syllabus, if he indeed acknowledged that such a thing was necessary, was an improvisation from class to class. Whatever took his fancy, whatever he happened to be reading. Perhaps that was the secret to his gift; his zeal for whatever new enthusiasm had grabbed his attention at that moment communicated itself to his girls. If it was Faulkner that day, they might walk out of class struggling with Benjy's chapter of *The Sound and the Fury*. Or perhaps Wolfe (either one), or Seamus Heaney, or Stephen Crane. Today, as I curled into a ball and listened to him, I determined he was talking about a short story by Ernest Hemingway, "Hills Like White Elephants." The girls were enraptured; the school authorities, no doubt, would have been livid. Today's lesson was supposed to cover the subjunctive voice. Not much of that in Hemingway in any event. No matter, I thought, drowsing off to sleep. Papa Hemingway loved cats.

I was awakened from my nap by being scooped up under the ribcage by Denis Pearson's strong right hand as he grabbed his battered, bulging briefcase in his left. Class was ending, the girls were gathering their books and leaving. Did they, I wondered sleepily, manage to get to grips with the Hemingway story? Did they appreciate how radical, even scandalous it had been when it had been written? I did. I remembered well.

"Tuesday," Denis was saying as the girls filed out, "remember Tuesday is the review session for the exam—we'll hold it right here, anything you want to go over, for as long as you want to go. And for the couple of you who still owe me the last essay please email it to me by Friday."

Denis turned aside, going along a lateral corridor away from the girls filing straight ahead toward the stairs. "Let's see if Miss Renata has finished with Modern Europe, eh?" Denis said to me as we strode along. He didn't bother to try to conceal me—didn't stuff me under his lapel, say, or into one of the jacket pockets at his side. Instead he carried me front and center, a little like a football. I almost hoped that we'd meet Margaret along the corridor, but I knew she was probably back at her station at the front of the stairs, glaring at the girls as they went past.

When we got to Renata's classroom, the class was already dismissed. Renata was sitting casually on one of the desktops, next to a student who had stayed behind. She looked up when we walked in.

"Hey," Denis said, "look who was sleeping under my desk again."

Renata looked up and smiled, but a wan, slight smile. She seemed concerned. The girl stayed seated at her desk. She stared stonily forward, not looking at either Renata or Denis.

"Sorry, am I interrupting something?" Denis said, letting me slip out of his hand to the floor. "I didn't mean to intrude."

I walked over to the student's desk, and after making a little show of parading, I leapt lightly onto her desktop.

"No, no, that's fine Mr. Pearson," Renata said, a little too brightly. "I was just having a word with Lupe. Do you know Lupe?"

Denis Pearson and María Guadalupe Hernandez-Vega

did not know each other; stiff introductions were made. I looked carefully at the girl's face. She was mastering her emotions with difficulty, and it was clear that tears were not far beneath the surface. But her eyes were dry. This pricked the interest of the scientist in me, and I looked carefully at the girl's face. It was beautiful, but something different from the other girls who came and went from Renata's and Denis's classes. How had I not noticed this girl before? The straight, coarse black hair, the breadth of forehead, just that fine slope to the nose-bridge... I placed it, finally, the category—this was an Indian face, Mesoamerican. Her almond eyes, still straining to control their composure, were as black as Renata's.

"Lupe's joined us halfway through this semester, so we're still trying to adjust," Renata said to Denis. "She's come to us from El Salvador, by way of Estado Piñela Prep in Washington." Although they were talking to each other, literally over Lupe's head, they both seemed to keep one eye on the girl. "But Lupe and I have a little problem, which is a paper that was due a week ago but that doesn't seem to be done yet. Is it, Lupe?"

Still silent, the girl shook her head slowly.

Renata sighed. "I wish you'd let me help you, Lupe. I know it can be very hard to change schools in the middle of the term, and everything. I know your placement tests were off the charts—genius level, really! But with so much material to catch up to the class on... There must be some *reason* you've not been able to work on the paper." Renata sighed again. She spoke low. "I would hate to count the paper as a fail, but I might not have any choice."

Lupe, looking forward, blinked twice. A tear escaped, leaking from her left eye and running quickly down her cheek. She impatiently brushed it away. The motion caused her black hair to swing, and the slight breeze it made wafted a subtle fragrance of rosewater through the air. I breathed the scent, fascinated.

"You know," Denis said, sounding a little too loud and

36

hale as he spoke, "I sometimes have situations in my classes where because of circumstances, a paper assignment can't be completed. You know, extenuating circumstances." He coughed, and continued. "So sometimes we just do a special exam instead of the paper. Call it even. You know?"

Renata looked at him sharply. "Well, I'm still new here, but I didn't know that the faculty could make a unilateral change in curriculum." She tilted her head. "Doesn't that cause trouble with the administration—you know, accreditation standards, all that?"

"Nonsense! It makes perfect sense." Denis laughed. "I have done it myself many times."

Renata laughed also. It wasn't lost on her that Denis had not actually answered her question about whether substituting an exam for a paper would get a teacher in trouble. He apparently just didn't care.

"OK, look," Renata said, bending back toward Lupe. "How about we try that? Do you think you could do that?"

Lupe's face brightened. "Yes," she said.

It was the first word she said, but her voice instantly grabbed me. It was light, musical; her accent was something altogether new to me. I willed her to speak further, but that's all she said.

"All right. So this is a history class, and that means we'll have to come up with an exam topic that would be relevant to the course." Renata smiled up at Denis. "I'm afraid we don't have the kind of latitude with topics that you must have in your comp classes, Mr. Pearson."

Denis grinned broadly, and made a courtly gesture with his hand. "Well then, I'll leave you history scholars to settle the details. Bye!" he said, and swept out of the room.

Both Renata and Lupe watched in his wake for a moment, silently. Their eyes met. Lupe was the first to smile; then they both giggled bashfully.

"Yes, I know what you're thinking," Renata said. "He *is* very handsome, isn't he?"

"Yes," Lupe said, visibly relaxing.

"And can we come up with a topic for the exam? The course is on Modern European history—perhaps you could write something about El Salvador?"

Lupe's eyes looked puzzled. "But, Miss Beaumanoir," she said, "El Salvador is in America, not in Europe."

"True," Renata replied thoughtfully. "But it is certainly part of the general flow of Western history. Wouldn't it be interesting to think about how the themes of modern European civilization have affected El Salvador?" Renata brushed an errant hair from her forehead. "You see, Lupe, the challenge is that you don't have time to do new research, so we have to pick something that you already have the facts on. What's the name of the town you come from?"

"Ahuachapan," Lupe said. "It's in the mountains, near Guatemala."

"And do you know about the local history of Ahuachapan—from, say, the stories that your parents or grandparents might have told you? Or things in a town that, you know, everyone just *knows?*"

Lupe's eyes gleamed. "Yes, yes, there are many things like that. And the old people, they have always told us stories," she said. "I could write about that."

Renata smiled. "Good. We've talked about a lot of themes in the latter part of this class—the reform movements, the revolutions of the 19th century, the struggles between socialism, capitalism, and totalitarian and liberal systems—can you pick a few of those themes, and discuss how they affected the recent history of Ahuachapan, El Salvador?"

Lupe smiled and nodded affirmatively. She stood and began gathering her papers, moving aside the kitten who had curled up on her desk.

"Is this your cat, Miss Beaumanoir?" she asked.

"Yes. Kikki," Renata said. "She seems to like you."

I made kitten stretching motions, and then rubbed my nose against Lupe's fingers as she held her hand out to me. She was a very interesting specimen; if I made friends, I thought, perhaps I could hear her speak more in that marvelous voice of hers.

Renata gave parting instructions on where and when Lupe would take her special exam, and began gathering her class materials—and her small cat—back into her canvas bag. As I situated myself in the bag I noticed that the heavy envelope had been opened, the flap unstuck, but I couldn't paw out the note inside it to read before Renata hoisted the bag onto her shoulder and I was obliged to poke my head out the top again.

She hurried out of the Everett Building and up the slope to her house. She pulled me out of the bag and put me on the kitchen floor.

"You'd better wait here, Kikki," she said. "I'm in enough trouble with Preen as it is." She grabbed a copy of her article off the counter and put it in her bag before pushing out the door again, and locking it behind her. I jumped onto the sill of the window facing Ridge Street and watched her walking quickly in the noontime light back toward Everett, wearing her big sunglasses and her white headscarf against the sun. I saw her, in the distance, pass close by Trace Cuthbert coming across the lawn the other way. They didn't seem to speak to each other.

I watched Renata reenter the Everett Building, and I mentally wished her luck and fortitude in her meeting with Dr. Preen. Normally I would have not lost much time scampering after her—locking me in the house wasn't really to be taken seriously, and with my mastery of the nooks and cracks in the Everett Building's walls I'm sure I could have been perched again on the ledge above Claude Preen's crew cut before Renata ever arrived. But not right now. There was something else to do. I could follow her to Preen's office after.

I scrambled back up to the table where Renata had placed her bag when she had lifted me out of it—and where the thick, cream envelope lay, which I had managed with a deft swipe of a paw to slide out of the canvas bag along with me. Now I set to reading whatever it was that it contained. Kitten's paws are not the most efficient instruments to use to open human mail, but then again envelopes were not really developed with them in mind. It took a few tries to flip the envelope over, so I could paw open the unglued flap. Another couple tries, and a sharp pink claw managed to snag the card inside the envelope and pull it out. The perfume scent was even stronger on the card as it emerged from the envelope and lay on the table. I walked around the tabletop to read it right-side up.

It was in Latin, course. The Vampire Council all spoke perfect English but they just liked to be difficult:

Renata, Comtesse de Beaumanoir, es hoc citati coram Concilio Vampire in civitate sumptus Charleston respondere tibi tenuere dicetur tempore appa...

Or, as any sane person would have written it in this day and age:

Renata, Comtesse de Beaumanoir, you are hereby summoned to appear before the Vampire Council in the City of Charleston to answer such charges laid before you as shall be explained at the time of your appearance...

So it was a summons. Renata was to be put on trial before the Vampire Council. I looked at the time and date—she was summoned for Saturday, at midnight of course—two days from now. And not a word of what the charges were supposed to be. That didn't seem good.

I sat on the table, considering this development. I thought about not following Renata to Preen's office—after all, it was a foregone conclusion what would happen, and there was little I could do to help. Preen would be solicitous, smiling, supportive—right up to the moment when he informed her that her article was crap, that her teaching wasn't good enough and that he wasn't going to renew her contract. President Hutchinson be damned. It was too bad for Renata, but not too surprising. And the summons from the Vampires in Charleston was a more urgent matter, requiring some careful thought. What was going on? They had obviously discovered Renata's attempt to start a new life and career here among the mortal humans—they had her mailing address, after all—but what was the big deal? What kind of transgression was *that*, after all, really? Or were there other transgressions they had discovered—or invented? And, most important, what if anything was to be done about it? I had to think it through, and for a small cat, thinking is best done in a patch of sunlight on a living room carpet. You might see me there, all afternoon, and you might think I was sleeping, not thinking, but you would have been wrong. I would be on the case. The Vampire Council is serious business—possibly a matter of life and death. Or, given that vampires like Renata are technically already dead, a matter of death and even worse death.

But I roused myself. Something told me that I didn't want her to face Preen alone, even if she may not know that I was there. Was I just being nosy? Maybe—but I would say, rather, concerned. A quick kitten paw on the back door latch, and I was out of the house, scampering up a shortcut along the edge of the lawns back to the Everett Building, as fast as my kitten legs would allow. That patch of sunlight would have to wait.

By the time I again reached my vantage point on the ledge over Claude Preen's window Renata was already seated in the chair opposite his desk, and he had already

started the interview. I could tell they had just begun—
Preen was still making friendly small talk, calling her by her
first name, and mispronouncing it each time. (He said,
"*RE*-nata," stressing the first syllable and giving it a long *e*.
When they were first introduced, at the beginning of the
academic year, Preen had asked her if she knew that her
name translated from the Latin as "reborn." Renata had
allowed that she did, but Preen hadn't let go of it. "*RE*-
nata, reborn," he had repeated a few times, thinking
himself clever. Thereafter, Preen continued to
mispronounce her name—I couldn't tell if he was doing it
out of thoughtlessness or malice. It hardly mattered. It
was typical Bully behavior.)

But now he was getting down to business. "I want to
thank you," he said, fingering the copy of Renata's article I
had seen on his desk that morning, "for getting me the
draft of your piece so promptly." He made a show of
searching for the right words, wetting his lips, and running
a cufflinked hand over his scalp as if to smooth his
already-perfect hair. But I could hear his mind—he wasn't
struggling to choose the right words. He knew exactly
where he was going with this.

He stopped fidgeting and folded his hands. He looked
at Renata with an expression of pained, but sympathetic,
disappointment.

"But," he said, "it just doesn't do. I'm sure you
understand that I can't accept this, uh, work as your
mandatory submission."

Renata regarded him coolly. Her legs were crossed
demurely, her hands folded on her lap. She had not
removed her sunglasses. She wasn't easily flustered, I have
to say that—that's one of the things I have come to like
about her. She has a backbone. She will stand her ground.

"No, Dr. Preen," she said evenly. "I don't think that I
do understand. Could you please explain?"

Preen exhaled noisily, and his eyes searched again about
the desktop as if an unambiguous answer to her query

were written there somewhere. He wasn't used to being challenged.

"Well, the subject matter, for a start," he blustered. "I mean, just look at this title." He adjusted his glasses and read from the top page of the manuscript, distastefully mangling the foreign words. "*Imperatoris Marmor*: The Myths of Constantine XI Palaiologos and the Development of European Chivalry.'" He took his glasses off dramatically, and glared. "What the hell is this—some kind of medieval, Byzantine topic? I thought we had agreed that you were writing something on *modern* Europe! Was I mistaken?"

She didn't flinch. "I think you must have been," she replied. "I think you may have *suggested* that I choose a topic on modern Europe. But we didn't agree to that. In fact, I think I remember you telling me that it was my decision. Yes—'Write about what you find most compelling'—I think those were your exact words."

Preen squirmed slightly in his chair. A Bully, confronted by inconvenient facts—especially those emanating from his own mouth—will always find a justification to explain them away. I did recall, however, that even from their first meeting Preen had made clear his preference that Renata write her required scholarly article about modern Europe—and more particularly, modern England during the Industrial Revolution. Which just happened to be Preen's own academic specialty. Indeed, from the bits of overheard conversation and stray thoughtstreams I had heard during the academic year, I had learned that Kjerstin Thorstad, the prior Visiting Lecturer, had suddenly abandoned some fairly advanced work on Scandinavian resistance to the Nazi invasions, and spent the year researching topics related to the English Reform Act of 1832. Guided, I had no doubt, by the firm mentoring hand of Claude Preen.

Preen wasn't put off, however—he simply shifted tack and continued in full flow. "But *myths?*" he demanded.

"*Chivalry?* Miss Beaumanoir, this article was supposed to be a substantial work of substantial *history*. Something that, not incidentally, was supposed to showcase your capability to fit in with our community of scholars here at Forshay College. But *this*," he said, searching for sufficiently damning superlatives, "this, Miss Beaumanoir, while this kind of foolish nonsense might be acceptable in some departments, might even be greeted with great enthusiasm by our colleagues in say, psychology or, God forbid, the *English department*," he continued, "I won't tolerate it in this department. I refuse to treat this *mythology* as serious history, Miss Beaumanoir."

No more "RE-nata," apparently—it was back to "Miss Beaumanoir."

Renata did not respond. Preen smirked, clearly believing he had recovered the moral high ground and, even better, believing that he was going to get his way. He continued his diatribe. "And Constantine the Eleventh…well, I won't even try to pronounce that next name again. Remind me, Miss Beaumanoir, my recall of this Byzantine mishmash is a little spotty—are we talking about a mythological king, or a real one? Indeed, are there any actual *facts* in your article at all?" He wasn't holding back at all now.

"Dr. Preen," Renata said evenly, "I'm a little surprised. The fall of Constantinople in 1453 was one of the seminal events that shaped Europe—modern Europe, especially. And so surely you must be well acquainted with the history of the last Roman Emperor in the East, when the Turks finally took the city in that year—you know the one…"

Preen's eyes flashed up to meet hers, daring her to continue with her next phrase, which could only have a single purpose—to embarrass him. But his eyes met only his reflection on the opaque lenses of her sunglasses.

"…*Kōnstantinos Endékatos Dragasēs Palaiologos,*" she finished, in perfectly inflected Greek.

Preen's face colored red.

"I don't know what the attraction is with this Byzantine stuff," he growled. "It's a dead end. A dead end! Why do you insist on it?"

Renata paused, thinking. "I honestly don't know, Dr. Preen. I find it compelling, just as we discussed all those months ago. Even irresistible. But why? I really can't tell you why," she said. "I just do."

Preen considered this admission for a moment, seeming to take the offer of candor as an admission of weakness. As he paused, I noticed the same stirring in Renata's thoughtstreams that I had felt that morning at the Sisters' Store. Renata's mind suppressed the feeling, though, intent as it was on Dr. Preen. Preen glanced up at length. He shook his head vigorously.

"No," he said finally. "No, I won't countenance this." He tossed the article back onto his desk as if it had been a dead rat. "It's wholly unsuitable. Wait," he said. "Let me show you something." He pulled open a drawer at the side of his desk, and drew a pamphlet out of a file. He slid it onto the desk in front of Renata. "Do you know what this is?" he demanded. "This is what a reprint of a scholarly article looks like. A reprint of my article, published last summer. Published in the *Atlanta Chronicle of Modern History*. One of the country's leading historical journals, as you probably know, and one that I have some significant influence on. This," he said, jabbing the cream-colored pamphlet with his finger, "this is what we're aiming for, Miss Beaumanoir. This is what enhances reputations—of historians, of their departments, of their colleges. But you come up with…that." He paused, and shook his head. "Here I thought, all along, that we were writing a substantial piece to publish in the *Atlanta Chronicle of Modern History*. I trusted you to formulate a proper topic. You assured me that you were making progress, all year. But this," he said, motioning to Renata's manuscript. "The *Atlanta Chronicle* won't take this."

"But there must be dozens of journals," Renata

protested. "And I wasn't aware that *I* was writing for any specific one."

Careful, girl, I said to myself. Don't push it.

But Renata was blustering on. "In fact," she said, "I sent an email query to the *Journal du Musée du Moyen Age* in Paris last month, and they emailed me back just this week. They seemed to be very interested in the topic and wanted to hear more…"

Preen put up both hands, palms out. To his mind, the debate was over. "The debate is over," he said. "Frankly, Miss Beaumanoir, I'm surprised—surprised and disappointed. Nine months—nine months of work, since the beginning of the fall term. And this. This is the result. It just won't do. And I'll have to take the matter up with President Hutchinson. You understand that, don't you? This has a direct bearing on your contract, and the President will have to know."

Renata was still holding her ground, but I could see that she was beginning to waver. She made one more attempt. "Dr. Preen," she said, "please. Is there anything you can tell me about the article, to improve it? Anything specifically that I could change? What parts in particular did you find faulty?"

Preen glared at her, and stood up. "If I were you," he said deliberately, "I would tear the thing up, and start over." He paused for emphasis, then leaned forward. "Throw it away, and start over." He stared at Renata. "Wherever you may happen to be at the time."

His meaning was clear to Renata. She stood to gather her bag and scarf. The interview was over. Time for her to go.

His meaning was clear to me too—though perhaps not the one he intended. I could hear his thoughtstreams, and it was obvious to me that the reason he couldn't name a specific part of the article to critique was for the very simple reason that he had never gotten past the title. That had been enough for him to make up his mind. The son of a bitch never even read it.

They parted without further words, without a handshake, nothing. Preen stood and watched silently as Renata left his office. I silently scampered over the ledges and back to my vantage point in the corridor, in time to see Renata emerge from the door of the outer office. She stopped in the corridor for a moment, composing herself. I could not remember ever seeing her so deflated. She gave a sigh in the empty corridor, unheard by any but an unseen small cat on a high ledge. She slipped her white scarf over her hair once more against the afternoon sunlight, and walked slowly away. As her footsteps clicked down the dark corridor of Everett, I considered slipping back into Preen's office. I could scratch his furniture, shred some papers. I could even pee on his desk blotter. But the vengeance a small cat could exact against a bullying chairman of a college history department seemed just too inadequate. I thought better of committing such mischief, and skittered away after Renata along the high ledges, silent as a shadow. Preen's turn would come, I thought, soon enough.

CHAPTER FIVE

"You've gotta eat something, honey."

Lucy had appeared over the table where Renata, Fulda Myerson and Fulda's five-year-old daughter Maia were gathered around a plate of the Sisters' Store special empanadas. The evening sun slanted golden light on the ridge above the town, outside the store window. It was spectacular. But Renata wasn't looking; she was fingering the food on her plate, toying with it distractedly, not eating it. At least she had taken her sunglasses off, and her eyes, though a little tired, looked more or less human. She mouthed a bit of lettuce from the side salad.

Fulda was helping Maia arrange a pink and silver tiara on her head. "Would the Princess like some more milk?" Fulda asked.

Maia made a show of regal deference. "No," she said. "But you're supposed to say, 'Your Highness'."

Fulda glanced at Renata with a look on her face indicating that the peasantry had reached its limit on royal privilege. "Here, hop down and go look at the toys," Fulda said, helping her daughter down from the chair and giving her back the pink magic wand with the silver-glitter star at the end, that Fulda had taken away before the meal.

Maia skipped across the store to the low glass case where Beth and Lucy displayed dolls and carved figurines, her pink taffeta skirts billowing behind her.

Fulda was a chemistry teacher at the College, some years Renata's senior and one of the permanent faculty—in fact, it had been a lab section of hers that I had cut through on my trek across Everett that morning. Her husband Michael worked at some job I don't really understand in the College administration—the development office. Was that also money-raising? Does the College administration actually do *anything* other than money-raising? Who knows. But I liked Fulda. She was thin and small and dark-haired and intense. She had heavy-framed glasses and wore slightly baggy shirts. She looked like she should be a chain-smoker who talked about Sartre and existentialism and the class struggle, but she wasn't—she was a nonsmoker scientist like me. And she always claimed that she had picked out the name "Maia" for her first daughter long, long before she ever met Michael Myerson, much less married him. So it was his fault, not hers, that her daughter had ended up with the alliterative name Maia Myerson.

"Is she supposed to be a princess or a fairy?" Renata asked, puzzled.

"She's not *supposed* to be anything, according to her—she *is* a princess," Fulda answered. "It's amazing how imagination and reality just seem to blend together for a kid that age, like there's just no difference between one and the other. She *is* a princess because she *believes* she's a princess."

Lucy came and sat down, keeping a wary eye on the child. The really fragile stuff was on a higher shelf on the back wall, but still—little hands could move very quickly. "It's a wonderful age," Lucy said. "I grew up on a farm, and there weren't many other kids around. I can remember how vividly I believed in all my imaginary adventures."

Fulda laughed. "If only it were just imagination. You should see all the princess stuff we have—paraphernalia of every type. Closets full! I could be the costumer for a childrens' opera company."

"Princesses," Renata said absently. "I've known a few princesses."

"Really? You mean personally?"

Renata glanced up at Fulda, recovering herself after a pause. "No, I didn't mean that," she said. "I meant, from history. Historical figures. You know, research…you can get very close to your subject researching medieval history."

Fulda laughed again with a sudden thought. "Hey, you know what would be great? What if Walt Disney came out with a new line of princess toys, except that the 'princesses' were all women from history, like Eleanor of Aquitaine and Joan of Arc and Boudica and Margaret of Anjou. Do think little girls like Maia would like the helmets and bloody swords to go with their princess dresses?"

The women laughed together. "It would make Halloween more interesting," Lucy allowed. Throughout the conversation, Lucy's eyes still keenly tracked the progress of Renata's fork. Taller than Beth, and thinner, she had her lanky blonde-and-gray hair tied back under a colorful bandana, and the sleeves of her blue denim shirt rolled up to display a black ink web of tattoos disappearing up her arms. Her blue eyes flicked sharply from the plate to Renata's face. "Look, Renata honey, I've been watching and you haven't eaten anything. What's wrong? You have to eat."

Renata glanced up at Lucy with a sallow smile, a picture of misery.

"You had to see Mr. Preen today, didn't you?" Lucy asked. "Bad news?"

Renata smiled again. "Bad news—what else? But that's not the problem. I got a letter today—I need to get down to Charleston this weekend, and I don't have a car."

"I thought you had a car," Fulda said.

Lucy had helped Renata many times over the course of the college term with the ancient Buick that stood parked on the street out front of Renata's house, tires bald, suspension rotted, its body pitted with rust. I pictured the car now, leaning toward the curbside with an air of exhausted capitulation. "You ever seen it?" Lucy said. "It wouldn't make it off the mountain, much less all the way to Charleston."

Fulda turned around toward the lunch counter that ran along the back of the store, where Forshay's police chief was sitting. "What do you think, Paul?" she asked. "You know the car—green Buick, parked on the curb on Ridge Street."

I suppose tall, gaunt, gray-haired Paul Moorland was the "chief" of police—why not, since he was in fact Forshay's entire police department? He was staring at the newspaper spread out on the counter next to his wide-brimmed hat, even though it was too dim to read back there. He had been listening to every word, and everyone knew it. He answered without looking up, his gray mustache so bushy I couldn't see his mouth move. "Not road worthy," he said. "Safety violation."

Renata sighed, pushing away the plate for good and sitting back. "Well, he's right, the car's a wreck. Beyond repair. I need a ride."

Fulda, not put off the empanadas by Renata's lack of appetite, had crammed half of one into her mouth. "How about Denis? He's going down there this weekend, I think."

Renata tried not to seem too eager. "Really? What for?"

"He told me he had a weekend meeting at the College of Charleston," Fulda said, chewing. "But I really think he's just going down there to see friends." Fulda looked hard at Renata. "Do you really think you should be leaving the campus, though? You know how they are about adjunct faculty. The rules about leaving campus during term are stricter for you than they are for the girls."

"Well, I guess I'll just have to watch out until I'm a matron like you," Renata said, "and the rules don't apply anymore."

Fulda made a pantomime arrow-in-the-heart gesture. "Oh, that hurt!" She wiped the crumbs off her mouth. "Seriously, why are you going there, the week before finals of all times? Not bad news, I hope? You could talk to President Hutch or Margaret and I'm sure they'd give permission."

"Well, it's kind of personal," Renata said, evasively. "I actually can't really get official permission to be off campus. I hope you'll cover for me if they ask—I'll be back by Monday for sure."

Lucy spoke to Fulda. "Death in the family," she said definitively. Lucy suddenly stood up, her gaze spying something out the store windows. "Speak of the devil," she said in her low, singsong voice. "There's Denis Pearson now, leaving class." She hustled to the door. "Watch the store for a minute, would you? And mind that Maia doesn't hurt herself."

I slipped off the chair where I had been sitting unobtrusively, and hopped up on the window sill. Lucy was already across the green, still wiping her hands on a white towel as she called out to Denis, honey. Everyone was honey to Lucy.

Renata and Fulda regarded each other across the table. "How did Lucy hear about that?" Renata asked.

Fulda chuckled. "Oh, don't worry about it," she said, "no one's prying. But Forshay's a small town. And Forshay College is an even smaller one." Fulda reached out and put her hand over Renata's. "It just means that you've kind of begun to be part of this place, that people think of you as part of the family here. Besides," she said, "whatever it is, maybe we can help."

Renata smiled. I could hear the human strand of her thoughtstreams suddenly grow loud and rushing, briefly overwhelming the vampire side of her mind—heavy emotion.

"Lucy's right though, you should definitely eat more," Fulda said. "Your hand's as cold as ice."

Lucy was already back in the store, trailing a bemused Denis Pearson in her wake. He was carrying his battered briefcase, and a small strapped bag over his shoulder. He was grinning like he had been let in on a great joke.

"So Lucy says that you're inviting me to go away with you for a sexy weekend," he said, taking a seat at the table.

Renata smiled back brilliantly. The rushing thoughtstreams again…I think that if she had been capable of blushing, she would be burning crimson. Luckily, vampires don't blush. All Denis saw was Renata maintaining her poise perfectly.

"Not quite, Denis," Renata said. "I need a ride to Charleston, and I hear you're driving down." She batted her black eyelashes. "Do have a spot for little ol' me?"

He laughed. His laugh really *was* very pleasant. I didn't understand why Renata couldn't mate with Denis, instead of big dumb Trace Cuthbert. But people are always more complicated than you think—in 6,000 years I've at least learned that much.

"Sure," he said. "No problem. I'm driving down around one o'clock tomorrow, to try to beat the beach traffic, if that's OK with you."

"Sure, that would be fine. Thank you, Denis."

Denis got serious for a moment. "Look, I heard about your loss," he said. "Just let me know where I can drop you off—it's no problem. Are you staying with family?"

"I have a place to stay, don't worry about me," Renata said. "Thank you."

"And Denis," Fulda added, "Renata hasn't *technically* gotten a pass to be off campus this weekend, so don't say anything about it. Especially to Preen."

53

"Or Margaret," Lucy added. I saw Renata's shoulder's give a slight, involuntary shudder. I was getting leery of Margaret myself.

"OK," Denis said. "No one'll find out." He thought for a moment. "But we shouldn't leave from the campus or the village then, or everyone will know you're gone. Can you get out to my house off-campus, quietly? You know where it is—out on Dellinger Road, up the ridge about two miles?"

"*Denis!*" Fulda exclaimed. "What's the matter with you? Of course she can't get out there, with a weekend bag and all—she doesn't have a car! That's the whole point."

"Oh yeah," Denis said. Why is it that such smart humans can be so dopey sometimes? I'd like to think that he was just distracted by Renata's beauty, and that pretty soon he'd sweep her off her feet so she'd forget all about Trace Cuthbert. But he just sat there quietly for a moment, thinking. And I'm just a cat—it's not like I can make any suggestions. Luckily, someone else came up with a plan.

"Well," came Paul Moorland's slow, deep voice from the lunch counter, "if the little lady would like to stop in here at about 12:30 I reckon I could give her a lift out." He had neatly stacked his coffee cup and the small plate with the remaining crumbs of the slice of Beth's pecan pie he had been working on for an hour, and was slowly, painfully straightening his lanky limbs. He took up his hat and gave Renata a gallant, wrinkly smile from beneath his bushy mustache and eyebrows. It was Forshay—no one minded that Paul Moorland had been eavesdropping. It would have been more impolite had he not bothered to take an interest.

"Thank you so much, Mr. Moorland," Renata said. "I really appreciate that."

"Happy to oblige," Paul said, and then took his leave. He briefly touched a finger to his forehead in salute.

"Ladies."

In the brief silence that followed, Denis found Renata, Lucy and Fulda all staring at him.

"What?" he said.

"That," Fulda said, "is a serious gentleman."

Denis grinned. "Hey, give me time," he said. "I just need to get more life experience."

"Maybe you'll get some this weekend," Lucy said, peering at Renata. But Renata was distracted once again, and couldn't be baited.

"Well, let me get going," Denis said, getting up. "One o'clock—is that OK, Renata? I can go later if you want, but I can't go earlier. Trace cancelled our tennis game this afternoon. Said he was sore or bruised, or something. So we're going to play tomorrow morning."

Renata looked up at him silently for a moment, as if uncomprehending. Then she smiled. "That's fine," she said. "One o'clock. And tell Trace I hope he feels better."

It was the sudden lights that awakened me, or what I took to be lights. I groggily shook off the sleep and tried to look around, but it was still dark. It was deep night, the moon was nowhere to be seen, and the living room of Renata's house was still and quiet. But I was sure I had seen lights. Could it have been late traffic on Ridge Street, or the sweep of headlights from a car in the campus parking lot? I was tired; my mind dismissed the question as unimportant. It had been a difficult day—more so for Renata than for me—but nonetheless too difficult to be distracted from sleep by unexplained lights. I stretched my white paws until the pink pads showed, and then curled myself again into the warm spot in the basket of clean laundry I was using as a bed. But the lights started again— not from the outside, though. They were coming from the inside of my mind. I sleepily tried to focus on them:

shifting shapes, rapidly moving forms, whirling colors and shimmers—all light, every variegation of light. The images were peculiar, at once realistic and fantastic. I realized then with a start what they were—my mind was reading the thoughtstreams of a vivid dream.

I groped at this information. The lights and images were certainly a human dream—I have seen human dreams frequently enough in my 6,000 years; in fact I often get glimpses of several dreams at once when I spy on the large lecture classes taught by some of Forshay's more especially dull professors. But location is important. My ability to read thoughtstreams degrades with distance, and I can hear only the strongest minds when the subject is not immediately proximate. What humans could be around and sleeping so soundly as to produce these vivid, REM-sleep dreams? The next two Visiting Faculty houses on the row were, I knew, vacant. Could there be somebody asleep in a car parked in the street?

My curiosity roused me; I climbed out of the laundry basket and crept to the front window. The street beneath the dull gleam of the streetlight was empty, save for Renata's rusted hulk of a Buick. No one could be there.

As I crept away from the window, the dream-thoughtstreams intruded again—stronger now, and more insistent. I crept past the laundry basket and followed them, followed the strengthening signal of the thoughtstreams as they grew more vivid until, with amazement, I found myself in the bedroom, looking down at the sleeping face of Renata herself. *But,* I said to myself—nearly said it out loud, too, so shocked was I at this contradiction of a settled truth, of something that I knew to be true—*but, vampires don't have dreams!*

Another piece of received wisdom, all shot to hell.

And it was true—I *knew* it to be true! Vampires are dead, and the dead have no future. Vampires are dead, and sundered from their lives—they have no care for the past. Just as vampires' minds reflect little beyond their present moment, so too have their minds lost the capacity to dream. They have no past to reflect upon, no future to anticipate. Vampires are immortals in a landscape without past or future. Without memory. Without dreams. And Renata—despite dosing herself with thanadoxicil—was indisputably a vampire. As I watched her sleeping face and I read the wildly shifting images of her thoughtstreams, I knew that I was observing something that could not be. It just could not be. I knew this could not be happening.

And yet, here it was.

I stayed and listened to her thoughtstreams—listened and watched. It was uncanny. Was it the effect of the thanadoxicil, or the effect of the on-again, off-again dosages that Renata seemed to have been taking? My own mind was rushing now, trying to find a scientific explanation for data that it knew should be inexplicable. She had let the thanadoxicil fall to a very low concentration just the other night—that was the cause of the scene with Trace Cuthbert—but how could that give her mind a mortal human ability, one that a vampire mind should be incapable of having? I wondered—perhaps it wasn't the drug? Perhaps this was something else about *her* that was unique among vampires? My scientific brain, stumped by the new data, strained to find a fitting hypothesis.

Then suddenly, out of the thoughtstreams, I felt the same shudder I had felt twice earlier that day, the shudder that had seemed to be a deep memory trying to rise to the fore, the very kind of memory that vampires are not supposed to have. That vampires *cannot* have.

Renata was speaking in her sleep. I was getting distracted by my scientific niceties, I thought; I should pay attention to the dream. Observe and record the facts, I commanded myself—imagine what I could learn! I crept closer to Renata's sleeping form, and listened to her dream-thoughtstreams intently.

"*Yes,*" Renata was saying. "*Yes, I will. I pledge to you.*"

Audibly, she was only mumbling, but her thoughtstream articulated the words clearly. I heard them distinctly. But then, I had to listen again, thinking I must have been mistaken, for they were spoken in a language that I had not heard for six hundred years. "*I pledge to you,*" Renata repeated—sweetly pronouncing the words in the Middle French of the 14th century.

The images swirled through my mind as she spoke. Images of horror: bodies strewn in the streets of a village, flies clouding about them in naked sunlight. Then the rushing view from the back of a horse; Renata was riding, riding, following a whitened track through a forest, dark although it was still daylight; the horse rode and rode but the pathway seemed to spool away beneath her too slowly. *Too slowly! She must hurry!* And then the face of the boy— his hair was still so smooth and pretty as she cradled his head in her lap—she stroked his hair, though his eyes had the listless emptiness of those at the verge of death. Black boils had burst on his face as well as along his arms, and the stench of the pus filled the dark, close room where they sat. Heedless, Renata was cradling him, rocking him gently, stroking his hair. "*Yes, I will. Yes, I pledge,*" she repeated, and repeated again, as she let go of the boy, relinquishing her grasp on him to the other person—there was another person in the room! Another person who could help! Who could save her son! "*Yes, I pledge,*" she said. "*I can give him another life,*" said another voice, another voice in the room, "*I can give him another life, but you must pledge. You must promise. You must pledge.*" "*Yes,*" Renata said, "*yes, I pledge.*" The body of the boy was dragged away; Renata reached out after it, tried to see it, looked up for it. But suddenly a face filled her field of vision, a face rushing toward her, the face of that other person who had been speaking—so close now, so close, *so close!*

And the picture of that face filling my mind so startled me that I involuntarily leapt up and cried out in a snarl. I was standing trembling with arched back and raised fur next to Renata's bed when my cat's-scream woke Renata out of her sleep. The dream faded, and that beautiful, terrifying face dissipated, that face that had drawn so close—a white-haired, white-skinned face at once so horrible and so lovely, that I knew I would never forget it again.

I could not tell whether Renata recalled the dream as she wearily sat up in her bed, gazing across the dark room. Her mind had reverted back to the stolid pulse of dull vampire thoughtstreams. I quietly leapt onto her bed and sat upon the sheets beside her. I listened further to her mind as she absently stroked my fur; I listened, trying to understand, trying to follow any thread that remained in her conscious mind that might explain the terrifying dream I had just seen. But Renata's mind did not disclose anything—whether it would have been capable of doing so or not.

Just the same, Renata never got back to sleep again that night.

CHAPTER SIX

The hood of Denis Pearson's sporty red Saab was up and Denis was leaning over the engine as Renata walked up the driveway. I heard the quiet swoosh of Paul Moorland's police cruiser backing away and then sweeping unobtrusively down the street from Denis's house. I thought we had gotten away from the College unseen.

Denis closed the hood and wiped his hands on a rag as we came up. "You brought your cat?" he said.

Renata was carrying her trusty canvas bag over her shoulder, and my head was, as usual, peeping out the top. This time my paws weren't looking for footing on a welter of books, folders and student essays—instead, she had packed a fine black silk dress, rolled up, atop a pair of dark black shoes. She was wearing a yellow summer sundress, light and cheerful and absolutely the wrong thing for the occasion she was going to Charleston for. And, tucked at the bottom of the bag, was the polished oblong wooden box containing her hypodermics and the small bottles of her precious supply of thanadoxicil. I was doing my best to keep my head above the edge of the bag, without clawing the rough silk of her dress.

"Yeah, sorry," she said. "But I can't really leave Kikki

at home. I can't ask anyone to come and feed her, because then they'd know I was off campus. If anyone finds out I'm dead." Renata held the bag out and I tried to make my best innocent-kitten face. I may have even mewed. I am sure I was irresistible. "Besides, Kikki is very good in cars. She'll just curl up in the bag and go to sleep."

Denis grinned. "Well, OK, if you're sure about it." He tossed the oily rag aside and opened the car doors. "Old Kerouac here's all checked out and ready to go."

"Kerouac?" Renata asked.

"Ah—my car. It's a very bad English teacher joke," he said. "You can put your stuff in the back—I'm afraid the trunk's full."

Renata stowed me and her bag in the back seat, and settled herself in the front passenger seat. Denis went into his house to wash his hands and lock up. Leaving the door open to air the heat out of the car, Renata put her head back on the seat and seemed to doze momentarily under her big sunglasses. She seemed tired and worried— I had been concerned about her since the day before. Although she had taken advantage of everyone's misunderstanding and pretended that the black-bordered envelope that Margaret had given her was just an ordinary notice of an ordinary death, I could tell how anxious she was. The Vampire Council, despite its eccentric ways, was not to be trifled with, and I understood that they had methods of making sure their decisions are respected. Very effective, terrible methods. I was also watching Renata's right arm as it lay in the midday sunshine—her skin was pale and white, and I watched for any sign of burn, any reddening. I knew that she had not taken her thanadoxicil since the night she clobbered Trace; her next dose would have normally been due last night, but she had skipped it. She had to let the drug work out of her system, because she couldn't appear before the Council like this: like a mortal human. Hopefully she had calibrated everything correctly—the dosages, the time to sundown, the drive time to Charleston. With a little luck, it would already be dark, and Denis would have already dropped her in the city, before her vampirism took the upper hand again.

Because by now you will have surmised that that is exactly what thanadoxicil does—it suppresses the vampire characteristics of a vampire, and allows the vampire to appear to be just an ordinary mortal human. It allows the vampire to go about in broad daylight, to interact with humans like just another normal mortal—it even suppresses the powerful blood-hunger for which vampires are so famous. But it is temporary, at least in its present formulations. A couple days, at most, and then the compound degrades and the vampire's normal body systems recover. The vampirism returns. And the transition can be a confusing, dangerous time for the vampire, like a junkie in withdrawal or a psych patient coming off meds—full of risk for the vampire and those around her. The blood lust returns suddenly and urgently, accompanied by a rush of energy, and an urgent sexual hunger—Trace Cuthbert's bad night a few days ago was just a symptom of Renata coming off thanadoxicil, though Trace didn't understand. But I had long understood that the Vampire Council had banned all vampires from the use of the drug. I had always heard that it was the risk of disclosure that vampires were present, the risk of provoking a fearful, violent backlash by the mortal humans against them, that lay behind the Council's proscription. If the Council had been able to find Renata at the College, it must have discovered that she was using thanadox and passing herself off as mortal. I had to assume the Vampire Council would view that as a serious matter.

Denis returned, and hopped in the driver's seat. "OK, let's get this show on the road," he said brightly, firing up the engine. Renata roused herself out of her doze and closed her door. Her arm, I noticed, had tinged ever so slightly pink just in the few minutes it had lain in the sun.

I hoped for Denis's sake that she had gotten her calculations right.

The drive off Forshay Mountain and into the Piedmont was absolutely a pleasant one, and I'm sure I would have enjoyed it if I had not been so concerned about the minutes ticking off the clock. Denis drove the back roads deep into the countryside of South Carolina, and didn't join up with the Interstate until he got to somewhere past Chester. He seemed to be in a holiday mood, flashing his smile at Renata, not minding when he got hung up behind the occasional slow tractor or vintage pickup truck blocking the two-lane road in a no-passing zone. The two did not talk much; after some trivial chat, Renata's drowsiness caught up with her and her dozing face slipped against the backrest, placid and untensed, still wearing her sunglasses. Denis, to his credit, took this in stride—not like some humans who seem to think that any break in conversation is a personal affront. Perhaps he just thought she was distraught at the alleged death in her family. Whatever the reason, Denis drove quietly as Renata dozed. My nerves eased a little as we finally got onto the fast Interstate south. The car hugged the fast lanes through Columbia and onto the flat pan of the Low Country. The miles peeled away as the red Saab sped through the stands of pine and past rushy expanses of pasture. I took advantage of the hypnotic thrum of the car engine to slip out of the canvas bag, creep into the front passenger seat and curl myself on Renata's lap. I noticed Denis's eye flick a glance toward me and smile a slight, tilted smile as he drove. Their thoughtstreams were both calm, smooth. I took the opportunity to sleep.

I woke when Denis nudged Renata on the arm. "Hey, Renata," he said, trying to get her attention. "Hey."

She pulled herself up in the car seat. I slipped back into the rear seat and looked out the windows. The sky had clouded over as we had neared the sea, and it was now late afternoon. I could see the tall supports of the Cooper

River Bridge off to the east ahead, like a monstrous stringed instrument. We were almost there.

"Hey."

"Yeah," Renata said, lifting her sunglasses and rubbing her eyes.

"You know, you never told me where you wanted me to take you," Denis said. "We'll be hitting the exit to Meeting Street soon."

The traffic was thick, with some cars streaming out of the city in the Friday afternoon rush hour, and other cars streaming into the city for Friday night entertainment. Renata looked out the window. "You can just drop me where you're going," she said. "I'll get a cab."

He looked askance at her. "You know, you don't have to be like that," he said. "You can level with me."

"It's all right, Denis," Renata said. "Really. I'm not trying to be difficult, but it's, well, a little embarrassing."

"OK." Denis was silent for a few minutes. The car nosed off the highway, looping around the exit ramps, and joined the parade of traffic going south on Meeting Street. "So, I'm going to the College down on Calhoun Street," he said. "So if, for example, you were going further along there, like to the hospital, I could just drop you and double back."

Renata turned to him, surprised. "The hospital? What makes you think I'm here to go to the hospital?"

Denis glanced at her quickly but looked away again. "Trace. Well, I knew about how you and Trace were…together. And he mentioned that you were acting very strangely the other night." The glance again. "And he saw your needles, and your…your medicine, in the bathroom at your place. So I, well, I just figured that you might be down here for something about that."

Denis's halting speech had gotten my undivided attention. I did not realize that Trace Cuthbert was capable of observing anything above Renata's breasts or beyond her buttocks. I guess having someone you just had sex with bash your head in might count as their "acting strangely." But if Trace had seen Renata's thanadoxicil equipment, then pretty soon everyone in Forshay was going to know about it, and draw their own conclusions. None of which was going to be correct, but they would draw them just the same. And I couldn't imagine that rumors about needles and drugs in her bathroom was going to help secure Renata's future at Forshay College.

Renata, as usual, was handling the situation with aplomb. "Denis, you're so sweet," she said with her French lilt, lightly touching his hand laying on the gearshift. "I am so touched that you're concerned. I do have a medical condition that requires injections, but I don't advertise it." She looked forward again through the windshield. "But no, I'm not here for that. I have to see some of my people. There's some trouble, I have to deal with them, and some of my people can be—well, a handful. And that's all I'm going to say."

Denis looked across at her again. "OK," he said. "You win." He grinned. "Don't we all got people like that?"

The red Saab finally worked through the traffic into the College of Charleston campus, tucked in its historic and genteel buildings on the west side of the city. Denis pulled into a parking garage on St. Philip Street. Renata opened her door and turned to gather her bag, and her cat. Denis lightly grabbed her arm.

"Wait," he said. He pulled out one of the business cards Forshay College gave its professors. (The college administration seemed to have visions of its faculty dropping calling cards on polished salvers as they visited monied aristocracy, though from what I had seen for most of them the reality of their lives consisted more of visits to the Sister's Store while in town and dining at McDonald's while on the road.) Denis turned the card over, took out a pen and wrote an address and two phone numbers on it. "Here's the address of the place I'll be staying—it's a residence hall here at the C of C. And here's my mobile number, and the main number at the residence hall too. You need anything, you just call. OK? I mean that."

Renata smiled and took the card. "OK," she said. "Thanks."

"I'm planning to drive back up Sunday afternoon, but I'm flexible about the time. Just call me and let me know when you want to go back, OK?"

"OK."

"OK then."

Renata got out of the car, shouldered her bag, and walked to the stairs out of the garage. Denis stood by his car, watching; he put his hand up in a silent wave, but Renata didn't look back. I couldn't read her thoughtstreams, but I could tell she was upset. Her mind was rushing, the thoughts whooshing past. In a way it would be natural for her to be worried and upset—she had to face the Council tomorrow, and she must have known how much trouble she was in. But I wondered whether, in some way, she was also frustrated that she couldn't tell Denis the truth. That she couldn't just talk to him honestly as a friend. That she still had to keep her real self out of sight.

The afternoon light was fading quickly as we left the garage and walked briskly away from the College of Charleston down St. Phillip Street. Charleston is not a taxicab kind of city; it's not like London or New York that way. We had walked all the way down St. Phillip Street to Wentworth, and back out to Meeting Street, and all we saw were tourist horse carriages and bike-pedal rickshaws. Finally Renata spotted a taxi pulled up near Society Street outside a theater. We hopped in.

"I'm already waitin' on a fare," the driver said.

"It's OK," Renata said. "Drive."

"But," the driver started. He turned around, a dignified black man with short silver hair and driver's cap. Renata had removed her sunglasses now that the evening was beginning to darken. The driver caught her eyes, and something he saw, something he *sensed* there, stopped his reply. He put the cab in gear and pulled out. "Where?" he asked.

"Drive," Renata said. "I'll direct you."

I saw the driver glancing at Renata in the review mirror from time to time. He looked worried. Renata looked out the window, at the old bricks and the slantwise sleeping porches and the live oaks. When she glanced back I caught a glimpse, just a glimpse of the same hard gleam starting in her eyes, the look they had had that night with Trace Cuthbert. "Here," she said. "Take Bay Street uptown. Till I tell you to turn."

The cab was making a big circle, doubling back toward the north of town where we had only recently gotten off the highway. My mind finally caught a sliver of thoughtstream that escaped her intense concentration, just a hint, but I suddenly realized where she was leading us. In a way, Denis had been almost right. We weren't driving to the hospital. But Renata was directing the cab to the Doctor.

The house was an old frame house, way up north King Street, hard against the highway overpass and Sans Souci Street. The paint was worn away until the wood was almost bare, the white of the whitewash surviving only in the grooved weathered grain of the planks. In the dying light it looked like the whorls of smudged white fingerprints left by a giant hand. The house looked abandoned; there was no lighted window, no light on the porch. Even the streetlight outside above the concrete curb had burned out. The cab driver, still anxious, dropped Renata in front of the house and wordlessly sped away, not even waiting for his fare. Renata hurried up the wooden steps of the covered porch, and when the door opened at her approach she entered the dark house without hesitation.

I had only met the Doctor one previous time, many years before. That was when he lived in New York, in a top floor apartment along Riverside Drive far up the West Side. He wasn't trying to avoid attention back in those days. In fact, there was a polished brass plaque by the separate entrance to his office suite along the back of the building: *Dr. Arnie Civitas, Specialty Internal Medicine.* Nothing evasive or even self-conscious. I remember how proud he was of the magnificent midnight views that were framed by the glass-curtain windows on two adjacent sides of his living room. One window faced downtown, with the brilliantly lit skyscrapers of Midtown rising out of the blocks of darker apartment buildings nearer by, their black bulk sprinkled with hundreds of lighted yellow windows. Through the other window the apartment faced the Hudson River, flowing black and silent beyond the park and the Drive, with the light of New Jersey glowing beyond the Palisades and with the occasional running lights of a barge moving downstream with the current. The Doctor was controversial even then, but in a different way from now. I remember his feeling at the time that controversy was something to be embraced, to be celebrated, not suppressed. Perhaps the vampire world had absorbed some of the sense of the times from the mortal human world—it was the late Sixties in New York back then, and the humans were good-naturedly challenging every kind of accepted wisdom. Summers of love, miniskirts, ringing electric guitar feeds through analog amps. Even the nickname "The Doctor" was a nod to hip London, where the original TV series *Dr. Who* had started its epic run but hadn't yet made it to America—you had to be in the know. Renata had sought the Doctor out then, when she had newly arrived in America—after many stages—from Europe. She and I had been together barely a decade then. She had seemed naïve and trusting to me, and seemed to be seeking something more from the Doctor than medical advice. It may have been just that I was still getting to know her, and I ascribed her seeking the Doctor's support to inexperience because I had no greater sense of her depth. But in any event, there were many other vampires in those days who also sought him out, looking for the guidance, advice and counsel of the Doctor—the famous creator of thanadoxicil.

I don't really know what happened in the years after that golden time, in the years after the Vampire Council suppressed the Doctor and his movement. Renata left New York to wander from place to place in America. I came along, riding in successive generations of canvas shoulder bags. The Doctor must have dropped out of sight. I never heard a whisper of a rumor of his whereabouts for years—and if Renata had known, I certainly would have plucked the information from a thoughtstream or two somewhere along the line. No word of the Doctor directly, for all those years, although the supplies of thanadoxicil somehow arrived regularly in their small, polished oblong boxes. I had never quite figured out how the Doctor managed to get them to her without anyone—without *me*—discovering his method. It was not until Renata had started at Forshay at the end of the prior summer that a letter had arrived in Renata's mail, not coded or hidden at all, bearing the Doctor's greetings and a Charleston return address. He wasn't hiding any more. He must have known that the Vampire Council had located him—or else he intended to face them at last. Why else would he have moved to the same town, to Charleston, right under the Council's pallid vampire noses?

Renata and I moved slowly into the dark interior of the Doctor's house. I could see the hard glittering of her eyes now in the faint light from the window, and heard the slight hiss in her breath—the vampire breathing was beginning. The thanadox had nearly faded. From across the dark room, as my cat's eyes adjusted to the darkness, the pale face of the Doctor emerged from the gloom.

"Child," he said, "I knew you'd come. I knew it when I heard that the Council had summoned you." His voice was a sibilant rasp, hardly above a whispered hiss—the common conversational voice of vampires talking to one another. "You must know what danger you're in."

Renata was clearly struggling to retain her composure as the remaining effects of the drug wore away, and her vampirism reasserted itself. She looked tired, and seemed moody. "Doctor," she said smiling, "I knew you had taken a house on King Street, but I had forgotten it was so near Sans Souci Street." She chuckled. "*Sans souci*— 'Without Cares' Street. You have a talent for irony."

The Doctor did not laugh, he did not smile. "I always forget that you're French," he said. "I never felt comfortable in that language myself. It confuses me. And I was always confused why, if you're French, you don't carry the French style of your name—*Renée* would be the French form, wouldn't it, Renata? But no matter. No, I chose the house because it was near the highway on-ramp. I have a car now, you know—a pre-owned Japanese import. Beige. It's so nondescript that it's practically invisible." He narrowed his eyes and peered closer at Renata's face, continuing to talk. "However I don't think that the Council will really give me much of a chance to escape, not if they are serious about coming after me. At least, I don't think I'll be escaping in a beige midsize sedan."

The Doctor reached out and laid his palm against Renata's cheek. He took her wrist in his hand. He made her open her mouth and he peered in—he was, after all, a doctor. "Child," he said, "you're not well."

Renata gave a pained smile. "Yes, I know."

He frowned. "You can't come on and off thanadoxicil like this," he said. "Going from one state to another is something that takes adjustment. You made the round trip in just the last day, didn't you?" He glared at her silence. "Didn't you?" he insisted.

Renata nodded. "Yes," she said. "First it was just a mistake, but then I got the summons from the Council right after I had gone back on. And I had to come off the stuff again to come down here and appear at my trial." She closed her eyes, rubbing her fingers over the eyelids. "I have such a headache. I feel awful."

Renata's legs buckled under her, and she took a stumbling step forward. She dropped the bag from her shoulder, and I leapt out and onto the carpet as the Doctor rushed forward to steady her.

"Here," he said, guiding her to a dark velvet couch that lay along the shadowy wall. "I want you to rest for an hour. Nothing's likely to happen. Not for a while anyway."

She seemed disoriented as he laid her onto the couch. I had not seen her have such trouble with the effects of coming off thanadoxicil before. "My bag...my cat," she said.

The Doctor pulled the straps of the canvas bag, dragging it over the floor, and stood it up next to Renata's arm where she lay on the couch. Then he caught me in his stare.

In all my years of experience with vampires, I have never gotten completely used to their gaze. I can understand why vampires are objects of fear and horror for mortal humans—much as are snakes for small rodents or birds. The vampire's eye is unblinking, steady, flat, unemotional. It pins you in place like a butterfly speared in a collector's box. It paralyzes. And the Doctor was clearly a vampire of unusual power, because even I—a cat of, as I have already mentioned to you, extensive talents— even I found myself paralyzed. If the Doctor had meant me harm, I could not have moved to save myself. But he just regarded me in his icy stare, as Renata slipped into a feverish slumber.

"Your cat," the Doctor hissed. "Oh yes, I have heard

about your cat."

CHAPTER SEVEN

I was still frozen in the Doctor's stare, caught in the gaze of this most famous and powerful vampire. He smiled. Renata's breath had quieted as she fell asleep. It sighed and hummed gently from the couch. The Doctor walked closer to where I sat upon the dark Persian carpet.

"Yes, I know the cat," he said, still staring at me. "I know what you are."

There was something about the way he said it. It daunted me. The beginning of a tickling dread began to tighten my scalp, as the import of what he was saying dawned upon me. Was it possible that I had disclosed myself without meaning to? Could I have been so careless? I could find out.

I could try to talk to his mind.

What do you know? I said mentally, my cat's eyes widening in my silence.

The Doctor chuckled. "Oh yes, I can hear you," he said in a hiss. "I'm afraid I can't respond in kind—I'll have to talk back to you the conventional way. But yes, I can hear every word you put in my mind." He seemed very pleased that we had found this common ground.

Then tell me what you mean, I said.

The Doctor paused, serious now. "I know what you are, even if Renata doesn't," he said. "I know that you are a Timeslider."

I was shocked. How could he know? How could *anyone* know? I paused; I couldn't formulate a response. I knew that my hesitation was only confirming his statement. I am ashamed to say that I became flustered—me, of all cats!—and broke off our stare to wash my paw. I needed the moment to collect myself. But I realized that the Doctor knew he had me. It was useless to deny it.

Yes, I am, I said. *And I'm sure you know how dangerous a thing that is to know. I won't endanger you further by asking how you came by this knowledge. But just for the record,* I said, *we don't use that word.*

"What word do you use?" the Doctor hissed.

We don't use any word.

"Then how do you…"

We don't.

Now it was the Doctor's turn to pause, taking this in. So I continued.

And you are correct that Renata does not know what I am.

The Doctor had by now approached very close. He pulled a chair up to a table and sat; I considered it only polite to leap to the tabletop so we could continue talking, face to face.

And furthermore, I said, *I do not intend that she should know.*

The Doctor frowned, his pallid forehead creasing above his unblinking vampire eyes. "Why is that?" he said. "I think you must have figured out that she is in danger from the Vampire Council. That she and I are both in danger. It might be a great comfort to her to know that so close by is a—well, one of you."

That would enhance her danger, not lessen it, I said. *You must realize that I can only protect her if she does not know what I am.*

"In that case, how can she not have figured it out for herself?" the Doctor said. "How do you know she doesn't know? For instance, what reason can she possibly understand that her kitten is still a kitten? That it doesn't age? You must have been with her for years!"

Yes. Since 1953, I replied. *The springtime. We're just now starting to get to know each other.*

"Better than fifty years," he said. "And so, the ageless cat? What is her understanding of that?"

I glared back at him, impatient for a moment. I thought he was being willfully obtuse.

I don't really know, I said, narrowing my eyes. *Perhaps she doesn't notice. Or she forgets. Or perhaps she assumes that she has had a succession of very similar cats over the decades. But,* I finished, a bit harshly, *as a doctor, you must be aware of the effect of immortality on vampire memory. How it leads to time-confusion—how some vampires even experience the illusion of living the same life, day by day, over and over again, in era after successive era. I mean, there have been studies!*

"Yes, I apologize," the Doctor said. "I have heard that you are a cat of science. I didn't mean to be impertinent. And I, too, know about the limits of her memory. Do you know that she really believes that we first met each other in New York? In 1966?"

That isn't the case?

The Doctor shook his head. "No," he said. "No, we have known each other long before that, even if Renata no longer retains a memory of it. I even knew her when she was a mortal human—before she became a vampire."

When was that?

The Doctor declined his face in thought for a moment. "It was in 1351, in Brittany. Two years after the great plague year. Though I do not think she died of the plague." He reflected a moment longer. "In life she was a noblewoman of France, you know."

Yes, I replied. *The Comtesse de Beaumanoir.*

The Doctor smiled and shook his head again. "No, she was a noblewoman, but no countess. That title was invented for her by Vesta Letalia, the chief of the Vampire Council. A powerful, ruthless vampire." The Doctor held up his left index finger. "You have noticed the ring Renata wears, on this finger? Red, with the white star on it?"

I have seen it.

"The Order of the Star," the Doctor said. "An emblem of an order of chivalry founded by the French king, during the wars we call the Hundred Years' War. The ring belonged to Renata's brother-in-law, Jean de Beaumanoir, a famous Breton knight in the service of the French king. The captain of Josselin, later the Marshal of all Brittany. Or at least that's the story as best as I have pieced it together over the years. She clings to that ring, has clung to it for centuries. She somehow knows that it's important, but she cannot remember why." He paused and looked down at me; it seemed, as incongruous as it would have been, that his flinty vampire eyes had been invaded by a hint of melancholy. "In every age, every century, I have to meet Renata anew, as a stranger," he said. "I have to win her friendship all over again. To win her trust. And in every new era, I try to refine and improve the ancient compound—what we call thanadoxicil now, because it sounds so modern. Perhaps someday I will succeed in creating a formulation that is not so transitory." Though his sentiment seemed wistful, his gaze continued steady and unflinching. "But meeting Renata anew each time is an effort, because her memory is so thin. Each time, she remembers nothing of me from before."

I took this all in thoughtfully, but a question lingered. *Doctor,* I asked, *you yourself are a vampire, yet your memory seems flawless—why? Why are you exempt from the time-confusion?*

He smiled again, but sadly. "Cat," he said, "I am not exempt. My memory is far from flawless. As you have pointed out, I am a vampire, and like other vampires I have little basic memory. But I know you can hear the thoughts of my mind. When you listen to my mind, what do you hear? Do you hear a mind like other vampires?"

I considered his question, and realized—as he must have known I would realize—that the thoughtstreams I heard from the Doctor's mind were different from a normal vampire's. They had the same hum of mortal-human undertone that Renata's had. They were, like hers, distinct from the ordinary, flat thoughts of an ordinary vampire. *No,* I said. *You and Renata both have unusual minds—unusual for a vampire.*

The Doctor nodded. "Yes, I thought you would have noticed this. In fact, I imagine that you have noticed this about Renata's mind more and more recently, haven't you?"

Yes, I replied. *I have remarked on it in the last few days. The human traits of her mind have become progressively more pronounced.* I thought of mentioning Renata's strange and inexplicable dream to the Doctor, but decided to hold back, at least for now. I pressed him for more information. *What does it mean?*

The Doctor became thoughtful, and cast his eyes down, frowning. "Part of it I can explain, or at least try to," he said. "But not all of it." He looked back down at me, the cold gaze fixing on my eyes again. "You see, Renata and I are both vampire adepts," he said. "Sometimes they call us memory adepts. Are you familiar with those terms?"

I slowly shook my head—surprised, because in all my centuries among vampires, and all my years with Renata, I would not have thought there was anything I had left to learn about either. *No,* I said, *I have never heard of that.*

The Doctor sighed, thinking. "It's a little tricky to explain," he said. "An adept is like a genetic anomaly. It is a vampire who retains certain of the mental abilities of a mortal even after passing into the vampire state. Including, most important, some level of memory."

So vampire adepts are not subject to the time-confusion? I asked.

"It varies by the degree of the adept," he said. "For some, the memory ability that is retained is very slight—for all practical purposes, they may be like other vampires. For others, however, the memory can become strong—

stronger even than it had been as a mortal. And the skill of the adept can be developed with training."

So a vampire can learn to be an adept?

"No, an adept can be trained to retain, even recapture memory," he said. "I have trained myself over centuries that way. And an adept can be trained by an adept master—another, more experienced adept that has bonded with the novice adept, and can guide the novice adept's mind down pathways leading to enhanced memory. The bond between the master and novice is a strong one, perhaps unique in the vampire world.

"But actually being an adept is innate, inherited. In fact, it is a characteristic of a human even when he or she is still mortal—before changing to the vampire state. They say that there are markers of an adept that a trained expert can discern in a mortal human. Some say that adept mortals have an unusual magnetic field, like a halo surrounding their bodies that is sometimes visible in the dark like the Northern Lights. Some say adepts can be detected by scent—a slight but distinct fragrance from bodily secretions—the sweat, the saliva, the tears of the adept. A smell like flower petals—roses. But any adept, especially a powerful adept, is exceedingly rare. And, depending on the adept, that rare case is considered by the Vampire Council to be either extremely valuable—or extremely dangerous."

I was silent for a long moment, confused. He wasn't making any sense! *I'm sorry, Doctor, but you've lost me. Why would the ability to retain memory, and to avoid time-confusion, pose a danger to the Vampire Council?*

The Doctor smiled again. "You would not think it should, would you? You might even think that such talents would be welcomed, nurtured, encouraged for the benefit of all vampires." A pensive frown crossed his brow. "But that is not the case, I'm afraid. Normal vampires, those that have the ordinary vampire mind we're familiar with, are detached and passive, generally attentive only to the most immediate stimuli of their environment. But their detachment makes them highly suggestible. Because vampire adepts have so much broader a command of memory and intellect, they are able to change the behavior of ordinary vampires by suggestion—and a truly powerful adept can effectively control the mass of ordinary vampires, bend them to his will. So to be an adept—or to control an adept—well, that could bring a vampire great power over his vampire brethren.

"And you see," the Doctor continued, "Renata is not just any adept—she is a uniquely talented adept. One in a million. Maybe like none ever before." He glanced at the sleeping figure of Renata. "And I do not know whether she has realized that she is an adept—or how rare an adept she is—or whether she once knew but decided to refrain from training her memory. To reject her gift."

I considered this. It would explain the Council's general suspicion and hostility toward Renata and the Doctor, I thought, on the theory that if you're not with us you're against us. But it didn't really explain one thing. *Doctor,* I asked, *the Vampire Council must have known that Renata was using thanadoxicil for a long time—months, if not years. And you are certainly not undertaking any pains to remain concealed. So why is the Council taking these actions now? Why the summons? What's changed? What are they up to?*

"That," the Doctor mused, "is one of the problems. I do not know. But something has prompted them to renew their efforts to extinguish me, and they seem to be suddenly impelled by an extreme urgency. And now they have expanded their attention to Renata, as well. I'm afraid that any infractions they may say she has committed, whether by using thanadoxicil or living among mortal humans, those must be a pretext. It would not justify convoking the meeting of vampires that I believe is supposed to occur tomorrow night. But exactly what Vesta Letalia and the Council are trying to do? I don't know. I do know that I am worried about Renata. She may be in for a very bad time with the Council. Somehow I have to figure out why exactly the Council is after her—and what exactly they want with her."

How do you do that?

The Doctor shook his head. "I don't know that either," he said. "In fact, I was hoping that a Timeslider might help me figure it out."

We both paused, looking over to where Renata lay. The last of the thanadox must have degraded because she was wholly vampire now. Her skin lay milky in the feeble light from the street; her lips and quivering eyelashes stark black against it. I felt for a moment as if the Doctor and I were babysitters, sitting a vigil over a feverish child.

"You are very loyal to her," the Doctor said.

I thought for a moment. I had never really thought about it that way, but I decided that the Doctor's observation was just. *Yes,* I said. *I am loyal.*

"She was loyal to me," the Doctor said. "Of all the vampires who joined my movement in New York all those years ago, she was the true believer. I often wonder if she was the *only* believer." The Doctor turned his stare back at me suddenly, so fiercely that I again felt a twinge of involuntary panic, just for a moment. "And now," he said, "she is the only one left. After everything the Council has done to break us down, she is the one who remains. And I," he declared, with a slight lift of his chin, "will be loyal to her."

Doctor, I asked, *you mentioned the relation of master and novice adepts—were you Renata's master?*

The Doctor smiled sadly. "No," he said, "I was not. Not for want of trying—I sought to lead her as a master, when I first met her as a vampire, centuries ago, and each time I met her again. But I never could," he said, "because she already had a master."

Who was that? I asked.

The Doctor shrugged. "I do not know. I never discovered. But an adept can only have one master—once the adept has pledged himself to his master, it is a bond that can never be broken. And no vampire can ever displace that master."

I fell silent, trying to take in all that the Doctor had said. I let a few moments pass. If there had been a clock anywhere in that house I'm sure the ticking would have filled the silence. I knew that the night was wearing on, Friday night late turning into Saturday morning early. I could catch the thoughtstreams from the Doctor, but like Renata's they weren't the normal, cool thoughtstreams of vampires. Rather, they carried the same undercurrent of clashing, clamoring struggle as mortal human minds, with their contending desires and emotions. I realized that the Doctor must be feeling such emotions for Renata. A vampire emotional over another vampire! I thought. And now two vampires with such un-vampirelike minds, both in the same room! How extraordinary!

"She's fully a vampire again," the Doctor hissed, "like me, like all the normal vampires." His flinty eyes gleamed as they caught my gaze again. "You know what she has to do."

Yes, I said. *Does it have to be soon?*

"It has to be tonight—I can tell that she hasn't been feeding properly while in the human state. That's one of the problems with moving from state to state so frequently—one must feed, either as a human or as a vampire. Well, she has failed to feed in the human state. So she must feed in the vampire state."

Tonight is going to be awkward, I said. *Look at her. And besides, there is no one chosen.*

The Doctor shook his head. "It must be tonight. If she doesn't feed she will become sicker. And if she feeds tomorrow night, she will be sluggish. Sluggish, full of blood, digesting—when she has to face the Council!" He tapped his lips with a long, bony white finger. "How about the human who she came to the city with? That black man, in the red car?"

81

No, I said flatly. I had better quash that idea right away.

"But why not?" the Doctor persisted. "He's so convenient. And no one would know."

No. Absolutely not. I tried to raise myself tall, and to make myself look intimidating. However, I only succeeded in making my tail fur bristle up—not the effect I was reaching for. *Please think of her—of her position,* I said. *She is trying to fit in at that new college. She is living in a small town now, and everyone knows each other there, and he's one of them. Renata would never forgive us if we let that happen.*

The Doctor relented. He glanced over at Renata, then stood. He towered over me, his pale face dim in the darkness. "So be it. But if it is not to be that human, then it must be another. And in that case, I had better wake her now." His eyes glinted coldly. "Because," the Doctor said, "she'll need to hunt."

It was after 1 a.m. when I finally caught up with her. After a year of living the happy, if prosaic, life of the pet of an ordinary human college teacher, I had started to forget some things about vampires. For one thing, they're fast. On a clear night they can sweep down the darkness of a city street like shadows thrown by the moon, their feet barely touching the ground. They move like the wind, and as silently. If you were pursued by a vampire, you would never know—your first clue would be the cold of the vampire's fingers, already upon your throat.

But if you are a small cat, keeping up with a vampire in the full rush of midnight is no easy task. I lost Renata in the shadows almost immediately after she slipped out of the Doctor's house, swathed in her black silk dress and carrying her high-heel shoes. But when I saw that she was headed back downtown, I had an idea that I might know where she was going.

The blocks along East Bay Street and Market Street had been the center of the tavern district in the days of the pirates, as they were in the days of the cotton trade—and as they continue to be even today, in the days of the weekend tourists. I was enjoying my loping jog down the back alleys of King Street toward the bars—the closer I got, the stronger the smell of fish and oysters from Charleston's famous seafood restaurants. I was hungry; I hadn't eaten since the day before. But I couldn't stop, not yet. There would be time to tip a trash can full of fish heads after I had found Renata.

It didn't take long, once I got to Market Street. One nice thing about my peculiar talents is that I did not have to actually visually inspect every bar and restaurant along the strip—it was enough to pause in the window or doorway, narrow my eyes and listen to the thoughtstreams emanating from the milling crowds within. I had observed Renata hunting before, and I knew her technique. I knew what to listen for. And I heard it, more quickly than I thought I would, in a run-down, nautical-themed bar a couple blocks off Market. I let myself into the bar through an open side window when I heard it, through the din of excited Friday night brains, a very loud, very clear beacon. It said, *"Who's the babe?"*

I quickly spotted the source of the thoughtstream—a scruffy white guy of about thirty, in a torn, tight t-shirt and blue jeans, and a ratty do-rag covering short, shabby hair. He was talking to two other men, one a white guy with dark hair, the other a light skinned black guy with his hair cut very short. They were several years younger than the scruffy guy—early twenties, maybe—and similarly dressed, but at least they were clean-shaven. The two younger guys wore dark wrap glasses, despite the dim light of the bar. The younger guys were also wearing various items of leather and chain: belts, straps, keyrings, and other bits I couldn't identify because they had no identifiable purpose—except to make the owner appear to know something about motorcycles. And I suspected that neither of these guys did.

Over on the other side of the room, sitting at a table under one of the few glowing lights in the bar, I spotted Renata. She had her white scarf over her thick black hair, and her large dark sunglasses were in place. The rough black silk of her dress had been shrugged far to the outside of her shoulders to display a long expanse of white skin above the neckline. The light above her gave warmth to her pallid skin and made it seem to glow, the long unbroken plane of flesh seeming as perfect and untouched as newfallen snow. She gazed impassively toward the three men at the bar. She was gorgeous.

I noticed that the boys were starting to quarrel. I crept closer.

"Look," said the scruffy one, "I don't know who you are, or who you *think* you are, but you're out of line!"

"Hey, hey, no worries, man," the white guy said. "You saw her, you talk to her."

"Yeah, we not here for it," the black guy said. "We just a couple a demons."

"Demons?" Scruffy asked.

"Yeah, we just a couple a demon dudes havin' a laugh," the white guy said.

The scruffy guy couldn't make out if he was being insulted. He tipped a pull from his longneck. "Yeah? Well fuck you."

"Oh man," the black guy said.

"Oh yeah," said the white guy.

"He messin' with us?"

"I don't know, should we ask him?"

"Yeah, ask him."

"Hey, you messin' with us?"

"Yeah, you messin' with us?"

The scruffy guy stood his ground, and fixed the younger guys with a practiced stink eye. "I don't have time for you *children*," he said. He held up his bottle to the bartender, and pointed across at Renata. The bartender uncapped a longneck beer and carried it to Renata, gesturing back toward the scruffy guy. Renata accepted the beer, and placed it on the table before her untasted. She then turned her face toward the scruffy guy and unveiled a dazzling, radiant smile. She was impossibly beautiful. Her smile was electric. It stopped the three men cold.

Scruffy was the first to recover his footing. "Later kids," he said, grabbing his bottle, "gotta go talk to a lady." The two younger guys dutifully stayed behind, watching carefully as Scruffy pulled out a chair at Renata's table and joined her.

I didn't need to stay too close, or try to listen in on what Renata and the scruffy guy were saying. It hardly mattered. My only concern was security—I was watching, most of all, for any truant girls in Forshay College t-shirts that might make an appearance in the bar, and notice their junior history lecturer hanging out with the rough end of the locals. But Renata knew her business, and had chosen this bar well; no Forshay girls were likely to make it out to a dive this far off the tourist track. I had nothing to do but wait.

The bar closed at two, and Renata and the scruffy guy walked out slowly into the dark. I followed. I saw the man motion toward the back of the bar, toward the parking lot, but Renata pulled his arm the other way. She wanted to walk out along the pier by the harbor. They walked; I followed at a distance. Across Bay Street, across Concord Street, along the piers on the water with their seaside restaurants and clubs, deserted now in the depth of the night. The hulking Greek columns of the Custom House emerged in the scattered light of midnight, and glowed whitish against the sky. I saw Renata climb down from the pier into the scrub and shingle along the harbor's edge. Scruffy followed. He was getting affectionate. He grabbed her hand, pulled her to him. There was no light except the crime lights from the restaurants on the pier above, and the lights from the shipping cranes across the harbor. The pair quickly disappeared into the shadows near the water. Then—nothing. Stillness. Silence. I waited, knowing that Renata could take care of herself, but thinking—it had been a long time. Maybe she had forgotten how? She must certainly be out of practice. I crept closer, trying to see. Still, not a sound. I hopped off the edge of the pier and into darkness of the scrub brush on the beach, inching forward little by little in the darkness as if stalking a mouse. I was nearly upon them by the time my eyes had adjusted to the deep shadow.

Renata had her dress off; it was folded neatly on a patch of dry sand to keep it clean. The scruffy guy, however, though he may initially have enjoyed the fact that she was naked, was definitely enjoying it no longer. Renata had him pinned to the earth, a knee driving into his gut, her arm jammed into his gaping, struggling mouth like a gag. As I watched, one of his arms worked itself free; he lashed it toward Renata again and again, struggling to get her off him, trying to get her away. Renata caught the arm in her free hand and, with a casual twist, broke his arm at the elbow. The elbow now pointed the wrong direction. The scruffy guy was trying to scream; his eyes were clenched and his back arched and he was maddened with pain. Renata was not making the move I expected, the move toward the kill, but instead just hung there, poised with her victim writhing, struggling. I was alarmed. There was no need for this delay, I thought. Even a cat knows it is bad form to play with a mouse for too long. This had gone on long enough. I leaped across the sand and bracken until I faced Renata full on. My cat's-eyes' retinas glowed green, reflecting the harbor lights. Her eyes caught mine and locked. She knew. It was time to end this. Her fangs had extended, and as she lunged at last they flashed in the near darkness like white lightning. And then her face was gone, plunged into the man's throat; all I could see was the mass of her tousled raven hair. I heard the deep gurgles as she drained the blood from the lacerated veins in the guy's neck, swallow after swallow, until the scruffy guy finally went limp. She looked up at me again, our eyes meeting for a moment with the blood black smeared on her mouth, drops spotting the white skin of her naked torso. And then, with a sudden movement she was away, silently disappearing into the night, the image of her still lingering before me unreal like the ghost image of a light that had flashed in the darkness, an afterimage, a hallucination.

I heard the thud of another set of feet hitting the wet sand from the pier. I faded back into the shadows and saw a dark figure, black-clothed and silent, creep up on the scruffy guy's corpse. I saw the figure produce a knife and, with a single, practiced motion, slice the scruffy guy's throat from ear to ear. I heard the knife hit the sand next to the body as he dropped it there, and then the black-clothed figure, too, was gone. I scampered out of the scrub and under the pier, then back out into the open of Concord Street just in time to see the figure climb into a car that was pulled up under a streetlight, Renata's folded black dress tucked under his arm, and drive away. A midsize beige sedan.

CHAPTER EIGHT

I could only perceive the daybreak because of the pencil-thin white lines that began to glow at the tiny gaps in the heavy black drapes. I was back at the Doctor's house, and I was bone-tired. Vampires under the spell of their blood-lust may not feel fatigue as they cover miles and miles in a single night, but not so small cats. We get tired indeed. My paws were sore and rubbed raw from scampering over asphalt and concrete and cobblestones, all the way down King Street and then all the way back up. I had lost the Doctor's car in the night almost as fast as I had lost Renata. I finally gave up trying to keep up with these creatures. Let them swoop and fly lightly up and down midnight streetscapes. I was a cat, not a vampire. I would make my own way at my own pace, back to the place I knew they were headed anyway.

And indeed, they were at the house when I returned in the dark of the predawn morning. Renata was already asleep, lying on the same couch where she had lain a few hours earlier after her fainting spell. The Doctor had put her into a white flannel nightdress, with curious and complex white-on-white embroidery and lace decorating the hem and cuffs. Whose nightdress might this have been? I wondered; what story must lie behind it? I thought of the Doctor, his severe vampire face glowing white like a hazy moon in the darkened room, as he tenderly dressed the drowsy Renata in the garment. His surprising, un-vampire-like sympathy continued to pique my scientific curiosity. He was indeed an interesting specimen.

The Doctor must have retired to a bedroom somewhere in the dark fastness of the second floor, long before I returned to the house. I considered for a moment making a quick exploration of the house—finding out what was where and who was there—but somehow, I lacked resolution. Perhaps I simply felt it unseemly—the Doctor was a creature of such refinement that an uninvited look around seemed gauche. Or perhaps it was a vague fear—if a vampire were so unpredictable that he could tuck in another vampire for a nap, in a pair of borrowed jammies, what other unpredictable actions might he be capable of? Some of them, no doubt, might be unfortunate for a small cat. Or perhaps I was just hesitant to leave Renata alone again, even for a moment. The image of her face at the pier, the blood of her victim smearing her chin, kept coming back to me again and again. I don't know what kind of pain that image would cause her if she were ever to see herself so—I could only hope that any feeble vampire memory of what she had done would dissolve when she could once again take the thanadoxicil. So I had curled myself on the top of the couch backrest and put my nose into my tail, sleeping until the daybreak had sent its tiny slivers of light through the drapes.

But once I realized that the day was in progress, my mind suddenly became anxious. Perhaps I am by nature a worrier. It is surely not so unexpected that a cat with a scientific mind might like to think ahead, to anticipate troubles rather than simply deal with them as they come. And I could see that there were troubles laying in wait today. Not just Renata's rendezvous with the Vampire Council that night—but also what about the dead body they had left by the pier? Sure, it's fine for vampires to justify it by saying that Renata needed to feed, and having got her fill of blood she could sleep it off behind the blackout curtains of a dingy old house. But in the other world, the world of mortal people—somehow I thought that Charleston law enforcement would likely see it less as a question of food than a question of homicide. I worried about the complexities that that small fact might add to our day.

I hopped off the couch and began to search for a way out of the house. Renata did not stir from her sleep as I crept about. The Doctor was right about how a belly full of fresh blood makes a vampire sluggish and drowsy. The night before the front door had been left slightly ajar by the Doctor, knowing that I would return; but this morning it was immovable, tight and deadbolted. The Doctor must have locked up during the night—no way out there. I searched around the unfamiliar baseboards, the windowsills behind the drapes, the crown molding by the ceiling.

It turned out that there was a loose panel in the metal storm door in the kitchen (the kitchen being, it seemed, a particularly disused room). I carefully pressed myself through the edge where the aluminum panel had come unattached from the frame, and found myself in bright-gray morning light that had spread up the rivers from the sea, a few miles south. I blinked a few times and stretched, washed a paw with my tongue, and quickly skittered around to the front of the house.

I was looking for a newspaper. I wanted to see what—if anything—the morning paper had to say about a mysterious killing on the East side, a stone's throw from the harbor and in the middle of the tourists' fun zone. I trotted down the street, and checked the concrete driveways of the neighboring houses. Many of them had a rolled newspaper tossed onto them, like a fish tossed up by an overnight tide, but each was tightly stuffed into a plastic bag. I tried to claw at one, to see if a small cat could shred the plastic and free the paper—but no use. A morning paper is not intended to be read by a curious tiger-striped kitten. I would have to find a place where someone had the paper open and was actually reading it. I paused for a moment, nose up. It took a moment, but a light southeast breeze off the Cooper River carried the scent I was hoping for. A whiff of coffee, sausage, frying potatoes.

The source of the scent wasn't hard to find. A little diner called Hannibal's, several blocks downtown, catering to the local trucking traffic going onto the highway up to Columbia or over the bridge to Mount Pleasant. Work vans of local mechanics and artisans crowded the small parking lot as they began their Saturday workday. I waited unobtrusively by the concrete steps for a few moments, and then slipped through the door behind a pair of oilstained workboots that walked in for breakfast.

Getting a glimpse at a newspaper was going to be a little more tricky. I had two choices: I could find a vantage point where I could see the open page, or I could find someone who was reading, and listen to his thoughtstreams as he went through the stories in the paper. The first option was preferable, because I have found that people never seem to be interested in the same things that I am, and there is only so much time I can spend listening to someone's mind making a careful recitation of yesterday's baseball boxscores, or the latest celebrity drug-and-fornication headlines. It was a small diner, however. If I took a vantage point that was open enough to see a newspaper on the countertop, I was just as likely to be visible myself, and I could find myself slung by the scruff back out onto the sidewalk. I looked around, hanging cautiously back by the chairs along the wall.

The man with the workboots had sat at the counter. He pulled a copy of the *Post & Courier* out of his back pocket, and unrolled it as the waitress brought him coffee. I crept close enough to hear his thoughtstreams clearly. I was in luck—this was apparently a methodical workman, a man who did every job by starting at the beginning and continuing through until the end. And that applied to newspapers as much as it must have applied to—based on the stitching on his workshirt—air conditioner repair. I sat quietly under the stool at the counter next to him. The headlines first, then the stories. A Friday night murder is juicy news; I didn't have to wait long to hear his mind echo the story. It was the top local item on page one.

LOCAL MAN SLASHED, MURDERED

A local brickmason was found dead with his throat slashed early this morning near the Market Street entertainment district in Charleston. Police say that Mark Hurley Johnson, 35, of Mount Pleasant, was found on the harbor beach near Concord and Cumberland Streets at about six o'clock A.M., although he had apparently been dead several hours. Johnson appeared to be the victim of an assailant wielding a knife, police said, and the cause of death has been tentatively determined to be loss of blood from the deep throat wound. Police say witnesses had observed Johnson at Cap'n Bridie's Bar a few blocks away earlier in the evening. Police are asking anyone who has any information about the incident to please contact them at the Charleston police Crimestoppers line...

I was no longer listening to the thoughtstreams—I had heard enough. The story had only mentioned the deep cut the Doctor had made in the man's throat; there had been no notice of two deep puncture wounds to the throat, or any strange, semicircular bruising there. And no mention of the absence of blood at the scene even though the police were putting the cause of death to exsanguination—the result, they no doubt reasoned, of the body having lain below the tide mark on the shingle and the waters of the harbor having washed around it as the tide rose and fell overnight. Renata had chosen her killing ground very well indeed.

The story also said, "witnesses had observed." That was a little worrying. Witnesses had been talked to, witnesses surely must have noticed the striking, raven-haired woman that Mark Hurley Johnson had been lucky enough to leave the bar with. *Witnesses—hmm.*

Nothing I could do about that at the moment, though. The air conditioner man had turned around in his stool, his back to the counter, so he could stretch out as he finished the paper and cross one oilstained boot across his opposite knee. He had not noticed that the waitress had slid his eggs and sausage to his place on the counter behind him. A kitten-light leap from floor to chair, and then from chair to countertop—it only took me a moment to paw a sausage patty off his plate and grab it with my mouth, trophy-like, as I leapt away from the counter. The door to the diner opportunely opened to admit another customer and I slipped out the open door with my breakfast, before any of the humans noticed anything amiss.

Now, I can tell that there is something that is puzzling you. As pleased as I was about the police treating the dead man as no more than a garden-variety murder victim, I can almost hear you objecting, *Now hold on there—that guy was killed by a vampire! He becomes a vampire too, now, doesn't he?* Well, that's a common belief, but it is a complete misunderstanding of vampire biology. I honestly don't know where these urban myths get started. The simple answer is that, when a vampire stalks, kills and drains its victim, all that's left is a dead victim—some mushy biomass. And I'm sure that, with a little thought, you can appreciate this from simple logic. After all, even though vampires may not feed as frequently as mortal humans—they need a full meal only every month or so, not the daily three squares that seem to be the fondest hope of mortal humans—even with such occasional meals, what would it mean mathematically if every one of those meals were itself given vampire immortality? And each of those meals in turn had to feed itself, creating still more vampires? You'd have a geometric progression, a vampiric-Malthusian epicycle, and pretty soon you'd up to your ass in crowds of hungry vampires. It would be as if, for every sausage patty you ever ate, you created a phantom, immortal pig that followed you around. How many thousands of phantom pigs would be trailing about after you at this point in your life? Absurd. So, just to set the record straight: vampire food is just vampire food. Vampire reproduction—the initiation of the newly dead into the vampire world of undead—ah, that's different. That's a complex, intimate, even erotic interaction between dead beings. That one's harder to explain. That's something even I have never directly observed, although I hope some day I will. Maybe it's something we can discover together, sometime.

I ate my stolen sausage patty, and sauntered back uptown toward the Doctor's house. I was feeling a little better; at least one of my worries had been assuaged. No one had been alerted to the presence of a vampire killing in Charleston last night. If they had, our situation might well have become more complicated in ways that would be hard to predict.

But there were other nagging concerns. Renata and the Doctor were wholly in the vampire state now, and both were in a properly creepy, darkened house sleeping the daylight away. And Renata would present herself as a full vampire to the Council tonight. But what about after that? After her summons, her trial—whatever it was that was going to happen tonight—would she get away? *How* would she get away? It seemed like an odd commonplace to think of her ride home, but it was becoming strategically crucial. Here is Denis Pearson, going to his English teacher seminar over at the College of Charleston, and planning to give Renata a lift back to Forshay on Sunday afternoon—what shall we say, four-ish? And, Denis, did I mention that Renata was a vampire now who can't emerge into daylight—and who it might not be *completely* safe to drive with after dark, depending on whether or not she was still hungry? And what about the Doctor? It still seemed to me that he was intentionally stirring trouble, inciting conflict with the Council. Would he have to flee too? Would they need to flee together, or would they need to split up? Either way, if it turned out that they had to run from the Vampire Council, wouldn't it be better to do so in the daytime, when vampires cannot follow? Some careful planning—not to mention, some carefully timed shooting-up with the Council-proscribed thanadoxicil—was going to be needed to get out of this safely.

I decided what I should do next. If we needed to split up from the Doctor, and if Renata might not be able to drive in the car *with* Denis, then Renata would need to be prepared to grab Denis's car for herself and drive back *without* Denis. Only if the situation demanded it, of course. If Denis knew all the facts, I'm sure he would understand. Besides, he'd just get a bus back to Forshay on Monday. But in the event we had to move fast, I couldn't take chances with fumbling around Denis's room trying to find his car keys. By now I had reached the Doctor's house. I regarded it for a moment, lying in the morning sunlight, quiet, rundown, sleeping. The Doctor and Renata would be OK for a couple hours. I'd better go do a little reconnaissance now in Denis's room at the College.

It didn't take me very long to get back down to Calhoun Street. I had checked the card that Denis had given Renata before heading out, so I had the name of Denis's residence hall and the number of his room. By the time I got there, the College was stretching its legs for a quiet Saturday morning—the weather was fair, if a little cloudy. The late spring air was already warm and moist, but the heat of full summer—the kind of hard heat that would make the streets oppressive—that heat had not yet arrived. People were already on the streets: walking tourists, maybe heading out for the free breakfast included with their weekend room package, the horse carriages, the inevitable joggers. The happy buzz of awakening.

The residence hall was in one of the College buildings between Wentworth and Beaufain Streets, and Denis's room was up on an upper floor. A little patience was all it took to gain entrance. Students were walking out the front door of the hall in a constant stream. I found the stairs, and quickly ran up to Denis's floor. Next step—to find his room number. I had to make a slower circuit of the floor, pausing occasionally to check the sequence. One girl student exclaimed, "A kitty!" and bent to stroke my fur; I stretched and purred for maybe a minute, just enough to be polite, and then slipped away before her enthusiasm could summon anyone else. Last thing I needed was someone in authority being alerted. On the second circuit, I located his door. Locked. There were several rooms along the hallway that had doors ajar, though, and each had windows that were wide open to the soft and warm breeze off the river. Thank goodness this dorm did not seem to be air-conditioned. There was no other way, if Denis's room was locked. I crept into an adjoining room, leapt onto the sill of the open window, and slipped gingerly onto the brick ledge outside the windows.

I was lucky—counting two windows down the row to where I assumed Denis's windows were, I saw a gap where the sash had been left up for air. I didn't hesitate; if you had been watching from below all you could have seen was a quick shadow across the window ledges, and a tiger-striped tail swiftly disappearing inside.

In Denis's room the shades were still down, although the sunlight and shadows of the leafy trees standing outside the window played across them in patterns of light and dark. I paused for a moment surveying the darkened room. Something was amiss. Or rather, something was missing. Denis's battered leather briefcase stood bulging on the spare desk along the wall. But his weekend bag with its canvas shoulder strap was not there. There were no shoes tumbled on the floor, no trousers over the straight chair at the desk. No toothbrush by the sink in the corner bathroom. In fact, there was no Denis.

And, no car keys.

I found myself looking around the room again, as if somehow I might have overlooked a grown man in a small dorm room. Like someone checking again and again and again that she has turned off the stove, before driving away to catch a plane at the airport. But to no avail—he wasn't there, and it didn't look like he had been there last night. The narrow bed along the far wall was unrumpled and neat. The clock on the desk read a little before eight a.m.—I doubted that Denis would have made his bed and cleaned so thoroughly and then left, all so early in the morning. He had not stayed here overnight. There was no use remaining in the room any longer. But I was still thinking about his car.

It was just as quick for me to fly back across the sill of Denis's window, across the window ledges along the outer wall back into the adjoining room, and out the door of the residence hall. This time no one spotted me; no one paused to pet the cute kitty. Orienting myself, I saw the parking garage where Denis had left Renata the previous day. The door to the stairs was too heavy for a cat my size, but a quick run up two rampways put me on the level where Denis had parked his red Saab, the very spot where he had parked. This was the spot, I was sure of it. But the car was not there.

I sat down on the cool concrete of the parking garage.

This was a problem. I felt I needed to know where Denis and his car were, today, *now,* because of how urgently Renata might need that car in a few hours. But how to find out where he had gone? I had the cell phone number that he had written on the card he had given to Renata—photographic recall of symbolic information is another of my talents, something I just have a knack for—but even if I had a cell phone, my paws weren't very good for pushing the little buttons. And besides, what information would Denis give to a caller that rang him on his mobile number and then made soft mewing noises over the line? He'd probably just hang up. That's what I'd do.

I still needed a way to track him, to find out where he had gone with his car, and where we might find him at, say, a couple hours after midnight tonight. I couldn't think of another way to do it. I decided that I would have to do a timeslide.

Now, I know you heard me talking to the Doctor before, and you heard what the Doctor called me. And yes, this is the one of my special talents that that name is taken from. We don't really like the name, though, not because it isn't accurate—it actually is a pretty acute description of the motion involved—but because it is so *incomplete.* As if by calling us "Timesliders" you have managed to describe us totally, as if we were doing simple conjuring tricks and no more. But this is a technique that me and my kind have mastered as an evolutionary adaptation over millennia, one which allows us to pass through time, backward and then back forward again, as we will. I avoid using the technique too often, though—not because it's not useful. But because it's extremely dangerous. And because it's exhausting.

I don't even have to look, I can feel your incredulity. You're sitting with your arms crossed, scoffing. But why should timesliding be so hard to fathom? I admit that I couldn't explain how it's accomplished, any more than you could explain how your brain goes about formulating a thought, or regulating your autonomic body functions, or establishing consciousness itself. A fish doesn't explain how it swims, a bird doesn't explain how it flies. They have adapted to their ecological niches, and take their talents as given. And in the same way, so have my kind adapted to a niche, although our adaptation extends across the whole fabric of spacetime. Why should this be so shocking? And why should you expect me to explain *how* it happens? It just *happens*. But the fact that it does happen? Yes, it happens.

Think about it—what is time, anyway? What is *now*, and what was *then*, and what is the future? Information. It's all pure information, not matter—that's where people seem to get so mixed up. What are *you*, in this moment, if not information? Just look at your face in the mirror, or look at your hand, or pinch your arm—you know that all the cells of your body have been dying and regenerating millions of times over, day in day out, since the day you were born. And you know that the molecules that make up your skin, muscles, fat, bone—all have been sloughed off and replaced, millions of times over your lifetime. But so what? Does that mean you today are no longer who you were last year, just because the matter that makes up your body isn't the same? You know that your body is 60% water, but where does the water go? Do people have a crisis of identity when they take their morning piss? Or bond emotionally with the pond at the water treatment plant that contains the molecules that once were part of them? No. Of course not.

But if the physical atoms that make you up are not the unique part of you that is you, then what is? It is obvious, if you think about it: it's the way those atoms have been arranged—arranged to make your face, and your hands and your arms and your skin. To make your brain, which in turn makes the electrochemistry that makes your consciousness, which in turn orients you in time. It is the arrangement, the recipe, the information. When one atom in the neurons of your brain substitutes for another, slots into its place, the physical reality changes but the information embedded in that neuron is retained. And as it is with you and your body, so it is with all of the matter that makes up our material world, in all the universe, in every era of the universe—it is the information that creates our moments, the uniquenesses of our world, the time we find ourselves in.

And the information doesn't die. It does not become degraded, because it is not subject to degradation. Information passes through time whole—and you already know that too. The examples are all around you. You know that we still swoon to the poetry of Keats and Shakespeare and Sappho, still breathe the prayers of Muhammad and Jesus, still abide under laws inscribed by Jefferson and Justinian. The information is not the physical books of the library, not even the electrochemical markers embedded in the brain cells of the memory artist. The information stands apart.

And because time is a thing of pure information, timesliding as well is a matter of pure information—a matter of projecting my information, my present information, into the matrices of all information of all moments, past and future. Because if information cannot be annihilated, then all those moments of time still exist, all those moments have always existed—or already exist, if they have yet to happen. Timesliding is only a matter of finding those moments, of reading them, of coursing into the information of those moments, whenever they may have appeared to us to have happened or to have yet to happen, in our ordinary reckoning of time.

All of which is a lot of high-tech explanation for how I proposed to solve a low-tech question: where did Denis park his car? So I let the timeslide start. I felt the familiar sensation as the intention of the time shift gave way to the shift itself, to the curious perception of time reshaping around me as I searched for the timeframe I needed. It's hard to describe. It isn't exactly like dreaming, or seeing visions, or hearing auditory hallucinations or anything like that—although I imagine that the sensation must be similar. I have to focus, to concentrate on the crease in time that I need—a momentary lapse, a loss of attention, and the timeslide could veer into an unintended direction and send me into an irrevocable void. It's necessary to have something to focus the timeslide on—a memory, an object, a face—to anchor the timeslide into context. A timeguide, we call it. Here, it was easy—I focused on my recollection of Denis's car. A rushing, humming noise filled my brain as if I were trying to listen to the thoughtstreams of a million people at once, a sound like a powerful racecar rushing through a highway tunnel at high speed, roof open and windows down. The sound was my mind processing the time information, moment by moment, examining and discarding millions of bits per second. The tension was extreme—as moments in time roared through my mind I knew that the tiniest failure of concentration, the slightest waver in my attention, could send my information down an unintended, unexamined course in spacetime to who knows what result—the information that once was one small if talented tiger-striped kitten could be shot into the sea, into the white-hot core of a star, or scattered like dust through the cold of intergalactic space in some remote era. But I am practiced, skillful—my mind focused and I stalked the moment I sought, like I might stalk a mouse. I was seeking the moment when Denis came back out to his car last night, his weekend bag over his shoulder and his car keys in his hands, got back in his car and started it up. And then I found it, I found that moment; I streamed my present into that present, and I had slid into the time I was seeking.

And then, because the visual information was the key information I needed, the sensation *became* visual, reality blurring and distorting at the edges with halos of rainbow colors rimming the images in the timerush, as if I had been swimming all day in an over-chlorinated pool. I saw Denis driving his car last night; I followed him as he—or his information, the information that was that moment last night—drove away from the College, back up Meeting Street, back onto the highway, then slowing, exiting, looping through a back neighborhood of North Charleston beyond Mark Clark, a neighborhood of tiny, ancient plank houses set on concrete blocks at the corners. Shaggy, overgrown trees swept above unkempt yards. He pulled the red Saab into the grassy unpaved driveway of one of the houses, and cut the lights. As he got out of the car, a light went on in the kitchen of the house, and a woman in a bright blue housedress appeared in the yellow light of the screen door. The door opened with a squeak and then slapped the doorframe as she rushed down the steps into the grass, the fireflies rising and flashing from the overgrown weeds of the house next door. Denis's arms were open, and he folded her into his full embrace.

"Hey, Mama," he said softly.

CHAPTER NINE

Now, of course, at the same time that I followed
Denis's information from tomorrow into yesterday, I also
physically translated myself through the crease in
spacetime as well, from yesterday back to today—and so I
found myself outside the tiny white house with the
squeaking screen door, at a little before 8 a.m. on Saturday.
But I'm not going to try to explain the physics of that to
you, not now anyway. I'm having enough trouble getting
you to follow the easy stuff. Suffice it to say that I was
there and that I was tired out from the timeslide—even
such a shallow timeslide into the recent past. It still beat
walking or taking the bus, though.

The screen door was loose enough that a small cat's
paw could prise it open. I let myself into the small but
spotless kitchen. I heard Denis and his mother talking,
over on the other side of the kitchen where they were
sitting at the small table. She had made him an enormous
breakfast of eggs and buttered grits and sausage. It
smelled delicious, but I had already had my sausage that
morning.

"That's not true," he said to her. "You've seen the
house—it's way bigger than I really need. There's plenty

of space."

"Plenty of space for a wife, and a bunch of kids, honey." She got up to fetch the coffee pot from the stove. She poured more coffee into each cup. "I know the master plan, you don't have to tell me." She sat down in the kitchen chair, awkwardly. She was a heavy woman, wearing the blue housedress again; when she had walked to the stove she had gone slowly, carefully, as if her legs were stiff and her feet hurt. "You want a woman to fill that extra space but it ain't your old mama you have in mind."

"Now, Mama, that's not true," Denis protested.

"Then tell me," she said, "how's the master plan working out?" Though her face was heavy, her eyes were quick. She caught him with a glance over the rim of her coffee cup that was as lithe and nimble as a girl's.

Denis sighed, then smiled. "You know, Mama," he said, laughing softly. "There's still no one. I would have told you otherwise."

"Uh-huh," she said. "Up there in Forshay, up in those mountains, you really think a black man like you is going to find a woman? I *know* Forshay, I know it from way back. I know what they thinking about you up there. A black man all alone."

"No, mama, that's a long time ago. All that's changed. You know that." Denis opened his arms, displaying his blazer, white shirt, tie. "Look at me," he said. "I'm a teacher. A professional. And at a damn fine college, too. I mean, look," he said.

She shook her head. "All I know is that some time, someone's going to get nervous about a handsome black man like you being alone with a lot of young white girls all the time."

Denis exhaled loudly in frustration and got up from the table. He walked the small kitchen, back and forth. I pressed myself back into the walls.

"You always talk this way, whenever I mention it. But

it's not true—you're just making an excuse. You act like it's still 1952, and the Klan owned the town, and Forshay was something out of, out of *In The Heat of the Night*."

"Maybe it is," she said. "Things don't change so much. Those bad things really happened—that past ain't going to change, ever."

He came up behind her, put his hands on her shoulders. "But the present *has* changed." He spoke softly. "Look, I'm just worried about you. You should stop working. What do you need a job for? You should get rid of this old house before it falls down around you. Move up out of the city, with me, where I can take care of you."

It's one of the things I have always noticed about mortal human conversations like these, family conversations, at least ones that are truly *felt*—the words come out, fly back and forth through the air, ricochet, clash, sometimes even fall into shouting and tears. But all the time the music of the thoughtstreams from the people plays behind the words, like the soundtrack in a movie, rising and falling, inchoate but tuned together, singing. So it was with Denis and his mother—they stopped talking, but I heard the thoughtstreams keep playing, the orchestration full of love and fear. She reached up to her shoulder, touched his hand. Their music filled my mind.

He broke the pause. "I could do my Poitier," he said. "I could walk around Forshay College telling people, *'They call me Mr. Tibbs!'*"

His mother laughed. She patted his hand, and Denis returned to his chair. "So please," he said. "What do you say?"

"Are you going to stop asking if I say I'll think about it?"

"You always say you'll think about it."

"And you always keep asking."

He smiled. "So I'm a handsome black man, huh?"

She beamed back. "Oh, you don't have to play with

your mother, boy, you know you're handsome."

"Poitier handsome?"

"Well," she said, rising slowly to clear his breakfast plate, "don't start getting notions." Denis chuckled quietly. He stayed at the table, finishing his coffee. His mother worked at the sink, her back to him, silently. They lingered like that for some minutes. They were calm, comfortable in each other's silence.

His mother suddenly spoke quietly, not looking up from the soft swish of water on dishes. "Denis," she said, "so is there anyone? Any girl?"

Seeing her back turned to him, Denis did not make any attempt to hide the expression that came over his face. Of course, I could see him—he still had not noticed the striped kitten, quietly sitting in the corner of the kitchen. The expression wasn't one of alarm, exactly, or fear— more like a sudden, intent watchfulness, as if he needed to tread with extreme caution. I could see that his mother was sharply intelligent; he would do well to tread carefully. Denis regained his easygoing manner quickly, though.

"Sure, there are girls," he said. "I have lots of dates."

"Didn't say 'girls', babe," she replied. "I said 'girl'."

"You mean, a special one?"

"Uh-huh."

"No."

"Hm." She went on washing for a while longer. "Tell me about the 'girls', then. Are they nice girls?"

"Sure."

"From the College?"

"Sometimes. Not often though. I try to be careful about that. And never students, of course."

"Uh-huh." She was quiet again for a while. "Are they pretty?"

The look of worry crossed Denis's face again. "Pretty? Well, gee, Ma, I think so. Sure. I like them—otherwise I wouldn't date them, would I?"

Denis was clearly wondering where she was going with

this. I could hear his thoughts—he was thinking she was still worried about race and danger, a black man in the Carolina hills at the old white-girls' school—and as he was struggling to formulate another comment, another way to reassure his mother that, sure, he dated black women, lots of black women, don't worry—she beat him to it.

"And these girls…you're nice to them?"

"Sure, Ma, of course."

And…they're nice to you?"

Stopped him dead. It was interesting to see the articulate Mr. Pearson speechless for once, his lips slightly agape as his mother calmly finished the dishes.

"They're…what? Nice? Ma, what do you mean?"

She put the last dish in the rack, wiped her hands on the dishtowel and turned ponderously back around to face him. That glance again—her eyes seemed to have the fixative power that Margaret Viper's did. "Denis Pearson, don't be stupid," she said flatly. "You know *exactly* what I mean."

To his credit, Denis recaptured his equilibrium quickly. He laughed. "Ma! Yes, the girls are 'nice' to me—I mean, sometimes. It depends! And anyway," he said, "a guy shouldn't talk about his personal life like this with his mother."

She was shaking her head. "I just wonder, honey, you know—you're thirty-five. You know how long married I was at your age?"

"Yes," he said, dutifully.

"So I just worry."

"Mama," he said. "Don't worry. I'm not gay. Being an English teacher doesn't automatically make you gay."

"Well, you never know," she said, "all that Shelley-Keats-Byron. A mother might worry."

Denis was laughing again. "Man, you are a treasure," he said, half to himself, walking up to her and embracing her. He towered over her—I never realized how tall Denis was, or perhaps I hadn't realized how small his mother was. She seemed to disappear into his arms. "And I happen to know you're an educated woman, Ma, with plenty of Shelley-Keats-Byron of your own. Well, to lay it out on the table—so there's no *misunderstanding*," he said. "Number one. I'm not gay. Number two. I have lots— well, a couple—of girlfriends. And yes, they occasionally spend the night. Not that that's anyone's business. Number three. There isn't any one in particular. Not yet, anyway. If there is," he said, finishing his piece and kissing the top of her head, "you'll be the first to know."

She pushed out of his embrace. "Well, if that's how it is, then it's just as well you're here for the lunch at the church," she said. "Reverend Loomis will be pleased to see you again—you so *professional* and everything. And there'll be a dance tonight after the service. You can go to that—see if you can do better on the girlfriend front."

"Ma, I can't."

"No?"

"No, I've got to be back in the city tonight."

"You said before that you didn't really need to attend that talk at the college," she said. "And besides, if you have so many girlfriends in your pocket, what are you doing way down here in Charleston on a Saturday night, all alone?"

Denis paused expertly. "Who said I was alone?" he said.

That got her attention—now it was her turn to be stopped cold. "Oh?" with a little, rising lilt, was all she managed.

"Yes," Denis said, knowing he had won a round. "Yes, I'm actually down here for the weekend with a woman I know from the college in Forshay." His mother was rapt; he knew he had her. "A beautiful French woman."

"Oh?" His mother had to pause to think; she twisted the ties to her housedress. "Well. Then you certainly must not disappoint her," she declared.

"That's right," he said. "And if you moved up to

Forshay, you'd have all the gossip about me first-hand."

"Well," his mother said, "it certainly seems like I maybe should *visit* soon."

Denis laughed. His mother left the kitchen to dress for the church picnic. I waited where I was, watching them fetch the picnic makings: a cooler filled with ice and Pepsi, an enormous plastic tub of cole slaw, a peach pie with the circumference of an automobile tire. All the food was put into his mother's elderly Buick. I was satisfied—Denis's car keys were in a bowl on the kitchen counter, the red Saab was going to stay put in the grassy driveway where I could keep an eye on it, and after a morning helping his mother set up the picnic at the Mt. Moriah Primitive Baptist Church (or so I assumed from the stack of church bulletins neatly piled by the telephone), I had no doubt that he would be insisting that he actually needed to get back to Charleston a little *earlier* than he had said. I wasn't concerned—I was confident my getaway car would be back in place in good time, and I had a perfectly acceptable ride back to Charleston if I was patient. No need to risk timesliding again. I sat in the kitchen doorway, curled my tail around my paws, and watched Denis and his mother pack up the last few things. Denis caught sight of me.

"Mama, I didn't remember your having a cat," he said, gesturing to me with his chin as he carried a box of paper plates.

His mother stooped down a little and squinted. "Now, where'd she come from?" she said. "Don't remember seeing that little puss around here before." She had dressed herself in a flowing, light-pink dress and headwrap. She gave the keys to her son, and he politely helped her slowly into the passenger seat. "Hope that little cat keeps safe from that mean dog the Hoskinses have, two yards down. That's a mean dog, noisy and mean."

As they drove off, I could hear that dog barking at the car. And it continued barking—at the trees, at the sky, at the air. At anything. I figured Denis's mother knew her neighbors, and if that dog meant trouble, maybe I should preempt it. I slipped out the screen door, and trotted up the rutted roadway to the house where the dog was barking behind a chain-link fence. It was thickset dog, heavy-shouldered, its black and brown brindled coat gleaming over a sheath of muscle. It redoubled its barking as it saw me approach, leaping side to side and then crouching from the shoulders, salivating and showing its fangs. The whites at the edges of its eyes had bloodshot from the exertion, making its eyes seem to glow an eerie red. I walked up impassively, and sat on my haunches in front of it. The dog started flipping out.

Now, the thoughtstreams of animals—dogs, for example—are not like peoples', but they are not as different as you might think. Dogs think like dogs, in the logic and symbology of a dog's perceptions. It's not so hard for me to push myself into their thoughts, but it's rarely necessary. They're dogs after all—why would I want to? This dog, however, was a problem—he was trying to leap his fence now, and was working himself into a frenzy. If he were to escape, he could be dangerous for another dog, for a child, for himself. He wouldn't be dangerous for me—I was in control of this situation. But I had to act. I had to shut this dog up.

So I projected a sound into the dog's mind—a sound only it could hear—a sound that started mild, like a low hum, but that I sharply raised until it roared at an overwhelming volume, as if a jet engine were suddenly screaming inside the dog's brain. The suddenness of the sound knocked the dog over with a sharp yelp. I cut the sound, and in the silence that followed, like the ringing silence you hear following the concussion of a nearby gunshot as your hearing struggles to regain itself, I projected my message. A short and clear message, though not in literal, verbal language—since this was a dog. The gist of it was expressible easily enough, though: *SHUT UP! AND DON'T MESS WITH ME!* I glared at the dog for a moment while it cowered, circling back from the fence and laying on its belly. I stayed where I was, and nonchalantly washed a paw. The dog was silent now. Satisfied, I turned and trotted back to Denis's mother's house, to wait by the car for Denis to return. I was planning to nap while they were gone, and it was good to have quiet again.

The sun had already set by the time Denis drove us back to the College of Charleston. I had reckoned without the stubborn politeness commanded by the ladies of a Baptist church picnic. It was hours before Denis— handsome, professional Denis—had been able to extract himself from the blandishments of the church ladies, not to mention their repeated offers to attend the dance and social that evening where their daughters would be found. He must have employed all his powers of evasion in ducking the event. He seemed more than a little frazzled by the time he finally got back.

I had been sleeping in the Saab, having crawled in through the half-open window on the driver's side. I had tried to keep my nerves in check as it had gotten later and later, but as I have already said I am a worrier, a planner, and we were starting to get seriously off my schedule. Luckily, since I was on a timeslide, and was a few hours off-kilter from my native timeframe, I could easily spare myself some worry by letting the time gap close, and slipping my timeframe back into its natural present. I watched the accelerating shadows lengthening across the long grass of the yard, and the sunlight bending from yellow to copper to rust with abnormal speed. I was back in my normal timeframe, and soon I saw Denis pilot his mother's Buick back into her driveway, carry the cooler and boxes back into the house and, with his weekend bag slung over his shoulder, kiss his mother good-bye and get into the Saab. I had the presence of mind, despite my nerves, to keep out of sight as Denis started his car and drove off.

Once back in Charleston, and the car again securely parked in its parking spot, I shadowed Denis back to his residence hall. It was already dark—maybe 8:30 or 9:00, I thought—and I wanted to get back to the Doctor's house. I wanted to trail Renata when she left for her appointment with the Vampire Council. I knew that there should not be any particular danger from the Council before her hearing. If nothing else, the Council would never pass up such a fine chance to lord it over other vampires, and a proceeding like this, with all its opportunities for ponderous speeches and vampire moralizing, must seem like too much fun for them to sacrifice. But all the same, it made me uneasy. It was the Doctor's presence in Charleston that concerned me. It seemed that there was some game being played between him and the Council, and I couldn't quite make out what it was. It made things unpredictable—and if things were going to be unpredictable, well, I just wanted to be nearby Renata. I only needed to see where Denis stowed his car keys—after all, that was the point of the whole day's excursion, wasn't it?—and then I could be off.

Denis didn't notice me as I trotted along the shadows a pace behind him, skittering through the residence hall door, up the stairs. He unlocked his room and I slipped through the door as he was drawing the key out of the lock. He was distracted, absent. He wouldn't have noticed me if I were the massive dog from his mother's neighbor's yard.

But then I heard a voice outside in the dark corridor. A low, muffled voice, a voice I recognized and that I had heard only recently—though the voice was sounded in a strange and artificial way, as if it were a poorly-modulated film soundtrack. As if it were echoed from inside a deep, stone well.

"Mr. Pearson?" it asked.

I saw Denis pause at the door. A twinge of fear swept over his face for a moment before he turned—perhaps from the break in his reverie, or the strangeness of the voice, or perhaps the instant, instinctive suspicion attendant on being accosted in a strange hallway. The classic gangster movie set-up.

"May I talk to you for a moment?" A figure appeared by the half-open doorway—a tall figure in black, wearing a long coat, a broadbrimmed hat, dark glasses. "Maybe we can go inside?" A long-fingered hand reached up to remove the hat in a gesture of guilelessness. The hand was white as ivory. "Please—it's about Renata." Denis stood dumbly a moment longer, as if trying to understand what the voice was saying, to comprehend its strange timbre. "You see, I'm her doctor."

Denis opened the door wide and gestured for the Doctor to enter. I found a hiding place by the bed. Denis reached over to the light switch.

"No, actually, if we could just leave the light off," the Doctor said. "I really should not be here. I would not want anyone to see me."

In the dim light from the window, my cat's eyes glowed—I could just see the surprise on Denis's face. He swung the door to but didn't let the latch catch. He walked over to the window.

"OK if I let the shade up?" he said. "Just to let in the light from the streetlights?"

The Doctor nodded. "I won't stay long, Mr. Pearson. I wanted to give you a few things." The Doctor had been carrying a bag—a doctor's bag, I supposed, but it looked just as much like Denis's weathered briefcase. The Doctor unsnapped the leather straps, and withdrew a leatherbound portfolio from the bag, and a smooth, polished oblong box. He handed them to Denis.

"What are these? What am I supposed to do with them?"

"Medical records," the Doctor said, a long white finger poking the leather portfolio, "and medicine. I think Renata might have told you that she has a medical condition that requires periodic injections. Yes?"

Denis nodded.

"Well, I asked her to meet me here in Charleston to give her these. I am leaving town shortly, and she'll need them. This medicine is not readily obtainable in this country—or really anywhere." The Doctor stopped, as if wondering whether he was giving too much information. He licked his lips, and continued. "She missed our appointment this morning—she had to see...relatives, I think. She left me a message with your room number here, and said I could leave these things with you." The Doctor reached over and lightly clasped Denis's forearm. "It is important. She will need to find another doctor, and when she does those records could save her life."

Denis looked down at the items in his arms, dumbfounded. "And the medicine is in the box?" he asked.

"That's right. A few weeks' supply. There is no other source for it."

Denis paused again, and looked up. "And it's not obtainable in this country?" His eyes widened slightly in the dim light from the streetlights as an implication dawned on him. "It's illegal?" Denis whispered.

The Doctor was apparently prepared for this question. He continued to speak levelly, the reverberating voice humming on. "No, it is perfectly legal—just not fully approved yet by the relevant government agencies," he said. "Renata has had good results from this compound. As her doctor, I am not willing to leave her without it just to appease some bureaucrats until they reach the same conclusions that the science supported long ago." The Doctor replaced his hat and moved toward the unlatched door. "But you understand, Mr. Pearson, how confidential this must be. For Renata's sake."

Denis paused a moment longer, then answered in a decisive voice. "Sure. OK, no problem. I'm giving her a ride back up to Forshay tomorrow. I'll keep these things for her here, and give them to her then." Denis carefully placed them on the desk next to his briefcase. "I'll let her know that you stopped by and gave them to me, Dr., uh…" Denis smiled nervously. "Don't think I got your name."

The Doctor had already swung the door open and was leaving. "Just tell her her doctor was here. And thank you, Mr. Pearson," the Doctor said.

I could see Denis make a movement toward the door, as if he were going to call after the Doctor, but he stopped himself. Instead, he turned and thoughtfully regarded the leather portfolio and oblong box next to his briefcase. After a moment, he walked back to the door and meditatively pushed it closed until it clicked. He flicked the wall switch, and the overhead light suddenly bounced his room from the dim glow of the window into bright, almost comical clarity. Denis stood still in the middle of the room for a moment, his chin on his chest. He then shucked his blazer off his shoulders and hooked it on a coathook by the closet. And from his trouser pockets he pulled a jangling chain of car keys, and slipped them in the jacket pocket.

That was all I needed to know.

The window I had come in through that morning was still ajar, and I launched myself from my hiding place and bounded onto the sill. Denis gave a startled yell as I scrambled out to the ledge—carefully, because even a talented cat's eyes have to adjust from the light to darkness—and scurried across the same ledge I had gone before. I heard Denis behind me in his room, the sound getting faint as I gained the adjoining window which was also, helpfully, still open. "Goddamn cat!" Denis was swearing. "Give me a heart attack, why don't you!"

I was on the street in a flash, scampering back toward

King Street with my striped tail high. I didn't know if the Doctor was going to the Council with Renata, but I couldn't have kept pace with a vampire at night anyway. I figured that even if I didn't get back to the Doctor's house before Renata left, I would surely intercept her heading downtown. I tried to relax as I loped along—I knew where the car was, I knew where the keys were—all the things I could control myself, I had. But the Council was the wild card. Nothing I could do to try to control that. The Council was up to Renata to handle.

CHAPTER TEN

I didn't know where in the city the Vampire Council met, but I had a general idea. I knew it had to be in the oldest part of the city, the most historic and fanciest part—nothing else would do. That was the direction I had headed after leaving Denis's room, and it wasn't long before I had my answer. As I trotted along, I noticed that the shadows in the streets were full of flitting figures, dim, evanescent, gone before your eye could fix upon them. They were like illusions, as hard to pin down as shooting stars. But they were there, and they all were seemingly headed one direction. I followed, keeping well clear of them. I found myself at the verge of Washington Park, just north from St. Michael's famous church steeple at Broad Street, where Chalmers runs into Meeting Street. I crept unobtrusively onto a low wall running along the verge of the park, in the shadow of the Historical Society, and settled down to watch. Across Meeting Street rose another one of Charleston's Greek temples, this one Hibernian Hall. It was dazzling white tonight, bathed in floodlights that lit it from within and silhouetted its Ionic columns. There was a formal party happening, a ball of some sort. Elegant Charlestonians in black tie and evening gowns were moving slowly in and out from the sidewalk. On the upper level, girls in their colorful gowns, elaborate make up and jewelry excitedly laughed and called from the lighted windows to friends they spotted walking below. Handfuls of happy sound sprinkled down upon the springtime street below, like scattered rainshowers in a warm breeze. And as I watched, the ephemeral black shadows slowed and fell into walking pace among the black-dressed men moving toward the midnight ball at the Hibernian, casually mingling into the straggling holiday crowd before, just as casually, they would split off, crossing the street and disappearing around the corner toward the darkness of Washington Park. I had not spotted Renata. However, I had no doubt—I had lost count of the shadowy gathering figures after I got to fifty. Such a large gathering of vampires could only signify something momentous, something like the convening of the Vampire Council—indeed, this must represent a fair percentage of all the vampires in this Hemisphere. I reluctantly turned my back on the pleasant scene of Hibernian Hall and the ball going on there. I trotted up the sidewalk and around the corner, and into the deep shadows cast at the verge of the park by the heavy oaks. I watched as the silent black figures swept to a knot of desiccated palmetto, tucked under the canopy of trees on the side beyond the obelisk. When the black figures reached the palmetto, they disappeared. Creeping forward to the knot of foliage I saw a pit entrance, a fissure in the surface irregularly edged and blended with leaves and the bracken of ground shrubs. The entrance was so cleverly concealed that you would walk straight by it if you did not already know it was there. I waited, watching the black-clothed vampires make their rapid and silent descents into the entrance, until the frequency of the passing vampires had diminished to a trickle. I decided that I would have to take the risk of running into a straggler. I made a dash and slipped into the entrance.

The pathway down was a slick stone staircase, the steps wet with condensation. An earthy smell of humus filled the close air. My eyes widened in the darkness as I descended, deeper into the earth. The staircase twisted first one way then another as it went down, as if the designers meant to disorient those who trod it so they could no longer tell which direction they faced. A silent whoosh brushed past me as a vampire flew on; it did not stop, did not acknowledge me; perhaps it did not notice me. Several twists further, the silence beginning to ring slightly in my ears, my paws touched the smooth and slick paving stones of the bottom. There was no light, but in the darkness I felt the slight movement of air ahead of me—the passage must lead that way forward. I moved on, trotting now, navigating by sound and feline smell and the touch of my paws in the darkness.

Up ahead, a dim red light emerged. The glow was razored across on one side by a sharp black edge—a corner in the passageway. I raced ahead, poking my face around the corner, and found myself looking at a portico almost identical to the Greek temple of the Hibernian Hall at street level, dozens of feet above me at the surface. It was situated in a widening of the earthen passageway. This subterranean version was lit not by clean white floodlights but by struggling dim torches, ranged along the ragged walls of the earthen opening. The portal beyond the dark-shadowed columns lay open, and as I watched I saw that last vampire sweep between the columns and through the portal, into a dim, torchlit interior. This must be it—the council chamber. An offhand thought occurred to me that it was just like the Vampire Council's sense of entitlement that it would insist that its meeting place must be at least the equal of the very best human locales in Charleston—even if they had to construct an identical replica directly below the original. But I didn't have time to pursue the thought. It seemed that the gathering of the vampires inside was complete, and that the proceedings were ready to start. I uneasily scooted forward, and nosed my way inside.

The interior of the building, beyond the columns and the portal, opened into a vast space of uncertain dimension. The interior was in complete darkness, except for the feeble pinpricks of additional torchstands spaced at regular intervals. For a convocation of vampires, of course, there would be no need for any light at all, but again it did not surprise me that the Vampire Council's sense of the dramatic required torches. Mood lighting, I thought. Despite the dim, red glow of the torchlight, I couldn't see far enough to make out the far wall of the chamber, which disappeared into darkness at the outer edge; the surrounding dark gave a disconcerting feeling that the whole room was hovering in mid-sky, untethered to the earth, the torches standing in for dim, reddish stars in the firmament. I crept forward toward what appeared to be the center of the chamber—there was a raised dais of some kind, and before it at a lower level, a wooden platform. As I approached I saw that there was ranged on the dais, each sitting on a tall black chair, a row of about a dozen vampires—the Council itself, already entered and seated. And before them, on the lower platform, a lone figure stood between two dim flaming torches—Renata. I found a perch in the shadows thrown by the torches, near enough to hear, and looked behind me. There were tiers of benches disappearing into the blackness, surrounding the Vampire Council and the platform where Renata stood, like the banks of seats in a stadium. And glittering from each tier of benches glinted the hard shine of multitudes of vampire eyes, catching the torchlight. The chamber was filled, and the crowd packing the galleries seemed to quiver with a suppressed energy that, despite the hush, vibrated with menace. It was like the rising fear one felt in stumbling upon a hollowed log in the woods, and perceiving it to be thick with a moving mass of bees. It seemed that all the vampires in the Western world had come to watch the trial. There were hundreds. I felt my fur crawl and involuntarily stand up, bottle-brushlike, along my tail. I did not like the looks of this.

A figure in the center of the Council panel rose. She was a tall, striking vampire, with a flowing black gown looped over one shoulder, the other white shoulder bare, and long, perfectly white hair parted exactly in the middle, the wings of hair on each side framing her slender face. Her eyes shone fierce from a face of surprising beauty; she had an immobile serenity, like a marble carving. I peered at the face; strange as it was, it seemed familiar to me. I felt that I had seen it only recently, but could not place it. I racked my memory nervously as the white-haired figure sought the attention of the crowd, but to no avail. As she stood, a hiss of vampire talk sizzled up from the indistinct ramparts of the audience like a sudden rainfall on the street. The figure struck the long table before her with an open hand, and the report echoed like a gunshot through the vast space.

"Silence in the chamber!" she shouted, using the loud and hollow voice audible to humans for dramatic effect. The hiss subsided, and she continued in the customary hissing vernacular of vampires. "The proceeding will start. The respondent is here?"

I looked at Renata. She stood stock still before the Council. "Here," Renata hissed, barely above a whisper.

The presiding vampire favored Renata with a broad smile, her fangs extended to add to the display. "We know each other, I think, Comtesse de Beaumanoir," she said.

"Yes, I know you," Renata hissed back. "I greet you, Vesta Letalia. But I do not use the title of Comtesse."

Vesta dropped the smile, cocking an eyebrow at Renata's response. A slight frisson murmured through the audience, then quickly died. "This is a formal proceeding," Vesta replied, "and we will use your formal name, Comtesse. We are who we are, after all."

Renata was silent; she gave a barely perceptible shrug

by way of answer.

"Do you know why you are here?" Vesta continued.

"No," Renata said. "I received the Council's summons. But there was no mention of a charge. There was, in fact, no mention of any purpose for my appearance here."

Vesta gave an ironic chuckle. "Oh, yes, of course—we are in the United States," she said. "There is a Bill of Rights! You must be read your rights, get notice and a hearing, the right to confront your accuser—have I forgotten anything? Any other due process of law?" The vampire audience hissed in an appreciative giggle, and Vesta's glittering vampire eyes scanned the galleries for several moments, indulging them. She turned back to Renata.

"No, Comtesse, you are not before a tribunal of the United States. The United States—just the latest temporary strongman in a long line of doomed, temporary strongmen of the mortal world. No, Comtesse, you appear now before the power of the Vampire Council. A power much more ancient and much more to be feared. And this Council will not compromise its powers and privileges. Not even for your scruples of due process." She softened again, lowering her voice a degree. "Come, Renata, you must have an idea why you are here."

Renata stood silent. She cast down her gaze, looking away from the Council. Vesta's face grew severe once more.

"Since you are going to be uncooperative, Comtesse, then this Council will be strict in its rigor," Vesta said tersely. "The charges against you are grave. You have been denounced as denying your vampire nature. As mingling freely with mortal humans, and as using proscribed tinctures and potions to conceal your true state. All of which actions put the vampire nation—*your* nation, Comtesse—into the gravest of peril, through the risk of disclosure of our existence and the extent of our existence." Vesta paused to look at a scrolled paper lying on the table before her. "It says here," she continued, a barely-suppressed mockery in her tone, "that you have taken a job. As a schoolteacher! Can that *possibly* be true?"

Renata was silent still. Vesta softened her tone once again, dropping the edge of taunt. "Renata," she said, "all this time I have observed you, tried to reach out to you. You have never appreciated your unique gifts, Renata. Do you not understand, even now, that you are an *adept?* That you have the special talents that are given to only a handful of vampires, perhaps only one in a generation? Have you forgotten *our* connection?" Vesta paused and sadly shook her head, her eyes closed. She forced herself to continue. "Renata, you must know in your heart that you are different from other vampires—don't you? Why is it that you have persisted in this stubborn and perverse desire to live among the mortals?"

But Renata did not answer. Her silence in the face of Vesta's questioning seemed as eloquent as any answer she could make.

"Renata, my darling," Vesta continued, her voice low, "how can you think that the mortal humans will accept you? They will discover what you are—you cannot hide your true nature. And even if you can maintain your ruse, what then? How can you explain yourself to them—a person with no family, no background, no past? No credentials, no papers—remember that, since you are so keen on the American due process of law. What will you be to them when they discover that you have nothing— not even a birth certificate that you can claim as your own? What will you be to them, but a fraud, and an undocumented alien?"

Renata raised her gaze back up, and faced Vesta angrily. "You ask me to deny that I have taken up a life among the mortal humans. Well, I do not deny it. Why should I? Is it proscribed? Against the law? Does the Vampire Council have a secret law against being a teacher? But of course, how would anyone know, because *all* the laws of the Vampire Council are held secret! And you call that justice!" A buzzing hiss arose in the gallery again, this time the sound angry, menacing. Renata spoke despite it. "You like to belittle the mortal humans and their due process of law, but what does this Council offer in substitute? Secret legislation, secret charges. If these are the ancient privileges of the Vampire Council, then I denounce them!" The gallery hissed in response, but Renata hissed louder. "I denounce them! I denounce them!"

In the fury of her speech, Renata's thoughtstreams bubbled with human emotion. Her danger, her courage in resisting Vesta' pressure—it did not surprise me that her mind would sound so agitated. But as she finished her speech, I heard the tremor in her thoughtstreams again that I had heard before, the push of that deep memory, but more insistent now—and suddenly, staring at Vesta's face, I remembered where I had seen it. The dream. I had seen it in that inexplicable dream of Renata's, the strange white face that had filled the dream with its mingled beauty and horror, just before it had awakened Renata. It had been this face, the face in that dream—the face of Vesta Letalia.

Renata repeated her denunciation, and the hissing in the chamber rose higher still. Vesta slammed the table in a fury to silence it. She spoke back to Renata deliberately, pointing a white finger in the dim chamber to accentuate her points. "The respondent should take care," Vesta said, "to consider the seriousness of this proceeding. To treat it, and the Council, with due respect. Of course the Council's laws are secret! If we disclosed our statutes, then the limits on vampire behavior would be freely known! And what would happen then? Clever vampires like you could know just how far they could go without running afoul of our laws. No," she continued, "it is better to keep the exact bounds in confidence with the executive body charged with the laws' execution, and to urge vampires to be guided by the basic precepts of the vampire nation: *Seek the darkness. Feed upon the unjust. Protect the nation."*

The galleries murmured again, hissing with approbation.

"But, Comtesse," Vesta said. "There is a further charge standing against you, and a far more serious one than being a schoolteacher. You stand denounced as attempting to resurrect the traitorous cult that followed the banished vampire known as The Doctor. Treason, Comtesse, treason against the vampire nation—*Ne comprenez-vous?*"

"Yes, I understand," Renata replied. "I had suspected that such was your ultimate motive. But the Doctor's movement is gone—destroyed, run off by this very Council, years ago. You are so disdainful of me, of my trivial ambition to be a teacher—but yet you ascribe to me the power to do miracles? You certainly cannot think it within the ability of a single, misguided vampire like me, to resurrect the whole system of the Doctor's movement that you so thoroughly destroyed?"

Vesta was restraining her anger with effort. She was clearly not accustomed to be talked to this way. Another Bully—Renata's life seemed just chock full of them.

"This Council is not convinced that the eradication of the Doctor's adherents was ever as complete as you say," Vesta said. "In fact, we were never even able to apprehend the Doctor himself. We have, over the years, heard rumors that he still exists, still even carries on his treasonous activities. But that might change. And do you know how it will change?"

Vesta paused, leaning forward in Renata's direction. Vesta's lips twisted into a smirk; a simulacrum of mirth played across her vampire eyes. She was enjoying herself. Renata was silent.

"Because, Renata dear," Vesta said. "You will lead us to him."

Renata was holding her ground, but I was getting concerned. There was something in Vesta's attitude, more than just the normal overconfidence exhibited by a Bully (even a vampire Bully), that seemed to hint that Vesta was holding back other tricks, other grand gestures for the audience. "But how can I do that," Renata said, "when I don't know where he is? I don't deny having known him. But that was before he was proscribed. I have not seen him since—a long time ago, now—more than forty human years ago!"

Vesta held her smirk for a moment longer. "Oh Renata," she said, "are you really going to take that tack with this Council? Do you think we have no knowledge of your affairs? We know everything you have done, and everywhere you have been, and everyone you have met." Vesta allowed a smile to peep through the smirk on her lips; the effect on her beautiful face was not appealing. "We know you have met with the Doctor. We know that you have met with him this very day, not thirty blocks north of where we stand right now!"

Renata stood silently, still, but I could tell that the tension was beginning to wear on her. I could see the muscles of her jaw tensing as she clenched her teeth. The hissing of the vampire galleries rose again, louder—hostile, condemnatory.

"It appears that the Comtesse de Beaumanoir has nothing to say in response to that," Vesta said. "The Vampire Council is not obliged to assay its proof—evidence that is satisfactory to the Council is by our laws deemed sufficiently proved, without necessity of disclosure. But, since the respondent here has made a point of raising *due process*," Vesta continued, licking her thin lips wickedly, "I am happy to demonstrate that we have reached our conclusions based on a firm foundation." She took the folds of her black gown over one white arm like a Roman toga, so she could raise the other in a magisterial gesture. "Summon the witnesses! Instruct them to approach the Council!"

There was a dim movement in the benches above, as

two figures made their way down the tiered seats on staircases I could not see. They emerged into the torchlight glowing around Renata on the platform before the Council. As their faces were illuminated in the torchlight, I knew that I recognized them too—in fact, I knew I had seen them only yesterday, and it took me just a moment to place them. They were the two guys in the bar on Market Street, who had been watching Renata attract her victim on her hunting trip the night before.

"Hey babe," the white guy said to Renata.

"Power," the black guy said.

"The witnesses may not address the respondent," Vesta said sternly. "You may address the Council. And only in response to the Council's inquiries."

"Check that, Vesta."

"Check that, babe."

Vesta regarded them for a moment with a quizzical expression. The two men had not removed their dark glasses, and in contrast to the high formality of the vampire attire that prevailed for the occasion, they were still dressed in their motorcycle chains and torn jeans. Vesta spoke to the ranks of vampires surrounding above them in the galleries.

"My vampires, you all may not recognize these witnesses," she said. "They have only recently joined the vampire nation, but have already undertaken important work for us in this matter, as you will hear. I present to you Harrison," she said, indicating the black guy, "and Chuck," indicating the other.

The two took a bow. The galleries hissed in appreciation.

Vesta turned the proceeding back to business. "Witnesses, the respondent has been accused of consorting with the criminal known as the Doctor, and has denied any such meeting. What do you know of the activities of Renata, Comtesse de Beaumanoir in this regard?"

"Hey, we followed her."

"We been following her all weekend, man."

"You saw what she did to the dude on Market Street? Brutal."

"Brutal."

"But we keep with her."

"All the way."

"The whole time in, didn't lose her once."

"Yes, yes," Vesta said impatiently. "And what else? Did she meet with the Doctor?"

"She drove down to the city with another dude," said Harrison.

"Guy from the college where she teaches, we think."

"But she ditched him quick."

"Ditched the dude."

"So then she's, like, racing back uptown in a taxi."

"Goes into an old, busted house."

"Old house."

"So we watch it. What do we do? We watch it."

"Yeah, the whole time."

Vesta was beginning to show her irritation. "The Doctor. Gentlemen, please let us know what you saw. Did she meet with the Doctor?"

"Yeah, so the house? Belongs to this old dude."

"A vampire."

"Yeah, a *old* vampire."

"So we check him out. And sure—it's the Doctor."

"For sure. We checked him out. The Doctor."

"And this lady, she was in the house with him. All day. Then she goes out."

"Goes out, to the bars downtown. So we follow."

"That's when she did that other dude. Brutal."

"Yeah, brutal, that."

Vesta held up a hand to stop the colloquy. "Your report, then, is unequivocal—the respondent not only met the Doctor, but accepted refuge with him. In this very city. Accepted the hospitality of a traitor to the vampire nation, under the very noses of the Vampire Council. Is that right?"

"Yeah, that's it."

"You got it."

"Righteous."

Harrison looked at Chuck with distaste. "Righteous? What the hell is that? What do you think this is, man, *The Mod Squad?* You watching too many reruns, man."

"Yeah?"

"Yeah."

"Well, fuck you."

"Fuck you too, man."

"Fuck you and the horse you rode in on, man," Chuck said.

Vesta's hand hit the table with concussive force again, as she shouted, *"Silete!* Silence!"* The two on the platform shut up. Vesta waited a moment for the inevitable hissing of vampire comment to die down in the galleries. Order restored, she continued. She leveled her gaze at Renata.

"Comtesse, you hear the witnesses. The Council does not find your denials persuasive—in fact, your perjuries become yet more crimes actionable against you, that you have committed here, before your own nation." Vesta pointed the finger again. "You have a choice! The Doctor has been under a sentence of annihilation since his movement was proscribed—forty years ago, as you point out. It is your duty to help the Vampire Council arrest him, to lead us to him, so that that just sentence might be executed at last."

Renata's voice, though only a hiss, sounded raspy with effort. "And, if I decline to perform that duty?"

Vesta glared forcefully at Renata. "Then this Council will be obliged to levy the same sentence upon you," she said, her flinty eyes glinting in the firelight. "Annihilation."

Renata's voice trembled further as she asked, "And how long do I have to give you an answer?"

Vesta chuckled, and the vampires on the Council

chuckled as well, looking one to the other. "You get no time," Vesta said. "You may answer in the affirmative, now and here. Any other response will be taken as refusal. Any delay will be considered a refusal." Vesta leaned toward Renata on the platform before her again. "It is not a choice, Comtesse. It is a requirement, or else you will be...terminated."

Renata still stood motionless as a stone, staring straight ahead. I could see her struggling; her fear was palpable. I had heard, over the years, oblique rumors and references to the powers of the Vampire Council, including its power of "annihilation," but I never understood it in detail. It was clearly not the power to levy a death penalty—what use, after all, is a death penalty against vampires, being already dead? There was no hint in the Council's array of what they meant by it, and its very ambiguity lent further terror to the sanction. Perhaps Renata knew, but her thoughts had never dropped that information at any time that I had been listening. I crept forward slightly in the dark, focusing myself on Renata's thoughtstreams now, hoping that something might flow past that could help me anticipate what might happen next—because I could not guess. I only thought it would be bad. Renata's thoughts were jumbled, chaotic—the scrambled mess of fear and anger that, I suppose, would be only to be expected given the circumstances. I happened to catch the echo of Vesta Letalia's thoughtstreams as well, even from a distance—they were emitting clear and confident and smoothly, over and over again, the word, *excindo...excindo*—destroy, destroy.

Suddenly, the tumult in Renata's thoughts stopped. The clashing rush and confusion was replaced with a calmness and confidence every bit the match of Vesta's. She had made up her mind. I knew what she was going to say before she said it.

"No," Renata declared loudly, using her echoing, human-tone voice. "With all respect to this Council, and to the vampire nation, no, I cannot do that."

The hissing in the gallery erupted in a fury. There was movement along the gallery benches, as if some of the vampires watching the proceeding in the dark had risen from their seats. Vesta stood angrily, motionless, regarding Renata now with unconcealed hate.

"Then so be it," Vesta said quietly. "Comtesse, you have demonstrated your contempt for this body with your willful refusal to comply with our most reasonable requests. Well—you who seem to yearn no longer to be a vampire at all, you may get your wish." With a flick of her finger, she motioned to the rest of the Vampire Council, who rose from their chairs with a portentous sound of scraping and creaking. The hissing gallery quieted to hear their pronouncement. "Renata, Comtesse de Beaumanoir, vampire of the 919th degree," Vesta said flatly, "you are hereby proscribed. You are hereby condemned. You shall be annihilated."

The sound of the galleries rose again, with hissing and, this time, a rhythmic beating of leathery vampire hands against the benches. Renata still stood, as if unhearing. I listened to her thoughtstreams, and they remained calm. Her resolution held.

Suddenly, another flash of thoughtstreams crossed my mind, like the brilliant beacon of a searchlight piercing into the darkness of the chamber. I looked for the source of this powerful mind, and saw another black figure approach openly down the steps from the portal. It was the Doctor himself, still cloaked in his black coat and wearing his black hat. He strode up to the platform, unafraid.

"There is no need to subject this vampire to this cruel proceeding," the Doctor announced, facing the Council. "Release her. I have come before you of my own volition. It is not her affair."

The Vampire Council murmured among themselves excitedly, resuming their seats as they spoke. Vesta remained standing, confronting the Doctor.

"I recognize you, Arcadius of Civitavecchia, vampire of the 12th degree, Doctor of Vampires," Vesta said, "though in truth you are no longer entitled to those usages. I will simply call you Doctor, *se siete d'accordo?* That should suffice for an old Etruscan like yourself—to be called as you are known among your treasonous adherents."

"D'accordo," the Doctor replied. "Call me what you will, Vesta Letalia. But release Renata."

"Now, why would the Council do that," Vesta asked, "when we suddenly, by this good fortune, have *both* you and the Comtesse before us here?" Vesta's sudden grin gleamed down at the Doctor and Renata.

"I ask you again, as a friend, Vesta, although you do not believe that, and as a loyal vampire, though you do not believe that either," the Doctor said. "Release her. You can hold me. I will submit to you. I will submit to your annihilation."

Renata's head suddenly turned to face the Doctor beside her at this, a look of despair upon her features. The tumult in her thoughtstreams rose again; it drummed in my mind like the beating of her heart. But the smile still played over Vesta's lips.

"Well," she said, "the Doctor wishes to bargain. But trade is only effective when each party can offer something that the other wants. Now that the Council has both of you," Vesta said, "what can you offer, Doctor, that the Council still wants?"

"You will have me," the Doctor said, "if you release Renata. And you will have peace."

Still smiling, Vesta shook her head. "No, Arcadius, I don't think you can offer peace," she said. "Peace is only possible if both parties want peace. And this Council is not ready for peace, not with you. Or the Comtesse."

Vesta paused, and a faraway expression seemed to overtake her beautiful face. Her eyes burned vividly as leaned forward from the dais. She seemed to hesitate as she spoke, as if the words she said held such great moment that her tongue could hardly form them. "But there is something you can give the Council," she said. Her hands involuntarily balled into fists at her side. "The Sable," she hissed. "Give us the Sable, Doctor. Give us the Sable, and the Council will release you both."

The other vampires on the Council turned confusedly to each other. The hissing in chamber grew restive once more.

"Vesta, the Sable is a myth. You know that. There is no proof of its existence," the Doctor said. My mind strained forward, trying to read the thoughtstreams of the Doctor, of Renata, even Vesta, for any hint of the meaning of this. What were they talking about? What the hell was the Sable?

Vesta exploded in rage. *"The Council will judge the verity of the Sable!"* she screamed. "You have insulted this Council once again, Doctor! You will be annihilated!"

"Then whatever secret the Council presumes I may have about the legendary Sable will be annihilated with me!"

"You will *both* suffer annihilation!" Vesta shouted, the tendons in her neck tensing. "You and the Comtesse! Immediately!"

"I warn the Council," the Doctor continued. "Release Renata. It will go better for you, if you do as I say."

At this, the galleries above erupted in noise. The hissing of vampire shouts rose in waves, and the shuffling of feet against the benches bespoke the audience rising from their seats to hurl their insults upon the Doctor. The bee swarm seemed ready to break.

"Enough of this!" shouted Vesta, her brow wrinkling as she scowled at the Doctor, slowly regaining her composure. "You insult the Vampire Council, and now you dare to threaten it! And what do you plan to do, Doctor? Have your disciples been magically restored? Do they come to drive us away at your command? Or has your genius with potions given you some new mixture that will destroy us all? All that is past—dead! Your time is over, Doctor!" Her eyes flashed at the two witnesses, still standing to the side of the platform beside Renata and the Doctor. "Seize them! Seize them now!"

It was perhaps indicative of the Doctor's reputation as the brilliant vampire chemist that Vesta had guessed that the Doctor would try a potion—or as we might say in these times, a chemical warfare operation. For before Harrison and Chuck could make a move the Doctor drew a glass vessel from his coat, about the size and shape of gallon milk bottle, but seemingly composed of fragile, hand-blown glass. He held it above his head with both hands; in the torchlight, the clear liquid within the glass vessel swirled threateningly, with a slow and viscous movement. The members of the Council scattered as he hurled the glass vessel directly at them.

"Away with tyrants!" the Doctor shouted.

The glass container exploded into a blizzard of shattered fragments as it struck, and immediately a fog flowed from the site of the shattered vessel and began to fill the chamber. Screams of alarm arose from the Council members and the gallery alike; a flurry of indistinct black figures was suddenly in motion, rushing from the rising white mist and pushing out the portal. I watched, fascinated—it was the scientist in me, I admit—if the Doctor had found some new wonder weapon effective against the dead beings which were vampires, then the event called for careful and dispassionate observation.

But I did not get the chance. The rushing sweep of fleeing vampires pushed me back against the bench where I was hiding; I leaped down toward the platform to avoid the tumult. I saw the Doctor grab Renata by the arm, and saw them race, not back toward the portal with the rest of the vampire crowd, but forward, toward the Council seats. As they leapt up onto the dais, I saw the Doctor confront Vesta face to face for a moment, and then he flung her aside and was gone. The Council fled out the portal with the rest of the vampire nation. Panicked, their suggestible minds in terror of the Doctor's reputation as the threatening white gas filled the room, they had not determined what I had already figured out using the simple expedients of scientific observation—the smell of the vapor, and the taste of the liquid—that the Doctor had achieved all this with a simple bluff. The glass container was filled with water, and contained a separate compartment that was filled with dry ice—simple ingredients, available to any chemist. Shatter the glass and the dry ice dropped into the water—and you had a smoke bomb worthy of any adolescent troublemaker. The bluff succeeded, however; as the vampires disappeared out the portal, I followed the Doctor and Renata out the other way, into the blackness beyond the dais, beyond the reach of the dim torchlight.

The Doctor and Renata were fast—I could barely keep up with them. My kitten paws stumbled over another wooden platform beyond the Council's dais, then stones again as I followed the indistinct black movement of the fleeing vampires into a further passage that seemed to lead out another exit from the building. Then squeezing through holes in the earth—we were following a tunnel now, my claws scratching at power cables, the passage leading up, then backtracking, and then up again. I was disoriented. And then suddenly, a light ahead—I saw the Doctor and Renata push out through a door and into a marble-paved room, filled with color and movement. I scurried through as Renata closed the door—a utility closet, so it seemed—and her downward glance spotted me. She bent and picked me up, and then, smoothing her elegant black dress, she and the Doctor secured their dark glasses in place. She took the Doctor's arm and stepped out with him into the perfumed air of the ball at the Hibernian Hall.

They walked through the crowd, occasionally pausing to smile and acknowledge a nod from a guest who fancied they were acquaintances. Perhaps the Doctor was acquainted with these guests—who knew? He was indeed a surprising vampire.

We were stopped only once, by a young woman who seemed both a bit drunk and a bit too enthusiastic over Renata's and the Doctor's all-black attire and whitened faces. She seemed to have decided that the Doctor and Renata were cutting loose with an individual, Goreyesque statement of style at an otherwise staid social function. Radical! How cool!

"Oh, Dr. Civitas, I *love* it!" she gushed with a slight slur. "So wonderfully *different!* And a cat! It's all so wonderfully *creepy!*" She turned her pleasant, smiling face to Renata. "And this must be your, your, ah, …" She trailed off. Even in her tipsy state, the woman's Charlestonian social training prevented her from plunging ahead and making the possibly grievous misstep of, say, mistaking a man's wife for his daughter. A mistake, by the way, I have noticed one could easily make in many prominent socio-economic strata in this country.

The Doctor pantomimed a sore throat, smiled pleasantly, and touching his watch he pointed across the room toward the door. It would not have been helpful for the Doctor or Renata to attempt to speak in their vampire voices, even if they were inclined to take the time. The woman, noisy but polite to the last, made her good nights to the Doctor and her *so*-pleased-to-meet-you's to Renata, even though they had never actually been introduced.

A few more moments, and the Doctor and Renata were out the front door of the Hibernian, down the steps and out past the black iron fence on Meeting Street. The ball in the Hibernian Hall seemed to be breaking up; well-dressed couples were waiting by the parking valet on the sidewalk, or drifting down the street on their own. I leaped down from Renata's arms as they mingled with the departing guests. I followed the Doctor and Renata as they moved away from the light illuminating Hibernian

Hall, and into the shadows up the block. Two blocks ahead, I noticed the Doctor's beige sedan parked on the street—illegally, it seemed, but then what does a vampire care about parking tickets? As they reached the car, I saw them look furtively back behind them, and then Doctor took both of Renata's hands in his and kissed her on each cheek with Continental courtesy. He was Italian, after all, and she was French. But the moment passed quickly. I thought I saw Renata flee in a sudden movement down a side street toward the West side—but then I wasn't sure— was it just a trick of the eyes?—because when I looked back at the Doctor, he had already gotten into the driver's seat of the beige car and started the engine and headlights, and as he pulled the car out onto Meeting Street going uptown I saw a passenger in the seat beside him—a passenger with long, gleaming black hair. As he drove on, I heard behind me the sound of two motorcycles revving, and then thrumming as they came up Meeting Street from the darkness of Washington Park. Harrison and Chuck, on throaty, powerful bikes. They fell in behind the beige sedan, now making no attempt at concealment. I realized that it had not been a trick of my eyes, but another trick of the Doctor's. The passenger was surely a decoy of some kind. A black wig rigged on a broomhandle, perhaps? Or maybe a store mannequin, prepared in advance for the occasion and dressed up like Renata? I personally hoped it was the latter—it would seem to confirm the Doctor's professionalism. And the two guys on the motorcycles made sense to me now too—Harrison and Chuck, being apparently recently-made vampires, had been pressed into service as Vesta's muscle. They had been mortal humans recently enough to retain some memory of the human way of thinking, and an ability to blend into human gatherings, even if they did need to stay in the dark and wear sunglasses all the time now. Immortality had not yet made them entirely blunt and stupid—although they appeared to trend that way naturally. But in this case, I felt sure, Vesta had not sent them to act as vampire spies. This mission had a more definite end. This time she was sending them to be vampire assassins.

And I realized now just as clearly that the Doctor was leading the assassins away to give Renata a chance to escape. I didn't know how long the Doctor could keep up the ruse—perhaps he planned to corkscrew back and forth through the streets of the city, or perhaps he planned to lead them up onto the highway, out into the midnight Low Country and away from Charleston entirely? But in any event, the assassins would at some point need to make their strike. They may prefer to do it at some remote spot, far away from prying mortal eyes. When they discovered that the Doctor was alone, they would come back for Renata—if they had succeeded in annihilating the Doctor first, whatever that meant. But what if the Doctor annihilated the assassins instead? The scientist in me was intensely curious to know, to observe how all this would play out. But, when I told the Doctor that I would be loyal to Renata, I wasn't lying. I let the taillights of the motorcycles disappear into the lights of the city street uptown, and I trotted along the side street I had seen Renata fly onto. I thought I knew where she was going. I had to get there fast.

CHAPTER ELEVEN

I caught up to Renata only a few blocks away. She had stopped in one of the small side streets just beyond King Street, past the art galleries and handbag stores beloved of the tourists. She was sitting on a worn painted-brick stoop in the back of a shop, beyond the circle of the nearest streetlight. I trotted up and sat on my haunches, squarely in front of her. I watched her. She glanced up, just the briefest flick of the glittering eyes, but enough that I know she saw me there. But then she turned back to the task occupying her attention. She gripped a silvery hypodermic in her teeth. As I watched, she rolled the skirt of her black gown far up to her waist and, canting her left leg slightly to reveal her milky-white inner thigh, she quickly took the hypodermic in her hand and thrust the needle deep into her flesh, at the crease of her thigh and hip. She emitted a hiss of pain, then slowly pressed the plunger until the needle was empty of the drug. She was shooting a dose of thanadoxicil directly into her femoral artery, I realized. The drug would swirl into her body almost instantly; her vampirism would begin to crash. I knew that she had to change states quickly to escape; blending into the human landscape would be her best hope to evade the assassins.

But mainlining the thanadox had to be risky—I wondered if she had asked the Doctor about it as part of their plan. In any event, I was impressed by her presence of mind, being able to not only locate a major artery while trying to make her escape, but choosing one where the inevitable purplish bruising would be hidden. Leave it to a vampire to have a practical working knowledge of human blood vessels.

Renata was already up, running again through the dark alleyway back toward the College of Charleston campus. She limped slightly, the leg which had received the injection dragging her back. She had already lost the fluid movement of the midnight vampire; now she was losing the speed. I could easily outrun her; I would scurry forward at a sprint and realize that I had passed her and left her behind. With a twist of my tiger-striped body I would double back behind her again, until my sprint overtook her once more. I could hear her breathing now, labored and apace with her footfalls. Her footsteps seemed thudding and ponderous compared to the silent glide of her movement a few hours ago in the vampire state. She was holding the black high-heeled shoes in one hand, swinging them as if pacing herself like a distance runner. Alas, however, her human state wasn't up to the physical strain. One block further on, I doubled back to find her off the sidewalk, kneeling in the shadow of a willow oak, retching a slick mass of congealed blood onto the grass beside the sidewalk. She paused and sat, her back resting against the tree trunk, strands of her black hair plastered to her forehead with very human perspiration. Her breath wheezed as she rested for a moment, and idly picked at the damaged black silk of her dress. I did what a kitten could do; I rubbed my nose against her ankle and sat with her.

She finally rose and struggled on. When we reached the residence hall on campus it was still heavily dark. I knew that hours must have elapsed since I had entered the chamber of the Vampire Council, but I had lost my sense of how many. Dawn would come soon, but how soon? Renata was shivering and sweating; I could see the effects of the mainlined thanadoxicil, but the vampirism was still there. She looked sick and weak this way, and I worried about her, exposed on the streets, with the vampire assassins knowing who she came to Charleston with.

She must have been thinking the same way. The door to the residence hall was locked; the lobby was dark. There was no chance to slip in with someone else entering or leaving. Without hesitation, Renata tore a strip of silk from her skirt and, wrapping it about the hand carrying the shoes, she went off toward a window to the side of the door, behind a low array of bushes. The shattering window made a shocking noise in the predawn silence, but no one stirred. With a heavy effort, Renata dragged herself through the broken window and dropped into the hallway within. Then she was off, running with labored step inside; I lightly leaped onto the windowsill and joined her in the hall, running ahead to lead her to the stairs and up to Denis's room.

She pounded on his door with her whole arm, less knocking on the door than bodily falling upon it in her weariness.

"Denis!" she called. Her voice was fully human again. "Denis! Denis! Denis!"

A scraping of a lock; the sticky dorm door pulled open. Denis's sleep-heavy eyes widened when he saw her. Black gown torn and shredded now, her face gleaming with sweat and flushed as if fevered, her breath heaving, Renata did not look good. Denis opened his mouth to speak, but was silent.

"We have to leave," she panted. "Now. The car. Get your keys. Come on, we have to leave. Now. We have to leave," she said. "Now."

Denis opened the room door, motioning her in. "OK," he whispered, "OK. Come on inside." He pulled her in, Renata resisting. "Let me get my stuff together, OK? We can leave in a minute."

"Now," Renata said. "We have to leave now."

Denis paused, walked to Renata and cupped her cheek in his hand. "Are you all right, Renata? You look awful."

Renata was silent. She looked at his face, her black eyes steady despite the streaming sweat and trembling. I picked up the discordant rumble of emotional thoughtstreams again. The emotional toll of the night was beginning to tell on her. Would she cry? I had never seen her cry, but the crash of the thanadoxicil overdose could have any effect. Renata touched his hand on her cheek for a moment, then lowered her hand. "I'll be OK," she said. "Get your bag, though. We need to hurry."

Denis moved quickly about the room, tossing his clothes and papers into the weekend bag. His hand found the oblong box on the desk, and the leather portfolio. He motioned at them, slightly embarrassed. "Your doctor stopped by last night," he said. "He left these." Denis paused, looking at her condition. He held up the box. "Do you, uh, you know, need some of this?"

Renata smiled slightly. "He came here," she said, wonderingly. She shook her head. "Thanks, I'll be OK. I just took some."

Denis had his bag and briefcase together. He grabbed his blazer from the coathook and pulled the keys from the pocket, swept his eyes around the room, and was out the door, Renata and I in his wake. Down the stairs, he pushed open the front door with a sidelong glance at the broken glass from the window, lying guiltily on the floor.

"Just go," Renata said.

We got to the parking garage and tossed everything into the back. I hopped in on the back seat; Denis fired the engine even before Renata was seated.

"So back to Forshay?" he said. "Where's your stuff, by the way?"

"It doesn't matter," Renata said. "Yes, back to

Forshay." Denis put the car in gear and was working his way down the ramps of the garage. They reached the exit of the parking garage. The car's blinker clicked, signaling a right turn, flashing into the empty dark street.

"No!" Renata said suddenly. "Not back that way!"

"What?" Denis asked. "I thought you needed to go back."

"Right," she responded. "But go a different way. Don't go the way we came." She looked at him pleadingly. "Can you go another way?"

Denis turned and looked at Renata for a long moment. I could hear his mind wrestling with whether he should demand some kind of explanation from her—about the sudden departure, about her ruined clothes and the loss of her canvas bag, about her obvious illness and stress. He thought of making a light remark—*hey, the weekend with your people must have turned out tougher than you thought, ha ha*—but then he dropped it. He broke off his glance with a slight shrug, and shifted the blinker to signal a left turn.

"Sure," he said. "We can go over the Ashley River Bridge. Go back up the long way."

Renata was still shivering slightly. She turned and faced straight forward through the black windshield. "Thank you," she said, her choked voice hardly a whisper.

We drove in silence for the rest of the night, the car wending its way quickly out of the quiet, dark city, over the gleaming black water of the river below the bridge, and onto the secondary highways running north. Renata had quickly dropped asleep, lulled by the hum of the tires in the darkness. When Denis pulled into a Waffle House outside of Summerville the darkness had only been slightly abated by a lighter blue glow on eastern edge of the sky. He woke Renata.

"Hey," he said. "I've gotta get some coffee if I'm going to keep driving. You want to eat?"

Renata stretched and opened her eyes. She was looking better; the violent, junkie-in-withdrawal reaction of the thanadoxicil had receded, and with it the shivering and fever. "Yes," she said. "I'm famished."

Denis sat at the counter with a second cup of coffee, a half-eaten muffin on the plate before him, and tried not to stare at Renata as she ate a three-egg ham and cheese omelet, a portion of country ham, a side of pancakes and syrup, biscuits and jelly, some sausage links, buttered toast, homefries and ketchup, some cling peaches, and then another side of pancakes. Renata smiled at him, chewing the last bites. Denis smiled back, and then nonchalantly gazed away through the still-dark plate windows at the highway beyond, as if everyone ate that kind of breakfast before dawn on a Sunday morning. Renata had changed out of her torn black dress in the ladies room, and was wearing a hooded sweatshirt and sweatpants that Denis had had in his bag. I was curled at Renata's feet, from the toes of which now dangled a pair of Denis's large running shoes like oversized loafers. Just a concession to the rule about wearing shoes in restaurants—Renata couldn't afford to be delayed by silly altercations about bare feet. The big shoes were comfortable for me, however; I could drape myself almost entirely inside them next to Renata's slim foot. No one was going to notice me. I dozed silently, waiting for Denis and Renata to finish, listening idly to the thoughts of the few other patrons. Dawn on Sunday morning—almost no one around, and those that were weren't thinking very hard.

And then suddenly, into my mind came another, different thoughtstream—flaring just briefly before it faded, like a radio wave from a far-off city blown by some atmospheric anomaly to broadcast loud and clear for just a moment on the other side of the world. I started when it came; and, strangely, I noticed that Renata's foot twitched at the same time. How odd—perhaps my jumpy movement had made her foot jump as well, but I didn't think so. Could she have heard the same thing I had? But, I knew that she did not share my talent to hear thoughtstreams. Another unexplained phenomenon. I listened again, trying to hear if it would come again—it had been a flash, like a beacon, perfectly clear, but I had not been able to discern any meaning from it. But in vain, however—the thoughtstream seemed to be gone. Renata's feet sought the inside of the oversized running shoes again; she and Denis were ready to leave. I hopped away from the shoe to avoid getting stepped on, and we all returned to the car.

Denis drove on through the Sunday morning emptiness of the local highway. The sky was finally lightening, and the grassy ground rushing by the car slowly resolved into gray visibility; the sunrise would break soon. Denis took the car back onto the Interstate, and for a few miles silence reigned in the car. The tires made their steady hum; Renata had put her dark glasses back on and slumped somnolently in the passenger seat. I was curled again in a nest in the jumble in the back seat, slowly relaxing. Perhaps this would be an easy drive back after all.

The rim of the sun broke above the horizon to the side of the car, and in the clear morning sky shot a flash of red light across the land. And simultaneously, the beacon-thoughtstream I had heard in the Waffle House flashed once again into my mind—but this time searing, screaming, overpowering; it was a crushing sudden sound in my brain. I started with a flurry of scratching, my tail-fur standing up and an involuntary hiss escaping my mouth. But most extraordinary—Renata, too, gave a sudden, sharp cry of surprise as well, and bolted upright. No question this time—she had heard the same thing I had heard: a thoughtstream in the mind.

But even more extraordinary is what she did next. She grabbed Denis's arm, and pointed at an upcoming exit sign. "We have to get off here!" she said, urgently.

Denis gently shook her hand from his arm, where it had interfered with his steering for a moment. "That's 95," he said. "That goes the wrong way. Besides, the *traffic* on that is *killer* on the weekends ..."

She wasn't put off. She grabbed him again, on the shoulder, trying to pull his face toward her. "No, we *have to get off here!*" she shouted. *"Here!"*

Denis's eyes were wide again. I have to say that the poor guy had been called upon for a lot this weekend, without his complaining at all. This was a very decent guy—and, true to form, he didn't complain this time either. He smoothly shifted Renata off his shoulder, guided the car onto the exit ramp to I-95, and kept driving calmly. Perhaps he was just following the perfectly reasonable strategy that, not knowing what Renata's condition actually was, it was best not to argue with a crazy lady. He continued driving, watching Renata from the corner of his eye.

But I understood now what she was doing—because the strange, insistent thoughtstream we had heard before had reemerged, and it was now sounding in our brains steadily, but with an intermittent rising and falling in volume. It had seemed to be a beacon, apparently, because it was a beacon—a homing signal, leading us and getting louder and more focused as we approached. Its sound had become a dreadful keening, filled with a strange, unnerving despair. Denis seemed to pick up the urgency from Renata's sudden intensity; the car accelerated through the morning truck traffic going north.

Suddenly, Renata pointed again. "Here, this exit," she said.

"Get off here?" Denis asked. "Why?"

"This exit—exit here!" Renata shouted.

"OK, OK," Denis replied meekly. "Getting off now."

Renata began to direct Denis through a series of local roads and turnings off the highway. We drove deeper and deeper into brushy countryside and new-plowed fields. The thoughtstream-beacon grew louder and louder all the time, more insistent, more despairing. It was filling my mind as Renata finally directed Denis to turn the car into the entrance of the Santee State Park.

"I don't think the park is open this early," he said.

Renata wasn't listening to him. "Go, hurry!" she said. "Faster!"

The sound in my mind was almost overwhelming now—it was blaring, drowning out every other thought and sound. And yet, as Denis sped the car around the looping access roads toward the great blue expanse of Lake Marion beyond, I thought I heard—or did I just imagine?—the distant thrum of two motorcycle engines, far away, and receding.

We found the beige sedan abandoned in the dusty, packed-earth parking lot for a picnic area near the lake beach. Denis's Saab skidded to a halt on the loose gravel, the tail swerving slightly as he jammed the brakes. Renata was already out of the car, racing toward the water, leaving the outsized running shoes behind and the car door open. I raced after her. The beacon was clear and perfectly directed: it came from straight before us. But now it was weakening, weakening rapidly. And it had shifted in aspect; no longer a loud, overpowering roar, it was now thin, sad, almost sweet—it resembled nothing so much as the mournful songs of loss and irrevocability that simple people sing to comfort themselves in the face of unknowable, unnamable tragedy.

The yellow sun was now shining bright and steady above the blue of the lake. Renata had raced far ahead of me into the bracken at the verge of the water. I saw the ruts of the two motorcycle tracks left in the sand, and I knew we had found the Doctor.

I don't know how they had managed to overpower him, but when I broke through the last screen of foliage before the beach, I saw that there had been a fight. The Doctor's hat lay on the sand to one side, his coat, suit, shoes and shirt—torn and bloodstained—were strewn across the strand where the vampire assassins had stripped them off the Doctor's body. A machete lay shining flatly in the steady sunrays, a thin ribbon of smoke rising from the vampire blood on the blade. And across the sand were other objects, still smoking where the sunlight had thrown its vampire-lethal brightness upon them—blackened ashes now, but still recognizably the Doctor's feet, then one arm, then another, then the stumps of his legs. They had overpowered him and dismembered him, leaving his body where it would be struck by the sun. I saw that Renata was on the far side of the sandy beach, kneeling over the Doctor's torso and head, which had been chained to stakes driven into the sand, and placed where the rising sunlight would strike his exposed head last. Renata was kneeling in the part that was still shaded by the overhang of trees. The smoke was rising fast from the Doctor's prone body as the sunlight rose and swept up it, and I arrived at Renata's side as the full rays of the sun blackened the Doctor's face in a riot of smoke, the echoing thoughtstreams from the Doctor's mind rising to one last, shrill climax before they suddenly fell still. The ashes of the Doctor's face subsided and collapsed into an indeterminate heap on the sand, thin streams of smoke still rising into the sun, and the great vampire was gone. And this, I realized, was annihilation.

After the sounds of the Doctor's thoughtstream beacon, the sudden absence seemed like silence, but it wasn't. I became aware of the thoughtstreams emanating from Renata beside me—tangled, unformed, laden. She still knelt above the smoking ashes, her face rigid behind her dark glasses, her body immobile. I crept away to the side to give her privacy, but I could not help but watch her. It was a situation, an event, which I would not have even believed possible not many hours before—but facts are facts, and one must accept them. Accepting the data is how scientific progress is made.

Denis emerged onto the sandy beach, and walked up to Renata. He gently put his hands on her shoulders.

"Hey, you all right?"

Renata did not answer.

"You want to sit here for a while?" Denis looked about the beach—except for some odd, lumpy ashes scattered about, apparently left from a water's-edge campfire, the sand looked clean and pleasantly bright in the sunny morning. I noticed the sound of quiet, splashing wavelets breaking at water's verge. "Beautiful lake," he said.

She paused a moment longer, then rose. She seemed to square her feet in the cool shady sand, putting her hands on her hips as she looked out over the sunny blue water. She looked determined, suddenly, almost fierce.

"Yes," she said. "Yes it is." Then she strode decisively into the direct, bright sunshine and stood, bareheaded, for a moment before she walked to the water's edge. She stood with her bare feet in the lapping waves of the lake on a bright, blue-skied Sunday morning. "Yes, it's beautiful. It's a beautiful lake." She then turned away, walked along the beach and gathered the Doctor's clothes and hat, and walked back to the car. Denis watched her go for a moment, silently. Then we followed her back to the car.

PART TWO

The Chantry of Beaumanoir

CHAPTER TWELVE

Michael Corleone sat on a bench on his windswept estate on Lake Tahoe. The ghostly memory train of Don Vito and the children in Sicily had already dissolved. The soundtrack lulled, and in the pause the camera tightened the frame onto Al Pacino's face—pensive, haunted, looking away into the past. Then the music swelled, the camera lingering a moment longer before the scene faded to black, and the wide screen of Fulda's television set began to fill with the slow crawl of the movie credits for *The Godfather Part II*.

There was a smattering of applause around the Myersons' living room, and as Fulda turned the lights back on the audience broke up, wandering back toward Fulda's kitchen and the dinner buffet she had laid out there, or gathering in small knots around the living room.

"God, that's such a great movie," Fulda said as she found Renata. "One of the greatest endings ever."

Renata sipped at a glass of cold white wine, and looked around the room. It was a faculty movie party for the end of term. By common custom it fell to a faculty member who had the good fortune to live in President's Row—the big, historic houses the College owned along Main Street

153

near the President's House—to host a party for the rest of the faculty at the end of the academic year. By luck in the housing lottery and by dint of Fulda's seniority in the chemistry department, Fulda and Michael occupied one of the choicest houses in the Row. A set of sliding glass doors led from the living room, with its bookshelves and big fieldstone fireplace, out to a stone patio and a flowery back yard; to the other side a bright coppery kitchen was filled with people and good cooking smells. A staircase of wide, hardwood steps led to a broad upstairs landing, with five bedrooms ranged off the center hall. More bedrooms than Fulda, Michael and Maia needed; two of them had been converted into home offices, one each for Fulda and Michael. Another had become a toy-strewn playroom for Maia—and, on the night of the party, for the young children of other faculty guests. About six of their children had been upstairs playing with Maia throughout the movie. The upstairs hallway must have been hardwood as well—I heard the shockingly heavy thudding of children's footsteps like thunder rolling along the ceiling each time they burst from the playroom and ran through the hall, their voices squealing with laughter.

There was also an overlooked cat flap in the side door to the kitchen, presumably installed by a cat-owning prior resident of the house, but seemingly ignored by the Myersons. As for me, I knew the cat door—and therefore the Myerson's house—very well. I considered myself invited to the faculty party, just as I considered myself automatically invited to every party at Forshay College, as a matter of simple right—although I prudently kept out of sight among the legs of the furniture that had been moved aside in the living room for the movie. I crept around, mingling in my own way you might say, and listened to the conversations both vocalized and nonvocalized.

The faculty all seemed to be there; even President Hutchinson had made an appearance early in the evening, although she had left before the movie had been played.

Ever the politician, she perhaps had judged that it would be better for her faculty's morale to have the party proceed without the president there. And so, after a few words of appreciation for another year of achievement, of goals met, and yet we do not shrink from the challenges to come, *blah blah blah*, she had left and walked up the sidewalk to where the white Greek Revival President's House stood, and where it seemed President Hutch had separately scheduled an alumnae fund-raising reception. I saw Claude Preen walking about the garden, presumably making a nuisance of himself. In the kitchen Denis Pearson was talking to Beth and Lucy, who had catered the food and then stayed on to help Fulda and Michael serve.

"Oh, before I forget," Fulda said. "There's someone here I wanted you to meet." Fulda took Renata's forearm and guided her out the sliding doors onto the patio. I scampered after them, the sliding door narrowly missing my tail as it shut.

"Silly cat," Fulda said. "She really follows you everywhere, doesn't she?"

Renata smiled. "Sometimes I wonder whether *I'm* following *her*," she said. "I thought she was back at my house. Kikki certainly has a mind of her own."

Fulda approached a knot of people chatting on the bricked patio near a flaring mosquito torch. One of the people was Claude Preen, I noticed distastefully. Fulda drew Renata up beside a stocky, bearded man of middling height. He was dressed casually but expensively, and from behind his breadth of shoulders gave him a pugilistic aspect. He turned, and his black beard drew aside in a bright smile as Fulda introduced him.

"Renata, this is John Random," Fulda said. "A farmer, believe it or not. And a lawyer—are you still a lawyer, in fact? But in any case a friend and benefactor of the College."

Random's voice was lighter, airier than I would have expected from a man who looked so tough. "I'm delighted to meet you," he said. "Fulda's told me about you—you're the history professor. The medievalist. Is that right?"

"Well, a history teacher, for sure, but no professor title," Renata said, shooting a nervous glance at Claude Preen. She added, "I've done quite a bit of research in the medieval period, but I don't know that I have really determined which era to concentrate on."

At this Preen rolled his eyes, and then cocked his head backwards to drain his highball glass, ice cubes clicking rudely on his teeth. "Love to continue, but I think I'll get a refill on this," he said with pointed brusqueness. "Beth is the only one in town who can do a proper Pimm's Cup."

Random watched sidelong as Preen strode away. "Don't know what that was all about," he said. "Hope it wasn't anything I said."

"Claude has strong feelings about which historical periods are worth the effort of modern historians," Fulda said, "or so I understand. Apparently, his view of history is that the modern world emerged fully-formed from the brow of Zeus around, oh, say 1815 or thereabouts. No need to ask what came before."

Renata fixed Fulda with a penetrating look. "For a chemist, you seem to take quite an interest in pre-modern history," she said.

"Just watching your back, sweetie," Fulda replied. "Besides, I've been looking into medieval chemistry lately. You know, we all think of medieval science as nonsense and magic and alchemy, but they weren't idiots. There's really some surprising stuff. I think there may be a lot that we've overlooked." She sipped her wine. "But John, you still haven't answered my question—lawyer or no?"

Random laughed, his eyes twinkling as his smile again creased the black whiskers. "I have to plead guilty to being a lawyer," he said. "Even had to sit for the bar exam down here in North Carolina instead of just waiving in. What a pain in the neck that was! But when I left New

York the plan was to leave law practice as well, so I didn't keep my license up for the first few years."

"So you used to be a lawyer in New York?" Renata asked.

"Yes—I was a partner at a big Wall Street-type firm in midtown. A pretty good one, too. But then, after 9/11— well, you know how so many people back then were saying how everything had changed, and how they were going to re-focus their lives, and stop living for transitory goals, and all that. Mostly, after the shock wore off, people got back to normal, and went back to the lives they had, best they could. But for some reason," Random said, with an open-palmed gesture of bewilderment, "I never could. I just couldn't settle back down to things. I had a good life and should have been happy with it, but I had this sense of, oh, I don't really know how to explain it—I guess of *significance* suddenly in the air after the catastrophe. And my old life didn't seem significant enough. So," he said, with a swig of beer from his glass, "I left. September 11th the towers came down; by October 11th I had resigned my partnership. And by the beginning of 2002 I was here in North Carolina, where I was able buy a good spread of good farmland. With the recession in 2002 I got it at a reasonable price, too."

"So that's it?" Renata asked. "Now you're just a farmer?"

Random smiled. *"Just'* a farmer? Now, that's full of interesting implications, isn't it?" he said, then laughing as Renata's faced showed embarrassment. "Hey, forget about it. But yes, I'm a farmer. But call me a farmer *plus,"* he said.

"Plus what?" Fulda asked. "You're not going to say that you're some kind of Renaissance Man who's out to save the world, are you?"

"No, but I am a lawyer again," he said. "It's mostly for real estate issues that come up with the farm and some other ventures I own. And for the workers I use—so many of them are from Mexico or Central America, with all kinds of legal issues. In fact I believe," he said, "that I can claim to be the fifth-best immigration lawyer in Forshay County. Of course, that's fifth out of five. But I'm working on it!"

Fulda and Renata laughed, and Fulda leaned in, her eyes darting behind her glasses from Random to Renata and back. "So John," she asked wickedly, "just how rich are you?"

John Random smiled pleasantly back. "Rich enough," he said.

"Numbers, please," Fulda said. "I'm a scientist. You need to give me the data set."

Random tipped his head back and gave a satisfying laugh. "Jesus, Fulda, you are something!" he said. "No, I won't give you numbers. But, consider this: I was a partner in a Wall Street law firm for 20 years. Tail of the LBO boom, all through the tech boom. I never married, never had kids. No kids means I never had to spend the money. And that, my friends, is the difference between rich and poor. At least in New York City." He scratched his chin thoughtfully. "To be honest, I really don't know how young couples manage things up there, even in the best of times."

"So where is your farm?" Renata asked. "Near the College?"

"Very close," Fulda interjected. "It's that land you see abutting the Forshay Golf Links, which is also, if I am not mistaken, owned by our simple farmer here."

Random laughed and raised his glass. "OK, correct. Add that to the data set. But everyone knows that."

"So you have a farm and a golf course," Renata said. "So you must like to farm and you must like to golf. Do just buy properties to do the things you like to do?"

"Well, in a way," Random replied. "I was certainly indulging myself with the farm. I really enjoy that, now that I have a clue what I'm doing. One hundred ten acres under cultivation, with apples, strawberries, and greens on one slope, and poultry, hogs and tomatoes on the other. All organic stuff, premium, and it's really good—I sell shares in the harvest to restaurants in Charlotte and Charleston and Atlanta, and I could sell double if I had the land. So I'm lucky—the farm's self-financing, for the most part. But the golf course, that's just for money—pure cash flow. I actually don't golf."

"You own a golf course when you don't even golf?"

"Nope. I don't like golf."

"Why don't you like golf?" Fulda asked.

"I don't know, but I never did. I could never understand the attraction. If I wanted to combine boredom with bad land-use planning, I'd just go to a county zoning commission hearing. Besides," he said, "I'm told that golf is an addiction—so I'd rather be the pusher than the junkie."

As Renata and Fulda chuckled, another voice spoke up. "But tell us about your other obsession, John," it said. "Or addiction, if you prefer to call it that."

John Random's eyes widened as Margaret Viper edged into the circle of the conversation. He put down his glass, and took both of Margaret's bony hands in his.

"Margaret," he said, his voice a compound of surprise and delight. He bent and gave Margaret a familiar, bristly kiss on each cheek. "Margaret, I was so hoping I would see you here," he said. "And yes, I was just about to talk about that—I'm not sure how I got off the track."

"My fault," Fulda said, with a sly grin at Margaret. "I was conducting a cross-examination about Mr. Random's real estate portfolio."

"Sorry," Renata said, "I think I'm suddenly lost. What are we talking about?"

John smiled at Renata. "A hobby of mine. Hobby—that sounds too, I don't know, insignificant. Interest? I wouldn't call it an obsession, but definitely a big interest of mine—it's why I asked Fulda if I could meet you." He paused, seemingly aware that he was rambling a bit. "History—especially medieval history. I could talk about it all day. It's the other reason I wanted to move out of New York," he said. "I didn't have enough space for all the history books in my city apartment."

"I've seen your library at the farmhouse, John," Margaret said. "Remember, you've promised it to Forshay College someday."

"Yes," Random said. "In fact, I was noticing your ring, Miss Beaumanoir." Random glanced at Renata's left hand and motioned to the white star ring she wore. "Order of the Star, is it not? The order created by good King Jean of France in 1351, I think?" Random glanced at her. "It's a beautiful reproduction."

Renata looked at him for a moment, not comprehending. "My ring?" she asked. "Yes, I think the device *is* the Order of the Star. It's something we've had in my family for many years—an heirloom, I think you say." She smiled. "Well spotted, Mr. Random."

Something in the way she said it made John Random pause for a moment and scrutinize Renata's face. I could hear his thoughtstreams, testing the proposition that Renata meant that her ring was not a reproduction, but that it was an authentic ring of the Order of the Star. Which would make it an extraordinary artifact, a museum piece without price. He said nothing, but soon a broad smile covered his face as he concluded that she must be kidding him. "Well, it's beautiful, anyway," he said.

"I can't say I understand what you two history geeks are even talking about," said Fulda. "And I'm not sure I'm finished asking you about your balance sheet, John."

I was watching, listening to all this from a few feet away on the floor. Suddenly I noticed that Renata had become aware that Margaret was staring at her. She had let her eyes meet Margaret's, and now felt her gaze involuntarily fixed by Margaret's stare. She was unable to look away. To be sure it was only for a moment, but I could tell it was unnerving to her. For in that moment I heard Renata's human thoughtstreams rise with a sudden panic, an irrational fear that Margaret had her in her thrall. Renata was breathing heavily when Margaret glanced away again to John Random.

"In fact," Random was saying to Fulda, skipping the question about his balance sheet, "I did a master's in pre-Renaissance Europe at Duke, years ago, back before law school. And do you know who my graduate advisor was? None other than Miss Margaret Viper."

Margaret smiled back to Random, with a flick of a sidelong glance at Renata. "You should have stuck with it, John, instead of going to law school," she said to him. "I told you that back then. As if the world needed more lawyers!"

I could tell that Renata was perplexed. "So, Margaret," she asked tentatively, "you did advanced work in history? At Duke?"

"Yes," she said, sweetly, or at least as sweetly as Margaret Viper could. "Long before you were on the scene, I'm sure, dear. But yes, I was doctoral candidate in Durham for several years."

"Don't let her modesty fool you," Random said. "When I knew her she was one of the most innovative historians in the country, bar none. It was a privilege to work with you, Margaret. And I've enjoyed keeping up with you over the years, even if I think we only actually saw each other again once, if I recall."

"Yes," Margaret said, "I think that's right. Even that was many years ago. Our Miss Beaumanoir would have been in nappies."

"Oh, that's an exaggeration," Fulda said. "We're not *that* much younger than you."

"I said Miss Beaumanoir," Margaret replied with perfect comic timing. "Not you, Dr. Myerson."

"Again with the age jokes," Fulda muttered. "I'm going to start taking this personally soon," she said, as

John and Renata chuckled.

"Forgive me, Margaret," said Renata, "but if you got your Ph.D at Duke in history, what brought you to Forshay? I mean, in a non-academic position?"

Margaret raised her chin slightly as she answered. "That's something I do not choose to share, Miss Beaumanoir," she said. "But you know as well as I do that good academic jobs are scarce, and a good job at a good college is not something to be put aside lightly. In fact, that reminds me," she continued, "perhaps I could have a word with you before the end of the evening, Miss Beaumanoir. A private word." Margaret's fixative glance caught Renata's again for a moment; I felt the shiver of fear involuntarily crease Renata's mind once more before the glance flicked away, leaving a residue of menace behind like a flavor on the tongue. Renata was silent.

"Look, maybe you two need to talk," Fulda said. "John, why don't we go get something to eat. I should get back to the house anyway—my party, theoretically, you know."

"Sure," Random said. "Renata, it was wonderful to meet you. I'd like to talk further sometime. And what Margaret says about my library is true—I have some interesting stuff. Maybe you could come out to the farm and see it?"

Renata smiled, nervously. "Sure, I'd like that," she said. "Any time."

"Excellent," Fulda said, triumphantly. "An invitation to Random Farm for my friend, from the rich and mysterious John Random—my work here is done!" She and John took their leave and walked back toward the house.

Alone facing Margaret, Renata found herself unable to speak. Margaret paused momentarily, a look of disapproval in her eyes. "I'll be blunt, Miss Beaumanoir. Usually, even a junior lecturer that is in excellent standing is careful to stay strictly within the rules of the College," she said. "But you've been on thin ice for some time, I think. I think Claude Preen has probably been pretty clear about that, has he not?"

"Yes," Renata replied. "Clear as day."

"Yes," Margaret repeated. "He's been very clear about it. Which is why I fail to understand, Miss Beaumanoir, why you persist in risking your position by challenging those very common-sense rules that the College abides by."

I could sense Renata regaining her resolve. If there was anything that spurred her, it was confrontation. A woman with the courage to push back against Vesta Letalia and the Vampire Council, I thought, could not be inherently reticent before the administrative secretary to the Dean of Students of a small women's college. I was glad to sense that her spine was stiffening at last. I only wondered if she would end by hurting her own interests.

"What, exactly, are you referring to, Margaret?" Renata asked.

"Oh, Miss Beaumanoir, I think you know," Margaret replied slyly. "Must I really give you a catalogue? Well then. One. A weekend trip to Charleston with Mr. Pearson, not only without authorization, but during the pre-exam period when junior faculty is expressly forbidden to leave campus—the period when your students may well have needed you. Two. Intravenous drug use. I don't know what it is you're taking or why, Miss Beaumanoir, and I don't know whether or not your condition would affect your ability to discharge your obligations to your students. But I rather think that you would have been under an obligation to disclose any such condition when you applied for this position. I don't think I would need to pull your file to discover that you made no such disclosure, would I? Three. Taking it upon yourself to change the curriculum requirements for final credit in the Modern Europe course. A special examination, invented pretty much on the spot I understand, as a substitute for the approved term paper requirement."

"Lupe Hernandez-Vega's situation is unique," Renata interrupted. "I think I was within my rights to make her that accommodation. And she completed that test beautifully!"

"Of course she did, Miss Beaumanoir. But no, you were not within your rights. You were very much not. That would have been a decision for the head of the department. But I don't think Dr. Preen was consulted, was he?"

Renata didn't answer. She did not have to. She glanced down darkly.

"Of course he wasn't," Margaret said. "In fact, he is not aware of the matter, even now."

Renata looked up sharply. "He doesn't know about the special exam?"

"To my knowledge, no," Margaret replied coolly.

"But you know. And you haven't told him about it?"

"No," Margaret said. "Why should I? Why should it fall to me to enforce discipline in the history department? I am just the assistant to the Dean of Students, and were this to become a matter for the Dean of Students I would be bound to intervene. And in that case, indeed I would. But short of that, no." Margaret paused, peering a little closer at Renata. "Miss Beaumanoir, I don't know why you constantly assume that I am your adversary. I have no interest in seeing you fail."

"Then what is your interest, Margaret? Why are you telling me all this?"

Margaret pursed her lips in an attitude of bemusement. The light glowing from the kitchen windows glinted off her glasses on the dark patio, obscuring her eyes momentarily, making her look blank and slightly mysterious. "Perhaps I am just a concerned member of the Forshay community, Miss Beaumanoir," she said. "Or perhaps I have a natural empathy for a young female history scholar. Thirty years ago, the opportunities for women in academic fields were not so open as they are now. A woman history professor in those days—despite all the winds of change blowing through the country then—was considered a novelty, a curiosity. But certainly nothing more. And when a university had already acquired its one curiosity, its woman professor—well then, the other women in the field were in a rather awkward spot, weren't they? How many novelty professors was a serious university to take on, after all? So perhaps, Renata, in some sense I feel a special kinship with you as a woman history teacher, even now. You are in a position that I might have liked to have been in, long ago."

Renata regarded Margaret warily, suffering a mild cognitive dissonance as she heard Margaret's words, trying to adjust to the idea that Margaret might not be unremittingly hostile. "So, Margaret," she said cautiously, "what are you going to do with what you know?"

"I've already done it," Margaret replied. "I wanted to warn you, let you know that you're not flying so thoroughly under the radar as you seem to think. That's all. These things I mentioned—they would get you peremptorily fired if they became generally known. Don't let them."

Renata nodded. "I won't," she said. "But I haven't really done anything wrong. Everything you mentioned, there were good reasons for."

"I know," Margaret replied. "I know that perfectly well—otherwise, believe me, I wouldn't bother trying to help you. There is one other thing though," Margaret said. "I think you did your university in France, isn't that right?"

"That's right," Renata answered. "Pantheon-Sorbonne-Paris 1. Both my undergraduate and graduate degrees. I put that on the application form when I applied for the job."

"Yes," Margaret said thoughtfully, leaning in close to Renata, and surprising her by taking her hands. "But let's not let anyone here inquire too closely as to just *when* you were awarded those degrees, yes?" Margaret said, giving Renata's hands a squeeze. "Time for me to be off. One other thing—I hope you don't mind, Miss Beaumanoir, but I took the liberty of appropriating the copy of your article that you gave to Dr. Preen. I thought I might show it to some of my old acquaintances at Duke University." She glanced again at Renata, playfully this time. "I don't think Claude is going to miss it, do you?"

With that, Margaret turned and left, and Renata and watched in wonder as the small woman bustled away. "Oh, Miss Beaumanoir," Margaret called coyly as she stepped off the patio into the darkness leading to Main Street. "Please say hello to your cat for me!"

Renata caught up with Fulda again as the party was winding down. Some of the faculty were already saying their good-byes. The gaggle of children who had been romping back and forth upstairs all evening had been wrangled back down into the living room by the student who was baby-sitting them. I was surprised to see who it was—and so, apparently, was Renata.

"Lupe!" Renata said, "I didn't know you were here."

"Yes, Professor Myerson asked me to help out," Lupe said, shyly, "since I didn't have to travel at the end of term."

Fulda came up to them and put her hands on Lupe's shoulders. Maia, dressed in her pink satin fairy costume, came up also and touched Lupe with the sparkly pink star of her wand. Maia giggled and ran away.

"Lupe's been a godsend for this party," Fulda said. "I can only imagine all these crazy kids running everywhere if she wasn't here to help. And since she's staying on campus for the summer instead of going back to D.C., I asked her to stay with us here in the house for the summer, rather than the dorm. We certainly have the room."

Renata smiled broadly, not quite knowing what to say.

"Look, Lupe," Fulda said. "If you can keep the rest of the kids quiet until after the Final Throwdown, then Miss Beaumanoir and I will help you bring your things over from the dorm and you can stay here tonight, OK?"

From Lupe's quick smile and nod of assent, I could tell that the dorms must already be deserted, less than a week after the exams were over.

"Throwdown?" Renata asked. "What's that?"

Fulda smiled. "You'll probably think it's silly, but a lot of the faculty are movie buffs. I mean, *serious* movie buffs. Have you ever wondered exactly what it is that keeps the River Theater down the street in business?"

I saw Renata grow thoughtful at the observation, but if she circulated about the campus as much as I did she would know that Fulda was exactly right. The River Theater had probably not had the seatcovers changed or the chewing gum removed since the 1950's, but since the bulk of the film repertoire shown there was movies from the '30's and '40's its slightly threadbare appearance seemed absolutely appropriate. Old movies at a classic theater in a small college town—my guess is that much of the Forshay faculty regarded that as a major perquisite of their teaching positions here. Better than free sherry in the faculty lounge.

"But what's a throwdown? I still don't get it."

"It's a contest, about movie trivia. Movie quotes, in fact," Fulda explained. "It's a tournament system, every pair pits a movie against a movie, starting with the more obscure ones, and the Final Throwdown is between two really famous movies. You follow?"

Both Renata and Lupe looked at each other, and laughed. "No," Renata said, "not in the slightest."

"Well, never mind—just watch, you'll figure it out," Fulda said.

Lupe went back upstairs to her babysitting, and Renata

watched, confused, the movie trivia contest that was already in full swing all around the living room. Pairs of challengers snapped out movie lines, laughing, with a judge looking on with each pair to keep score. By the time Lupe had gotten all the children together in one spot and quieted them down with glasses of milk and cookies, the movie contest had already worked its way to the final round. Blonde, moon-faced Arnie Richardson of the economics department, to everyone's great surprise, was one of the finalists, but everyone attributed that to his having drawn the movie *Wall Street* in an early round. Professor Richardson had virtually memorized that script. The other player was Beth from the Sisters' Store, who, while not technically a faculty member, was such a mainstay of the faculty Film Society that it would have been injustice to exclude her. She could have extemporaneously taught a course on contemporary film with no problem. Mike Myerson would play referee and judge for the Final Throwdown, on the grounds that, unlike his wife, he hated, *hated,* movie trivia, and it was funny to watch him suffer.

"OK, so are we ready to start this idiocy?" Mike Myerson barked. "I'll announce the movies and assign one to each of you. When I give the word, you have to alternate quotes from the movies—no pauses, delays, mumbles, stumbles, or claims that you had to tie your shoe. If you can't think of a quote immediately, you have to pass and the other guy goes. Each quote is one point. And don't get a quote wrong or God forbid make one up, because there's about a dozen movie nerds in this room who are just dying to take you to school. All right, ready?" A cheer went up around the living room. I leaped quietly onto a chair back to see better. Fulda was right, these people were serious about this. I noticed some money being laid out on a table in the corner. Really? I thought. Getting a line on the action at the faculty movie trivia contest? Really?

Mike pointed to Prof. Richardson. "You're *The Godfather Part I*," he said. Richardson smiled slyly; he knew *The Godfather*, too. Then, pointing at Beth, Mike said, "and you're *Casablanca*. OK, ready? Go!"

Beth got in first: *"Of all the gin joints in all the towns in all the world, she walks into mine."*

Richardson was right there: *"It's a Sicilian message. It means Luca Brasi sleeps with the fishes."*

Beth: *"We haven't quite decided whether he committed suicide or died trying to escape."*

Richardson: *"Leave the gun. Take the cannoli."*

"I came to Casablanca for the waters."

"Fredo, you're my older brother, and I love you. But don't ever take sides with anyone against the Family again. Ever."

"I'm shocked, shocked to find that gambling is going on in here!"

"Tell Mike it wasn't personal, just business."

"If that plane leaves the ground and you're not with him, you'll regret it. Maybe not today, maybe not tomorrow, but soon and for the rest of your life."

"I'm Moe Greene! I made my bones when you were going out with cheerleaders!"

"Major Strasser's been shot. Round up the usual suspects."

"My father made him an offer he couldn't refuse."

The contest went on and on, back and forth like a ping pong match, the flying quotations becoming ever more arcane, and after a while a little cheer going up after each successful quote moved the contest to yet another cycle. The faculty with children began to leave, slowly relieving Lupe of her charges. The contest was still tied at 57-57 when the last child (other than Maia) was bundled sleepily into his father's arms, and hoisted over the shoulder for the walk to the car. Renata nudged Mike Myerson.

"Mike, could you tell Fulda that I'm going to walk with Lupe back to the dorm?"

Mike gave Renata a martyred expression. "Sure, I'll tell her, if I ever manage to get finished with this fucking contest," he said. "These god-damned movie geeks are

169

liable to go on all night."

Lupe smiled, her wide black eyes shining with mischief as she joined Renata, and then the front door to the Myerson's house closed on the raucous contest behind them, and Renata and Lupe stepped into the quiet of the sidewalk on Main Street under dark leafy tree branches and a clear June night sky. I skittered along beside them, just keeping to the shadows along the sidewalk.

We learned later that *Casablanca* finally defeated *The Godfather*, 397 to 258.

CHAPTER THIRTEEN

Renata and Lupe were quiet as they walked the
sidewalk along President's Row back toward the dorms on
the main campus. I have often noticed that Renata—
despite her distinct streak of stubbornness—can suddenly
become painfully shy around people who, for one reason
or another, she has developed an attachment to. And I
could tell that she was developing just such an attachment
to Lupe. The two of them walked along without speaking.
Lupe had tugged a baseball cap out of the pocket of her
jeans; her ponytail was now pulled through the gap in the
back of the cap. I watched their paired shadows in the
moonlight slipping gracefully over the lawns and shrubs
along the sidewalk, the shadow of Lupe's ponytail
swinging happily along the grass. And as they walked, I
could hear their thoughtstreams singing contentedly from
each of their minds, Lupe's mortal thoughtstreams
exuberant and musical, Renata's vampiric ones more
muted, both shy, both happy, both trying to find a way to
speak. I tried to remember—did Renata ever act shy when
I was around? Should I be offended that she never
seemed to? But, nah, I thought—I knew she was attached
to me, just like I was to her.

Renata finally found words. "So, Lupe, what will you be doing on campus all summer?" she asked. "Are you working for the College? Doing extra coursework?"

"Just working," Lupe replied.

"Are you working for Fulda—I mean, Professor Myerson? Or did they get you a different job?"

"Two jobs," Lupe said. "I'll be working in the evenings in the library. And in the mornings, I'll be working for the Dean of Students."

"Dean of Students," Renata repeated. "You mean, you'll be working with Margaret Viper?"

"Yes," she said.

"Hmm. Are you nervous about it?" Renata pressed.

"Yes," Lupe said, trying to sound matter-of-fact. But she presently looked up and met Renata's eyes, and her expression was one of pure relief that she could finally admit to being scared.

"Well, Margaret's bark is worse than her bite," Renata said.

Lupe, still looking at Renata, seemed confused. "Her bark?" Lupe shook her head. "I'm sorry, I don't understand."

Renata chuckled gently. "You know, I'm a foreigner too," she said. "It took me years to understand American expressions. I was puzzled for a week the first time someone mentioned about barking up the wrong tree."

Lupe, relenting, softly laughed also. "Yes, I still have some trouble with English. With the vernacular," she said. "I am OK with the formal language."

"Ah, but the vernacular is the fun part," Renata said. "And you'll get the hang of it in no time."

This seemed to satisfy them for a while. They walked on silently. Then Renata spoke again.

"You know, Lupe, I read your exam," she said. "I thought it was good. Very good, in fact."

"Yes?" Lupe said. She cast her face, embarrassed, toward the sidewalk.

"Yes," Renata said. "I know that final grades aren't released for another month, but I don't mind telling you how you did in my class." I saw Renata steal a glance toward Lupe, but Lupe's face, shadowed beneath the visor of her ball cap, was still firmly set toward the ground. "I'm giving you an *A-plus*, Lupe."

I could see Renata glance toward Lupe again, still not able to see her face. But from the vantage of a small cat down beneath, keeping pace along the bushes, I could make out Lupe's features perfectly. Her lips were compressed as she walked along; her eyes, fixed on the blocks of the sidewalk passing beneath her, were wide and shining.

"Did you hear me, Lupe?" Renata asked.

"Yes," Lupe said, her voice barely choking above a whisper. "Thank you."

And that was all they said.

What is *wrong* with you humans, anyway? Maybe it is just my perspective—informed as it is by my unique ability to hear from the mind itself what is unsaid as well as what is said, and by six thousand years of experience with actual humans to boot. But I just don't understand why humans are so often unable to release their reserve, to uncoil, and to expose their feelings about each other. Renata and Lupe are perfect examples. It was perfectly clear to me how much Renata was coming to care about Lupe and her welfare. And it was perfectly clear to me that Lupe, feeling lonely and vulnerable at this new place, was drawn to Renata as an ally and even, possibly, a friend. Yet, here they were, walking along in stony silence instead of sharing their mutual affection, awkward and stilted like some dopey men portrayed in a beer commercial. And even in the beer commercials, the guys eventually manage to say "I love you, man" or something similarly profound. Amazing.

But the growing affection was definitely there on Renata's part. It may have been the exam. The exam had been there when she had returned to her house from the disastrous trip to Charleston, three blue books densely filled with tidy inked handwriting, tucked into one of the College's yellow internal mail envelopes and slipped through the mail slot in Renata's door amid the latest detritus addressed to Kjerstin Thorstadt. Renata had put the envelope aside, as Denis had walked her back into her house and had hovered about in her tiny living room for a long time, uncertain whether she was well enough to be left alone. Denis had quickly become a nuisance. It was an interesting exchange, for a scientific observer of human behavior. Renata's annoyance with Denis had grown as he lingered, and his temper had flashed as well. Renata eventually demanded to know what he had done that Saturday night in Charleston, since Fulda thought he sure as hell did not go to any English teacher conference. Denis had replied that, if she must know, he had spent the night with another woman he knew in North Charleston. Fine, Renata had replied, but she felt well enough now, and could he leave, please? And all the while, a small cat listened, rapt, to each of their thoughtstreams calling out signals exactly contrary to their spat. Poor Denis. He offered Renata a kiss on the cheek as he moved to leave but Renata ducked it, and so Denis had drifted away to his Saab, piqued with himself for picking a fight with Renata, still uncertain exactly what he had seen that day, and just as uncertain why he hadn't told Renata that the other woman he had been with in Charleston had been his mother.

Renata had changed into her nightgown and prepared for a long night of grading the stack of term papers waiting on her sofa—a couple dozen term papers, that is, and one special exam. One of my favorite comforts is to settle close to Renata and to listen to her mind as she reads, whether she's reading research materials, novels, student essays, whatever. Her vampiric mind has a clear way of thinking as she reads; it is almost as if she is reading aloud, smoothly yet swiftly enunciating every syllable. A cat with my special talents can enjoy an effect not unlike that of the old Victorians sitting in their parlors, reading Dickens to one another. Anticipating a nice long evening of such reading, I had curled onto her lap as she began to work. She had tossed aside the stack of term papers, and instead tore open the envelope with Lupe's exam.

And Renata had been correct about the quality of Lupe's exam. Lupe had expertly drawn together several threads—the 19th century revolutionary movements, the emergence of European imperialism—into an appraisal of the recent history of her city in El Salvador. Her exam assayed the coffee barons, the military juntas, the oligarchic families, the revolutionary labor leaders. In three blue books of finely nuanced prose, Lupe had developed her themes, balancing and critiquing them with such economy that topics the class had struggled with for weeks she covered in a few deft paragraphs. She related those broader themes of modern European history to the local context of her home city, bringing the historical narrative smoothly up to the Salvadoran Civil War of the 1980's. Renata's internal reading voice motored on, page after page, like a smooth-running automobile. And then, with one offhand phrase, introducing a paragraph intended to show Lupe's familiarity with the labor movement in her country, I heard the contented, even cadence of Renata's reading mind suddenly catch and interrupt itself, lose its train, and backtrack—once, again, and then again and again. *"After my father was disappeared and my mother was shot by the paramilitaries,"* Lupe had written, *"my brother and I had frequent contact with FMLN officials and local members of the labor unions, who helped provide for our education…"*

Renata had had to stop reading. She had risen and walked to a window, where she stood looking out into the blackness of the nighttime. I mewed in sympathy, but I don't think she heard me. It was half an hour before Renata could settle back down to her task of grading the remaining papers. But she did; she worked through the night and gave every single one of the undergraduate papers on her sofa a full and sympathetic reading. And when she was done, she once more read through Lupe's blue books, just to be sure—to make sure that the impression she had gotten on the first reading was still as valid after reviewing the other students' work. Her decision confirmed, Renata marked the last page of the blue book in red marker with unequivocal, bold strokes: $A+$. The poignant personal detail that had slipped into Lupe's exam had had nothing to do with the grade.

But Renata and Lupe discussed none of this as they walked on toward the campus, up the quad above Forshay village where the student dorms stood, and into the strangely quiet stairwell leading to Lupe's room in the South Dorm.

"That's all the stuff you need to move?" Renata asked, when she saw the small collection of a suitcase and two boxes on the bare linoleum floor of Lupe's room. "Most of the girls have a truckload of junk after a year at college."

Lupe grinned. "I have only been here for half a semester," she said. "Maybe by next year I'll have a truckload too."

Renata grabbed the suitcase and Lupe grabbed a box, and they lugged them down the stairs. The walk back up to President's Row was somewhat slower and more arduous, but they reached Fulda's front door again only slightly winded. The party was over at long last; when Fulda opened the door she was holding a broom and a plastic trash bag.

"Ah, you're back," she said. "Care to join the after party? The theme this time is white wine and garbage bags."

Renata smiled graciously. "As much as I would love to, I must help this young lady move her things into this stately house."

Fulda nodded. "Of course. But we'll be sure to save some garbage bags for you." She called up the stairs to

Lupe, who had taken the suitcase up to her new room. "Lupe, did I remember to give you a key?"

Lupe shook her head to say no, as she panted down the stairs. "Not yet, Professor Myerson," she said. "It would be very convenient if you did have one for me."

Fulda was already fussing about her pockets, looking for a keyring. "Here, I know I have one here someplace. I had Trace Cuthbert cut a new one for you yesterday down at the B&G shed." Lupe noticed a key lying on a low table by the front door, sporting a paper tag labeled *"Lupe"*. She picked it up.

"Is this is it?"

Fulda gave a slight frown. "Maybe those age jokes aren't so silly after all," she said. "Yes, of course, Lupe. It opens the front door as well as the door to the kitchen, OK?"

"OK."

"We have to go back for the rest of her things anyway," Renata said. "One or two boxes, and that's it."

Fulda looked closely at Renata. "Are you sure you're OK to carry all this stuff?" she asked. "Denis was worrying like a mother hen about you tonight. You must have really scared him last week in Charleston."

"I'm fine," Renata said. "I have my medicine now, so don't worry." And as she said these reassuring words to soothe Fulda, I noticed a sudden fillip in her thoughtstreams, a spike of anxiety. In the back of her mind, she was worried, and the mention of her medicine had brought it back to mind. But what was she worried about? That little oblong box that Denis had taken from the Doctor contained exactly that—her thanadoxicil. And then it struck me: that oblong box not only contained her current supply of thanadoxicil, but her *only* supply of thanadoxicil—indeed, quite possibly the only remaining supply of thanadox in the world. And, with the Doctor now gone, that supply could no longer be replenished. I wondered how many days' supply that little oblong box contained. Maybe Renata was right to be worried.

"I can carry them myself, Miss Beaumanoir," Lupe said. "They're really not heavy."

"I don't mind, Lupe. I'm happy to help."

Fulda touched Renata on the shoulder. "I think Lupe can get the rest of her things, Renata." She looked at Renata with concern. "We don't really know why you became ill last week, but wouldn't it be better to be careful?"

Renata nodded agreement. "OK," she said. "But let me at least walk Lupe back to the dorms."

Everyone could agree on this, and so the three of us— Lupe and Renata, walking again in companionable silence, and a small shadowy cat going before and behind them— walked back to the South Dorm.

"Are you sure you're OK, Lupe?" Renata asked.

"Yes, Miss Beaumanoir," Lupe said. "Thank you for your help, but the last boxes aren't heavy. I can carry them myself."

"You're sure?"

"Piece of cake," Lupe said, and grinned. Renata smiled, nodding in approval at the perfectly idiomatic use of American vernacular, and then turned and started across the quad toward her house on Ridge Street. Lupe quietly went inside the dorm and up the brightly lit stairwell.

I followed Renata as she walked across the grass of the darkened quad toward home, looking forward to a quiet night dozing on Renata's lap. But there was something nagging at me, something I couldn't remember. Six thousand years old, and you never overcome that odd trick that your mind plays on you, when something you are trying to remember is on the tip of your tongue but you just cannot summon it. Everyone knows that the only solution is to not think directly *about* what you're trying to remember, but to think *beside* it—the way you can see a dim star in the night sky not by looking directly at it, but by looking next to it. Of course, six thousand years to practice, and I still can't do it properly. It was still bothering me as Renata walked up the steps to her house and pulled open the screen door. I scrambled in behind her just before the door gently slapped closed against the jamb.

There was the usual scattering of mail on the hallway floor that had been dropped through the mail slot in the door. Renata walked over the letters distractedly, pulling off her headscarf as she drifted slowly toward the bedroom. I lingered a moment in the hallway, idle curiosity drawing me toward the mail on the floor. Credit card offers. A department store flier addressed to Kjerstin Thorstad or current resident. Another item for Ms. Thorstad—an attractive subscription offer from the *Atlanta Chronicle of Modern History*.

As I idly pawed the letters on the floor, I spotted something among them that was different. Not a letter, it was a simple sheet of notebook paper, folded in half, which had been shoved through the mail slot also, the day's mail having plopped on top of it. Blue ballpoint on lined paper. It was not sealed in any way—this note was easy for my paw to open, and lay flat so I could read it.

Dear Renata,
I am very sorry I tried to hurt your cat. I tried to call you but you dont have voyz mail. Would you let me take you out some time? I want to be your boyfriend.
Sincerly,
Trace Cuthbert

Trace Cuthbert. I reflected on the slightly childish handwriting on the notepaper, the missive's simple but strangely earnest locution. He seemed less like a threatening Bully, suddenly, than a big, sloppy, none-too-bright dog. Golden retriever, perhaps.

And then it came back to me. I remembered what I

had been trying to recall, what I saw that night, the night Renata that had—well, let's not sugar-coat it—the night she beat Trace up. I remembered what I saw after bruised and bloodied Trace Cuthbert had staggered out Renata's door and had made his slow and furtive escape—I remembered that other figure making a furtive escape that night, a girl in the dark, with a baseball cap over her ponytail. I decided not to stay with Renata back in the house tonight after all. It was a pleasant summer night— clear and dry. Maybe tonight I would keep watch outside the Myersons' house. Keep watch for a girl with a ball cap and a ponytail, perhaps.

In fact, I didn't bother waiting outside. I used the Myerson's cat door and just walked right in. And I didn't bother sneaking up on Lupe—I found her room easily, just up the staircase and off the landing next to Maia's room. The room was dark except for the glow of a digital clock that said it was a few minutes before two in the morning. The Myersons' house was dark and still except for the vague noises of sleeping humans—and the sound of a cautious Lupe trying to be silent while stuffing something into an almost-new Forshay College hand duffel. I walked into her room and rubbed on her leg. She started for a moment until she saw my glowing green cat's eyes in the dark.

"Oh, it's you," she whispered. "How did you get in here?" She paused and stroked my fur; I involuntarily broke into a purr which sounded alarmingly loud in the silent house. Lupe stood and gripped the hand duffel.

"You have to go, now," she whispered. "Go home, little cat!" She waved her hands a little to frighten me away, but I could see that her heart was not in it. I sat, acting unimpressed with her efforts to shoo me, and nonchalantly washed a paw. Lupe did not seem unhappy that I had not run; in fact, I think she was glad to have the company. And at least a cat is quiet—an especially important factor with all those hardwood floors in the upstairs hall of the Myersons' house that Lupe was about to negotiate.

I pranced down the staircase ahead of Lupe as she crept, barefoot and carrying a pair of sneakers, step by step behind me. We moved through the silent kitchen, spotless and tidy after Beth had closed down the party and cleaned up. Lupe's new key stuck a little in the lock of the kitchen door; the sound of the key in the stiff keyhole made a painful scratching that violated the stillness. But finally the door opened; we slipped out, and Lupe carefully locked it behind her. She gripped her bag and slipped on the sneakers without untying them, then began to run swiftly around the house and toward Main Street. I scampered after, a dark shadow flung across the moonlit lawn following her.

"No, go home, kitty," she whispered, pausing to turn around on me. I waited for her to resume her run, and then darted after her again, keeping once more to the shadows in the verges of the sidewalk.

I did not notice the long, low car until Lupe was almost upon it. It lay parked again where I had seen it that prior night, along the village street in front of the unlit movie theater. As I approached, I saw that the engine was idling but the headlights were dark. The car moved forward to meet Lupe as she jogged up the sidewalk, the car's worn muffler growling. Lupe put the hand duffel down on the sidewalk and leaned in the window of the car. I saw that the duffel was unzipped—in her hurry she had not bothered to fasten it. An opportunity for a small cat. I slipped into the bag just before she grabbed the handles again. Lupe pulled the rusty door of the car open and, bag (with cat) in hand, climbed in. The car, headlights still doused, slowly rumbled up Main Street and away from Forshay village.

I listened to the noisy growl of the car as it drove for several minutes before I thought it safe to make a foray out of the zip-top, and try to see where I was. I popped my kitten head out of the duffel bag, and discovered that Lupe still had the bag on her lap.

"Oh no!" Lupe wailed.

I looked at her sharply, and then realized she was talking about me. The driver of the car looked sidelong at her. I glanced over. He was a young man—younger even than Lupe—but with the same thick black hair, and the same sensuous curve to his nose and forehead.

"What?" he said. Then, spotting me, he said, matter-of-factly, "There's a cat in your bag."

"Yes I know, Rafael, thank you for informing me!" Lupe responded crossly. She looked back at me in the bag, and then stroked my head. "It is my professor's cat—she's been following me ever since the party tonight." She smiled over toward Rafael. "I think she likes me."

"Well, you better get rid of it."

"I can't get rid of it! My teacher would be angry with me if I lost her cat!"

"Well, hide it then. Put it in the trunk of the car or something. I don't think Alejo likes cats."

"Alejo doesn't like anyone. Or anything. Just money," Lupe said grimly.

"How much did you get?" Rafael asked.

"As much as I could," Lupe replied. "But it is not going to be enough."

"We'll just have to tell him this is all we have," Rafael replied.

Lupe looked away from me toward Rafael. "Don't be stupid, little brother," she said angrily. "These aren't some of your friends from a football game, who you can argue about the rules with. You made a deal with the *polleros*, and now they want to get paid. And they want to get paid all of their money. And if you don't pay them they will hurt you. This isn't a game, little brother."

It wasn't until Lupe had used the colloquialism for human smuggler—or "chicken-herder" (although something told me that, whoever Alejo was, you wouldn't use that word to his face)—that I realized that they had been speaking in Spanish the whole time. My mind sometimes gets lazy when I can follow a conversation both aloud and by listening to thoughtstreams. I've lived among humans for so long now that I have learned pretty much every language there is, or ever was—and what I don't know from the language I can glean from the thoughtstreams. It can sometimes be as confusing to understand many languages as it can be to understand few.

"So how much do you have in your little bag?"

Lupe did not need to look, she knew the amount exactly. "One hundred and twenty-seven dollars," she said. "It won't make much of a dent in the three thousand you owe him."

"I already paid him a lot," Rafael said hotly. "I paid him five hundred before I even left. And I have paid him two hundred more since then, and now this." Rafael glared angrily forward out the windshield as he drove. They came to a steep hill going over the shoulder of the ridge, and the laboring car lugged and complained as it slowly climbed. Lupe just shook her head sadly and looked out the window, away from her brother.

I strained to see out the window as well. The car was moving beyond the ridge of Forshay Mountain and into the valley beyond—there were dim lights of other towns glowing in the midnight darkness of the surrounding farmland and forests. He drove in silence for forty minutes or longer, and the view outside the car slowly changed from wilderness and pasture, to stretches of truck lots, heavy equipment behind razor-wire fences, abandoned, derelict storefronts and sad, leaning houses, all suffused with an unhealthy orangish glow from overhead sodium lights. I recognized the place—a neighborhood on the outskirts of a town not far by distance from Forshay village, but a world away in its hopelessness. The neighborhood had seen successive waves of economic hardship wash across it, as mill jobs disappeared, then the trucking and manufacturing jobs that the mills supported. Now the signs, what there were of them, were in Spanish. What businesses remained were mostly liquor and lottery stores, pawnshops displaying evil-looking guns behind dim, barred windows, and paycheck cashing outlets behind bulletproof Plexiglas. Despair seemed to run in the gutters of the street.

Rafael nosed the car to a stop along a dark street with a row of storefronts, all of which were abandoned except a bodega at one corner of the block, and a bar next to it. The bar had a small orange sign by the door that flashed on and off. Rafael and Lupe, her fist holding tightly onto the bag of money, walked nervously into the bar. I was unnoticed as I slipped in beside them, and followed them toward the back.

There were pool tables in the back of the bar, and behind the tables three very large, unsmiling men stood with cues in their hands, but not playing a game. Rafael approached nervously.

"I'm here to see Alejo," Rafael announced, his voice too loud. "I'm Rafael Hernandez-Vega."

The men kept Rafael and Lupe fixed in their stares, unresponsive. Eventually one of them slid out of the bar through a door leading to another room in the back. He returned and spoke in a murmur to the largest man, standing at the center of the pool table. This man's face was scarred, and he carried a thin black mustache over his cruel mouth. "OK," he said slowly. "Alejo will see you." He jerked his head toward the door. *"Allá."*

Through the door was a small room where two more men stood back against the wall. There was a battered desk in the middle of the room, piled with papers, and at a small clear space in the middle of the desk a dark, thin man hunched over a ledger book that lay in the pool of brightness shed by a desk lamp. This was Alejo. He did not look up as Rafael approached the desk. His hair was thinning and combed back straight to cover the balding spot, and with his head still bowed he looked no more threatening than a middle-aged bank teller, or an office clerk. The men behind him edged about nervously, their faces barely visible beyond the circle of light from the desk lamp. The room was otherwise dark. Rafael fidgeted, pausing to see if Alejo would acknowledge him. He waited as long as he could stand it. His nervousness and impatience overcame him.

"I am Rafael Hernandez-Vega," he announced.

I had crept in behind them, and I slunk into the darkness by the walls where I could watch the entire room. When Rafael spoke, I saw Alejo stiffen, his hands stopping where they were on the book. He lifted his face to regard Rafael, who stood straight as a soldier before him. Lupe stood cautiously behind Rafael's shoulder. Alejo's face was thin and creased, with hollow cheeks and skin that hung from the bone so loosely that there was a perceptible, sore-red gap at the lower edge of each eye socket, as if his eyes were an ill fit for his face. He had a long mouth with long, unsmiling lips, and the same pencil-stroke mustache as the heavier guard outside the door. Alejo slowly picked up a cigarette from an ashtray and took a long, silent pull from it. The coal glowed, and then he glared at Rafael as he exhaled. Despite his slight appearance and drooping face, Alejo's eyes burned with intensity. When he spoke, his voice was low, a growl of restrained violence. "I know who you are," he said. He no longer seemed like an office clerk. He was a picture of danger.

"I have brought you money," Rafael said. His breath was beginning to be labored. I could see that he was gripping the seam of his pants leg with the fingers of one hand as he struggled with his fear.

"Good," Alejo said, with no emotion. "You are supposed to bring me money. You owe me a debt." He paused, then motioned to the desk. "Lay it here."

Lupe hurriedly dug into the hand duffel and grabbed the money out of the bottom. She pressed it into Rafael's hand. Rafael took a step forward and laid the bills gravely in the circle of light on the desk and then stood back straight again, as if he were a votary laying an offering at the altar of a capricious and dangerous god. As, in a way, he was.

Alejo did not touch the money; he stared at it for a moment, blowing smoke into the light of the desk lamp. Without looking up, he slowly took the money from the desktop and stowed it, uncounted, in a drawer.

"How much is it," he said, still no inflection in his voice.

Lupe spoke from behind, her voice sounding very small in the dark room. "One hundred and twenty-seven," she said, uncertainly.

Alejo looked up, ignoring her. His red-rimmed eyes fastened on Rafael. Rafael struggled to retain his rigid posture under the weight of Alejo's glare. Alejo broke his gaze away casually, and laid down his cigarette.

"It is not enough," he said. "Not enough. You have a debt, and you should have paid it by now." Alejo made a show of flipping a page of the ledger book and peering at the numbers, as if finding the exact entry recording Rafael's debt. I couldn't tell, but I suspected it was a mere pantomime to menace Rafael further. After all, it was absurd to think that a gangster's handwritten book was to be given any credence, as if it were a legal business record, admissible in court—as if it were to be taken seriously at all. Every extortionist I had ever known kept his records in the same place, the only place deemed secure enough: his memory. The book, I was sure, was a prop. Alejo looked back at Rafael. "Three thousand dollars you owe me," he said. "You have to pay it."

When he heard the number, Rafael's childlike sense of injustice flared up, prompting him to speak out before he could restrain himself. "No," he said firmly, "I already paid five hundred. Before I left for Guatemala. And since then I have paid two hundred more, at least…"

The fist flashed out of the darkness so quickly that I was confused for a moment—it had seemed as if neither of the two men standing behind Alejo could have moved that fast. But the one on the left had indeed silently slipped forward while Alejo was speaking, and had expertly hit Rafael below the ribcage a vicious blow which landed with a sickening, heavy thud. Rafael groaned and doubled, then fell to one knee, unable to breathe. Lupe moved to help him, but was stopped by a look from Alejo's hate-filled eyes.

"Don't tell me my business, boy," Alejo murmured. "Don't tell me how to count." Alejo deliberately closed the ledger book, and lit a fresh cigarette, leaning back from the desk and watching as Rafael struggled back to his feet, his face wet from tears that he, in his boyish pride, would not acknowledge. Alejo calmly expelled the smoke; he took his sweet time. "Yes, I know what you paid. Five hundred to start, as per the contract. I happen to know that you have paid a good deal less than two hundred since, but let's call it two hundred. And now a hundred more. Fine—eight hundred. So what? So how much is the interest that you owe, eh? Have you figured that out, you fuck? Can you do that math in your head?" He stopped speaking again, smoking quietly, as if in calm meditation. Rafael seemed to have recovered, standing almost straight once more; but from a cat's-eye perspective on the floor I could see that the hand he still held against his bruised abdomen trembled with the strain of retaining his composure.

"You don't realize how much I am your friend," Alejo said. "The math doesn't lie. When I tell you that you owe me three thousand, do you not realize how much of a *gift* I am giving you? How much interest that is accrued—interest that I am fairly owed!—but that I am forgiving?

Because I am a generous man? Three thousand," Alejo spat. "Three thousand dollars. In the United States, that is nothing. Nothing! You can earn that in a few weeks, months. Where are you working now? It is strawberry time here, yes? So everyone has a job now. Where are you this week?"

Rafael's voice was raspy. "Random Farm, outside Forshay," he said painfully. "I have been in the crew there for two weeks now."

"See?" Alejo said. "You have work. So you must have money. And you—the sister—you are at that very nice college there. Right in Forshay—and might I say, how touching a family story it is, that you have been reunited again! Well, sister, college is expensive. You must be paying somehow. You must have money too. Money that, of course, you will share for your brother's need. Or else you must get money. Or you must get things that can be turned into money." Alejo looked down at the cigarette in his fingers, slowly burning. "I have been to Forshay," he said. "I have seen the College. I have seen the rich peoples' houses in the College. Yes," Alejo said, "yes, there is plenty of money to be gotten there."

Alejo seemed to be finished with them. He deliberately pushed back the scarred and creaky swivel chair he sat in, and stood. Though thin, he was tall; as he unfolded his long legs he rose to an unexpected height. His face was above the circle of light from the desk lamp; only his glowing cigarette and eyes were visible, and they glowered down at Rafael. "That car is worth something," Alejo said. "Why don't you leave me the car?"

Rafael shook his head; it was still painful to speak. "No, it is not my car. I borrowed it from the chief," Rafael said. "I have to return it."

Alejo shook his head, disappointed. "That was the wrong answer, boy," he growled. "Why do you have to make everything so difficult for me? I would have been generous with the credit I would have given you against the car—and then, yes, you would have the problem of explaining to your chief about the missing car, but that would have been a problem for you solve for yourself, like a man. But no," he continued, anger bleeding into his voice. "No, you embarrass me and make me use force. Well, then. I will have the car anyway. But now there must be—there must be a lesson taught."

Rafael stiffened involuntarily; he camouflaged it by straightening his back, fearlessly. "What lesson?" Rafael said.

Alejo smiled. "You will have a ride back to Random Farm," he said. "And your nice sister will have a ride back to Forshay, too, back to her College. But, there must be a lesson taught. And we will teach it," he said smiling angrily, and pausing dramatically, and then suddenly jabbing a finger toward Lupe. "We will teach the lesson...to *you*, sister!"

Another fist, a sharp jab striking Lupe this time, and she was felled. Rafael turned on her attacker, swinging wildly. The other bodyguard, ready for this, smashed a fist into Rafael's mouth, and his face became a foam of saliva and blood where his lip had split. Then two bodyguards were quickly dragging Lupe and her brother out of the back room, and back across the bar toward the exit.

"Get the keys," Alejo called after them. "Give these shits to the two new guys to deal with. Make the boy watch. Give a lesson to the sister, that'll show the little fuck. The new guys—they can take care of these little shits."

I raced out of the bar after the bodyguards, one dragging Rafael under the armpits, his heels tracing a scuff line across the sidewalk; the other holding Lupe like a flour sack over a shoulder. They pushed Lupe and Rafael against the hood of the long, rusty car. I watched from the verge of the shadows as the bodyguards rifled Rafael's and Lupe's pockets. I saw one find Lupe's new key to the Myersons' house; the other pulled out of Rafael's jeans a jangling keyring that held the car keys. He tossed it to one of the two figures who now emerged from the bar onto the dark sidewalk.

"Here," the bodyguard said. "Car keys." The other bodyguard tossed the other key as well. "Go. You heard Alejo." The bodyguards left and went back into the bar. The black glass door swung shut behind them, and the orange light beside it flashed its intermittent glow onto the street. And in the orange light from the sign I recognized the faces of the two newest members of Alejo's *coyote* gang, who were now charged with teaching a lesson on behalf of Alejo. I guess I shouldn't have been surprised.

"Yo, Harrison, can you drive this piece of crap?" the white guy said.

"No problem," the black guy answered. "Get 'em."

"What?"

"The two kids, get 'em. Let's get out of here."

"Check that, man," Chuck said. "I got 'em." He yanked open the rear door and pushed in Lupe first, then Rafael. Chuck shoved in next to Rafael, intentionally crowding them against the opposite door. He pulled out a long, evil-looking knife and brandished it at the boy. "Don't try any shit, man," he said. "I've been wanting to use my new blade all day."

Harrison was gunning the engine. "She don't want us to cut them," he said.

"Fuck you," Chuck said.

"Fuck you back," Harrison said. "Fuck you to hell, you fuckin demon."

"Just drive," Chuck said, holding the point of the long knife a centimeter above Rafael's cornea. "Just fucking drive and fucking shut your fucking mouth."

The car's engine gunned again, much too loud, and Harrison jerked the car into gear. It gave a comical lurch, then stalled.

"Can't you drive?" Chuck said.

"Piece of crap," Harrison said, starting the car again.

"It's *his* car. It's *his* fault we driving this crappy car. You gonna let him get away with this?"

"No," Chuck said.

"No," Harrison said.

"So what do you want?" Chuck said.

"So fucking punch the shitbag," Harrison said.

"Can I cut him?"

"No. Punch him," Harrison said. "Punch him and see if he's got the smell, like she said."

I heard the thud of a fist, and Rafael's groan as the punch hit home.

"Flowers," Chuck said. "Stinks like flowers in here."

"So that's what she said the smell was," Harrison replied. "She said to see if they smell like roses. Rosewater. So they got the smell."

"Well, one of 'em does, anyway."

"So punch 'em some more," Harrison said, "punch 'em both and figure out which one it is."

Harrison managed to put the car into gear again and, its normal throaty growl tortured into a shriek, the car finally moved away. I heard Rafael cry out as Chuck's fist found its target again, and then the car was down the street and away into the darkness and I was alone in the grimy street, under the flash of the bar sign, miles away from Forshay village and Renata and my cat food dish. But as I stood in the darkness of the sidewalk I wasn't thinking about those things. Only one thought occupied my mind: the Vampire Council's assassins had arrived on our doorstep.

CHAPTER FOURTEEN

It was late morning by the time I got back to Forshay. Or rather, by the time I got back to Forshay *and* managed to wake up. I had found myself stranded in that rundown town, at least thirty miles away from Forshay village. Since the vampire assassins had taken Rafael's car I had no ride back—and it was perfectly clear to me that I was also not going to make the return journey solely by means of my short kitten legs. So it was necessary to timeslide, and overcoming my usual trepidation I did just that, following the crease in time back along the drive that Rafael and Lupe had made over the ridge just a few hours before, and then winding the time forward again to the present. I found myself back on Main Street in front of the River Theater, with dawn just beginning to glow in the lower sky. Timesliding—even a short slide—always exhausts me. I slipped back into Renata's house and found a soft cushion on the sofa. I could have slept all day. Cats are pretty good at that even in more normal circumstances.

But I didn't—I couldn't. I knew I had to get out and see what I could learn—about Lupe, about her brother, about the assassins. By the time I shook off the heavy sleep and found my way out onto the campus, Renata was

192

already up and gone. Forshay village was quiet, with the College settling into its summer dormancy. Only a few people were about, town residents mostly, strolling in the summer morning air and talking with friends. But despite the scarcity of people on Main Street, I immediately picked up an excitement in their thoughtstreams—the electricity of good gossip. I knew the basic facts of the story before I had even walked halfway to the Green. I sat under one of the old, heavy oak trees to think it through, and curled my tail around my paws. It also seemed that Renata and Fulda were in the Sisters' Store—I would join them there in a minute.

What I had learned was this: somebody had beaten Lupe Hernandez-Vega the night before and left her, unconscious and bruised, on the grass just off Main Street in front of the student dorm quad. Trace Cuthbert had found her early in the morning as he drew the equipment out of the sheds for mowing, and he had carried her to the infirmary. The doctor had looked her over and pronounced her injuries ugly, but minor. She was going to have a nasty black eye, and she'd need to see the dentist because one of her back teeth was loose. But aside from that, it was only bruises on the abdomen, bruises on the face and some abrasions on her arms. All perfectly placed to be painful and visible, but not permanently damaging. Whoever had beaten her had made skillful work of it.

And it was that fact, indeed, that had ignited the excitement in the thoughtstreams of the citizens of Forshay—that this was a real crime, inflicted by real criminals, and not just the common run of student mischief that even the Pre-eminent Women's College of the Upper South was prone to. The police were conducting "investigations". There was a search for "suspects". This kind of thing never happens in Forshay!

But in none of the thoughtstreams, in none of the street conversations, was there any word of Rafael, or of his car, or of the two other uninvited passengers the car

193

had borne last night. The assassins were here, that was sure, and I was worried. I was also worried that they had contrived such an elaborate and indirect means to reach Renata: to do so through Lupe, and to do so by exploiting the problem that Lupe had because of her brother—a problem that Renata was not even aware of. It could not be coincidence—the idea that Harrison and Chuck just happened to be moonlighting for immigrant extortionists, who just happened to be operating near Renata's college— it was absurd to ascribe that to happenstance. And how had they managed to conceive such a ruse? It must mean that they had been watching the campus, and watching Renata, for some time now. Perhaps they had been planning this since even before Renata's summons to the Vampire Council. But why the indirection? Why not strike out at Renata immediately, directly, if that was their aim? She had not tried to conceal herself; indeed, she tried to live as openly as possible. What was stopping them from simply trying to dispose of her, as they had the Doctor? I didn't have the answers. But I feared that the assault on Lupe signaled a change in tactics, and that the vampire assassins' deliberate slowness—whatever the reason—may have already run its course.

I wasn't going to find the answer sitting under a tree, however. I uncoiled my tail and sauntered across Main Street to the Sisters' Store.

I let myself in through a gap on one side, near the large, arched opening where the ancient carriage doors once had hung, but which had many years ago been planked up. I silently joined the group I found in the main store sitting at a table, each with a look of quiet concern: Renata, Fulda, Beth and Lucy. No one was smiling.

"I just can't help feeling that I'm responsible," Fulda said. "I didn't even have any idea that she had gone out last night. I should have, I don't know, caught her or something."

Beth looked at Fulda and shook her head silently. They

had apparently been over this ground with Fulda already; there was no need to tell her again that it wasn't her fault.

A silent pause ripened around the table as I walked up and stretched next to the group. I aimed, then made a quick leap onto the tabletop next to them, and sat down. I was trying to break the tension; I wasn't sure if I succeeded.

"No, Kikki, not on the table," Renata said, grabbing me under the ribcage and lifting me onto her lap. I notice that she was wearing the white scarf on her head, and on her face sat the large, dark sunglasses despite the early hour and the low angle of the sun. Her hands were cold. I wondered if she had begun reducing her doses of thanadoxicil, stretching her remaining supply. I wasn't there last night when she would have injected herself, but it seemed like a good guess. I would have to keep an eye on her; over the last decades I was only just learning the effects of the drug as the Doctor had prescribed it—what effects irregular and insufficient doses of thanadox might have was impossible to say. Renata distractedly stroked my fur; I set up a soft but audible purring.

"Good old Kikki," Lucy said. "She always seems to know when she's needed."

"Yes," Renata said, smiling meditatively. "She wanders about, but always comes back."

Lucy and Beth smiled a private joke at each other, looks of beatific devotion crossing their faces. Fulda was impatient.

"I actually have to get back to the lab this morning," she said. "Actual, honest-to-God experimental research, if you can believe it. So where is Lupe now? Can she have visitors?"

"She's in the College infirmary, according to Paul Moorland," Lucy said. "He said they were holding her there. They didn't need to move her to a hospital."

"Paul stopped by here? Already?" Renata asked. "I was hoping to talk to him."

"He came by at 5:45," Beth said. "We were still getting the store open. He mainly asked us about what we saw, whether there was any traffic on Main Street, anything suspicious. You know—as witnesses," she said. She looked slightly abashed; I knew that deep down she thought, as a native New Yorker, that she was too worldly to be distracted by such small-town excitements as a local crime. But she was indeed excited, and could not conceal it. Perhaps she was beginning to think like a Forshayan at long last. "Paul had just come from the infirmary, and the doctor said she really wasn't hurt badly, just scared." Beth rubbed her lips thoughtfully. "I don't think he mentioned anything about visitors. Did he, Lucy?"

Lucy shook her head doubtfully. The early morning shift was not her thing; she had only come down when she heard the police chief talking to Beth. He had had the blue lights of his cruiser revolving outside the window of their apartment above the store—why, she didn't know. Paul could have walked from the police station, down the block. "No," she said, a little sleepily. "He did say he would want to talk to you both, though—he asked us to let you know. He pretty much knew you were likely to stop in."

Fulda wrapped the remnant of her breakfast sandwich in a napkin, and gulped a final sip from her coffee. "Well, it's easy to find out about visiting hours," she said. "The infirmary is on the way to my lab in Everett." She grabbed her backpack and mobile phone. "You coming?" she said to Renata.

In reply, Renata stuffed me into her canvas bag, swung it over her shoulder and started toward the door. Fulda hustled to catch her up.

"Let us know if we can bring Lupe anything," Beth called behind them. "We've got some great carrot cake today."

*   *   *

"Oh, she'll be delighted to see you," sparkled Mrs. Rose as she let them into the infirmary waiting room. It was several hours later; the visiting hours for ill students had turned out to be surprisingly limited. The waiting room was a large space, situated on the basement floor and, as Fulda had said, but a few steps from the small suite of research labs that the College made available to the chemistry and biology faculty. The windows, unlike the broad and airy vistas afforded to the spaces on the upper floors, were narrow and crowded to the tops of the walls, a small airspace just above ground level. The prevailing light in the room was, consequently, artificial—splashed brightly by glaring florescent fixtures onto the white-painted concrete walls. The space looked sterile and antiseptic; it would have seemed hostile, if not for the comforting presence of Mrs. Rose.

To generations of Forshay students, Mrs. Rose was a substitute mother, a warm security blanket with a Southern country accent and white nurse's smock. White-haired and plump, with pink cheeks that were always on the verge of smiling if they were not, in fact, already smiling, she ministered to the girls who found their way to the infirmary with all the ailments afflicting college girls away from home. And although she seemed to treat her patients at least as much through the hugs she dispensed as with any medication, I had seen her in action a few times that year when more serious conditions required more serious responses. She was, dimpled cheeks and plump pink arms notwithstanding, a tough and effective professional. When Audrey Huddleston had managed to slash her thigh falling though a glass pane in a door of the Arts Building, there was nothing cuddly about the spurting arterial blood, or the pressure Mrs. Rose's bloodied fists applied on her leg until the screaming ambulance arrived from Lincoln County Medical. It was the only time I hadn't seen Mrs. Rose smiling.

There were a handful of beds in the infirmary rooms behind the waiting room and the suite of examination rooms. Mrs. Rose led Fulda and Renata down the corridor to the first patient room; the rest, with the student populace now gone for the summer, were empty and dark.

"She's right in here," Mrs. Rose said, opening the door of the room. "Lupe, look who's here, honey!"

As she entered I heard Fulda catch her breath sharply. Mrs. Rose shot Fulda a surprisingly severe look, then beamed warmly back at Lupe.

"Lunch will be in fifteen minutes," Mrs. Rose said. "Are you hungry honey?" She turned to Renata and Fulda. "You all are welcome to have lunch with her too, if you like. They always send more than we need—especially seeing that we just have the one patient."

Renata shook her head. "No, thank you, Mrs. Rose," she said, smiling back from behind her scarf and sunglasses. "We just had a bite at the Sisters' Store."

"Actually, I'd love something," Fulda said. "I have a long afternoon ahead of me at the lab, once I check in on my renegade student houseguest."

"I'll tell 'em to send us down some sandwiches, you can take 'em with you," Mrs. Rose trilled. "Let me know if you need anything else—I'll be just outside." Mrs. Rose bustled out and partly closed the door; even after she departed it seemed she left an air of warmth behind, like an aroma of fresh bread in a cozy kitchen.

But Renata was staring down at Lupe, propped on pillows in the bed. Lupe's face was puffy, with yellow and black bruising on the cheekbone on her left side, and the eye on her right side an angry purple and swollen shut. Her forearms were bloodied and scabbed, as if they had tried to shield her face as she was pushed to the ground.

"Well look at you," Renata said. "Don't you look beautiful."

Fulda did not attempt niceties. "My God, Lupe," she said. "You look like hell. What happened?"

Lupe would not let herself cry. But she also found that she could not speak just at that moment, and so sat in the bed, silent.

Fulda reached behind her for Renata's bag. "There's another visitor for you, you know," she said, pulling me out of the bag by my shoulders. I landed lightly on the sheets on Lupe's bed. Lupe's rigid expression softened when she saw me. She reached out and stroked my back, from nape to tail. I stood with stretched back legs and began to purr. Then I found my way to Lupe's lap, and sat down there as she continued to stroke me. Her face, discolored and bruised though it was, now was happy.

"I found your cat in my room last night," Lupe said, "in Prof. Myerson's house. She was right there in my room! How do you think she got there?"

Fulda was still blunt. "Where did you go last night, Lupe? You shouldn't be going out in the middle of the night! What made you do something so stupid?"

Lupe stopped talking; the brief happy light in her face fled and an expression of stubbornness overtook it with her silence. But as she stroked my fur, I could hear Lupe's thoughtstreams loudly. She wanted to tell, she wanted to tell Renata and Fulda what had happened so badly. But she couldn't. She was afraid.

Fulda sighed audibly. "I wish you would tell us what's going on. How can we help you, if you won't tell us what's going on?" Fulda glanced at Renata, then back to Lupe. "Was the policeman here—Chief Moorland? Did you tell the police about it, at least?"

Lupe said nothing, but she looked away into a lower corner on the far side of the white wall. It was enough of an answer.

Mrs. Rose knocked, and pushed the door back. "Lunch, honey," she said, bringing in a tray, and also suspending a plastic bag hooked from one finger. She handed the bag to Fulda, and placed the tray on a low table to the side of the bed. "And I see Miss Beaumanoir's cat is visiting, too! Well, let's put the pussycat back on the ground while you each lunch, honey—she'll be just fine. This cat certainly knows her way around Everett."

"Thank you, Mrs. Rose," Fulda said, motioning to the bag of sandwiches. "I need to get over to the lab, though. How long are you going to keep Lupe here?"

Mrs. Rose smiled steadily at Lupe. "Well, all those bruises sure are ugly, but they're no mind. The doctor wanted me to keep her here today, but I know that he was almost sure should could have gone right home." Mrs. Rose compressed her brow in thought for a moment, though she never stopping her smiling. "Probably until five, six o'clock, I think. Can you come get her then, Professor?"

Fulda looked at Renata. "My experiment is still going to be busy then," she said. "Could I ask you to pick Lupe up at five, Renata? Something tells me that the sooner Lupe gets back to her own bed, the happier she'll be." Fulda was trying, awkwardly, to make up for her prior brusqueness. I could hear her thoughtstreams rushing with anxiousness and relief; she really did feel guilty about what had happened to Lupe. Did it occur to Fulda that, despite what she said about getting Lupe back to her own bed, in fact Lupe had as yet not spent a full night in her room at the Myerson's?

Renata nodded her assent. "Five o'clock, not a problem."

"Renata, can you go back to my house and pick up some clothes for Lupe?" Fulda said. She handed her housekey to Renata. "Mike's at his office all day, so here's the key." She squinted at Lupe's black eyes. "Maybe some eye makeup too, what do you think?"

"Prof. Myerson," Mrs. Rose said, "by the way, Paul—er, Chief Moorland, he stopped by and asked if he could have a few minutes of your time. I told him you were headed to your laboratory—he'll meet you there in an hour. Hope that's OK?"

"*Paul*, eh," Fulda smiled at Mrs. Rose. "Has Chief Moorland been a-callin' on you, Mrs. Rose?"

Mrs. Rose laughed delightedly. "Oh! I sure *wish* he was calling on me!" she cried, "a big ol' apple dumpling like me! He stops in every day, but I think he's more interested in the dispensary we have here. Chock full of Schedule I controlled substances. I could be a high-end drug dealer if I chose!" she said, trilling a laugh.

"Well, I just wonder what took Paul so long to track me down," Fulda said. She bent down to the bed and gave Lupe a quick, embarrassed kiss on her brow. I could hear Fulda's thoughtstreams calming; she was feeling better, now that she had seen that Lupe was safe. "We'll see if Chief Moorland doesn't order me to keep a certain college student under house arrest from now on."

Renata did not kiss Lupe; I could hear her thoughtstreams, too, and they were not calming at all. Too fraught to do anything but press Lupe's hand gently, Renata made a brave smile from behind her sunglasses, and took her leave. "Kikki can stay with you this afternoon," she said. "That little cat will have no problem finding her way back to my house."

Lupe smiled back at Renata, gratefully. "Thank you, Miss Beaumanoir," she said.

"Renata," Renata said. "Please call me Renata."

Lupe smiled more broadly. "Thank you, Renata," she said. "Kikki is like a real friend."

"Bon," Renata murmured, still holding Lupe's hand. *"Dormez."*

Still nestled on Lupe's lap, I watched Renata and Fulda leave Lupe's room. Lupe did not touch the food on the tray, and Mrs. Rose was wise enough not to insist. The sounds of the infirmary, despite the antiseptic white light, began to take on the rhythms of a comfortable home. There was an indistinct hum from machinery, somewhere; perhaps the refrigerator behind Mrs. Rose's nurse's station? Mrs. Rose busied herself by her desk, tapping on a computer keyboard, occasionally singing quietly in a sweet, soft voice—switching back and forth between Baptist hymns and Nashville pop. Lupe's hand ceased stroking my fur; I listened as her breathing grew deep and regular. Her eyes were shut, and her bruised face had fallen to the side, the mouth a little open. I paused to listen again to her thoughtstreams—she, too had calmed, at least enough to sleep. But I perceived a deep well of fear and worry still lurking in her mind. Well, that would be only natural. Lupe had much to be worried about.

But as Lupe slept peacefully under the watch of Mrs. Rose, I crept off her bed, and toward yet another of the cat-sized passages that honeycombed the Everett Building. I scampered through a gap in the wall at the back of infirmary, and was quickly squeezing through another gap, into the chemistry research lab where Fulda's experiments were ongoing. I suppressed the urge to trail after Renata—worrier that I am, I didn't like the idea of letting Renata out of my sight with the vampire assassins at large, even at high noon. But that could wait—I could catch up with her when she went back to Fulda's house. What I really wanted was to hear what Paul Moorland would ask Fulda about. A quiet leap, then another, and I was on the ledge along the top of the wall again, unseen along the back of the laboratory, waiting for Moorland to come. When he arrived, Fulda spoke to him in the front of the room, but I could hear clearly enough. It was routine questioning, really—when did you notice she was gone? (not until the morning), has she ever done this before? (how should I know, she only just moved in), and so on. Nothing enlightening. I watched, silently, until Moorland had asked his questions, nodding his head in a gentlemanly way, and then left.

Fulda continued working, her white lab coat about her, and surrounded by a laptop computer display and rows of test tubes along the bench filled with ambiguous liquids, showing a gradient of color from light to dark. I was captivated by the activity, excited as a little boy watching tractors at a building site. It was the scientist in me. I tried to listen to Fulda's mind as she worked, but the information was unfamiliar—chemistry is not my strong suit. Still—the glamour of science, eh? I could have watched all day, even if I did not know what she was doing.

But, after an hour, I decided I had to turn away. Before going to find Renata I would return to Lupe's bed for a while longer, where if nothing else perhaps my purring could ease the healing process. As I moved to creep away along the upper ledge and back to the gap leading to the infirmary, I glanced back at Fulda's crowded lab bench once again, and spied something I had not noticed before. Odd—under a stack of printed spreadsheets and plastic-bound lab books, there was a soft leather portfolio. It looked like the leather portfolio that Denis had had in Charleston, the one given to him by the Doctor. From my vantage on the upper ledge I could not tell for certain if that was what it was. But it could have been. Perhaps Denis had shared the portfolio with Fulda—he had certainly told her about Renata's medicine, even if he did not seem to appreciate what condition it was intended for. It was interesting, very interesting indeed. Fulda was fixed in concentration as I left her. Perhaps I would try back another time, and see if I could figure out what she was cooking up in her lab.

Renata was not at the Myerson's house yet later that afternoon, as I nosed my way in through the cat flap. The house was silent; Mike Myerson was working, apparently preparing to go off on some out-of-town mission for the college development office. A fund-raising emergency, perhaps. I listened carefully for any sound of Maia or a babysitter, but there was none. The child had been apparently bundled off to a day-care facility for the day.

After the bright afternoon sunshine, the interior of the house seemed dark as well as quiet. My padded feet crept quietly through the kitchen, and I paused occasionally to bend my head cautiously around the next corner of the room, the tip of my tail twitching. But I seemed to be alone. Well, Renata would arrive soon; she was not likely to encounter trouble before that. Out of idle curiosity, if nothing else—I am, after all, a cat—I decided to make a quick patrol of the Myerson's magnificent house while I waited for Renata.

The kitchen, usually a cat's favorite, seemed to have been cleaned to an utterly unnecessary degree. I sniffed about the ceramic tile floor, hopped about the countertops, gingerly pawed along the top of the stove— but nothing, no interesting smells at all. A whiff of ammonia cleanser here and there tickled my nose, and almost made me sneeze. Disappointed in the kitchen, I leapt off the countertop and trotted into the living room. The pieces of furniture which had been haphazardly pushed to the verges of the room the night of the movie party had been arranged once more in their proper places. I sat for a moment on a coffee table, appreciating the authoritative eye that had decorated the room. This certainly wasn't Fulda's doing. I suspected that Beth and Lucy must have been the guiding intelligence.

Interior design, however, even executed at the most practiced level, can only hold my interest for so long. I continued my tour, hopping from the coffee table to the sofa, and onto the polished dark hardwood floor of the corridor. I thought I would go into the formal dining room off the front hallway. That room hadn't been used for the party, and so hopefully had not been scoured clean; maybe something smelled interesting in there.

But as I skittered past the side table and chair in the hallway, a movement flicked in the corner of my eye. Just a brief glimpse, but it was definitely something. I trust my peripheral vision—and to the scientist even optical illusions must have an explanation. I stopped, wary, crouching in the hallway, waiting to see if I could catch sight of the movement again.

Yes—there! I looked up. Above the side table in the hallway hung a mirror in a heavy gilt frame. The movement was in the mirror—in the reflection of the mirror, as if a shadow moving across the room were being reflected in the glass. I glanced behind me across the broad hall; all was still. Two straight-backed chairs stood against the opposite wall, waiting with puritanical severity to seat guests entering at the front door. Unwelcoming as they looked, they were quite empty. No shadows crossed the wall above. My eyes glimpsed the movement in the mirror again. Coiling like a spring, I leapt lightly onto the side table, and cautiously peered directly into the glass of the mirror. I saw movement suddenly flash again, once more as if a figure had crossed in front of the mirror across the hall. I craned my tiger-striped neck around again, but the hall behind me was again still. The severe guest chairs sat immobile against the far wall, empty. There was no one there.

Cat, a voice sounded clearly in my mind. *I thought you'd come by here.*

I turned around quickly once more and looked deep into the mirror. The figure that I had glimpsed before now stood clearly in the reflection—a familiar figure, wearing a familiar black suit, although it carried the wide-brimmed hat in its hands.

It's good to see you, Cat, the Doctor said in my mind.

I was flabbergasted. The Doctor! But he was dead!— or annihilated, to be technical, since he had been dead all along. I fought the impulse to look behind me and see if he was standing there, but a slight motion of my head must have betrayed me.

It's OK, Cat, the Doctor said, *take a look behind. It's a perfectly natural impulse.* The Doctor took a step over to the reflections of the chairs in the mirror, and sat his tall frame rather stiffly in one of them. *I'll wait.*

I struggled to regain my composure, but I have to admit that I did sneak a look back over my shoulder—the chairs, the hallway, still stood empty, as I knew they would be. *Doctor, forgive me,* I said. *It startled me to see you... I never expected to see you again! I mean, you were annihilated!* I paused, inarticulate for a moment. *Is it really you?* I asked. *Or is this some kind of trick?*

The Doctor chuckled. *I guess you could call it a trick. And you have to agree, it's a pretty good one! And even better, I have now learned your trick of telepathic communication. At least while I'm in this state. It's very convenient,* he said, with a smile. The Doctor grew serious. *Yes, I was annihilated—what you saw at Lake Marion was no illusion. And yes, it really is me. I am really here. Or, at least, my information is here. While I'm in the process of reassembling myself.*

Reassembling yourself? I repeated. *You mean, you can be reborn?*

The Doctor smiled again. He was clearly enjoying this. He was like a university instructor just aching to explain a particularly knotty problem to a seminar room of his best students. *Reborn? Well, that's a poetic way to put it, Cat,* he said. *But no, I think 'reassembled' is the better way to describe the phenomenon. It's just a matter of engineering the physical matter to correspond with the information. It's the information that must be preserved to preserve the identity. You know that. The physical matter can be replaced.*

I thought about this. *So you weren't annihilated?*

The Doctor shook his head gravely. *No, of course I was annihilated—as you yourself saw! In fact, that wasn't even the first time the Council has had me annihilated—although they don't remember that. Vesta, for all her talents, doesn't quite have the memory skills she thinks she does.* The Doctor's eyes flashed fiercely for a moment. *And I'll tell you, being annihilated hurts like hell! So I'm looking forward to getting my hands on those two nasty sons of bitches who did that to me, someday.* The Doctor struggled for a moment to calm himself, at length reverting back to his donnish demeanor. *But the information that is me has remained intact.*

How? I asked.

I had help, the Doctor said. *In fact, I had the help of a Timeslider.*

I was stunned, puzzled. *But Doctor,* I said, *I didn't do anything to help you! I was hardly able to make sense of what I was seeing!*

The Doctor chuckled again and continued. *I know, Cat. But I did not say it was you—I said I was assisted by a Timeslider.* He fixed me in his vampire gaze for a moment. *Another one.*

I felt a slight rising of panic—my scientific faculties were being rapidly overwhelmed by new and inexplicable information. *Another one?* I demanded. *Who? Do you have any idea, Doctor, what kind of incredible coincidence it would be to have two Timesliders anywhere concurrent in the same neighborhood of timespace? It's practically impossible!*

The Doctor was silent for a moment before answering. *Don't you realize, Cat,* he said gravely, *that the unusual events you have been observing are* not *a matter of simple coincidence? As a scientist, I would have thought you would have discounted the notion of coincidence anyway. Or at least calculated the probability sufficiently to discount it. No, these events have not been mere coincidence. Not at all.*

Then who is the other Timeslider?

The Doctor shook his head. *I can't tell you that. The Timeslider will reveal itself to you, when it decides to do so, if it decides to do so. Have patience, Cat.* The Doctor smiled again. *I hope you appreciate all the forward planning, if nothing else. You must have noticed that I was able to hand off some materials before I was annihilated—including some items that may be useful 'timeguides', as I think you would call them.* My face must have shown astonishment to hear the terms of art of my kind being spoken back to me with such familiarity. The Doctor smiled. *Yes, my Timeslider has been very forthcoming, and very helpful. And what do you think of the mirror phenomenon? It's quite an elegant solution to my current problem that my Timeslider has taught me. I only need the smallest crease in timespace in which to preserve my information. The light that bounces from the mirror to your eyes travels at 299 million meters per second, give or take, but just that slight gap in time is all I need.* He smiled broadly. *Information is wonderfully compact,* he said. *I could hide in any mirror—any reflective surface, in fact—until my reassembly is ready.*

I thought about it—I *thought* I understood, vaguely, what he was talking about. My anxiety lessened as the scientist in me started to take over, began to roll the idea around in my mind. The idea of tucking information into that tiny gap in time left by the transit of photons at lightspeed. If nothing else, the idea sounded amazingly cool.

But, Cat, listen to me, the Doctor said, pulling me back to the conversation. *There is a reason that I happen to be in this mirror in this house,* he said. *It would have been far more convenient to stay down in Charleston, by the way—there must be about a million mirrors available down there. But I'm here, of all places, because we need to talk.* The Doctor leaned forward in the straight chair earnestly. He had my attention.

Look, he began, *being disembodied can sometimes be to my advantage. I have been able to gather some information that I might not have been able to, otherwise—and, please don't pester me about how I was able to gather that information or what being disembodied has to do with it. We don't have time right now—just accept that I have learned something. Something very big. Cat,* he said in a low murmur, *I believe I know what Vesta is up to. She is looking for something. Or rather, someone.*

The prickle of anxiety started again in the back of my mind; I couldn't respond. I did not need to, though, as the Doctor continued.

Do you remember at the hearing before the Council in Charleston, when she asked us about the thing she called the Sable? he asked. *Vesta was in earnest, and I have learned that Vesta believes that she is close to discovering the Sable. And Cat*, he said, betraying anxiety, *I'm concerned that she may be correct.*

At this point, I'm afraid I lost my temper. It must have been the cumulative effect of these manifestly impossible phenomena that had been assaulting my cognitive faculties: first seeing the Doctor again—sentient in any case, even if he was in a disembodied state and living in a mirror, of all things—and then news that I was not the only one of my kind in the vicinity, and now the reference to this Sable (whatever that is!), which the Doctor himself had told the Council was a legendary fantasy—yes, I had not forgotten his throwaway speech to Vesta when she raised that puzzling name. Of course Vesta was looking for the Sable—she had asked the Doctor that very question at the Vampire Council a week ago! All these conspired to make me very cranky.

Look, Doctor, I snarled into his mind, *I've had about enough of this! Please just tell me what the hell is going on! With all due respect to your Timeslider friend and your mirror tricks, please just get to the point!*

The Doctor glared at me severely for a moment, then with a long, noisy expulsion of air from his lungs (my mind wondering in passing how he did that given that he was only a reflection in a mirror, but I let it go), he relaxed back into his chair, and laced his fingers over his knee calmly. *Point taken, Cat,* he said. *You've been remarkably patient, I should say. You certainly deserve a full explanation.*

And with that, the Doctor began to speak, steadily—I don't know for how long. He explained the legend that the Vampire Council maintained of the Sable, a lost vampire adept who was reputed to have been the greatest adept ever known. The Sable was said to have disappeared centuries ago, but the Vampire Council believed that the Sable had been swallowed up by the stones of the earth— somewhere—and lay hidden, ready to come forth again to lead legions of the vampire warriors of the Council in a final battle to subdue the mortal world. He explained that his belittling of the legend was in part posturing, an attempt to lead the suggestible minds of the vampires listening in the galleries away from belief in the Sable. And it was in part his conclusion, based on the evidence he had had in the past—there was no proof that there was any such thing as the Sable. But could the Sable actually have existed—or could still exist? Yes, the Doctor said. He could not exclude that possibility. And that was the worry. Because now, suddenly, Vesta seemed convinced that she was close to discovering a route to find the Sable, and that Renata was somehow the key to that route.

I don't know if you have been aware, the Doctor said, *but Vesta has been watching Renata in Forshay, every night, for the whole academic year. She has kept vigil in the woods above the College, on the mountain, trying to draw out Renata's memory with her mind.* The Doctor looked grave. *She stands in the forest, reaching out with her mind—acting exactly as a vampire master would act with her novice adept.*

But how do you know, Doctor? I asked. *I've been watching at night as well, and I've never seen her. Never heard her mind, either—remember, I have other senses I could bring to bear!*

Perhaps she knows you're present, Cat, and avoids you, the Doctor said. *But listen, I think I now understand why Vesta and the Council think they are so close. It's the article!*

The article? I asked. *What article? What are you talking about?*

The article that Renata was working on for the history department, the Doctor said, *the one that that jackass Claude Preen rejected. Remember the title? 'Imperatoris Marmor'—the 'Marble Emperor.' The legend of Constantine XI is the very same legend as the legend of the Sable—the legends say that Constantine was swallowed into the walls of Constantinople in 1453 as the city fell to the army of the Sultan, and he is now waiting for the day to emerge again and take the field against the enemies of his people! Vesta thinks that Renata's was drawn to that topic, because somewhere she retains a memory, a memory that could lead to the Sable!*

I was confused. *But Doctor,* I said, *this seems pretty farfetched—that was a history paper. A scholarly essay—even if the Council had read it, all the sources of information would have been fully attributed. The information is available to anyone. There are no secret 'codes'.*

They aren't looking for a code, the Doctor said impatiently, *and they don't think that the article was important in its own right. They seem to think it is a signal—to me, to other members of the Doctor movement, to the Sable itself, I don't know. But they think that Renata knows. Or that the knowledge is somewhere embedded in her memory, even if she is not presently conscious of it.* The Doctor paused, his long white fingers nervously working around the brim of his hat. *And there's something else, Cat,* he said anxiously. *Who is this new student of Renata's, who she is so taken with?*

Lupe? I said. *What does she have to do with any of this?*

I don't know, the Doctor said. *I heard about her beating. And I don't think that is a coincidence either. In fact,* the Doctor said, *I think that Vesta believes that the girl herself may be the Sable. Or the next step leading to the Sable.*

I had to stop to think about this. What the Doctor was saying was absurd—laughable. But there was an itching, a tingling in my mind told me it was not absurd. It would certainly explain several things. And Lupe's beating was certainly not imaginary. Nor, I had to admit, did I believe in coincidences. The vampire assassins were doing this for a reason.

OK, I said. *But what does it mean? What do we do?*

We have to find the Sable first, the Doctor declared. *Before the Council does. Before Vesta does.*

The legendary, mythical, nonexistent Sable? I said mockingly. *How do we do that? We don't even know what—who—we are looking for.*

That's why I need a Timeslider, he said. *I need you to find it for me.*

This was a little much—did he have any idea what he was asking? *That's a pretty big request,* I said. *Why don't you ask your own Timeslider to do it for you?*

The Doctor regarded me quietly. *I would if I could, Cat,* he said, *but you know it doesn't work that way. The timeguide and the Timeslider must have a bond, a connection. My Timeslider, true, has a bond with me. But it has no particular bond with Renata. Not yet, anyway.* He eyed me frankly. *Cat, you have a bond with Renata. I think you may not appreciate the strength of that bond. You could find a way into her history. And if the Council is right, it is her history that holds the answer.*

Then I need a timeguide, I said. *I can't timeslide back five minutes without a timeguide. And what you seem to be talking about is a timeslide a whole lot deeper than that. The timeguide,* I demanded. *What are you proposing as the relevant timeguide?*

The Doctor sighed. *That is the problem, Cat,* he said. *I don't know. No one knows. Only Renata can show you the timeguide. But we have to find it—we have to find the Sable before the Council does.*

Or what? I said. I admit I was still a bit petulant; perhaps it was discovering that I wasn't as unique as I thought I was. *What happens if Vesta finds the Sable first?*

I heard a noise in the back of the house, in the kitchen. A key scratching at the kitchen door.

Best not even to think of that, the Doctor said. *I'll take my leave, Cat—hopefully the next time we meet I will have a material presence again. But find the timeguide!*

I glanced over my shoulder as I heard footsteps in the corridor.

"Kikki!" Renata's voice came to me. "What are you doing here?"

I glanced back at the mirror just in time to see a fleeting shadow move outside the frame.

Lupe was dressed and seated on a chair in the infirmary waiting room long before five o'clock. She was cradling me in one hand, and holding a small plastic bag filled with ice to her swollen eye with the other. "Just keep it there, honey," Mrs. Rose cooed, "that there swelling will go down by tomorrow. But you'll have a mighty shiner for a week!"

Mrs. Rose squeezed Lupe's shoulder as Renata walked into the infirmary.

"I came a little early," Renata said, "just in case the doctor had already given his OK."

"Oh, Renata, dear, we're glad you did," Mrs. Rose said sunnily. "Lupe's more than ready to head back to Dr. Myerson's house!"

Lupe let me leap to the floor as she rose slowly from the chair. She began walking gingerly toward the door. Renata looked questioningly toward Mrs. Rose.

"Oh, just take it slow, honey," she said to Lupe, then turned to Renata. "Doc Stevenson said it was actually better not to baby her too much—you know, let her walk around and such. Liable to get very stiff and sore, otherwise. I mean, even sorer than she is now."

Renata took Lupe by the elbow as they left the infirmary. "I'm OK, Miss Beaumanoir," Lupe said. She made a show of gaining speed and confidence as she walked the corridor from the infirmary and up the handful of steps to the exit. But I could hear the wincing in her mind as each step gave a twinge.

Outside, however, she cheered up—it was late afternoon; the sun was golden and the oak trees along Main Street fairly glowed. Lupe plunged ahead with vigor, baseball cap planted firmly atop her ponytail. I watched worriedly as the slanting late sun slowly reddened Renata's bare arm as she kept a hand lightly on Lupe's back. We made a slow but happy walk up President's Row to the Myerson's house. Up the staircase to the second floor landing, then to Lupe's room. Lupe sat heavily on her bed. Renata sat beside her.

"You know, Lupe, I hate to keep repeating this, but Dr. Myerson's right," Renata said gently, delicately taking her sunglasses off in the dim bedroom. "It would be better if you told us what really happened."

I had just leapt onto the bedspread and sat beside Lupe, and could hear the sudden, jarring shift in her thoughtstreams—from the contented (if tired) happiness of walking through the June afternoon with Renata to being, once again, confronted with the problem of the attack on her. Her thoughtstreams became loud, blaring, confused—she was clearly near the end of her tether, on the verge of panic. I rubbed my nose on her limp fingers lying on the bedspread, trying to comfort her. But the effect seemed to be opposite—the stoic façade of her features finally crumbled and the tears finally ran, and she fell against Renata, who, surprised, only barely had time to open her arms in embrace. Lupe pressed her face against Renata's blouse and wept; Renata held her, looking down at Lupe and trying to keep pressure off her black eye. The air was slowly suffused with a faint odor of roses.

And, after Lupe recovered enough, they talked—Lupe talked to Renata until the sun slanted down and the window outside the bedroom became dark. The sky faded to luminescent blue as the summer evening bloomed with fireflies. Lupe told Renata everything, or what she thought was everything. She told Renata things that Renata had already guessed from that stray line in her final exam, and things that been presaged by no kind of hint. Lupe told Renata what she remembered of her mother, who died when she was only three. She did not remember her father—the story of what had happened to her parents was one she had assembled from random comments, here and there, over the years. She had finally asked a union leader in Ahuachapan, a friend of her father's, if she had put together the story correctly. She had, for the most part— except that both her father and mother had been living in the capital when they died, not the mountains. Her father disappeared soon after she was born. Her mother lived in San Salvador for three more years with her, and was shot only a few weeks after she had delivered Rafael. Lupe knew that Rafael could only be her half-brother, and she never found out who his father was. It had never seemed important to her—relatives had brought them back to her mother's neighborhood in Ahuachapan, where the war had already wound down. She grew up happy enough, raised by the women of the neighborhood, playing on the packed-earth streets in the dresses sewn for her by her many, many aunts. Or so they said: every woman in the neighborhood seemed to be her aunt. Occasionally, an old *abuela* would suddenly stop her on the street and place her hand against Lupe's cheek, looking at her tight-lipped, but searching intently from within the deep eyes in her wrinkled face for the shadow of someone lost, a niece, perhaps, or just a neighborhood girl—Lupe's mother, gone now for reasons that no human words could seem to explain.

Lupe told Renata about Rafael's trouble with Alejo's gang, who he had met on the Guatemalan border. Rafael had called her from cell phones at first; Lupe had scolded him, telling him that he was foolish to trust the *coyotes*, who only prey on young migrants like Rafael. But Rafael was reckless, and did poorly in school; the governors of the Estado Piñela school would clearly not send Rafael abroad to join his sister at their prestigious prep school in Washington, D.C. So he had decided to follow his sister by himself, thinking that he, at seventeen, was more than a match for any dangers on the road north. She did not know where he had gotten the first five hundred dollars; she preferred not to think about it. She suspected that he had been in trouble; she was certain he had fallen in with more and more dangerous people. Soon the cell phone calls had stopped, and it was months before he got word to her that he had made it to the United States. It was a postcard she had received in Washington, with a skeletal address that read, "Escuela Estado Piñela, Wash DC". No return address; Rafael had had only the slightest recollection where she was, but he had no idea at all of his own location. Another postcard arrived weeks later; this one at least bore a return address in Texas. Lupe had written back to the address on the card, telling her brother about her transfer to Forshay College, and explaining as best she knew (because her own sense of the geography had been vague) where North Carolina was, and where Forshay might lie within it. She had not heard back. Not until, near the end of the term, a farm worker, a Central American by his face and accent, had quietly walked up to her on Main Street and handed her a note. Rafael, it explained, had been journeying for months trying to find his way to where Lupe was; he was working with a migrant crew which had, miracle of miracles, just moved into Forshay for the early season farm work.

And it had soon become very apparent that the very crew he had joined—or had been steered to—was also under the control of Alejo. Alejo or his men had appeared at every stop as they had moved north; every town seemed to belong to Alejo, and the purpose of every job of work seemed only to pay Alejo his debts. And all of the workers had debts.

Lupe finally stopped, exhausted by the unburdening. She was trembling; the tears were starting again. Renata gently removed her ball cap, and softly stroked her hair.

"It's all right," Renata said, soothingly. "We can help Rafael. But," she added, "we have to tell the police about it."

Lupe shook Renata's hand from her head. "No! We can't tell the police!" she moaned. "They'll take him away!"

"Then what should we do, Lupe? Do you have the money for Alejo? Would Alejo leave Rafael alone then?"

Lupe, eyes downcast, began to sob again. "No," she cried. "There is no money. It is an impossible amount of money! And no matter how much Rafael pays, it is not enough." She wiped her eyes, and looked up at Renata, her blackened eye looking horrible in the dimness, her good eye wide and pleading. "Please, we have to help him," she said. "He is my brother, and if we don't help him they will kill him."

And that was all—no problem-solving, no analysis, no scientific methodology. I sat on the side of the bed as Renata embraced Lupe, rocking her gently and murmuring in French. After some minutes, Renata laid Lupe down on the pillow, unlaced her sneakers and pulled them off. She covered Lupe with a fold of the bedspread, and pulled a chair for herself next to the bed. Lupe was drained, wrung out. She looked at Renata for a moment; Renata touched her hand.

"Don't worry," Renata said. "I'll stay here. Kikki too. All night if you want."

Lupe was too tired to respond. The long black lashes of her good eye gently knit together as she fell asleep. I walked over the spot on the bed where Renata had been sitting; I always liked to find a warm spot to curl up on. But it was cold, not warm; that worried me. Renata had nodded asleep in her chair, as well. I watched the stars wink in the patch of night sky at the top of the window. I saw the door open quietly as Fulda looked in; she smiled when she saw us. She took another blanket from the end of the bed and tossed it over Renata. "Cold as ice," Fulda whispered to herself as she patted Renata's hand, and then left the room. The stillness of the summer night filled the house. Despite my worries, all seemed to be safe for now. I let myself drift asleep, never a difficult thing for a cat.

I was awakened again in the deep of night—not by dream-thoughtstreams this time, but by a sense of movement. I blinked my eyes sleepily open in time to see Renata framed in the starlight at the bedroom door, pulling a robe about her shoulders. I was still sleepy; and all things being equal a cat asleep will remain asleep. I turned a circle, attempting to nestle once again against Lupe's legs under the blankets, but something was wrong. I could not get comfortable. It took me a moment to realize the reason. The bed was empty; Lupe was gone. Again.

Renata had apparently also seen the empty bed. It was a moment before I could shake off the sleep and gather myself sufficiently to follow her out of Lupe's bedroom, and pad down the wooden stairs after her to the kitchen.

Which is where Renata found Lupe—in the kitchen, sitting at the table, unable to sleep. Renata drew up a chair silently and sat next to Lupe. I followed, and leapt quietly onto the kitchen counter behind. A glass of milk sat on the kitchen table before Lupe, untouched. I wondered why—perhaps it was some semi-conscious recollection of Lupe's, drawn from who knew what American situation comedy: when kids in suburban American homes go to the kitchen, they get a glass of milk. It didn't really matter that Lupe didn't like milk. We sat quietly for a long time in the still house, wakefully watching the black night outside the kitchen windows. Lupe stared off into the distance beyond the blackened panes; Renata's black eyes remained fixed on Lupe. An electric motor inside the clock on the wall whirred gently; there was no other sound.

And then, suddenly, there was. It was just a touch at first, something out of place. A tap, a click. But we all heard it—and then another sound, a metallic scratching. Close. I saw Lupe's eyes—the swollen one as well as the good one—swing to the lock on the kitchen door at the unmistakable sound of a key in the lock, of the lock being turned, of the click of the doorknob turning open. Lupe gasped. A chilly breeze entered the kitchen with them. They spoke low in the quiet kitchen.

"Hey babe," said Harrison.

"Hey, Renata babe," said Chuck.

"Man, you sleep sound!" said Harrison.

"Like a rock," said Chuck.

"Thought we'd have to watch for you all night."

"Just watchin'. Outside your house, watchin'."

Harrison held up the house key, with its tag reading 'Lupe'. "Had to bring this back, Sweets," he said. "It's got your name on it."

"Yeah. So we bring it back."

"Right. Honest, we are."

"It's OK, though," Chuck said. "We cut our own copy."

"Yeah," said Harrison. "Just want to let you know. In case, you know, we want to visit you."

"Just friendly. You know."

"Yeah. Us. Friendly."

Renata stared at them, seething. "Get out of here," she hissed in a forced whisper. "Get out. You have nothing to do with her."

Harrison laughed. "Tough chick!" He nudged Chuck.

"Yeah, *awful* tough!" laughed Chuck quietly. "What are going to do about it, Comtesse? Shot through with that junk from the Doctor, you don't have no power anymore—how you going to make us go?"

Renata sprang to her feet and pulled a butcher knife from a block by the stove. She stood, brandishing the knife at them. Chuck dropped his smile.

"Don't, Comtesse," he said. He dramatically drew out his knife. "See this? I got a pointy, too, Comtesse. So, don't start anything you can't finish. Because I got no Doctor junk in my blood." Chuck bared his teeth; the white canines looked sharp, ready. He was poised to extend the teeth, poised to strike. He closed his mouth, and smirked.

Harrison jerked his head at Chuck. "Let's go," he said. He tossed the key onto the table, where it rang loud, far too loud, in the quiet kitchen. Chuck made a show of leaning forward toward Lupe, and breathed noisily through his nostrils as if enjoying a pleasant fragrance. "Nice smell," he said mockingly. His eyes glinted as he stared at

Lupe.

Harrison grabbed his shoulder, withdrawing. "We just stopped by, just to let both of you know," Harrison said, licking his lips and smiling, "that we're here."

Harrison and Chuck gave them each their most charming smiles. Then, silently, they slipped open the kitchen door and disappeared.

Lupe rushed to the door and twisted the deadbolt knob; the lock shot to with a clack. She stood for a moment, panting, wildly looking at Renata through her disheveled eyes.

"You...you *knew* them!" she exclaimed, accusatorily.

Renata was silent for a moment. "Yes," she said at length. "Yes, I know them—I have trouble with them, too. Not exactly like your brother, Lupe, but trouble enough." She reached out to Lupe's hand. "Come on, I'll put you back to bed."

Lupe eyes widened with concern as she looked at Renata, trying to process this new information. Renata smiled. "Come," she said, "it's OK."

At length Lupe relaxed, and let herself be led. I leaped down from the counter, and headed the barefoot, three-man parade quietly back up the stairs.

"It's funny, you know," Renata said softly to Lupe as they walked up, "between me, you and your brother, you're the only one whose papers are valid."

But of course Renata did not stay with Lupe all night— she couldn't. In the quiet still dark before dawn, Renata stole away from the Myerson's house and swiftly made her way back to her small place in the Visiting Faculty housing on Ridge Street. When I nudged my way into the house through the window, she already had the dose of thanadoxicil ready in the bathroom. Or, I should say, the half-dose—if that. I rubbed against her bare ankle, as I usually did, as she slipped the silvery needle between her toes, but she did not react, just continued grimly concentrating on her task. I crept away, not so much with hurt feelings for being ignored (as a scientist I thought I understood what drove this particular output set of behaviors) as with simple concern. I could see from the small, smooth wooden box that she had open on the edge of the sink that Renata tonight was administering her last dose of the drug. A day's worth, at best, and then the vampirism would return, ineluctably. I saw that Renata had pulled out a suitcase and made a halfhearted attempt to pack. Pack? The incongruity of the impulse saddened me. It was a human impulse, the impulse of a creature with a past to value and a future to protect. A vampire, though? A vampire is immortal, a being dissociated from time. Why pack, when there is no loss that can ultimately hurt you? And why provide for a future, when the future is immeasurable, without effort or reward? A vampire would never pack. Pack. Pack for what?

She sat on the edge of her bed, fully-clothed, breathing shallowly as the thanadoxicil slowly suffused her body. I watched over her, worried, as she had watched over Lupe only a few hours before, feeling as powerless to protect Renata as Renata must have felt powerless to protect Lupe. Her vampire thoughtstreams, superficially placid and glassy, thrummed with the strange undercurrent that had lingered there for so many days now that it seemed to be an old friend. Was it a suppressed memory, like the Doctor had suggested? The Doctor had said that it had been Vesta who had been calling it forth. I thought of the dark mass of Forshay Mountain rising above Ridge Street, the blackness of the woods on the side of the ridge above the campus. Was Vesta there tonight? Was Vesta, even now, standing somewhere under the canopy of black trees, trying to pry the hidden memory from Renata's mind? Was it Vesta who had caused Renata to have that vivid dream that previous night?

Renata had folded her hands on her lap as she sat. The background rumble in her thoughtstreams grew louder, like a rumor of approaching thunder. It put me on alert—could it mean that the long-suppressed memory might break through the barrier of Renata's vampire state on its own? Was Renata really so powerful an adept that she could summon her own memory by pure will? The disruption in her thoughtstreams grew more intense; she stared ahead intently, as if in a trance. But no memory emerged. Her mind remained the flat black of a vampire mind, despite the grumbling undercurrent, and I learned nothing.

I gave up and sat back on my haunches, disheartened. I licked my forepaw to distract myself from my disappointment. Suddenly a movement caught my eye, and I looked up again. Nothing seemed to have changed, though; Renata still sat, immobile, raptly staring ahead. But then I saw the movement once more—my peripheral vision again serving me well—and saw that it was Renata's hands, nervously working. I looked closer, and saw that she was worrying the red enameled star ring on the index finger of her left hand, twisting it, fidgeting the ring round and round. I stopped cleaning my paws and looked closer, my cat's eyes narrowing. The ring. The way her hands sought it out, involuntarily, autonomically, as if the ring were a talisman, a relic of enormous importance, instinctively understood. Could this be it, then—the timeguide? Could it have been here, out in the open, unseen, all along?

I knew what I had to do. I had to act on this idea, and act immediately. If the vampire assassins had been so bold as to accost Renata and Lupe openly tonight, then the Doctor must be right—Vesta and the Council must be ready to strike. And we had to figure out what they were after. There was no chance any more to delay, no other alternative. I had to timeslide, now, with the star ring as my timeguide.

A deep breath—I knew I was going far back this time. What did John Random and the Doctor say about the ring? That it was an emblem of an order of chivalry, from 14th century France? Well then, I said to myself, that is apparently where this timeguide will be taking me. I crept closer to Renata; I have found that the closer I get to the timeguide the better—even touching it, if it is a physical object, though I did not think I could touch Renata's hand without breaking her reverie. I steadied myself, crouching and creeping closer as if stalking a mouse, fixing the ring with my eyes. The ring gleamed in the soft moonlight flowing into Renata's bedroom, the light glinting off the bezel of the ring as Renata absently twisted it round and round. I stared; I felt my mind focus on the ring; I felt as if I were going *into* the ring, diving beneath its handsome metallic surface and swimming into some more fluid reality lying beneath. And as I stared, the world tilted and swirled, the colors of the ring expanded to fill my entire mind and the rushing, overwhelming sounds of the timeslide accelerated, filling my ears with almost intolerable noise. It was splitting my head, as if a ramjet had suddenly taken residence in my skull. The sound became more and more painful. I focused on the ring; I had to stay focused on the ring. The timeslide went on and on, gaining momentum. Faster and faster. The whine of the jet engine in my head grew and grew. The pain began to fatigue my mind; my kitten jaws clenched and every fiber of muscle in my body tensed as the ring led me deeper and deeper through the crease in timespace from which it had sprung. The pain intensified as the timeslide stretched on and on. I did not know where I would land—in fact, I did not know if I would survive. My eyes grimly clung to their gaze at the ring, unwilling even to blink as the obliterating noise of the timeslide screamed in my mind, and the great colored whorls of time closed over me.

CHAPTER FIFTEEN

It was night, and the moonlight bathed the countryside all around in white. I stood still for a moment, watching, listening. I was exhausted and still trembling slightly from the effort of the timeslide. I saw that I was standing on a sandy road that ran through fields and trees; the road glowed silvery through the dim landscape. I sat on the road for a moment, resting. I felt a sudden, uncanny impression that I was just back in Forshay, looking over the moonlit campus of the College once again from the low sweeping branches of the oak trees. But I knew that wasn't the case. I relaxed the focus of my eyes and let them gaze unfixed, allowing the sense of the place to flow over me, trying to get my bearings.

I rarely timeslide this far back. I am much more comfortable as a denizen of my own natural time—that is, the time which I have lived through to in the conventional way, to the early decades of the 21st century, as it stands now. But I have enough experience with deep timeslides to recognize how it goes with one's first impressions of the different time and place. At first, all seems familiar—there is the land and air, and the sun and moon shine in the sky, and the grass looks the same, and the trees. But after a short time, a disquiet takes hold like a sense of *déjà vu*, imbuing the new scene with a curious strangeness. It feels peculiarly both familiar and unfamiliar. It is as if you were looking at an old family photograph, and reaching back into your childhood memories about the place and time depicted. Your perceptions may feel askew, you may even feel strangely unfamiliar with yourself, as you remember your world as you knew it as a child—as you recall how your old neighborhood looked, and the smell of the wet boots in the school coatroom on a rainy day, and the way snowflakes felt on your eyelashes and how the snow stung your fingers as you mashed it into snowballs after you pulled off your mittens, but how you never really remembered feeling cold—all the mixed perceptions of phenomena that are at once familiar and strange because they belong to a different time.

I saw shadows moving up ahead along the road, and I roused myself into a trot to follow them. The road seemed to be leading into a village, and the shadows ahead of me seemed to be the black moonlight shadows cast by the figures of a tired horse, and an equally weary person leading it on foot. I saw them follow the road down a decline to a bridge over a rushing river, where they paused in crossing and I took the opportunity to catch up with them, scampering up the whitened road in the moonlight shadows cast by my own legs and tail. As I trotted near them, I caught the thoughtstreams—thoughtstreams musical and complex, full of the kaleidoscope emotion of mortal humans. And I recognized the voice, a voice so familiar despite the difference in quality, and the difference in time: the figure on foot, leading the horse, was a very human, very mortal Renata.

As I drew near, I saw that she stood facing another figure on the road, a figure in a cowl and cloak who seemed to have confronted Renata, stopping her. They were arguing. The horse stamped and blew out its breath in irritation at the delay. I cautiously made my way about the animal's hooves, trying to hear the conversation.

It took my brain a moment to adjust to the language. The archaic vocabulary of Middle French, just like in the dream of Renata's that I had overheard.

"Leave us alone and let us pass!" Renata demanded. "I'll bring him to Father Bertran in Josselin!"

The other figure laughed a low, feminine laugh. Then the figure spoke, her voice sounding hollow and off-pitch in the deep night silence. "What makes you think that Father Bertran has remained behind, when the rest of the village has fled? Lord Beaumanoir has taken his knights to fight the English, and Montfort and his traitors. And the ladies of the chateau have scurried away from the river to the hills, as if that will protect them from this new pestilence. There is no one in Josselin anymore—not your sister, not Lord Beaumanoir. None are there, none but the dying, and those already dead."

Renata pushed the woman in the cloak roughly off the sandy track. "Father will be there," she said fiercely. "Stop following me, whoever you are! I have no need to your arts—magic, from the devil! Witchcraft!"

The other figure forced her way back in front of Renata, impeding her again. She laughed once more and took the cowl off of her head. The moonlight caught the white cascade of her hair as it shook loose from the heavy black garment, and the hard eyes in the beautiful alabaster face glittered fiercely back at Renata. I was not surprised, for I had already heard the flat and smooth vampire thoughtstreams of Vesta Letalia beyond those musical human thoughtstreams of Renata. Vesta took a step toward Renata threateningly.

"Don't insult me, Renata de Rohan," she said. "I am no witch. I am no fantasy of the ignorant. I offer you help." She pointed at the horse. "He will die, no matter how many priests you take him to. Unless you come to me. *I* am your aid," she said, "why do you think I mean you harm?"

As Vesta spoke, she had gestured to a bundle of clothes tied to the saddle. I looked closer and saw that the bundle was, in fact, a person, a boy, his head laying motionless against the neck of the animal and his arms tied about it so he would not slip off. The boy's eyes seemed to be slightly open, the whites showing behind the tiny gap in the slack eyelids, but the eyes were unseeing. His face was ashen; the high moonlight made it seem paler still.

Renata's eyes widened in fear. "I don't know you," she said in a terrified whisper. "You have followed me here— you have followed me and watched me since the Great Death four years ago. Since the first pestilence, and the death of my husband, and the deaths of my other dear children. Matthieu is the only one left. My only son now. And you followed me when I was still on Cedran's estate. And you followed me when I left the estate after the Great Death, and came to my sister at Josselin. I now I see you following me still. I have seen you waiting for me on the road at night. You followed me and Mattieu since before this new plague," Renata said. "And you follow me now. What do you want? Who are you?" Vesta reached out gently toward the horse's bridle, her hands a gesture of calm. The horse shied. Renata recoiled in fear, pulling the horse away, wiping away tears that had begun to stream from her anguished eyes. "You are unnatural!" Renata exclaimed. "You come from the evil one!"

"Foolish woman!" Vesta scowled. "I am no demon, no evil thing! I can save Matthieu! Give him a new life!" Vesta leaned her face forward toward Renata's, breathing deeply as if inhaling a fair perfume. Vesta closed her eyes momentarily, as if she had lost interest in Renata and her dying son.

Vesta made a sudden grab for the bridle. Renata gasped, pulling the horse's head sharply aside. The horse started, neighing loudly in the stillness of the road. It crouched back on its hind legs, ready to rear itself up and bolt. Renata cried out as Vesta struggled to grasp the reins. Renata pulled away and with a sudden movement grabbed the ropes that bound the unresponsive Matthieu to the horse, and hauled herself onto the beast's back. Her feet scrambled to find the stirrups as Vesta fought to control the animal, a keening scream of anger building from her throat.

"No!" Renata cried, "leave us alone!" She dug a heel fiercely into the horse's ribs, and the animal broke into a clumsy run away from Vesta, the reins tearing out of Vesta's hands.

"You'll return to me!" Vesta called after them, her voice hoarse and hollow. The hooves of Renata's horse beat a tattoo over the planks of the river bridge, and then it broke into a gallop up the sandy roadbed on the opposite side. "Go to your priests, but you will return to me!" Vesta pulled the cowl back over her head and walked off the road toward the verge of the woods across a moonlit field. I paused a moment watching her move swiftly away, my mind catching a thoughtstream as she disappeared. *The adept will belong to me,* Vesta's mind said. I turned and dashed along the midnight road toward the village, trying to catch up with the horse.

It was not a long way to run, even for a small cat. I saw the walls of the great rampart of Josselin castle as it rose above the village against the river Oust. It had occurred to me that I knew this town—that Renata and I had visited this town, although six centuries in the future. We had taken a tourist barge down the river—well, the canal, I guess you would call it, since it had been incorporated into the Nantes-Brest Canal. It would have been in the 1960's some time but before she had left France, when Renata had become attached to an optimistic group of vampires, followers of the Doctor and users of thanadoxicil. They had made a great fuss that weekend about going about the town as tourists in the broad summer sunshine, in white linen suits and hats, and wearing the big sunglasses that Renata continued to favor long after she followed the Doctor to New York. I remembered great delight when they discovered that the pharmacy that they had stopped in to buy sunburn ointment turned out to stand on the *Rue Beaumanoir*. There was no murmur of deep memory in Renata's thoughtstreams that day, not that I remember anyhow— no inkling that she had walked the streets of that same village centuries before. But the village that I was seeing before my eyes now, in 1352, looked very different from the one I remembered from that happy visit in the future. The castle looked different; the battlements were rougher than the ones I remembered, those of the Renaissance castle that had been built on the site a century or so later. The walls now before me under the moonlight were scarred by fire and stone missiles. The village that lay beyond seemed deserted; it lay motionless under the moon, and the gates through the fortifications lay open. As the road crossed the river again, I saw mounds on the riverbank, smoke drifting from them across the moonlight shining on the river water. The breeze shifted momentarily, and a whiff of the stench reached my nostrils—diseased bodies that had been dragged from the village to the riverbank were being burned.

Renata had said that she was going to seek out the priest. It did not take me long to find her. The echo of her hands beating against the door of the chapel alongside the castle rang through the silent town. The horse stood before the church when I caught up to them, its head hung in weariness. The street was dirty and cluttered with dark piles of garbage in the moonlight. Against the walls of the houses lay pieces of broken oxcarts, trash, heaps of stained straw and ordure, and other still, dark objects that I chose not to examine closely. Renata stood in the street, calling to a window on the upper floor in the parish house. The face in the window looked down at her, seeming almost dazed in fear.

"I can bless him from here," the face said in a small

voice. A hand appeared in the window, tracing a sign of the cross.

"No!" Renata demanded. "I am the sister of Lady Marguerite, I am the sister-in-law of Lord Beaumanoir! I am of the House of Rohan! You will not hide from me, Father! I demand that Mattieu be treated!"

Father Bertran raised a small glass vessel to the open window. "Move the horse under the window," he said. "The holy water will drop on him from above." He shook droplets of water from the glass.

"Open the chapel, Father!" Renata shouted. "Matthieu must have the sacrament! I *command* you!"

The priest seemed to shrink away from the window slightly as she yelled, but he made no move to descend the stairs and open the door. "My lady," he said weakly, "if your son is touched with the plague, then he is dead already. Leave him behind, and save yourself. Pray for him. That is all we can do." The priest crossed himself. "The watch will find him in the morning. He will be respectfully burned."

Renata shrieked in frustration. "Then I will take him to the chateau, Father," she cried, "and find Lady Beaumanoir! And you will be forced to do your office! I will come back, and you will embrace the victims of this plague yet!"

"The chateau is empty, but for a few servants," the priest said petulantly. "And the servants will drive you away if you take a sick boy there. They do not welcome the plague, even in those of noble station. They will drive you to the burning place yourself!"

Renata bent down and gripped a rock lying in the street. She hurled with all her might at the window. Father Bertran ducked behind the window sill as the rock thumped against the wall of the parish house. "Be off, Lady Renata!" the priest shouted out. "The pestilence has upended this world! You mighty nobles are laid low!" He put his face out the window once more. "I have done

230

what I can! Flee, and may the Holy Ghost protect you!"
Father Bertran flung the glass vessel of holy water from
the window, the water spinning in droplets from its mouth
as it flew before shattering on the stones of the street. He
quickly pulled the shutters of the window closed behind
him. Renata's second rock thumped against the wooden
shutters, exactly where the priest's face was a moment ago.

Renata stood in the empty street, her breathing labored
from throwing the stones. I heard her mind rushing, the
despair and panic rising and subsiding as she tried to
decide what to do. She began to lead the horse down a
side alley by the church. I followed close by, keeping to
the shadows, avoiding the waste and corpses that littered
the verges of those plague-stricken village streets. At
length she came to a small building, built to the side of and
adjacent to the church, its windows dark, but the door ajar.
She pushed it open, and then untied Matthieu from the
horse's neck and eased him from the saddle. She pulled
him into the darkness of the room, and laid him along the
floor. She returned to the horse and carried in the bundle
that had been tied to the saddle—blankets, candles. She lit
a candle from the tiny flame that winked in the corner of
the room, and the interior became visible. I looked about
the spare stone room. Two benches, a tiny altar, a cross.
In the flickering candlelight, I saw carved in the stone
above the altar the words, *Puissent ces prières defender les âmes
de ceux du nom de Beaumanoir*—'May these prayers defend
the souls of those of the name of Beaumanoir'. It was a
shrine, a chantry, presumably one dedicated by her
illustrious brother-in-law.

But Renata was not praying. She poured clean water
from a leather bottle onto a scrap of cloth, and wiped the
boy's face. I could see the boy clearly now for the first
time. He was handsome, about seventeen years old. But
his face was thin and wasted, and the bulges on his neck
and the black necrosis of his skin over the swellings told all
that needed to be said about his condition. Bubonic

plague. Renata passed her hand over his forehead, smoothing back his fine brown hair. She showed no fear of the disease. Her thoughtstreams calmed as she tended her son. Suddenly, I heard her light, clear voice begin to sing, softly, keeping a rhythmic time to the strokes her hand made over his forehead, gently passing over Matthieu's hair. I started when I heard it—I had never heard Renata sing before. As I may have mentioned before, vampire minds do not carry music. But this was Renata as she was before, as a mortal human. And as a mortal human, she had an achingly sweet singing voice.

Matthieu would not recover—I could see that. Perhaps Renata had brought him to this private place to give him a modicum of peace as he died, away from the panic he would surely have inspired in those remaining uninfected in the village. He did not regain his consciousness; as the sky lightened outside, his breath remained labored and shallow, his eyelids trembled slightly and lay slightly parted, but his eyes were still sightless. Renata stood when she saw that the dawn was coming outside the chantry. She looked down at her son, adjusted the blankets about his chest. "I will come right back," she whispered to him, unaware of the cat who overheard her. "I'll find the alchemist."

I should probably explain a little more about the timesliding—even though you seem like a clever person, and seem to be catching on well enough. But it would be good to explain; there's no sense making you work harder than you need to in order to follow along. Some of this will probably intuitive enough to you, and some will surely seem strange indeed. But, whatever—if you find it hard to follow, just skip this part. Don't tease your mind with it if you find it hard or boring.

OK, so there are a few things to keep in mind. First,

just because I happen to be timesliding in an era some six hundred years earlier than my present era, it doesn't mean that my understanding of the events occurring during that timeslide are immediately available to me. Like all of my kind, I exist in a timeframe that is my native timeframe. It acts like a horizon; I cannot see beyond it. Events unfold in my native timeframe the way they do for anyone—and they are just as full of surprises. But when I utilize my talents, and slide back to an earlier era—ah, then things become tricky. Can I remember the events of my native timeframe—that is, events that will occur in the future? Interestingly, I can, although the memory feels strange during the timeslide, since it is not really a memory in that timeframe at all. It feels rather like a premonition of things that will happen in the future, which is, after all, what such a memory amounts to. After millennia of practice and training in the higher arts of timesliding, I am able actually to recall those memories of my future with some specificity and clarity. The ability to remember things that have yet to occur is one of my signal talents while timesliding. But listen—it still feels weird.

And second, when I am on a timeslide, my native timeframe continues to move along the arrow of time in the conventional way, and I am aware of that time's passage. And so one of the odd things about timesliding is what my kind call the breakoff. My mind in my native timeframe might interrupt a timeslide to summon me back to that native timeframe—back to the present, as it were. The crease in timespace remains open once the timeslide is established (at least going back in that direction), and when a breakoff occurs the timeslide is merely suspended, like dogearing the leaves of a book or bookmarking a web page—I go back effortlessly to where the breakoff occurred. Because, in fact, the timeslide would have occurred long ago—six hundred years ago, in this case. But I cannot jump ahead in the timeslide—when I rejoin the timeslide it is as if no time has elapsed in that timeframe. I can't jump ahead—I can only follow the timeguide as it takes me along the crease in timespace as it will, no faster nor slower. I suppose it would be *possible* to jump ahead in the same timestream, if I were to use a different timeguide and establish the pathway of a *second* timeslide adjacent to the first. It would even be theoretically possible to commence a new timeslide from within a prior timeslide, assuming one could discover an appropriate timeguide to follow. But I have certainly never attempted either of those things, and so far as I know none of my kind have ever attempted such foolhardy experiments, either. Imagine the risks! What if the slider's path led him face to face with himself from another path? Two timeslides crossing, within the context of one and the same timeslider? How could the information not become corrupted, damaged, even destroyed? Although time paradoxes don't really pose a risk in a normal timeslide—all that science fiction stuff about time travelers changing history because they snapped the wrong twig in some remote era in the past— that's all fantasy. Except in the case of the future and the past interacting directly, in the person of the timeslider. Who knows? I couldn't imagine what it would mean—the possibilities are too terrifying to contemplate!

But one thing that these features of timesliding does imply is that, even though all of the events of my timeslide must have unfolded centuries ago, my knowledge of them is only revealed to me in the memory I acquire of them in my native timeframe as I experience the timeslide. And all the time, time in my native timeframe moves along. In other words, time is not on my side. If I don't discover the facts that I'm hoping to find in my timeslide quickly, I could be too late to save Renata from the Council.

I can of course control the timing of breakoffs from within the timeframe of the timeslide—I can always choose to send my conscious mind from the past back into the present time, volitionally. The weird thing is when my mind in the present time breaks off a timeslide involuntarily. But those breakoffs happen when they will happen; they don't really feel as if they are under my control, although it is a future iteration of my mind that does it. Whatever. We just accept them as part of the life, and we trust that our present-time minds trigger breakoffs for good cause. Well, sometimes yes, and sometimes…not so much. At any rate, that was how, as I sat curled uncomfortably on the stone floor of the Chantry of Beaumanoir, in Josselin, in the Duchy of Brittany, in the Year of our Lord 1352, trying to decide whether to follow Renata on her search for that alchemist or to sit by Matthieu as his life drained away, I felt the familiar, momentary disorientation that told me that a breakoff was happening, as if I had jumped up onto a chair too fast and become lightheaded. I knew that I was being called back to my native timeframe.

It happens fast. I blinked, blinked, and blinked again, and found I was back in Forshay.

Back in Renata's living room, to be precise, on the night that the vampire assassins had accosted her and Lupe, the night that Renata had tried to pack her bags. The darkness was slowly being dispelled outside the windows but in the bedroom Renata slept on, the gentle sound of her breathing flowing through the open bedroom door. The remaining time before daylight stretched ahead, and the thanadoxicil she had taken had made its transformation, rendering Renata a human once again, not a vampire. She was a human again, but it was, perhaps, for the last time—the Doctor's smooth, wooden box in the bathroom lay quite empty. I watched, wondering if the half-dose of thanadoxicil, like the half-packed suitcase on the floor, would define the last I would ever know of Renata Beaumanoir as a simple human being in my native timeframe. I wondered if the Doctor might complete his reassembly in time to replenish her supply, and forestall her passing into the vampire state again. There was no sign of him yet. If he didn't resupply her, she would have to leave Forshay—and leave behind the new home where she had just begun to feel as if she belonged. I let Renata sleep peacefully past sunup. As I shook away the effects of the timeslide, the circumstances of Renata's present situation reemerged in my memory with a seriousness that afflicted me. I felt that I was powerless, that something was about to be irretrievably lost. The whole thing was making me sad in a way that was inconsistent with impartial scientific observation.

It was a knocking at the door of her house that finally roused her, despite my intent to let her enjoy the few remaining hours of peaceful human sleep that might be allotted her. I jumped down from a laundry basket which I had appropriated as a nest and skittered to the window of the living room where I could see the steps to the front door. Renata was a few steps behind me, drawing on a bathrobe.

"Chief Moorland," Renata said as she opened the door. "Well, I guess you had to get to me eventually. I suppose you want to ask me about that terrible event with Lupe Hernandez."

Paul Moorland made his slow and courtly greeting, drawing off his trooper's hat and letting a small semblance of a smile play briefly beneath his hanging moustache. "Ma'am," he said. "Apologies about the hour. Needed to talk to you rather urgently."

Something in his manner alarmed Renata. "Urgently," she repeated. "You could have talked to me anytime yesterday, Paul—I was with Lupe the whole time. I spent the night comforting her, at the Myersons'!"

"Yes, ma'am," Moorland said equably. "Understand. No hurry on that matter. I will need to get your statement on that when you can. But," he said deliberately, "I need to talk to you about something else."

"Not about Lupe?" Renata asked, surprised.

"Well, yes," Moorland said, "it is about Miss Hernandez-Vega. But not about the assault on her. My department is investigating that." *His department,* I thought. He is the only police officer in Forshay; he is a one-man department. Moorland was playing for effect, I realized, trying to sound official—bureaucratic and efficient, as policemen do when they need professional distance. Now I was getting alarmed about where Moorland was going with this. He fixed his steady gray eyes on Renata. "Miss Hernandez has disappeared again. Last night. And," he added, "there's been a serious robbery."

Renata was not completely taking this in. "Robbery?" she repeated.

"Yes," Moorland said. "The infirmary. There was a break-in there last night, and the dispensary was looted. A great deal of drugs were taken, Miss Beaumanoir, including some very dangerous ones. Thousands of dollars worth."

Renata's jaw was beginning to clench; I could see the subtle outline of a muscle pressing beneath the smooth skin of her cheek. I could tell she was beginning to get stubborn. "What are you suggesting, Paul?" she demanded. "Lupe was asleep in her bed in the Myersons' house when I left last night. You aren't saying that you think she is responsible for the break-in at the infirmary?"

"You just said you spent the night at the Myersons'," Moorland said quietly.

"Well, I'm *here* this morning, Paul, so I obviously left!" Renata snapped. "What are you trying to say?"

Moorland continued deliberately. "What time did you leave the Myersons', Miss Beaumanoir? That's all I'm trying to establish."

Renata stared at him speechless for a moment. She seemed flustered; perhaps she was simply still sleepy—or perhaps she was trying to gauge just how much she should say.

"It was very late—early, I mean," she said. "An hour or two before dawn."

"And the girl was in her room when you left then, right?"

"Yes, that's right."

Moorland looked down briefly at a notebook he held in his left hand; he flicked a page and read a note that was there. "Miss Beaumanoir, did anyone come to the Myerson's house last night?"

"No," Renata said flatly. No hesitation. "Fulda looked in on us around midnight. I was still awake, but Lupe was asleep."

Moorland had her fixed in his gaze again. "No one came to the door? No one entered through the kitchen last night?"

"No."

Nodding, Moorland looked down at his notepad again, making a further note in the pages there with a pen. Without glancing up, he asked another question. "Why did you leave and come back here, Miss Beaumanoir?"

"I had to get my medicine," Renata said. "I hadn't been planning to stay with Lupe last night, so I didn't have it with me."

Moorland scribbled a bit further in his pad, and then slipped it into his tunic. He replaced his hat and touched the brim with a finger. "That'll be all, ma'am. Thank you for your time. Apologies, again." He turned to leave.

Renata grabbed his forearm. "That'll be *all?*" she demanded. "Wait a minute! Where is Lupe? Are you looking for her? Is she all right? Why do you think she committed a break-in?"

"Ma'am, I can't go into all that," Moorland began.

Renata's face was intense. She wasn't going to let him go that easy. Paul Moorland sighed. He slipped his hat from his head again.

"We don't know where she is for sure," he said, "but we're pretty sure she was trying to get out to the Random

Farm, to be with her brother."

"You know about her brother?" Renata asked, uncertainly.

"Yes, ma'am," Moorland said. "We know about that situation. About her brother's trouble with Alejo Ramirez's syndicate. We've been talking to John Random about it for some time. This is the third season that gang has been causing trouble with the workers at his place."

Renata looked at Moorland dumbly. Moorland drew the connections for her.

"We're trying to establish a timeline, Miss Beaumanoir," he said. "You say you left at, say, between four and five in the morning, OK? And Miss Hernandez was still at the Myerson's? So we can draw a conclusion whether the timing might exclude the possibility that Miss Hernandez had anything to do with the break-in."

"I see," Renata said guardedly, regaining her voice. "And so it must show that Lupe couldn't have done it, right?" she asked.

Moorland was still acting the dutiful public official, but there was a sad look in his gray eyes. "No, afraid not, Miss Beaumanoir. Security cameras at the infirmary recorded the intruder just before six o'clock this morning. Small, slight person, long hair in a pony tail, baseball cap. Forshay College sweatshirt." He put his hat back on his head. "I'm sorry, Renata," he said quietly. He turned away and walked purposefully back down the sidewalk of Ridge Street toward Main, where his cruiser was pulled up at the curb, idling.

Renata seemed rooted in place, as if the suggestion that Lupe might have committed a break-in and robbery made no kind of sense. But it *did* make sense—at least it made sense to me, a kind of plausible, if sickening, sense. After all, I had heard more than Renata had. *Get money,* Alejo had said to Lupe and Rafael. *Get money, or get what could be turned into money.* No, it made sense all right.

But Renata only paused for a moment before she ran

to the telephone in the narrow hallway. I strolled after her, settling on the floor and watching quietly as she untangled the dirty brown cord and punched the streaked and sticky buttons on the dialpad. When we had moved into the house at the beginning of the year, it seemed clear that the landline phone had been neglected by the last several occupants at least. It was not connected to the network; there wasn't even a legible phone number on the worn, peeling sticker near the cradle for the handset. When Renata had lifted the receiver to test it, the thick plastic object had met her ear with stubborn silence. I had half expected to see a string of cobwebs stuck to the phone as she raised it. It had taken some effort to get the phone connected. Buildings & Grounds had sent Trace Cuthbert over, who had to crawl along the baseboards on his hands and knees, following the scuffed and worn phone line, looking for the phone jack (hidden, it turned out, behind a rickety bookshelf). "Most of the teachers don't even bother with the house phones anymore, just their mobile," he had said to Renata. But she had shaken her head. She didn't carry a mobile phone. She didn't use a computer either; at least, not then. Much hectoring—followed by much patient explaining—on the part of Denis and Fulda had eventually gotten Renata sufficiently conversant with an Apple laptop that she, grudgingly, had acknowledged that it was a useful tool. Despite her youthful human appearance, Renata could behave like an elderly technophobe. She still refused to carry a cell phone. At the hall telephone, waiting as her call rang, she had drawn her fountain pen out of her bag and unscrewed the top in case she needed to write down a note. A beautiful silver pen with a filigreed nib that she had acquired in Paris, in 1897. The cutting edge of Renata's technology.

"What do you mean Fulda's not there?" Renata was barking into the receiver. "Mike, where the hell is she? How can she be at the lab? At…" She juggled a glimpse at her watch. "At 7:30 in the morning? Doesn't she know

what's happened? Don't *you* know what's happened?"
Renata tucked the phone under her chin, and squaring up a
scrap of paper on the dirty side table. "Is there a phone at
the lab? What's the number? No? I *tried* her mobile; it
must off. Man, that's just *great*. No. No, Paul Moorland
was just here. He says they think Lupe's headed over to
Random. No, don't tell me to calm down! *I'm* calm!
Dammit!" She hung up the phone, grabbed her bag and
pulled an overcoat, scarf and hat off the coatrack in the
hallway.

Her jumpy eyes lighted on me for a moment. "Well, if
there's no phone in the lab I guess we better go in
person," she said. "Let's find the lady chemist." She was
already heading out of the house, the screen door swinging
open behind her, before I registered what she was doing. I
leapt through the door before it banged to, and galloped
two or three paces to catch up. As I ran through the
morning air my kitten nostrils caught a scent, incongruous
with the beautiful June morning, just a hint, but
unmistakable—the slight smell of burning hair. Renata's
arm had apparently caught the low morning sunlight, just
for a moment, before she had slid it into the overcoat. It
was just a flash, I realized, but enough to singe a few arm
hairs. The thanadoxicil had become dangerously diluted in
her system. We would have to be very, very careful, I
thought, jogging hard along the pathway to the Everett
Building to keep up with her.

Renata pushed through the side door of Everett that
led to the basement corridor. She passed by the infirmary,
the glass doors now crisscrossed with yellow crime-scene
tape that Paul Moorland must have been waiting years to
use. I glanced through the glass doors as we passed and
caught a glimpse of Mrs. Rose, calmly sitting behind her
desk and surreptitiously smoking a cigarette. The narrow
window to ground level was open a crack, and the smoke
drifted up and out above her. I smiled inwardly as we
passed by the infirmary and the yellow crime tape—despite

the festoons of yellow tape on the front door to the infirmary, neither Mrs. Rose nor Paul Moorland had thought it important to seal the back entrance to the infirmary, further down the hall. Sure, it was a crime scene, and there were important standards of evidentiary integrity to maintain, but Mrs. Rose had to use her computer, didn't she? And, besides, everyone knew Mrs. Rose. After all, this was Forshay.

We reached the chemistry lab suite at the end of the hall. I felt a little strange walking in the main door of a space I had spied on earlier—I wondered if I was supposed to act like I had never been there before? But then I decided that no one was going to be paying attention to a cat's reactions anyway, and in fact it would do better for me to stay out of sight. Cat fur in a chemistry lab couldn't be a good idea, and I could tell that Fulda would be stricter about contamination than Chief Moorland. I slipped along the baseboards of the laboratory, unseen, where I could hear the words and the thoughtstreams as well.

Fulda was engrossed with the same row of liquids in test tubes that I had seen the day before. She held one with a metal clamp, alternately warming the blunt end of the tube in a burner and then peering at it through a pair of plastic lab goggles. Renata had to call her name twice before she noticed she wasn't alone.

"Renata," Fulda said, surprised. "What are you doing here?" She gave the test tube a gentle shake, and examined it again. "Amazing," Fulda muttered.

"Lupe's gone," Renata blurted, sounding out of breath. "I called your house. Mike answered but he wouldn't come. We tried to call you…"

Fulda had put the test tube back in the row, and walked over to Renata, removing the goggles. "Slow down," she said, "what are you talking about? What do you mean Lupe's gone?"

"She's gone," Renata repeated, the catch of a sob just

barely mastered as she spoke. Words tumbled out as Renata quickly explained to Fulda about Lupe's disappearance, the break-in at the infirmary, the stolen drugs, the *coyote* gang, the police, everything. Fulda cursed under her breath as she pulled out her mobile phone, and discovered that she had left it switched off. A dozen unreceived messages popped up as soon as she powered on. "Look, Michael couldn't come because he couldn't leave Maia. And I can't leave this," she said, gesturing to the lab bench. Even behind her sunglasses, Fulda could tell that Renata was indignant. "I *can't,*" Fulda insisted. "You have no idea how important, how unbelievable this thing is that I'm onto here." Fulda turned back and looked at the row of test tubes again, almost tenderly. "It could really change everything," she said, in a low, amazed voice.

Renata would not be put off. "We have to find Lupe," she insisted. "She could be in serious danger."

"If the police already know that she is going to John Random's, why don't we just call him?" Fulda asked. Renata did not answer; the human edge of her thoughtstreams were a rush of contradictory emotions—including, I noted, a bitter annoyance at Fulda's unwillingness to leave her experiment. In her rush to get Fulda's help to undertake a search for Lupe, Renata's thoughts had rushed from expedient to expedient, with worst-case scenarios continually multiplying and intruding themselves into her thoughts. Her brain was full of imagined disasters involving Lupe, but as to the idea of just calling John Random—it simply hadn't occurred to her.

Fulda, answering her own question, had punched a speed-dial button on her phone; a few seconds later, we heard Fulda's elliptical conversation with John Random.

"They've found her," she said to Renata, who visibly relaxed. I heard the contending thoughtstreams in Renata's mind calm slightly. "She's with John and Paul

Moorland out at the farm now," Fulda continued. "They say she got a ride out there with Trace Cuthbert this morning."

"What about Rafael?" Renata asked, "her brother?"

"That's who John said they're out looking for now," Fulda said. "They don't know where he is. Or the drugs. There's no sign of either."

The thoughtstreams in Renata's mind began racing again. "We have to get out there," she said. "Lupe and Rafael would be together if everything was OK. Something's wrong. We should get out to Random Farm right away."

Fulda put her hands on Renata's shoulders, and looked squarely into Renata's face. "John Random is out there. Chief Moorland is out there. Hell, even Trace Cuthbert is out there," Fulda said. "Lupe is OK. They'll find her brother. Calm down." She moved her gaze side to side slightly, as if trying to see behind Renata's big sunglasses. "You really don't need to go out there."

Renata shook her head, and took Fulda's hands from her shoulders. She clasped Fulda's hands in her own as she pleaded. "No, you don't understand," Renata said. "I have to get out there. I have to. This is all my fault. Please, you have to help me."

"Your fault? How is any of this *your* fault?" Fulda replied. "You're one of the good guys. You've been helping that girl stay out of trouble for two days now."

"I can't explain," Renata said, "but none of this would be happening if it wasn't for me. Can't you just drive me out there?" Fulda was quiet. "Then what about Michael, can he take me?" Fulda shook her head.

"He has to travel this afternoon," she said. "New York, for another damn alumnae fundraiser. He'll need to leave in a couple hours. And he's already ticked off that I won't go with him this trip." She looked around the lab absently. "As it is, I'm going to have to find a safe place to let Maia wander around in here. Or else leave her at the

Sisters Store for a couple hours, if I can sweet-talk Beth."

Renata still held her hands. She looked very troubled.

"We could try Denis," Fulda said. "He's still on campus. He was good for a ride to Charleston, right?"

And as Fulda disengaged herself to call Denis on her mobile phone, I saw Renata relax once again. The strain and worry about Lupe seemed to be taking an undue toll; she already seemed to be tired, drooping, despite the early hour. She dropped onto a small stool by a table away from the lab bench, and rested her forehead on her hand. Fulda took a few steps away, walking the phone closer to the row of high, narrow windows on the far wall; the signal in the basement laboratory was stronger by the windows. In the temporary lull, I slipped out of my concealment and moved stealthily toward the lab bench. I had seen something there that had caught my attention when we had walked in, and now I wanted to—I needed to—satisfy my curiosity.

I had seen that Fulda had left the leather portfolio on the side of the lab bench, its pages open.

A quick jump onto the bench—perfectly executed, absolutely silent. I padded past the racks of laboratory glassware, pausing occasionally still as a statue, to be sure neither of the women had noticed me. I reached the portfolio, and tentatively laid one paw on the pages. They crackled slightly. I bent and sniffed. Not paper, but vellum. I focused on the words snaking across the broad pages—not printed, apparently, but all handwritten, the black ink slightly coppery in some places with age. There were tight paragraphs on each page written, I discerned, in Latin, in a precise and tiny medieval miniscule. The spacing between the words was so small I could not immediately make out the sense of the writing. Then, I noticed a sheet of paper beside the portfolio, a sheet of English, neatly printed off a laser printer. I moved to that side to glance at it—apparently, someone had translated the text for Fulda. My eyes registered a random sentence from the middle of the page.

> *...and, thence, to the second distillation, the mixture to be reheated again upon fire until the crystals descend from the liquid...*

As I curled my tail about my haunches, settling down to read the page, I felt something smooth and cold catch under a rear paw. I raised up suddenly in surprise, and spotted in the corner of my eye the glint of a glass pipette, dislodged by my foot and rolling toward the edge of the bench. There was nothing I could do—I couldn't catch it, and so instead I froze still again as the glass item shattered noisily on the laboratory floor. Renata looked up, and Fulda glanced back at me sharply. *"Off, off"* she stage-whispered from the window, covering her phone with her hand and pantomiming sweeping gestures. "Get that cat off the bench!"

Renata made a reach toward me, but I was too quick. I leaped off the bench before she could catch me, and scampered away. Fulda walked back to the lab bench, putting away her phone. "Well, nothing really damaged," she said, "just a broken pipette. But still, it's dangerous for that cat in here. Where's she got to?"

Renata couldn't see me, hiding again as I was along the baseboards on the far side of the lab. "I think she ran away," Renata said. "I don't see her anywhere."

"Comes and goes as she pleases," Fulda said, "just like our Lupe." Fulda put the sheet of typed translation into the pages of the portfolio and closed it, laying it aside. "I got hold of Denis," she told Renata. "He had already heard about Lupe, and the infirmary and the rest of it. I think Moorland must have called him or stopped by. Or maybe he just heard Forshay gossip. In any event, Denis was already coming to the village. He said he'd give you a ride out to Random Farm."

"Thank goodness!" Renata exclaimed with relief. She

pulled on her overcoat again. I took the opportunity to leave my hiding place, and paraded boldly down the aisle between the wall and the lab bench. I mewed loudly at Fulda and Renata, all innocence.

"There's your naughty cat!" said Fulda. "Better grab her before she gets into some real trouble in here."

As Renata grabbed me under the ribcage I went limp, acting the part of the compliant little kitten as she stowed me in the ubiquitous canvas bag. I popped my head out the top as Renata put the bag to her shoulder and hustled out of the chemistry lab. I wasn't afraid that Renata or Fulda might scold me for walking on the lab bench, although I suppose they had the right to. I knew that Renata was right—we had to get to Random's Farm. I just didn't feel like having to go timesliding to get out there—even if I weren't already engaged in an epic timeslide into the 14th century. Aside from the dangers involved in making two simultaneous timeslides, why exhaust yourself riding the creases of timespace, when there's a nice English professor to give you a ride? Besides, I was quite getting to like Denis's red Saab.

Renata hurried upstairs through the Everett Building, through the center corridor toward the main door. Denis had said that he would meet us outside in front, in ten minutes.

"Miss Beaumanoir," came Margaret Viper's voice as we passed her desk by the staircase. "Miss Beaumanoir? Please, wait."

Renata stopped, as Margaret hurried up from her desk to catch her. "It's Dr. Preen," Margaret said. "He asked me to find you—he said he had to talk to you right away."

"Margaret, I can't," Renata said pleadingly. "I have a real emergency. I don't have time for him right now."

Margaret reached out and touched Renata's hand. "I

know, dear," she said soothingly. "I know. And we both know why he wants to talk to you—he's going to fire you." Margaret patted her hand. "Get it over with. Right now. Don't string this out." Margaret gave Renata a sly smile. "Everything is going to be fine, believe me."

Renata exhaled loudly in exasperation. She let Margaret draw her back toward the history department offices, setting her on her way to Preen's office like a mother sending a child off to the school bus stop. I looked back at Margaret from my bobbing perch in the canvas bag; far from being annoyed to see a cat in the Everett Building, Margaret gave me a wide sunny smile.

Don't worry, she said, directly into my mind, *everything's under control!*

Renata walked through the anteroom of the history offices to Preen's office. It was too early for any secretary to be there yet. Renata advanced directly to Preen's inner office door. Her knock on Preen's door was perfunctory; she didn't wait for a response before entering.

Preen looked up when she entered, startled; his demeanor immediately turned to pique when he saw who it was. He was used to stage-managing entrances and exits; this didn't fit his script.

Renata sat down opposite him. "I'm in a hurry, Dr. Preen," she said flatly. "Margaret said you needed to see me urgently. OK. What?"

He smirked back at her. "You know, just the disrespect you show by not even removing your sunglasses when you talk to me—no fair-minded person would think me wrong to be offended by that."

"I have a condition that makes my eyes highly sensitive, Dr. Preen," Renata replied. "I don't think my glasses should make a difference to our conversation."

Preen leaned back in his chair, crossing his arms. "Humor me," he said. "We're not playing high stakes poker here. Besides, the light in here is quite low."

Renata looked about the office blandly, as if to confirm

the dim light. Out Preen's treasured windows, the sun was beginning to tip the elms and willow oaks far across the quad with light, but with the early hour the lawns and trees close by still lay in the deep sloping shadow of the Everett Building. "Sure," Renata said. "Whatever you say." She slipped off her scarf and sunglasses and shook free her hair a bit. The flesh around her eyes was bruised-looking, discolored, and her eyes were bloodshot and fierce red. I could see that her irises were beginning to glitter crystalline, as the thanadoxicil was struggling to keep the vampirism submerged. She fixed Preen in a hard stare.

"Jesus!" Preen exclaimed.

"Yes," Renata said flatly. She put the sunglasses back on. "I think maybe we'd both be more comfortable this way."

There was a pause while Preen tried to reorient himself. He shuffled some papers before him, as if looking for an item that would help him pick up the thread of a prior conversation. "Well," he said, "the reason that I wanted to see you—and I appreciate your dropping by so early, *RE*-nata…"

"Let me save you time," Renata said, annoyed at the mispronunciation of her name, yet again. "You want to tell me that my contract isn't being renewed for next year. That I'm fired. Well. Fine. You've made no secret that you intended to do that, so I can't feign surprise. But," she said, leaning forward and putting her elbows on his desk. "I want you to explain why. A reason. And don't tell me it's about the article I wrote, because that's pure bullshit, Claude. My article is perfectly competent scholarly work, and you know it. Assuming you've ever read it."

The challenge in her voice clearly provoked him, as I could tell it was meant to. His face passed from a look of stunned seriousness to something jocular, as if he was prepared to entertain her with a string of funny wisecracks. "A reason?" he asked. "A reason? And not your article, then? OK, I'll play along. Let's see, hmmm," he said, smiling theatrically and tapping his chin. "How about, oh, I don't know—how about fraud?"

Renata did not respond. Preen dropped the levity.

"How old are you?" he asked.

Renata stumbled, confused by the question. "What's that got…," she started. "I really don't think that that's relevant."

He pulled a folder from a stack of papers on his desk and opened it. "Let's see, I'm looking at your file, Miss Beaumanoir," he said. "University of Paris, I think you said, right?"

"Yes," she responded.

"Yes," he said. "What year was that again?"

"What year?"

"Yes," he said. "What *year* did you take your degree, Miss Beaumanoir?" He waited only a moment before waving his hand at her silence. "That's right, don't answer, don't even bother. Because guess what? We finally got a response from an inquiry we made a few weeks ago. The University of Paris *does* have a record of one candidate— full name, Renata Rozenn du Rohan Verane de Beaumanoir—taking a degree there. A doctor of humanities, I think the nice lady at the university registrar said—I had a little trouble with her accent. But the year that degree was awarded, well, that I could understand perfectly. In fact, I made her repeat it twice." He leaned forward on the desk on his elbows. "It was in 1679, Miss Beaumanoir."

Renata leaned back into her chair. "There must be a mistake," she said, though without conviction.

"Oh, there's no mistake," Preen replied. "It just seems that there is a logical quandary. Because, as I see it, there are only two possibilities. Possibility one, is that you are something over three hundred years old. And let's not inquire too closely on that, because perhaps it is impolite for me to ask a woman her age, yes? Or, possibility two, is that you have lied about your principal academic credentials, Miss Beaumanoir. That you obtained this job through deception and false pretenses. That you are a liar, an impostor, and a fraud."

He leaned forward again, peering intently at her.

"Any answer, Miss Beaumanoir? Any answer at all?" he asked. "Because, frankly, even with your sore eyes, you don't look anything like three hundred years old." He picked up the file again, and swiveled his chair to the side so he could cross his legs. He flipped through some more of the papers stapled into the file. "I could go on," he said. "You asked for reasons; would you like me to?"

"It's a mistake," Renata said softly. "I *do* hold a degree from Paris. I *am* a doctor of humanities."

"Well, how about this then?" Preen said, finding another fact from the file. "Your application says that you are a native of France. But according to Citizenship and Immigration Services, your residency status is a little— shall we say—confused? Homeland Security has no record of a permanent residency. Or even a visa, for that matter. No record of you at all. And yet, on your application, you claimed that you were a permanent resident, green card and all. Another mistake?"

Renata sat silently. I was getting worried. It wasn't like her not to fight back.

"Or this," Preen nattered on. "Your references. When we checked them more closely, they all seemed to be the same person, one Arnie Civitas, who you said was a tenured professor at the University of Parma, I believe. Too bad, though—I think we discovered that in fact he turned out to be a doctor in New York City. And some strange kind of doctor, as well, some kind of unorthodox treatment practices—not accredited by any medical authorities. Certainly not an academic, as far as we could tell. Really, Miss Beaumanoir, it's really not much of a reference for an academic position, is it? Some quack doctor up in New York?"

Renata put her hands on Preen's desk, and rose from her chair. Preen's insult to the Doctor, I saw, had finally gotten a reaction out of her. "He was a great and learned man," she said, her voice just controlling a slow fury. "His reference is the best one could possibly have. One that you could never obtain, Claude, even if you did live for three hundred years."

Preen also rose from his chair, and for a moment the two of them stood facing each other over the desk, like sumo wrestlers about to commence a match. But then Preen smirked, knowing that it was over, and that he had won. "Well, I guess that's that, then," he said. "You have your reasons. I trust you don't care to dispute any of them."

"I dispute them entirely," Renata said angrily. "You have everything wrong."

Preen chuckled. "No, I don't think so, Miss Beaumanoir, I don't think so." He sat down in his chair again and looked up at her coldly. "No. This is over. You're out."

Renata stood at his desk for a moment longer before turning away. Preen glanced up, curious that she seemed to be resisting the impulse to have the last word. As she silently put the white scarf back over her hair and walked toward the door, Preen found that it was an impulse that he, in fact, could not resist.

"Oh, RE-nata," he said. "If you want to wait for a moment, I can return your, uh, article to you." He poked about the piles of paper about his desk. "I'm almost positive I had it here. I know for sure I didn't bring it home to read…"

Renata didn't slow her walk to the doorway. "Fuck you, Preen," she said over her shoulder, and slammed the door behind her.

We found Denis in the corridor by Margaret's desk; Margaret and he both watched Renata with concern as she walked toward them.

"Bad?" Denis asked, but he could tell from her downcast face what the answer was.

"We have to go find Lupe and her brother," Renata said. "I'll tell you about it as we drive." She smiled at Margaret. "I really didn't need that right now, but you were right, Margaret—I'm glad it's over with," she said.

Margaret smiled. "Just go, dear. Do what you need to do," Margaret said. "Don't worry about a little prick like Claude Preen." Denis and Renata laughed to hear Margaret use such language, and hurried down the corridor to the main exit from Everett. As we left I heard Margaret speaking to me wordlessly again. This was getting to be a regular occurrence.

You take care of her, Margaret's voice sounded in my mind.

I will, I replied. *I will.*

CHAPTER SIXTEEN

My eyes blinked, and the streets of 14th century Josselin came into focus again. I realized I had been released from the breakoff. I found myself trotting through the early morning light a pace behind the dirty hem of Renata's skirts, edged with mud and worse from the foul street. The plague village of Josselin did not look any less bleak in the daylight than it had appeared the prior night in the moonlight—the morning watch was abroad already, collecting the corpses that panicked villagers had dragged into the street the previous night. They were a group of three burly men, dressed in dirty, shabby clothes. Their faces were obscured by rags tied behind their heads.

"The doctor," Renata said to the first. "The alchemist. Where is he?"

The man turned and looked at her suspiciously. Renata did not look infected, but he knew that looks could be deceiving. The plague struck quickly—the saying in the plague years was that in a single day you could eat breakfast with your family and eat dinner with your ancestors. The two other members approached carrying a wasted corpse pulled from the gutter by the wall, one holding its hands and the other its feet. They hefted the body onto the heap on the two-wheeled cart they pulled.

"Lord Beaumanoir engaged a plague doctor before he left," the man said, "but I've never seen him." He turned to his two companions. "You seen a beaky around here?" he asked.

"Nah, he never came," said one of the others. "Probably just kept the payment and stayed away. He would have known that Montfort's army had drawn the lord and his men-at-arms away from here, so who'd be here to check?" He adjusted the stack of bodies so they would not slip. "I can't blame him. I'd never stay here, handling all the pus and blood from these poor dead bastards, without the tincture from the Tuscan."

My kitten ears pricked up. Tuscan. That sounded familiar.

"Yes," Renata said. "You mean the alchemist, right? Where's he? Is he still in the village, or has he also fled?"

"Still in his shop, I should think," said the first man. He dug under the folds of his filthy cloak, and drew out a tiny clay bottle, stoppered with wood. He inclined his head of matted hair confidentially toward Renata, and spoke low through the rags over his mouth. "They say, lady, that that Tuscan speaks to demons," he said, indicating the bottle. "That that's how his tinctures have the power to ward off the pestilence."

"Or maybe he's a devil because he's an Italian!" called the third man, with unwonted heartiness. He was the largest of the three and stood behind the cart, ready to heave the laden vehicle forward again. "Like those Visconti devils, the lords of Milan—bastards!"

"Ignore him," the first man said. "It's a personal grudge. He hates Italians." He glanced over his shoulder and spoke loudly in the direction of his hulking companion. "Even though that crazy Italian's tincture is all that's keeping him from becoming a putrefying piece of meat like the ones in the cart!" The big man thought that this was impossibly funny, and he put his head back to roar delightedly into the still morning air, the sightless eyes in the cartful of bodies at his knees making an incongruous audience. The first man turned back to Renata. "My lady, you should not be going about in Josselin at all, much less going about alone. Go find the alchemist—he is an honest man. He will not overcharge you for the tincture, even though I can see you are rich."

They pushed the cart along, and Renata walked briskly the other way up the street. I briefly heard the muttering of the third man as he scoffed at the second one's claim that the lady had been the sister of Lady Marguerite—all the nobles had fled the plague days ago and why should any of them return to the village now, before all the shit had been cleaned up? I saw Renata hurry around a corner; I scampered off after her.

She drew up before a shopfront, set in a leaning stone house in the narrow street. The door was crooked and did not fully close; a faded apothecary device of mortar and pestle was painted on the weathered wood of the lower door panel. Renata pushed through the door impatiently, her brusqueness born more of urgency than any arrogance of her station.

The apothecary shop was dark. There were windows, but they had been covered over with wood and dark cloth. Even as daylight spread jarringly bright and sunny over the horrors of the plague-stricken village, the gloom of night clung within the shop. Renata called out. The shop was still. She called again, louder.

My mind sensed the thoughtstream before I saw the figure emerge from the dark recesses of the store. I heard a flat, toneless thoughtstream—it was a vampire mind, I knew. The face emerged into the hazy bar of light intruding from the open door. The man walked quietly to the door and closed it, shutting in the darkness. He opened a small stove that burned in the stones of the wall, and drew a flame from it on a straw. He lit a candle.

"Are you Arcadius, the alchemist—er, the apothecary?"

Renata asked nervously.

The face smiled. "I am," the man said. "I am both in fact, Lady Renata." He voice was hollow, I noticed, and his French a bit stilted, over-formal.

Renata stopped, for a moment. "You know me?" she asked.

I looked carefully at the familiar face, somehow less surprised to see the Doctor at this particular point in timespace than curious to see whether the physical expression of his features had changed in any way over six centuries. But no—the pale face with its undistinguished features looked the same peering out of the gloom of this storefront in Brittany as it had all those ages in the future when I saw it in the house near Sans Souci Street in Charleston. The Doctor continued to smile at her.

"Yes, my lady, I know you, though I realize you do not know me. I was briefly with your husband some years ago, in the service of our Charles of Blois. I served as a healer as well as a soldier—your husband trusted my...well, my somewhat special talents. We were lucky, and we pushed back the English and the traitor Montfort, at least for a time. Although we did not know that we would have to fight the same enemies over and over again. It seems that this war never stays won, I am afraid." He paused, his manner somber. "I was sorry when I heard the plague had claimed him, my lady. In losing Cedrane Verane, Brittany, and France, lost a brave man."

Renata dropped her glance for a moment at the mention of her husband. But she recovered herself quickly, reasserting her pleading gaze at the Doctor. She could not prevent two tears from involuntarily running down her cheeks; the wet tracks caught the candlelight. "Please, Doctor," she implored. "I thank you for your remembrance of Cedrane. But I need your help. Our son, Matthieu...I need you to save him!"

"Yes," the Doctor said, turning away toward a workbench behind him. "I understand. It is it plague that has touched your last son now as well, is it not?"

Renata stood mute in the darkened shop. I saw that her tears were running faster now, her lips tight as she struggled to master herself. I heard her thoughtstreams singing with sudden emotion—the multiple losses of her husband, and then one child and another child, all were made raw once again by her remembrance of them, and now the impending death of her last child on top of that seemed to push her mind into a rushing orchestration of grief and sadness.

The Doctor turned again. In one hand, he held a small clay bottle, the twin of the one the morning watchman had displayed. The Doctor took her unresponsive hand and, opening it, pressed the bottle into her palm. "This is the tincture you would have heard about," he said softly. "You must dose yourself with it. Do it immediately."

In his other hand was a scrap of white cloth, ragged as if torn from a bedsheet. The Doctor carefully reached out with the cloth and dabbed at the tears running down Renata's face. He soaked the cloth in the moisture, wiping it gently over her cheeks, and then brought the cloth to his nostrils and inhaled deeply. I had already noticed the smell—the odor of rosewater had grown stronger with each moment that Renata silently wept.

So it is true, I heard the Doctor's mind say to itself.

I don't know why—perhaps I had become so accustomed to talking telepathically with the Doctor in my native timeframe that it seemed only natural to respond to him—but before I could stop myself, I had spontaneously answered him, speaking into the Doctor's mind.

Yes, I said. *It is true. She is an adept.*

The Doctor started at the words invading his mind, his eyes moving wildly across the shop. "Did you say anything?" he demanded of Renata. She did not speak. The Doctor's glance passed by a small tiger-striped kitten—who must really have been looking rather untidy, after all the timesliding and breakoffs—without pausing, without really even seeing me.

Renata's grief was being overpowered by her anxiety, however, and she had found her voice again. "Do I give this tincture to my Matthieu?" she demanded.

The Doctor shook his head sadly. "No, lady," he replied. "The tincture will keep you safe from the plague because the disease has not yet infected you. But, for the boy…" The Doctor looked into her eyes; despite his effort at sympathy, his irises glittered harshly. "There is nothing to be done. Your son will die—you must accept that."

The Doctor's words seemed to have a concussive effect on Renata, and the shriek of frustration that loosed itself from Renata's lungs shocked me—having known her only with her vampire voice, I had never heard such sound come from her. It was as if the sweetness of her song voice had found its exact opposite counterpart in the expression of savage rage. She hurled the clay bottle at the Doctor; it shattered somewhere unseen in the shadows of the shop. A bitter smell rose from the broken bottle, mingling strangely with the perfume of roses flowing from Renata's tears.

The Doctor seized Renata's hands, shaking them firmly downwards once, twice, thrice, trying to snap her temper. "Lady, no! Not this!" he said sternly. "Listen to me—it is too late for your son. You must comfort him, you must help the transition of his soul. For that, you must only trust in the holy Redeemer. But," the Doctor continued, "you must protect yourself. I will find you another dose of the tincture." The Doctor tried to look behind him while still clasping her hands. Renata tried to shake out of his grip, the tears spilling over her cheeks again.

"My lady," the Doctor said urgently, "you must tell me—have you been visited? Did you meet a white-haired woman? Did she speak to you?" The Doctor leaned closer to Renata, the urgency of his question rasping his voice. "Answer me! Lady Renata! Did you?" She turned her face away from his, struggling now to get away. "You must stay away from the white woman," the Doctor said. "She is not to be trusted! She cannot help your son! Do not speak to her!"

Renata finally broke from the Doctor's grasp, and ran. She smashed through the door, which banged against the stone doorjamb so violently that the force slammed it shut again and set the shop back into darkness. The sudden movement of air snuffed the candle. The pungent smell of the smoking wick added to the strange mix of fragrance in that close room.

My cat's eyes adjusted to the dark again, and I leapt from the floor onto the workbench where the Doctor's bottles and canisters stood in rows. I stared at the Doctor, waiting until the green glow of my retinas attracted his glance. I saw the coldly glittering eyes turn toward me in the dark; his stare chilled me slightly, as it always did.

The chantry by the chapel, I said into the Doctor's mind. *The Chantry of Beaumanoir. She is hiding there with her son.*

I watched as the Doctor's eyes grew wide with amazement. "The cat," he whispered to himself.

I ignored him; I didn't know what Renata might do in her anguished state, and I had to be gone to follow her. I didn't have time to watch the Doctor work through the realization of who his conversationalist was. *She did meet the white-haired woman. She met her on the road to Josselin,* I continued. *I don't know if the white woman will come back. But if there is anything you have that can help, bring it to the chantry.*

"There is nothing I have," the Doctor whispered, to me this time. "A cat," he repeated to himself. The Doctor seemed dumbstruck, as if he could not believe that he was talking to a cat. Well, tough titties, I thought to myself, that's your problem. I was a little disappointed. Even though I knew that the Doctor could have no memory— or rather, no premonition—of our future association, I had thought the Doctor would have risen to the new situation a little more assertively, shown a little more grace.

Or might have at least offered a suggestion.

Well, that's that, then, I said. *We'll just have to fend for ourselves against Vesta Letalia.* I jumped off the workbench and scampered over toward the door of the shop, standing at the sill and looking every bit the picture of a small and domestic cat, who just wants to be let out into the garden. *Doctor, if I can ask you to get the door for me,* I said.

But Renata had not taken any rash action. In fact, when I found her back at the chantry, she seemed resigned, almost at peace. Matthieu lay still. Despite the summer weather outside, the stone floor of the chantry was cold, and Renata had folded Matthieu into several blankets to shield his body from the stones. She sat beside him, singing softly to him, listening to his shallow breath and wiping the black sputum from his mouth when he coughed. I sat a respectful distance away, watching her and listening to her mind. There was a sweetness to the day we spent there, despite the melancholy. Matthieu was dying, and his mother sang to him—that was all.

But I could not escape the realization that so far I had learned nothing about the Sable—who it was, even what it was. The episodes in Josselin were illuminating; the Doctor had already told me that he had met Renata when she was still a mortal human, and that she was an adept. It was remarkable to see these events first-hand. But I was anxious that my mission was failing—I had come to learn something about the Sable, but instead I only learned about Renata.

But what I did learn about Renata was so fascinating, I could not leave the chantry. I learned so much that I had never understood before, listening to the music of Renata's mortal life play on as her mind drifted over the memories of the life she had led. Her mind recalled its memories in bright colors and music, even as she sang to her boy. As she sang she let her memory drift, and I saw the face of her husband Cedrane—a handsome face, as she remembered it the day he first rode off to war. He was younger than I thought he would be, and slighter of frame. His white surcoat billowed in a wind as he turned in his saddle to wave good-bye again to her, laughing and pushing his windblown brown hair from his eyes as if he were merely riding away to a fair. And then each of her children came to her mind, her younger ones first: Alexandre, and Rozenn, and Marie—none of them older than twelve before the black plague carried their souls away, and they rested with their father beneath four raw scars of dirt torn in the grass of Cedrane's estate. The farm was a ruin—overgrown with weeds, fallow, the livestock dead of the plague or stolen by the groups of the desperate who roamed the countryside. The pestilence had carried away so many that there was no one left to farm. Matthieu stayed alive, though; he survived, and the light of his father's smile still shone out of Matthieu's eyes as he slowly grew into a man. A year they held out, huddling in the broken house, a year and then another year, and she watched as her cheerful and happy son slowly starved thin and wan. They could not remain. She was proud; her family had not approved of her marriage to a man such as Cedrane—a poor knight, and native speaker of Breton, not French. But her sister's husband was now the great man of Brittany, Jean de Beaumanoir—or Jehan, in the Breton rendering. He was famous, a hero—the year before he had issued a challenge to settle the war in Brittany by a *pas d'armes*—a battle of champions, thirty champions of France and Charles of Blois, thirty champions of the English and John of Montfort. It was a pointless, glorious work of blood. The French and the English knights had hacked and disemboweled each other all day, with swords, daggers and axes; all were either killed or maimed. It was only a question of which side was the last to hold out, and only when the English champions dragged the mangled bodies of their few survivors from the field was the issue decided. So the French had won—who cared? The Battle of the Thirty had not ended the war, or brought peace to Brittany, or expelled the English from France. But the *trouvères*, the song-makers, loved the show of it, and Beaumanoir quickly became the rock star of the age, a sensation. He was the most celebrated knight in France, invested by King Jean with the Order of the Star. Certainly the great Jean de Beaumanoir would welcome his unfortunate sister-in-law into his protection. And so Renata and Matthieu had come to Josselin, poor relations welcomed, not coldly, to be sure, but still with some reserve. Beaumanoir had instructed the priest in the village to assume the duty of Matthieu's education, and to prepare the boy for holy orders. Father Bertran had been no more effective at that task than he had been the night before, providing succor to Matthieu as the boy lay unconscious tied to the horse.

And so Renata after a time determined to leave Josselin, and return to the estate twenty miles to the west. She did not care that Montfort's army was once again in the field, as the spring came and the campaigning season took hold. The English raided throughout the countryside, pillaging, burning. The English brought their forces out of their fortified camps in *chevauchée*, or scorched-earth raiding. They said that if they could not garrison a large army in the country, then they would prevent the country from having the wealth to support an army of the enemy. Be that as it may—to Renata it seemed that the soldiers were mere undisciplined brigands. They stole what they could, and destroyed what they could not steal. There was no food in the country any more; the scarcity of bread and meat raised prices to dizzying heights—and merchants took only gold. Renata and Matthieu made the slow walk back to Cedrane's ruined estate, Renata preferring to hide hungry near the graves of her husband and children than to stand back proudly, denying their hunger as her sister's children ate their fill in the chateau of Josselin.

But the plague was not finished with them. Like a black finger, it reached out and touched Matthieu, and passed over Renata entirely. There was no one at her farm. Her only hope was to bring the boy back to Josselin, to seek relief in the mercy of God, the liberality of her sister, and the medicine of the alchemist, although not necessarily in that order. But none had provided relief. All that remained now was to sit the hours of a vigil in the chantry as the day wore old, and Matthieu's breathing subsided little by little. And so we were waiting.

I felt the presence in the room before I saw the movement. The door to the chantry swung open silently, and a figure entered. Outside, the day had fled and blue evening light glowed in the sky. There was no need for me to look—I knew who it was softly approaching Renata as she sat on the stone floor beside her son.

"I have come myself, to help you," Vesta Letalia said, her voice rasping in the silence of the darkening room. "To help your son."

Renata looked up sharply at her. "You," she said flatly—I could not tell whether the expression in her eyes was fear, anger or resignation. Probably a compound of all three.

"I told you that you would find no help," Vesta said. "The priest says to let him die, yes? Offers prayers, from a safe distance? Ah, that is our Father Bertran, I'm afraid," she said, smiling wickedly.

She moved closer to Renata, slowly kneeling at her side. "And you went to see the sorcerer," Vesta hissed, "or, pardon, what do we call him in these modern times? The apothecary." Renata looked away, turning her black hair toward Vesta's face. "No help, was he? I could have told you that—that old Etruscan is a worthless faker." She leaned closer to Renata's head, her lips close to her ear. "Only I can help Matthieu." She moved closer still. "I

264

can give him new life," she whispered.

Renata's gaze stayed downward, fixed on her son. She reached out and laid her palm against his cheek. The sores had scabbed over, their edges inflamed red. However, Matthieu's face did not move. Teardrops began to fall from Renata's eyes onto the stone floor of the chantry. Vesta became more agitated as the fragrance of rosewater began to pervade the air.

"I can give him new life," Vesta wheedled into Renata's ear. "He need not die like this. But, you must pledge something to me."

Renata, sadly, looked back toward Vesta with resignation. I heard her thoughtstreams crying out; her eyes seemed to plead, afraid to learn what Vesta offered lest it be yet another false promise made by a callous universe. Another deception.

"What must I pledge?" she asked at length.

"Yourself," Vesta hissed vigorously, the scent of the rosewater in her nostrils. "You must pledge yourself to me." Vesta fixed Renata with her glittering eyes. "Would not a mother give herself for her son?"

I heard Renata's thoughtstreams whirring, racing—the logic of Vesta's offer seemed so plausible... I wondered if I should do something, intervene—but why? The events which happened had happened—and I could not presume to take such a decision away from Renata. And to be honest, I was curious—perhaps you think me perverse, but my inquisitiveness was aroused by the idea that I might finally, after all my centuries living with vampires and humans, actually be privileged to see vampire reproduction, to see the creation of a new vampire from a mortal. I had never seen such a thing. In fact, no one other than another vampire had ever seen it, to my knowledge. I was excited.

But the question that Vesta had posed Renata, whether she would give herself for her son? It was an idle question. Of course she would give herself. There was no

265

question of my intervening in any case—Renata had already decided before I could even finish my thought.

"I will," she said firmly. "But save Matthieu."

"Of course," Vesta said reassuringly.

Renata motioned toward Matthieu. "My son—you must save my son!"

"No, first you, my lady," Vesta said smiling. She reached out to Renata, taking one shoulder gently in her white hands. She turned Renata toward her, looking into Renata's face with an expression that would have been almost tender, but for the hard glinting of her vampire eyes.

Another sudden movement by the door—I turned and saw two other figures enter the room, black shadows of enormous size. They stepped purposefully toward Renata and Vesta; I heard the clank of metal as armor shifted against a sword scabbard.

"A few friends of mine," Vesta said. "Don't be alarmed. They will help us."

The two black figures suddenly reached forward and took Renata between them, one gripping each arm. I saw their faces as they forced Renata to the ground; their faces were sooty and grimed with the dirt of riding, each fully bearded. One carried the haphazard scar of a blade slash across his nose and cheek; the beard grew but sparsely over the damaged skin. Their eyes glittered with the harsh cruel brittleness of the vampire. They forced Renata prone onto her back on the stone floor. She cried out as they held her down. One of them put a chain mail glove against her throat.

Vesta rose. She cast off the black cloak she wore, and stood above Renata in a white garment that cascaded to her ankles, her white shoulders and arms bare, her white hair falling down her back. "You will repeat," Vesta said.

Renata struggled. "Matthieu!" she cried.

"Soon enough, my dear." Vesta dramatically held out her marble-smooth arm. With a hiss, she gaped open her mouth, her fangs suddenly extending like ivory daggers. She plunged them into the flesh of her arm and sucked, pulling a rivulet of black vampire blood to the surface that ran down her white arm.

"Are you a demon?" Renata gasped.

"No, Lady Renata," Vesta said. She approached. "But we have our bargain, remember? You must pledge. Do you pledge?"

Renata was still, terrified. The vampire soldier jogged his hand against her throat to get her attention.

"I said, do you pledge?"

"Yes, I pledge," Renata said.

"You must pledge," Vesta said. "You will repeat. Do you pledge?"

"Yes, I pledge," Renata said once more.

Vesta leaned over and held her bleeding arm above Renata's face. The black stream of blood dripped onto Renata's eyes and nose. Vesta reached out with her other hand, smearing the blood thoroughly into her eyes and nostrils.

"Get ready," Vesta said to the soldiers. She drew her arm a few inches lower, and the blood dripped into Renata's mouth. Renata's tongue worked against the bitter blood, but more dripped between her lips. Vesta saw Renata's throat involuntarily contract as it swallowed. She had swallowed the blood.

"Seek the darkness," Vesta intoned, *"protect the Council. And serve your master, Vesta Letalia!"*

Vesta gave the soldiers a nod, and with a sudden violence the one that held Renata's throat drove the gloved fist into her windpipe. Renata struggled against the soldiers holding down, her face working in gasps that were sickeningly silent as the mailed fist strangled her of air. A few minutes and her face went rigid, her eyes staring, unconscious. The soldier released Renata's throat and with a sudden lurch Vesta clamped her fanged mouth over Renata's mouth and nose, exhaling from the depths of her lungs into Renata's body, filling Renata with a new breath from Vesta's lungs as the last breath of Renata's mortal life left her. Vesta clung there motionless for several minutes, like a tiger subduing its prey. Suddenly Renata inhaled loudly, her chest began to rise and fall again, and her eyes refocused. With unwonted fury she sat up, casting aside Vesta and the soldiers. She glared at them with hard, crystalline eyes. Renata was a vampire.

"Matthieu," Renata hissed.

Vesta stepped away from Renata, and moved toward the sickly boy. This was certainly an easier case—no need for vampire soldiers to hold down Matthieu, or to strangle the mortal life from him. The plague was doing that for them. Vesta knelt down and, curious, reached out toward the boy's face with her hand. She gingerly worked a white fingernail under one of the scabs that crusted Matthieu's face, picking it free until a moisture of pus and blood was exposed beneath. Vesta moved her face close to Matthieu's, and inhaled. She did not say a word, but I could hear her mind—her thoughtstreams explained the look of triumph that crossed her face as she caught the fragrance of roses that wafted from Matthieu's exposed wound, distinctive despite being obscured beneath the stench of plague. Vesta quickly performed the same ceremonial on Matthieu that she had on Renata, slapping his face until the boy weakly made his pledge before expiring. Vesta's face covered Matthieu's for a long moment as she finally exhaled the breath into his lungs that transformed Matthieu into her vampire as well.

Another adept! Vesta's thoughtstreams exulted, as she withdrew and Matthieu's eyes finally blinked to life—to their new life. *A second adept, who now also serves me!*

It was deep into midnight, and it had been several hours since they had left the village. Vesta still led Renata and Matthieu further and further from Josselin, crossing woods and fields, deeper and deeper into the Breton countryside. They followed the opposite road from that which Renata and Matthieu had arrived on; this road ran east and north into the dark interior of the country, a country infested with the ravaging troops of Montfort and the English. Vesta led, with Renata and Matthieu just behind; many paces further back on the track were the hulking black shadows of four vampire soldiers, the heavy tramp of their feet occasionally sounding with the clank of armor. Renata and Matthieu did not ask Vesta where she was leading them, or why they were leaving Josselin—they were confused by their new state, seeing things for the first time with the eyes of vampires, feeling the unaccustomed lightness of vampire feet, struggling to articulate speech in their vampire voices. Matthieu at least seemed to have regained his boyish high spirits; in the playful mind reflected even within the torpor of his vampire thoughtstreams I recognized the same young man I had read from Renata's mortal memories earlier that day—a merry youth, full of energy and adventure who could barely keep from running in his excitement as they moved along the road, asking where they were going one moment, complaining of hunger the next. Vesta for her part kept up a rasping commentary for Renata and Matthieu, an explanation of what had happened to them and a litany of basic information and lessons about their new state. Vampire 101, you might say. I trotted along in the shadows verging the road, curious, listening to Vesta hold forth. It was no surprise to me that Vesta liked the sound of her own voice; a Bully with an information advantage will always act the know-it-all. But I didn't mind, not this time. It gave me a chance to compare notes, check the information I had gathered over centuries of observing vampires against the perspective of a vampire master. I was pleased to find that, in most things, I had gotten the information right.

Renata still seemed anxious as she followed Vesta. "But what happens now?" she asked. "What becomes of us now?"

Vesta, a pace ahead on the road, looked back with annoyance. "What happens now?" Vesta repeated. She shrugged, and turned back ahead, her rasping voice loud so that Renata and Matthieu could hear. "That is not your concern. You are my vampires, and I am your master. I may decide what you do. What you say. What you think. I decide what happens now with you." She turned back and favored Renata and Matthieu with a sly grin. "But I will tell you that you are much more promising slaves to me than the rotten plague vampires behind you," she said in a whisper. "To think that the Council had thought that the Great Death would be our great chance—all that death happening, all at once! Our nation could choose the best of the dead, and soon the host of our dead would become so great that the living world could not resist it!" She huffed in irritation. "But so it goes with such plans, sometimes. The plague makes the victims weak, and rots them from the inside. Most are not sound additions to the nation. But," she added, "luck has brought us another occasion of death. We are favored not only with pestilence, but with war."

I noted Vesta's remarks, filed them away to consider later. It seemed that maybe they were beginning to illuminate a few things for me. But I could tell from the flatness of Renata's mind that she was not following Vesta's words, or at least their implications. Her worry had not abated. "But are we dead, then?" she asked. "You promised us a new life, but you speak as if we are dead."

"Yes, Lady Renata, you are dead," Vesta replied in a loud voice, "but it is a *living* death. You live to serve your master—me, Vesta Letalia—and the Vampire Council." She looked over her shoulder at Renata, grinning fiercely. "That was your pledge."

But all Renata seemed to hear was Vesta confirm that she and her son were, indeed, dead. Renata turned to Matthieu, and placed a hand on his cheek. She did not speak, but I heard her thoughtstreams struggling to understand—trying to understand what had happened to them, what she was now, what she had done to herself, and to her son. Her mind was rapidly flattening whatever remnant remained of its former mortal emotional vividness. Somehow, however, she still seemed to retain her concern about the vampire who had been her son. She ran her fingers over the scabbed skin of Matthieu's face. "Does the plague still hold Matthieu? Why does his face still look so?"

Vesta, becoming impatient with Renata's questioning, brushed the query aside. "No, the plague can no longer touch him," she answered. "He is dead! Dead! He is beyond the reach of any pestilence! But he will keep the scars," she continued. "We all retain the scars we had when we first came to the vampire state, the scars we earned when we were mortal. It is only after that we become invulnerable to wounds." Vesta stopped on the road, turning to face Renata. "I'll show you," she said. She called to the vampire soldiers down the road, over Renata's shoulder. "Tancred! Before me, now!"

One of the shadows down the road picked up its pace, hustling forward, each step rattling the chain mail girding his body, until he stood before Vesta. It was the soldier I had seen earlier in the chantry, the one with the jagged scar across his beard.

"Master Vesta," he said obediently.

"Bare your arm," Vesta said, "and unsheath your dagger."

He pulled off his glove from his left arm and pulled away the sleeve of his tunic. His muscular forearm was massive. He yanked a long dagger from his belt with his other hand, flipped the blade and offered the hilt to Vesta. They had evidently done this demonstration before.

"Watch, my slaves," Vesta said to Renata and Matthieu. And with that she plunged the point of the blade deep into the soldier's bicep, and slowly drew the dagger down the length of the forearm to his wrist. The skin of the soldier's arm parted as the blade passed, like the rind off a ripe cheese; the wound filled with black blood that began to run down the soldier's hand, and drip ominously from his fingers. Vesta pulled the blade away.

"Now, watch," she said, drawing away so that Renata and Matthieu could observe. Renata and Matthieu leaned in toward the soldier's arm in silent fascination. Their vampire-bright eyes could see perfectly in the dim starlight of the road, and they watched with amazement as the bleeding lessened and then stanched, and slowly the hanging edges of skin on the soldier's arm began to knit together as if growing anew under their eyes. The wound closed, fusing from top to bottom into a smooth and unbroken new surface of skin, though discolored and slightly glossy. After a few minutes the only evidence that remained of the wound was a long, ugly, purplish bruising of the skin.

Matthieu's eyes shone with delight. "Can I do that?" he exclaimed. "Master Vesta, can I do that too, now?" He made a grab for the dagger which Vesta held loosely, the blood clotting on its blade. She pulled the dagger away and held him at bay.

"Not yet, not yet," Vesta said, smiling. She handed the dagger back to the soldier, who bowed his head briefly and withdrew to a distance from Vesta once again. Vesta put her hands on Matthieu's shoulders, and fixed her eyes on him. "Not yet, but soon, my young adept. You will very soon fight for your master." She continued to stare at Matthieu. Her gaze continued, longer than was natural, and I soon became aware of a subtle shift in the thoughtstreams swirling about me. Where before I had heard the distinct but separate streams of several, stolid vampire minds, now something substantial had changed.

Vesta's mind had suddenly become louder, a penetrating throb, while Matthieu's thoughtstreams had subsided, quieted, almost disappeared entirely, it seemed. I listened more intently, my mind searching for Matthieu's thoughtstreams. Finally, I found them—still there, but they were pulsing now, like Vesta's, throbbing in synchronicity with the thoughtstreams that Vesta seemed to direct into Matthieu's mind. I glanced up again and looked at her there, her eyes still boring into Matthieu's with their unblinking stare. At length she released him, and smiling briefly, she turned and continued down the road, swiftly. Matthieu paused for a moment, seeming to need to recover himself, before bounding along the road after her.

We continued for many more miles, eventually the talk ceasing and our group moving through the night in silence. The road crested a small hill, a copse of trees screening a pastured slope running down below. Vesta suddenly stopped, and silently raised her hand. She turned and motioned to the vampire soldiers behind her; crouching, they broke from the road and moved swiftly into the dark foliage.

"Come, my Matthieu," Vesta whispered. "Now we fight, and eat."

Renata and Matthieu followed Vesta into the clump of trees and underbrush, creeping ahead carefully until they could see down the slope beyond—could see what had attracted Vesta's attention. It was a military camp. Only a handful of mounted knights, together with their squires and attendants. Less than twenty men. The horses, tethered on one side of the cluster of rude tents, had not yet sensed our presence. The black shapes of the vampire soldiers swept like shadows down the grassy slope in the starlight. One of them drew his sword in perfect silence; the blade gleamed from across the field.

"Are they the enemy, Master Vesta?" Matthieu whispered.

"And what do you mean by that, my slave?" Vesta said. "They are mortal humans, so they are the enemy in that sense."

Matthieu's eyes widened as they crept out from the cover of the trees, and moved stealthily on the camp. "No," he said, "I mean, are they English?"

Vesta laughed softly. "English, French, Breton—who cares? What is the difference, anyway? The King of England speaks French in his court, while your villagers here speak more like the old Celts back in Cornwall than the French." She turned to Matthieu. She smiled evilly. "These happen to be *anglais, mon cher,* if it makes you feel any better. But we kill them now, just the same."

Renata gasped. Vesta glanced sternly at her. "That is your instruction as well, Lady Renata," she said. "We kill, and perhaps we choose new soldiers for our Council tonight." Vesta rose out of her crouch and ran forward toward the soldiers. *"Sequi!"* she hissed. "Follow!"

The sound of Vesta's rasping vampire voice spooked the horses; they shifted in confusion, neighing loudly. I saw a man, presumably on watch but dozing, leap to his feet before the tent nearest the horses, one hand gripping a sheathed sword, the other struggling to pull on his trousers. The man looked around anxiously as he moved to the tethered animals, searching for the source of the alarm. He saw nothing. He paused, still alert, but calming. There was nothing—no alarm. He turned to walk back toward his tent; he could stir the watch fire back to life. Suddenly the huge black bulk of a vampire soldier stood before him, sword raised. A cry began to rise in the man's throat but was cut short, as the vampire soldier's heavy sword swung down with shattering force on the man's shoulder at the base of his neck, bisecting his torso to the belly. The horses screamed at the sudden movement and the terrifying smell of hot blood.

The vampire soldier pulled the dead man's sword from its scabbard. Vesta, Renata and Matthieu had arrived at the scene. The soldier put the sword's hilt in Matthieu's hand. "Good luck, boy," he muttered, and swept away.

I had been running through the long grass, just behind Vesta. But when we got to the camp, the vampire soldiers had vanished, dissolved into the black night. The commotion by the horses had roused the company from their tents; they hustled out, gathering around the body of the watchman. A knight strode into the gathering from behind, clearly the commander. He had taken the time to pull on his gambeson if not a breastplate; at least he bore something of a military aspect. He looked down at the body, and then at Vesta, Renata and Matthieu. He turned to a soldier beside him.

"Dead?" he asked. The soldier nodded. "Who was it?"

"Eric Rood. An archer, my lord."

The commander nodded gravely, fixing his eyes on Matthieu. Matthieu held the naked sword before him, uncertainly. "A boy, and two women," the commander muttered to himself. He shouted at Matthieu, "Boy! Did you do this? Did you kill my soldier?"

"No, I think the white-haired lady done it!" shouted a voice at the back of the crowd. The soldiers laughed.

The commander continued serious. "Who sent you? Is this what Marshal Nesle sends against us now, boys and women? Or were you sent by that rat-bastard Beaumanoir? Fucking over-rated shit, he is."

Impulsively, Matthieu raised the sword over his head. *"Dieu et Saint-Denis!"* he shouted. Or rather tried to shout—he had not mastered the vampire voice yet, and his attempt at a battle-cry sounded pathetic. He swung the blade down awkwardly, the edge turning askew and dealing the commander nothing but a glancing blow and scratch down his cheek. The English commander touched his fingers to his face; his eyes darkening with anger as he saw the blood. "Bastard!" he shouted. He swung his fist and cuffed Matthieu's face.

"Cut their throats!" he shouted. "All of them—the two

bitches, and Master Pimply here too!"

What happened next happened so fast, I couldn't react for what seemed like an eternity—although it was probably no more than a few seconds. One of the soldiers crowding around Renata and Matthieu roughly pulled Matthieu off his feet, and pushed him onto the grass. The sword fell impotently from Matthieu's hands. Another of the English put a knee onto Matthieu's back and, grabbing his hair, pulled his head back as he drew a dagger from his belt. It was then that the blow hit him—the English soldier, that is. It was but a blur to my eyes, but the violent, rasping shriek that reached my ears left no doubt in my mind that it was Renata who had made the attack. The English soldier lay a dozen feet away, his body mangled. The other English soldiers still stood in a group, nervously, unable to understand what had just happened to their comrade, unable to understand that the slender black-haired woman who approached them again, with a curiously fierce light in her eyes, might pose a danger. It was just a moment's pause, before the melee began in earnest.

Renata attacked them—she attacked and attacked without respite. She tore into the English soldiers, pulling arms from shoulders, heads from necks, tearing faces and scalps. She was quickly covered in blood. The English panicked. They sprinted toward the horses, crying out that they were attacked by demons. Matthieu had retrieved his sword; he leapt onto one after another of the soldiers, cutting off their heads and watching the blood spurt from the carotid arteries with childish delight. Renata's way through the knot of soldiers became a mass of pulpy corpses. She fought her way to the commander. He swung the sword at her and missed. She leapt upon his face, tearing at his eyes. He beat at her back with the pommel of his sword as he screamed, "Demon!" Renata stilled his cry when her fangs cut into his throat and released a hot geyser of blood into her mouth. She drank her fill, and then stood, wiping her lips with the back of her hand.

She looked behind her, looked at the lifeless lumps strewn across the starlit field. None of the English were left alive. Matthieu idly thwacked with his sword against the dead, like a country boy hitting dandelions with a stick. He occasionally bent to suck the blood spurting from the dying men. I had fled from the fury of the vampire attack—no place for a small cat, surely—but now I crept back toward Renata as she regarded the devastation she had made. I heard a catch in her thoughtstreams, her newly-vampiric thoughtstreams, already beginning to hum with her unique, very un-vampirelike threnody. Vesta stood back, beyond the circle of the dead and dismembered English soldiers, her face still white and unblemished. The hulking shapes of the four vampire soldiers crept into view. Renata stood before them, bloodstained and panting, shredded flesh still stuck in her fingernails.

"Holy shit," muttered one of the vampire soldiers. They looked at the scene in silent disbelief.

Vesta walked forward, absently kicking at the corpses around her.

"A waste, slave," Vesta rasped at Renata. "Such a lack of skill. No finesse!" She bent and grabbed the head of one of the English, holding it before her angrily as she approached Renata. "What use is all this to us, now? You left not a single one to join our nation. All *spoiled!*" She heaved the head away from her in disgust.

"You!" Renata hissed. "What have you done to us? What have you made us do? What have you made us become?"

Vesta walked slowly forward. "I? I did nothing. *You* made the pledge, Lady Renata. And you are what you are now. Yes, you are killers. And, yes, we all must consume the blood." Vesta pushed her face close to Renata's. "But you are *my* killers! You and your son—you serve *me!*"

Renata lunged at her, slamming Vesta into the ground. Renata's blood-slicked hands sought Vesta's throat. Vesta struggled away. Renata lunged again, grabbing the snow-white hair and yanking out clumps.

"You—did—this!" Renata seethed, her hands ripping at Vesta's face and eyes. "I'll—kill—you!"

Vesta cried out sharply in pain. A long gash tore from her eyebrow to her chin, exposing her teeth and jaw. Renata fought on furiously still. She was berserk.

Vesta landed a blow with her elbow against Renata's head; Renata went reeling backwards against the grass. "Enough!" shouted Vesta. "How dare you raise your hand against your master! I command you! You serve me!"

"I do not serve you!"

"You serve me! Your son serves me!" Vesta stepped back, and called over her shoulder. "Matthieu! Who do you serve, Matthieu?"

Matthieu swung his sword fiercely in the air. "I serve you, Master Vesta."

With a rasping exhalation of breath, Renata sank to her knees. "No," she hissed.

Vesta leaned forward to Renata again, her hand massaging her cheek as the torn flesh healed itself. "You cannot escape this, Lady Renata. You are one of us. You do serve me." Vesta suddenly swung her foot in a vicious kick, catching Renata's jaw. Renata sprawled onto her back. "And if you do not like to serve your master, perhaps you would like to see how it goes to be a vampire, alone." Vesta summoned the vampire soldiers. "Get the horses. The French army is ahead of us. There will be battle. Perhaps a chance to win a greater prize for our nation than that pitiful slave there."

The soldiers untethered the horses of the dead English. Vesta chose a mount, and swung herself atop the animal. "Matthieu, come with me," Vesta said. "We go to find battle." Matthieu eagerly chose a horse—the biggest, blackest horse in the herd.

"Come find us, if you learn humility," Vesta said to Renata. "Don't think you can rebel from your master with impunity. What will you do? Go back to the Chantry of Beaumanoir? Will you stay in the dark there all your days, sucking blood from rats? Is that to be your realm, Renata de Rohan—that tiny, dark room in the chantry? Are you now the countess of the chantry? The countess of Beaumanoir Chantry? The Comtesse of Beaumanoir?" Vesta laughed spitefully.

"Leave me my son," Renata said.

Vesta shook her head. "No, he belongs to you no longer, Comtesse. He is mine. He is a powerful adept, did you know that? He could be great, as could you." She glowered. "But unlike you, he is obedient."

"He is my son," Renata said.

Vesta exhaled loudly in exasperation. "You will come back when you are ready, Comtesse. There is no one to help you. Try going back to Father Bertran, and see what he will do. Go back to Arcadius the Alchemist. No one can help you. You have only one course—to serve your master." She pulled her horse around. "You will come back to your master, Comtesse. You will come back and serve me." She galloped off. The hoofbeats of the horses bearing Matthieu and the vampire soldiers following her faded into the night.

Renata lay in the grass for several long minutes. Then she sat up, testing her face where Vesta's kick had struck it. It was bruised, but whole. I heard her thoughtstreams rumbling on; under the flatness of her vampire mind the accustomed human bassline played, as it still would six centuries hence in a small town in the North Carolina hills. The familiarity of it drew me out of hiding. I emerged from the behind tufts of torn and trampled grass, and trotted toward Renata. I sat openly, and looked at her. She looked back at me. "A cat," she hissed. "Perhaps you are demon also, cat?" She laughed bitterly to herself, and stood up. She looked about her in the silence of the devastated camp. The vampire soldiers had driven off the horses that they did not take to ride. In the starlight, the flattened grass over the field where Vesta, Matthieu and the soldiers had ridden shone bright, like so many streams of water. Renata began to walk in the direction into which they had disappeared. I watched her pull a sword from the ground as she passed, taking it with her as she walked into the grass trails left by the horses. I watched her briefly as she walked—and suddenly became conscious that another breakoff was taking me. I gazed at her receding figure, knowing that I would be back to follow her soon.

CHAPTER SEVENTEEN

I was in Denis's car again, his red Saab. My eyes refocused; I saw that we were driving—Denis, Renata and me. I remembered, then: it was the morning Lupe disappeared. Moorland had said she had gone to John Random's farm. We were going after her.

It was already after midday by the time we got out to the Random Farm. Neither Denis nor Renata had ever been there before, and Fulda's directions, which had sounded so simple, turned out to be a little incomplete. Denis had overshot the farm on the state highway, then backtracked, got lost on the unmarked local roads, and then puzzled various farm workers they had asked from the roadside about a place called Random. Mobile phone coverage was spotty, and as a general rule was least available when most needed. We eventually drove back to Forshay village, and started again. This time we found it, by dint of a closer attention to the directions, and by the lucky fortune of not overlooking a small wooden sign at an unpaved turn-off that read "Random Farm" with a small arrow. The tires on Denis's Saab crunched slowly down the eroded, rocky gravel road that led through several acres of dense and overgrown woods, before finally the terrain opened into cleared pasture. The road led to a packed-earth drive in front of a large but plain farmhouse, at least a century old. I could see that the house sat on a hilltop, under four massive oak trees. Beyond, down the slopes and reaching out into the distance, lay green fields—some serried with the patterns of cultivation, others spreading out in a solid bluish-green, looking cool under the cloudless sunny sky. Paul Moorland's police cruiser was pulled up in front of the house. But it was John Random himself who came out of the front door of the farmhouse.

"Hi, welcome!" he called. "We were almost giving up on you. Trouble finding the place?" He led Denis and Renata up the steps into the farmhouse. "Through here," he said, leading through a corridor of weathered planks and dark wallpaper. "We were out searching for Lupe's brother all morning. We were having some lunch before going out again."

Random led Renata and Denis into a wide kitchen, ringed with windows to the fields beyond. At a large circular table, under the pewter arms of a hanging light fixture, sat Paul Moorland and another man, a serious-looking Latino. Between them sat Lupe, her eye no longer swollen but now resplendent with a mottled purple bruise. None of the three was eating the food on the table before them; Moorland and the other man seemed to be talking in low voices to Lupe, who listened without answering. On the other side of the table, I noticed, sat Trace Cuthbert, having no trouble demolishing a ham sandwich.

Lupe broke into a broad smile when she saw Renata. She rushed from the table and flung her arms around Renata in a close embrace. "I was hoping you would come," she said. Renata patted her back gently for a moment, then led Lupe back to the table. I pawed at Lupe gently from the canvas bag, and mewed.

"Yes, and your friend Kikki has also come," Renata said.

John Random introduced everyone around the table.

The serious man sitting by Lupe was Steve Portillo, the foreman of the work crew that was harvesting the late strawberries and early tomatoes on the farm. Random brought sandwiches for Renata and Denis, then sat down as well. Paul Moorland spoke.

"Well," he said, "no sense having secrets here. Everyone knows what's going on. Miss Hernandez-Vega is cooperating. We'd like her to go back to Forshay while we look for her brother, but she refuses to go." Moorland shot a glance at Lupe, who looked back stubbornly. Moorland absently stroked his hand over his mustache. "Well, if that's so, I ain't going to make her go. But the boy seems to have run off. No sign of him. Or the drugs."

"I gave everything to Rafael this morning," Lupe interjected.

"Yes, young lady, I know you did," Moorland said soothingly. "We just don't know where they are *now*. And there's no car available that Miss Hernandez's brother could have driven—Mr. Portillo's car was stolen yesterday, we think, by the same gang working for Alejo Ramirez who's been causing all the trouble."

"I know it was them," Steve Portillo said, in blunt, unaccented English.

"He could have hitched," Trace Cuthbert put in. "Hell, if he caught a ride he could be in Georgia by now."

"Well, first things first," Moorland said. "As Mr. Cuthbert says, there's a chance that Miss Hernandez's brother's hitchhiked away from here. But given the light traffic in the area, that's not so likely. And without a car at his disposal to drive, there's still a good possibility that Rafael hasn't left, but is still somewhere nearby. And could be hurt, or in danger." Moorland looked around the table. "No question. We keep searching. Maybe we even call in more help."

"We've already pulled the whole crew out of the field to help," Random said. "And the crew's been around the property all day, anyway. If he's still here, I don't understand why we haven't found him already."

"Just the same," Moorland said. "I've already put a call into the chief at Lincolnton. They're sending some men. They should be here shortly." Moorland stood. "OK, let's get back out there and keep searching." He squinted at Lupe. "Not you, young lady. You stay here with me and wait for the others. And the rest of you, if you see someone who doesn't belong here, don't be heroic. You have the number," he said, holding up his mobile phone. "Back away, and call me."

John Random caught Renata by the elbow as the group was moving out of the kitchen. "Let's walk out this way," he said, steering her from the kitchen through another set of corridors. "I was hoping you'd come out and visit, though I wasn't expecting quite these circumstances. But, since you're here, I thought that you might just like to take a peek at the library Margaret told you about." He led her to a wing at the back of the house, clearly a newer add-on to the older structure. A set of double doors opened, and Renata caught her breath at the sight—an enormous room, two stories high, lined with bookshelves crammed with volumes. Light streamed in through a row of high arched windows above the bookshelves.

"Unbelievable," Renata whispered.

"Yeah," Random said. "I wasn't kidding when I said I had run out of space in my old apartment." Renata and he took a few steps into the library, Renata taking a volume or two off the shelves and turning them experimentally in her hands before reshelving them. She looked at the books as if they were objects of reverence.

Random glanced at her left hand as she held a book, and motioned to the white star ring she wore. "Your ring," he said. "I saw it the night of the movie party, remember?" he said. "I meant to ask you about it. I mean, why you wear it."

Renata looked at him steadily. "It *is* curious, isn't it?"

she said. "Not really the type of thing a person actually wears. It's not very practical." Renata held the ring up, twisting the large and unwieldy bezel around her finger once. She smiled back up to John Random. "I really don't know *why* I wear it. I guess I'm like you, John. I just love the past."

Random looked back at her for a moment, weighing her words, wondering whether there was something more behind them. I heard his mind put the thought away from him, with some little effort. He smiled at her. "Well, it's a beautiful ring, anyway," he said. "I guess we should head back to the others. Maybe once we take care of the current emergency, I can tempt you back out to spend some time here? If I've whetted your appetite?" He smiled on intently, his grin boyish despite the bristly beard. "Maybe I could you show you my LP collection too. Original vinyl—lots of cool rock classics. I could start my own oldies station."

Renata smiled back gently. "I'd like that," she said. Random pulled the doors to the library shut, leading Renata toward another door to the back of the house where the group was splitting up for the search. But I heard the sadness in Renata's thoughtstreams as she turned away from the library. All those books, all that history. The friendly invitation from the interesting John Random. But she could never come back here. Her time as a human was almost up.

The sun was now slanting low over the trees; evening was coming on fast, and we had still not found Rafael. I was still swinging from the canvas bag Renata carried under her arm. Trace Cuthbert was walking ahead, switching at the long grass at the verge of the fields with a stick; Steve Portillo followed resolutely behind Renata. Denis and John Random had been sent a different direction. Chief Moorland had given each of the teams one of the village police department's prized walkie-talkie sets, and more out of boredom and frustration than any real need Trace paused frequently to report their lack of progress. "Still no sign," he transmitted, over and over. The blarings of the radio static, too loud in the early summer fields, seemed to underscore the hopelessness of their search.

"We've been out here for hours," Trace said. "We should wrap it up. He ain't here."

Steve Portillo demurred. "We should finish checking this section, like the Chief asked us to."

"We've already been over there, man," Trace complained. "Back and forth, all afternoon, over the same ground."

Portillo smiled indulgently. "Yes, back and forth, each time ten paces further west," he said. "That's how you make a thorough search."

"Jesus," Trace muttered, swatting his workboot with the stick. "Well, we should bring Renata back. She shouldn't be out in the sun all day anyway, in her condition."

Portillo looked at Renata quizzically. "Are you sick, Miss?" he asked, appraising her overcoat, scarf and sunglasses.

Renata shook her head. "No, I'm fine. I just have to be careful about sunlight. Like Trace said." Trace glanced back at her for a moment, then turned and continued walking the pattern across the darkening green field. I noticed Renata's voice was becoming distinctly raspy; I wondered if the others noticed it.

"Well, the sun will take care of itself, soon enough," Portillo said. "It gets dark very quickly here once the sun sets."

Renata stopped suddenly; she stared at the ground for a moment, her hand at her forehead. Portillo stepped up beside her, concerned. "Are you sure you're all right,

Miss?"

Ignoring him, Renata called ahead to Cuthbert. "Trace! Trace, wait." She jogged up the few paces to reach him. "This morning, you picked up Lupe, and gave her a ride out here?"

"Yeah," Trace said, "I was coming out anyway. The College has a sustainability initiative, they call it, and I was truckin' out a load of compost and clippings and such…"

"OK, OK," Renata interrupted, "but when? I mean, was it still dark out?"

Trace scratched his cheek with a thumb. "Nah, I don't think so," he said. "No, definitely, sun was already up. It was real early, but light enough so I could see her on the roadside. It was light enough."

Renata turned quickly back to Portillo. "Mr. Portillo, where's the darkest place on the farm? I mean, if you wanted to keep something in real darkness, even during the daytime—is there a place you could think of?"

"Sure," Portillo said. "Probably the stone barn, back up near the house." He stopped and pointed back up the house at a collection of low, disused outbuildings that ranged down the slope from the farmhouse until they were tangled in the scrub of the woods. "They don't use those buildings, since they never ran electricity out there. Probably just a bunch of old tools stored in there. But the old stone barn—that one is half underground. They used it for cold storage before refrigeration. It seals up tight, with the doors closed. A natural spring runs under it. Very cool inside. Very dark."

Renata turned and began hurrying back up the sloping field toward the outbuildings. "Come on, we need to look in there," she said.

Portillo hung back. "But Miss," he said, "Mr. Random already looked in there. It's an obvious place to hide. It's probably the first place he looked, but he didn't find anything in the stone barn."

Because they weren't looking for Mr. Random, Renata's

thoughtstreams said. "I know," she said to Portillo. "But let's look again."

Trace Cuthbert didn't need a second invitation. He spun back, and began to stride ahead toward the buildings across the field. He punched the button on the walkie-talkie. "Still no sign," he transmitted. "Going to check the stone barn behind the house."

The walkie-talkie responded with a blast of static. "Say again?" Moorland's voice asked. Trace ignored it, smiling as he walked. Portillo followed along.

The stone barn was easy to overlook. Swathed in vines and clumps of brushy saplings, it almost disappeared into the undergrowth. As the shadows of the late afternoon deepened at the verges of the woods, the stone walls behind the vines and underbrush only became less distinct. Trace Cuthbert located a faint path that led to the entrance, and he happily swung his stick a few times at the vines by one side of the double doors. Steve Portillo, quietly following behind, gently pushed the other door; unencumbered by vines, it swung open easily.

"Entering the stone barn," Trace transmitted on the walkie-talkie.

"You know, Mr. Cuthbert," Portillo said, "it may be better not to use the walkie-talkie right now. If Rafael's in here, the radio noise may frighten him."

"Oh, right," Trace said. He tucked the walkie-talkie into his belt and pushed past Portillo into the interior. "Damn, it sure enough is dark in here," he said. "Can't see anything." From my perch in Renata's bag, I could hear Trace stealthily feeling his way forward in the dark. There was a crash, a clanging sound of iron tools—and, presumably, Trace—hitting a stone floor. "Fuck!" he shouted. "Goddamn it!" He backed out, holding his kneecap with a hand. "Look, go see if there's a flashlight in one of these other sheds," he said to Portillo. "Can't see worth a damn in there, it's so dark."

Portillo silently departed, shooting a glance at Trace

that I wouldn't have described as admiring. Trace found a spot to sit on a rock, and worked his sore knee. He did not notice Renata entering the stone barn, removing her scarf and sunglasses. I slipped myself out of the canvas bag and into the barn ahead of her. The humans weren't exactly covering themselves with glory on this part of the escapade; I thought that maybe a cat's eyesight might be a help in the dark interior.

And it did help—my eyes glowed green and luminescent as I leaped over piles of ancient, rusted farm implements, heaped in disarray across the floor and by the stone walls of the barn. I heard a dripping of water from the other end of the barn. There was a clear spot there, where the spring Portillo had mentioned ran through a fissure in the bedrock. On the far end of the stone barn the builders had incorporated it into the wall itself. The water trickled through the wall, pooled in a small basin, and flowed away in a runnel in the stone floor into the darkness. The running spring cooled the air inside the barn—natural refrigeration. Clever, these humans.

Renata was picking her way uncertainly behind me. The thanadoxicil was thinned, almost gone—she would be a full vampire again very soon. Her eyes were strained from the pressure of sunlight all day, even behind the dark glasses; they didn't yet give her clear vision in the dark. I saw her guiding her way by running her hands over the upended plow bottoms and barrows and other objects strewn across the barn floor, slowly moving toward the interior of the barn. Through the sound of the dripping water, echoing it, came the sound of low laughter. Even with my cat's eyes, I had to strain to see. But they were there. They knew they had a good hiding place—even someone who could see in the dark wouldn't see them until he was right on top of them.

"Hey, Renata," the voice hissed.

"Hey, babe."

"What took you so long?"

"Yeah, we been waitin', like, all day."

"Rude, man."

"Real rude."

"You get lost, or something?"

The vampire assassins thought this was extremely funny; they emitted a hissing gale of snickering. I crept forward until I could see the clear space at the far side of the barn. Rafael was seated on the stone floor in front of the assassins. There was the small duffel bag on the floor in front of him—presumably containing a couple thousand dollars of drugs this time, rather than a hundred and twenty-seven dollars in ones and fives. My eyes picked out the curve of a long knifeblade held against Rafael's neck, the blade dimpling the flesh. But, I saw, the knife wasn't held by Chuck. Instead, one of Alejo's men was there with them, squatting on the floor and holding the knife on Rafael. Chuck was behind him, his arm wrapped around the thug's shoulder—was he holding a knife on Alejo's man as well? Or did he just have him in an armlock? I couldn't tell, but Alejo's man seemed very uncomfortable.

Alejo's man bent his head toward Chuck over his shoulder. "See? Now someone's found us," he said in rapid Spanish. "I told you it was stupid to hide. We could have been far away by now."

"Shut up," Harrison said. "We do it our way. We wait until night."

"Why do we even need the boy?" the thug complained. "Just leave him here. Let's go."

"Shut up," Harrison said.

"Stupid," Alejo's man muttered.

"You watch who you call stupid, man," Chuck said. He jerked the thug's shoulder. Alejo's man emitted a quick yelp of pain.

Harrison stood up, and flashed Renata a broad smile. "Better late than never, Comtesse," he said. "Looks like we're all here now." Harrison motioned to Chuck. Slowly, Chuck, the Alejo thug and Rafael all got uncertainly to their feet, the two humans clearly blind in the black darkness. The thug's knife was still pressed hard against Rafael's throat. "Didn't think it would take you so long to figure out that we'd be in the *dark* place, though," Harrison said. "It's bright sunshine all day today, Comtesse. We figured you'd have found us hours ago."

Renata took a step closer to the group. "What do you want with him?" she said, her voice rasping into the sibilance of a full vampire voice. I glanced back at her; her eyes glinted with the hard and sharp flecking of vampire eyes. Renata the vampire was back, I saw. Renata the human—gone.

"I'm explaining that," Harrison said.

"You've got the drugs," she said. "Now let him go. Alejo's got more than his money back."

Harrison smiled broadly again. He looked at Chuck and laughed. "Yeah, Alejo. I forgot Alejo, man."

Chuck laughed. He jammed the arm of Alejo's man again, for good measure. The thug grunted, confused. He kept the knifeblade steady on Rafael.

"So, how about this, Comtesse," Harrison said. "How about, we let the kid go—give him back. We give back the drugs too, man. And then you give the drugs back to the doctors. Maybe the police will drop the charges on the sister, yeah?"

Alejo's man twisted his head back again with urgency. "What you talking about?" he demanded. His Spanish was slurring in his anxiety. "We already told Alejo we had the drugs. Alejo will *kill* us if we don't bring them!"

"Shut up," Chuck said.

Renata took another step closer—she was almost within reach of Rafael. I was worried—I knew that, vampire though she was, she must have been weakened by coming off the thanadoxicil. I didn't like her creeping toward Rafael, as if she were going to make a grab for him, as if she were going to challenge the vampire assassins now in the pitch darkness. She was in no condition to be doing this. There had to be another way than letting her fight the vampires, I thought.

"So is it a deal, Renata?" Harrison asked.

Renata slowly shook her head, her glittering eyes seeming to hold stationary as she did so. "I don't hear a deal," she said. "I get Rafael and the drugs back. And you get—what?"

Harrison smiled again. "Thought that would be obvious, Comtesse," he said smugly. "We get you. And the sister. This one," he said, nudging Rafael with impatience, "he's the wrong one."

There was a scratching behind us across the barn as the door was pulled open again. Two unsteady spikes of light from flashlights poked into the darkness, picking out the clutter of ironwork around the floor. "Renata!" Trace Cuthbert called.

Renata shot forward and wrenched the knife away from Rafael's throat. Rafael cried out in alarm, and stumbled onto one knee in the dark.

"Fuck!" shouted Chuck. He pushed Alejo's man forward toward Renata in the dark. "No, her, goddamn it! Get *her!*"

Alejo's man swung the knife blindly, lurching forward and groping with his arms in front of him. A straight-arm blow caught Renata in the side and threw her off balance, her feet slipping on the damp stones beneath her as she fell. Alejo's man had found her now, with his free hand; he gripped her hair with that hand as the other raised the knife above his head.

The flashlight beam caught the thug in the face. He winced at the light. "Christ! No!" shouted Trace Cuthbert, shoving forward toward Alejo's man as the knife arced downward into the dark. The flashlight dropped and rolled, its light beam now shining uselessly at the wall. I heard the sounds of pain and struggle from Trace and Alejo's man. Renata was still on the floor. I couldn't leave it like this. I couldn't just stand aside. I focused my mind, desperately struggling to formulate a plan.

Alejo's man struggled to his feet, the knifehandle slippery and hot and wet. Panting heavily, he pushed aside the inert Trace Cuthbert, his free hand again feeling along the floor, looking for Renata,

Then suddenly, from the other corner of the dark barn, a new sound. A sound that hadn't been there before. Breathing—no, louder than breathing, heavier. The catch of a deep growl, closely suppressed, then a throaty rumble, just for a moment. A heavy, deliberate footfall, quiet and padded, but palpable. There was something out there in the dark. Something big.

They felt the presence of the massive predator before they could see anything of it. It was the eyes that they first saw—the shock of those eyes stopped the assassins, and made Alejo's man drop the knife. They were a cat's eyes, to be sure, but huge—green discs the size of hubcaps, fixed on Alejo's thug for the infinitesimal moment before the snarl of attack rang out against the stone walls of the barn. Alejo's man felt the enormous weight of the animal crush him to the stone floor, felt the massive claw enter at his sternum and tear straight down through his pelvis. He felt the bloodrush and the slide of his entrails from his torn abdomen for a moment, before his consciousness blackened as dark as the interior of the barn and his ears rang with his own screaming, and he was dead.

The growling predator panicked the assassins.

"Go, man, *go!*" Harrison shouted.

"But it might be still light out," Chuck shouted.

"Fuck it! It's dark enough! Just *go!*" The vampire assassins flashed out of the barn, their tread touching lightly over the jumble of twisted iron, and through the doors. They were a black breeze brushing past Steve Portillo near the doorway.

"Mr. Cuthbert!" Portillo shouted, cycling his flashlight beam into the barn wildly. His flashlight beam fell on Trace's face. "Oh, God!" Portillo wailed.

Rafael had run out of the barn, clashing through the jumble of farm tools toward the source of Portillo's flashlight. "It was an animal!" he panted wildly. "It was a monster!"

Portillo grabbed the boy, steadying him, while his flashlight picked out the body of Alejo's man, slashed from throat to crotch, a mass of bloody organs slumped to the side of the body untidily. "Where's Miss Beaumanoir?" Portillo demanded. He swept the darkness with his flashlight again. She was not to be seen. "I have to get you back," Portillo said, fighting for coherence, "I have to call an ambulance for Mr. Cuthbert." He gathered the boy under his arm, and flashed the beam of his flashlight into the darkness of the barn once more. The beam caught only the eyes of a small, tiger-striped kitten, perched atop a piece of scrap iron along the stone wall of the barn. Portillo took Rafael and they hurried back toward the farmhouse.

I would amend that next-to-last sentence, by saying that it was a small, *tired,* tiger-striped kitten who looked back into Portillo's flashlight. I think you have already seen that timesliding has uses far beyond prosaic tasks like finding Denis's car keys. Not that that wasn't important. But just as I can ride the creases in the timeflows and translate myself to other places and times and back again, as long as I have a proper timeguide I can also translate another *form* of myself back and forward from other places and times. I can even translate other things, other creatures, back and forward as well. It is the information that moves, you see, the information that supervenes the constraints of timespace—oh, it's hard to explain. And dangerous. And tiring—I can't do it often. I think you'll agree, though, that this had been as good a time as any to make a timeslide, even if in another time dimension I was already timesliding in medieval Brittany. But, if I use myself as my own timeguide, there's less risk, and following the crease through time is much, much easier—

even to the extent of accessing the information of my own evolutionary antecedents, millions of years in the past. Besides, even though I'm a pragmatist, I do try to do things with a little style, a little thematic consistency. After all, I am a cat—so why not translate back in the form of another cat? For example, in the form of a saber-toothed cat from the late Pleistocene, a *smilodon populator* maybe—a big sucker, too, over a thousand pounds. Of course, the change to that form and back seems, to the time-constant observer, to have been instantaneous—but remember, concepts of sequence and simultaneity really aren't that helpful to understand timesliding. Well, I guess it is hard to explain. Maybe I should just leave it there. Let's just say, as I may have mentioned before, that I am a very special cat.

But a tired one now, nonetheless. I knew that I would have to get up soon, and locate Renata, and Rafael, and Lupe—my entanglements with humans seemed to be multiplying daily. But for now, I needed to catch my breath after the timeslide, so I sat for a quiet moment, licking the blood of Alejo's man off my tidy, kitten paws.

I heard a groan from the floor of the barn, and looked down. Trace Cuthbert was still alive. Don't think me callous, but I have lived a long time, and even without the flashlight I had seen where Alejo's man had thrust his knife. An abdominal wound—it would be fatal, that was certain. Portillo could summon the ambulance, but Trace Cuthbert was going to die. I did now regret, however, so bluntly labeling Trace as a Bully—I thought again and again at how he had pushed toward Renata as the knife descended. He must have known, even in that flash of light, even in that brief moment, the risk he took. It was not the act of a selfish, stupid Bully, but that of a human of a greater depth and complexity than I had given him credit for. I paused from washing my paw, and looked down sadly at Trace. The wound was painful, I could tell that from his thoughtstreams, and I felt badly about that.

Trace didn't deserve to die so nastily.

And then something marvelous happened, something I never expected to see a second time, much less so soon after having seen in for the first time in the dark chantry in my timeslide. Vampire reproduction, once again—or maybe better described as vampire generation, although I must admit that the process does look oddly erotic. At all events, I could watch the process unfold again, this time as a pure scientist.

As I looked at Trace's prone body, I saw a dark shape silently emerge from the tangle of iron by the far side of the stone barn, and swiftly creep across the floor to where Trace lay on his belly, the blood pooling on the stones beneath him. The shape noticed me watching, and with a toss of raven-colored hair my cat's eyes could make out the white face of Renata, eyes glowing now in full vampirism. She must have been hiding under the welter of tools and iron waste in the barn. She looked away from me and back down at Trace. With a heave, she rolled his body onto its back. Trace was still barely conscious. She shook him, to get his attention. His eyes, growing dull, struggled to focus on her.

"Trace," Renata hissed. "I have to thank you. You did not need to do what you did, but I must thank you."

He gazed at her absently, his expression unchanging.

Renata spoke again. "I can give you another life," she hissed. "If you want it. It is the only thanks I can give." She gripped his face between her two hands. "I can give you another life," she hissed. "But you must pledge."

Trace was slipping away. Renata shook his face with her hands, firmly. "You must pledge," Renata hissed, insistently. "You must pledge!"

He came back for a moment; his eyes found hers. "Renata," he whispered. He mustered a weak smile. "Yes, Renata. Yes."

It was all the response she needed. Renata pulled off the overcoat, and then tore away the sleeve of her blouse.

Extending her gleaming white fangs, she drove them deeply into her own forearm. Black, viscous vampire blood welled in the punctures; a black drop ran down her white skin. She raised her bleeding forearm over Trace's face and let the drops of blood drip into each of his eyes, his nostrils, and then his mouth. *"Seek the darkness,"* Renata hissed. *"Feed upon the unjust. Protect the nation."* She watched carefully as the blood dripped across his lips and tongue—watching for the movement of the palatal reflex in Trace's mouth—the moment she saw him swallow, she forced his body against the ground, her thighs straddling his hips and her elbows pinning his shoulders, as she pressed the heels of her hands against Trace's nose and mouth, smothering the last breath out of his body until, as his eyes finally rolled upward, dull, obtunded, she released her hands and clamped her mouth over his, exhaling hard into his lungs as the last breath of his life became her breath, a breath that brought a death that was also life. Trace's body convulsed and shook as Renata held it down. And then, as quickly as the convulsions began, they stopped, and Trace opened his eyes again. Opened eyes glittering as hard and crystalline as any vampire who had ever lived—or rather, who had ever been given the life of death.

"Welcome," Renata hissed. She released him and stood. She looked toward the doorway to the barn, still ajar. The light had faded completely now; it was full night. I could see a scattering of stars against the night sky beyond the leaves of the woods. She glanced at me, then back at Trace. "You can't stay here," she said to Trace. "Go to my house, on the campus. Or the woods on the ridge above my house. Go either place, and wait for me." She looked at me again. "We have some other business tonight."

With a silent rush, they were both gone—vampires flying through the night. I heard voices approaching the stone barn along the pathway from John Random's farmhouse, and soon could see what must have been a dozen flashlights swerving their way along the path, and two white-coated paramedics wrestling a stretcher over the uneven ground. I gave my paw one last swipe of my tongue—it would have to do. I looked back down at the floor of the stone barn—all that fighting, all that drama, and all there is to show for it was a lot of blood, a dead thug, and a duffel full of stolen drugs. Who knows how Paul Moorland would try to explain the disappearance of both Renata and Trace Cuthbert. They'll come up with some kind of explanation, I thought, as I slipped out the barn door ahead of the approaching party; they'll have to. But the true history is something they surely could not even imagine.

CHAPTER EIGHTEEN

But as I melted into the shadows along the darkened path and the group of people coming toward the stone barn slipped past, a worry took hold, a worry that quickly grew into a certain dread. Because as the party passed by me I searched among the faces there—Chief Moorland was in the group, as was John Random, and Steve Portillo, and the EMT's and a handful of other workers from Portillo's crew, even Denis Pearson trailed along behind. But not Lupe—she was not among them. I didn't like the idea that she seemed to have been left behind in the house, not with the Council's assassins on the loose. I skittered back onto the path after the group had passed by, and began to sprint back up the slope toward the farmhouse.

I saw red lights flashing from the ambulance while I was still a distance from the house. When I got to the turnabout on the dirt driveway, I saw that the paramedics had left the ambulance running. The engine vibrated, and snaps of radio traffic from the cab broke the steady buzz of evening insects. The headlights shone their beams across the grassy verge to the steps up to the farmhouse door. As I came down the end of the path, I saw a movement through the brightness of the headlight beams—two figures, walking briskly away from the house. They quickly passed down the steps and behind the idling ambulance. I raced to catch up.

As I got past the ambulance, I stopped—I could see the figures walking toward a car that was parked haphazardly across the driveway, a new white Mercedes CLS coupe that had not been there before. I could see that one of the figures was Lupe, walking uncertainly and glancing back under her ballcap across at the farmhouse, strangely illuminated in the dark by the headlights and the red strobes of the ambulance. The other figure was taller, a well-dressed woman in a businesslike straight skirt and heels. She placed a firm but friendly hand on Lupe's shoulder and moved her toward the car. I scampered silently through the shadows across the driveway until I was only a few feet away from the car. The tall woman turned as she opened the passenger door for Lupe, and her hair, pinned in a severe up-swept style, caught the reflected light of the ambulance headlights. The hair was white—sleek but brilliantly, shockingly white. I felt a tightness in my stomach as I looked from the hairstyle toward the woman's face, and saw the white skin of the exquisite features, and the round dark glasses over the eyes. Dark glasses at night...there could be no question.

"Are you sure we should just leave?" Lupe asked uncertainly.

"Of course," the woman replied brusquely. "In fact, it is imperative that I take responsibility for you right away. The Trustees of Estado Piñela have retained me for exactly that purpose."

"So, are you some kind of a lawyer?"

"Yes, of course I'm a lawyer," the woman said, "and a lawyer is exactly what you need right now, if I'm not mistaken."

Lupe still hung back from the car, hesitating. "But shouldn't we tell Mr. Random? Or at least Chief Moorland?" She looked back toward the dark copse of trees where the others had gone toward the barn. "I don't think I should leave without telling the policeman."

The tall woman gave a sharp, contemptuous laugh. "I don't think that Forshay College has helped the situation by involving the local constabulary," she said. "I think I will have my hands quite full enough fixing all the damage Chief Moorland has already been done to our situation." She looked at Lupe sharply, and slipped off the dark glasses. "Now, please. Get in the car," the woman commanded Lupe. "We're already wasting valuable time."

Lupe relented, and meekly got into the car. Faced with those hard, cutting eyes, and that hard, cutting laugh, who could have resisted? I had to say that Vesta Letalia made a very plausible lawyer.

I heard a shout behind me as the car doors slammed, and the powerful Mercedes engine came to life. "Hey!" Denis shouted, running up the path toward the drive. He emerged into the beams of the ambulance headlights as the Merc sped away from the farmhouse and into the wooded track back toward the main road. "Dammit!" Denis swore, his breath heaving as he held up from his run. He dashed toward the other side of the turnaround where his red Saab was parked, loping awkwardly as his hand tried to fish his keys out of his hip pocket. I sprang from the shadows and ran in front of him toward his car—I admit, it almost seemed like my car now—and hopped right in when he swung the driver's door open.

"You again!" Denis exclaimed when he saw me. "Shoo! Scram!" I jumped into the back seat where he couldn't get me. I knew he wouldn't waste time trying to find me. Denis quickly had the Saab noisily hurtling down the drive through the black woods, the red taillights of the Mercedes still visible intermittently through the dark leaves. We got to the main road and turned, following the white car, doing our best to keep up. The Mercedes was leading us back to Forshay. I tried to focus on Denis's thoughtstreams, but they were haphazard, excited, confused—I could only read that Denis knew something was very, very wrong about Lupe being driven off like that. Chief Moorland would have said something about it if Lupe were supposed to be picked up. No time to call for the others—if he waited, he would lose the car for sure. As it was, the white Mercedes was easily outpacing Denis on the straight stretches of road through the dark farmland; it was only when the road made an unexpected bend or a hairpin turn that the Mercedes was forced to slow and downshift, and Denis could make up the distance. The red taillights would glow, and we would catch up just enough so the Saab's headlights would illuminate the South Carolina plates on the back of the Mercedes, before the CLS would accelerate again and vanish before us with a roar.

The white Mercedes had seemed to have disappeared for good as Denis slowed and steered his car onto the Main Street of Forshay. He drove the Saab carefully down one side of the Green, and then carefully back up the other, scanning the scattering of cars still parked along the street. The college buildings and storefronts were dark, the quads empty. He didn't see it. "Damn," Denis muttered. "Must have lost them." He turned his car around to make another circuit. As he pulled the Saab around, the sweep of the headlights caught a flash of white in the distance. Denis stopped and backed up, putting the beams on high. Like spotlights the headlights illuminated the Mercedes, parked crookedly up at the end of Ridge Street just past Renata's house. The white car looked abandoned, the passenger door open. Denis turned the Saab and gunned it up Ridge Street. He pulled up with a jerk behind the Mercedes.

"Lupe!" he shouted as he launched out of his car. "Lupe!"

No answer. I scampered out of the Saab and nosed into the Mercedes. In the warm night air a subtle whiff of death, masked by Vesta's sharp, expensive perfume, seeped from the upholstery.

Denis had his mobile phone out; he had gotten Fulda on the line. "No, Lupe's gone again," he said. "Someone grabbed her into a car and drove back to Forshay, and now she's gone again!" He listened and then interrupted. "Call Moorland and tell him where I am—on Ridge Street, by Renata's house. No, I don't have his number…no, I'm going to see if I can find Lupe before they get too far." The phone beeped off, and Denis ran up the street.

But Ridge Street is a dead end—the row of Visiting Faculty houses and cracked asphalt peters out in the woodland that marches from the College campus right up the shoulder of Forshay Mountain. I knew it well; it was a pleasant place for a small cat to roam, full of tasty deermice and birds. But it was not a welcome prospect for Denis. The thicket of nighttime woods, beyond the reach of the streetlights on Main Street, stopped him in his run, and he stood momentarily before the woods, confused and undecided. He looked around him, clearly wondering which way to start searching. He walked back from the woods, and found himself in front of Renata's house. It seemed to offer itself as a place to start—he rapped on the door loudly. "Lupe!" Rapping again. "Lupe!"

Denis pulled the door open and entered the darkened house. "Lupe!" he called again.

From the darkness inside the house, Denis heard a response—a voice he knew, but with a strange, disembodied quality. "Hello?" he called, more softly. "Renata? Is that you?" I crept into the house after Denis. I didn't recall if Denis had ever seen Renata with the thanadoxicil fully, unequivocally worn off. This situation might be delicate.

In the dark house, I could barely make her out. She moved closer to Denis, her face looking whiter than ever in the dim light of the stars and the distant streetlights. "Denis? What are you doing here?" Denis's thoughtstreams jumped at the strange rasping of Renata's voice, but I could tell that he was forcibly thrusting his trepidation aside.

"Lupe," he said. "She got into a car with some stranger at Random Farm, and they drove back here. Has she been here?" Denis looked around the dark room. "Where's the light switch?"

Renata reached out to him, took his hand. "No, no lights," she said. "My eyes are sore."

I felt a leap in Denis's thoughtstreams—he was suddenly hyper-alert. Was it her touch? Was it alarm? Fear? I jumped up onto the side table where Renata puts her mail and her car keys so I could get a better view. I saw Renata slowly drawing Denis closer to her—they looked like nothing so much as two lovers, in the slow ballet of a first kiss. But then, I caught sight of Renata's eyes. They were not a lover's eyes. I focused my mind on hers; I needed to hear her thoughtstreams, what she was thinking and feeling. Was this another sexual rush from the thanadoxicil, the crash as the drug left her body like that night with Trace Cuthbert? Or was this something else? I listened to her mind. I did not hear any thrum of desire, of lust. I heard a pang echo in her mind, however. But it was a pang of hunger. Renata was a full vampire, and she was ravenously hungry. I watched, alarmed, as she drew Denis closer.

"Renata," Denis said softly. "Renata, look, we really need to find Lupe," he said. "I think she's in real trouble." He put his hand on her cheek and looked into her gleaming, flinty eyes. "Come on," Denis said. "We'll find her together."

Renata regarded Denis for several long seconds, her face inches from his. I seemed to see subtle movement in her jaw, as if she were working her teeth, nervously. They stood so close, it would take just the briefest of movements for her fangs to extend, for her to sink them into his coffee-colored neck, and he would be done. The moment ached in its tension; in my imagination I could envision it happening so clearly, so shockingly, that I found myself beseeching Renata's mind, thrusting my thoughtstreams into hers. *No!* I pleaded in her thoughts, *Not Denis! Do not do this! Not him!*

Suddenly, I saw her turn and look squarely at me. I heard her thoughtstreams shift, changing from the rumble and tug of her hunger, to an overpowering thought of Lupe. She stared at me, unblinking glittering eyes boring into my gleaming green cat's eyes through the dark room, staring as only a vampire can stare.

Where is Lupe? she asked me in my mind.

This time, I was not taken aback—ever since the trip to Charleston, I had believed that Renata had somehow developed my talent of speaking through thoughtstreams. The same talent that the Doctor had developed. Perhaps it was another effect of the thanadoxicil withdrawal. Or perhaps, indeed, she had learned it from me—who knew? That was a question for later, when I could attend to proper scientific inquiry; it would have to wait for now.

Vesta Letalia has taken her, I replied. *I don't know where. She drove Lupe here in a car, the white car that is outside your house.*

Renata dropped Denis's hand and rushed to the door, looking out at the abandoned white Mercedes.

The Council has come for me, her thoughtstreams said. *They have taken Lupe hostage because they want me. They want to punish me.*

No, I said in reply, *they want you both. They think that you or Lupe can lead them to something called the Sable. Or that you or Lupe actually is the Sable.* I paused for a moment, waiting for a reaction. There was none. *Do you know what the Sable is? Do you know what they're looking for?*

Renata didn't answer. She walked out onto Ridge Street and stood, white-faced and raven-haired under the summer starlight. Denis and I walked out after her. We stood silently in the street for several minutes.

The sound came into both of our minds at the same time, a scream, but not vocalized—a peal of fear and shock injected into both our thoughtstreams that we knew immediately must have come from Lupe's mind. She was nearby. Renata looked up the sloping woods of the mountain. Her eyes glanced back at me; they told me that Lupe was up there somewhere.

"The ridge," Renata rasped to Denis. "I think they took Lupe up the ridge onto the mountain."

Denis looked up uncertainly at the impenetrable black woods. "Up there?" he said. "How are we going to be able to find her up there?"

"We'll find her," Renata said. Renata's eyes flashed toward me momentarily. *I can't wait,* she signaled into my mind. She glanced back at Denis again and, in a single sudden motion Renata's cold lips pressed onto Denis's mouth in a brief, wide-eyed kiss (her fangs thoughtfully tucked aside, of course) and then she released him, leaving him speechless and dazed as Renata silently disappeared into the black forest.

Denis found himself alone with a cat on Ridge Street. He was sweating in the cool night, his skin tickling with a fear he had not noticed before. "She just wasn't herself," he muttered absently, as he pulled out his mobile to call Fulda again. I saw him smile in spite of himself as he dialed.

I didn't stay to listen to the call—I was already on my way into the woods to follow Renata, trotting through the gaps in the underbrush and around the knotty knees of tree roots, toward my familiar paths up the ridge. I knew some short cuts—I needed to get ahead of her, get a little head start. I'd then have a chance to slip back in time again. Because I was still painfully aware that my timeslide to medieval Brittany had not yet yielded the answers we most needed. I wanted to get back there again. Besides, my knowledge of Forshay Mountain allowed me to make some educated guesses about where the vampires were, and where they were going. There were a couple places I could think of up on the mountain, a couple of likely spots—I thought I knew where we were all headed.

I was blinking again—it took my eyes a few moments to recognize that I was back in Brittany. My mind shook off the fuzziness of returning from the breakoff, and I found myself still following Renata through the nighttime fields, the sword she had taken from the dead English soldiers dragging on the grass.

Renata walked for the rest of the night, grimly following the trails left by the horses ridden by Vesta, Matthieu and the vampire soldiers, across the nighttime fields, through forests, moving further and further away from Josselin. I trotted behind as Renata moved along, close enough for me to keep tabs on the dull flow of her thoughtstreams, but enough out of sight that she need not concern herself with a dubious cat following her—who could, for all she knew, have indeed been a demon. We hid as the day broke—even without Vesta's explanation during the night Renata's new instincts as a vampire told her that daylight was to be avoided at all costs. She plunged deep into the foliage of forest undergrowth surrounding the fields to wait out the day. When the night fell, we emerged once again.

While Renata huddled against the daytime—her eyes clenched and her thoughtstreams struggling with the strangeness of a new life that could never again see sunlight—I prowled about the locality, just curious. I even recognized some of the landmarks from that far-in-the-future tour Renata and I would take with her friends from Paris to Josselin and the Breton countryside. Although, I really did not need to explore much—I knew where we were, and I knew the history that we were in. I knew where Vesta was leading us.

We were on the outskirts of rural place called Brambily near a castle called Mauron, and the date was August 14,

1352. By the way, don't be too impressed that I can nail a place and a date. Just like an arctic tern has evolved the capacity to navigate by instinct on thousand-mile migrations, reading longitude and latitude from the planet's magnetic field, so also has evolution endowed my kind with a similar adaptation—I can sense my exact location in timespace just by instinct. Not by magnetic fields, but by other markers in the quantum environment. But I almost didn't need to use that time-orientation sense now—my memory was enough.

And that memory was memory that I had acquired in various ways—including, you might say, the hard way, by studying. I had lived through this same period of time in France as well, although it was in a different region, in Picardy, far to the east near the frontier with Burgundy. My only contemporary understanding of the Battle of Mauron came second-hand in those days. The news travelled at the speed of a horseman then, and by the time you received the news, anything you might have heard about would have been over—beyond the ability to make any rigorous, scientific inquiry of the current event. Unless one happened to possess an ability to slide through time. But the battle had been of only passing interest to me when it happened, a minor skirmish in what the historians centuries later would call the War of the Breton Succession, and which those same historians would consider a mere sideshow in something grander called the Hundred Years' War. A thoroughly ridiculous name, that, by the way—as if anyone at the time would have intended that England and France would make war on each other for a century. Indeed, no one then knew when the wars would end—if ever. I remember in Picardy the people had begun to think that, just as the plague had brought never-ending pestilence into their lives, so the nobility of England and France had arranged for their peoples forever after to suffer never-ending war. The Forever War, they might better have called it. In fact, it would not have occurred to the people then to give it any name, because they no longer recognized a time of war to be distinct from any other time. It was just the normal condition of their misery.

But the soldiers who had fought that day at Mauron would not have considered themselves fighting in a backwater, or a sideshow. In later ages, I did collect information about these events and committed the facts to memory, just as I have committed the basic facts of all human history to memory. The Battle of Mauron— August 14, 1352—Franco-Breton forces of 5,000 men under Guy Il de Nesle and Jean de Beaumanoir were routed by an Anglo-Breton force of 2,000, led by Sir Walter Bentley and Tanguy de Chastel. The French were caught in ambush by the English, who showered them with arrows from longbows. The French could have fled the field and saved their army, but they did not. Their leaders had been made companions of the Order of the Star by King Jean the year before, and, in being invested with that honor, they had sworn never to retreat in battle more than four *arpents*—about 600 yards—but instead to fight on until they were killed or taken prisoner. And they followed their oath at Mauron to disaster. Virtually all the French knights were killed or captured; 800 of the French army were killed in all. The French dead were strewn so thickly on the field that the body of de Nesle could not be found for two days. The historians said that the loss of their best knights was a blow from which the Breton-French side of the war never recovered. That may well be so. The English did push the French out of Brittany for a time after Mauron. And the Order of the Star was so decimated that it was effectively snuffed out, almost as soon as it had been founded.

But so it was that I understood where we were, and why Vesta had been trailing the armies as they approached each other—she seemed to have an instinct for the proximity of mass death, much like my instinct for orientation in time. And therefore, I was prepared for the scene that revealed itself as we emerged from the darkness of the forest, after the sun had set. Renata, however, was not.

The battlefield was only about a mile further on from where Renata had hidden in the woods from the daylight. The carnage had occurred nearby while she had slept, oblivious. We came upon the scene before night had fully fallen—we crested a low ridge screened by a few trees, and then stopped. Renata's mind tumbled in incomprehension for several long moments as she stood perfectly still. The last, glowing blue light draining from the evening sky looked lovely, but its loveliness stood in weird contrast with what lay beneath it on the ground.

Battlefields are always horrible to see, even though as a scientist I try to regard them for what they are—artifacts of human behavior, behavior that has certainly remained consistent over the 6,000 years of my experience. But this battlefield was peculiarly horrible. In the fading light the bodies were indistinct dark tangles, the end of one corpse indistinguishable from the beginning of the next. The darkening field bristled with the arrows that had fallen from the sky like razor-edged rain. Dead horses lay everywhere in heaps, giant sacks of hide and hair, some pierced with the same arrows, some bearing the slashes of sword or lance. The strewn bodies seemed to cover acres into the dimming distance. At the verges of the field, against the dark line where a forest verged opposite, I saw thin ribbons of smoke drifting upward from a few fires, lit by the English guards who watched the field. Renata moved forward, down the slope and toward the silent carnage; I ran alongside her.

As we approached the scene of the battle I saw the movement of a few indistinct figures among the dead. I remembered the historians describing how the Irish and Welsh knifemen would glean the battlefields after the main army, capturing those of the wounded men who were rich enough to hold for a ransom, and slicing the throats of those who were not. We were approaching two of those moving figures; I reflexively began to move away from them, to give them a wide berth. No need to foment trouble.

But Renata did not turn aside—indeed, she quickened her pace, moving directly toward the figures. It was only then that I looked more closely at them. They were not knifemen from the English army. Nor were they from the French. They were soldiers, yes—but not from any mortal army.

The one who turned and faced us as we approached was the vampire soldier with the scar across his beard. He gripped four swords stripped from the battlefield dead in one hand; he held the reins of a horse laden with armor and weapons with the other.

"Lady Renata," he said gravely, inclining his face in a slight bow. "Master Vesta said you would return to us. I see that she was right."

"Where is Matthieu?" Renata said brusquely. "What are you doing here?"

"We're gathering arms and armor," the other vampire soldier exclaimed. "For the vampire army!"

"The vampire army?" Renata asked.

The scarred one smiled indulgently at his smaller, and apparently dimmer, companion. "He don't know what he's talking about," the vampire soldier said. "Master Vesta just ordered us to collect this. Only the good pieces though—nothing broken."

Renata's thoughtstreams tried to force away the inaninity of the soldiers' conversation. "Where is Vesta, then?" Renata demanded. "Is she here also? Is she with Matthieu?"

The vampire soldier did not answer. Instead, he glanced up over Renata's shoulder as two horsemen galloped up behind her and pulled to a stop. He made a deeper, more formal bow than he had favored Renata with. Renata turned; Vesta and Mattieu looked down at her from the height of their saddles. They had obtained new mounts in the intervening time—giant horses: a dazzling white gelding for Vesta; Matthieu was astride a huge, glossy black mare with wide eyes crazed by the sight and smell of death. Vesta smiled as sweetly as she could.

"Renata," she said. "I thought you would find us. Have you come to take your place at the side of your master once again?"

I heard the echo of Vesta's thoughtstreams, reaching out to Renata's mind—and the mood of Vesta's thoughtstreams was not as sweet as her smile. The sound was not articulated in words; rather, it was almost as if Vesta's mind were exerting a palpable pressure on Renata's, attempting to bend it to Vesta's inclination, trying to overmaster Renata's will. I felt Renata's thoughtstreams push against Vesta's mind, the twanging of that familiar mortal tone underlying her vampire mind vibrating angrily. It was like a telepathic wrestling match. Vesta bore on, harder and harder; Renata resisted, just as hard.

"You will submit to me!" Vesta hissed through gritted teeth. "I am your master! I *command* you!"

Renata was breathing heavily with the strain of the mental effort. "You lied to us," she hissed threateningly. "You promised us life, but now we are dead. We are worse than dead!" I felt Renata's thoughtstreams give a sudden effort, pushing Vesta's mind out of her mind, shutting down Vesta's thoughtstreams. "You made us evil things!" Renata hissed.

Vesta's vampire voice gave a freakish, hissing screech as her thoughtstreams were squelched. She glared down at Renata angrily. "It is unnatural," she heaved. "It is unnatural for an adept to resist her master! I am *your* master! I *made* you! I *control* you!" Vesta raised her fists to her face and screamed again in frustration.

Renata brought forward the sword she had been

dragging since the earlier attack on the Montfortist knights. She hefted the sword and held it forward, toward Vesta. "You are not my master," Renata hissed. "I am not your slave." She looked away from Vesta and toward Matthieu, sitting atop the great black horse. "Matthieu, we are not bound to this one. We need not serve her."

Matthieu did not meet her eyes. He glanced uncertainly toward Vesta. I heard Vesta's thoughtstreams reach out to Matthieu's mind; they smoothly, easily, caressingly coaxed Matthieu's thoughts in the channels she chose.

"I serve Master Vesta," Matthieu said softly.

"Yes," Vesta said. She laughed softly. "Yes, my Matthieu. Did you show the Comtesse the armor you found upon the field?"

Matthieu's face shone with boyish pleasure as he pulled a huge black bascinet helmet from a cord that had hung it behind his saddle. He put the glossy black steel object over his head, and lifted the barred visor aside. The visor moved with some difficulty; the blow that had killed the man who wore it that afternoon had compressed the hinge.

"See, it goes like that," Matthieu said. "And we'll get black plate for the breastplate and cuisses, as well." He smiled excitedly. "And I shall be a knight of the vampire army. All black, like my horse!"

Vesta smiled indulgently. "Yes, you will be my lieutenant. My sable knight on his sable horse." Her eyes glittered fiercely back down at Renata. "I had hoped to have the service of two adepts. I see that you refuse to serve me as is your duty. So be it—you will be served justice for that crime soon enough. But see, I still have this adept." She smiled evilly. "He is my slave. And he will be a powerful adept."

Matthieu spurred his horse exultantly. He galloped away through the mounds of corpses, swinging his sword to knock the heads and hands off the dead. He laughed at the pretend slaughter, the despoiling of the bodies. "I am the Sable Knight of the Vampires!" he shouted as he rode.

Renata glowered at Vesta. "What have you done to him? Give me back my son!"

"Your son?" Vesta exclaimed, with mock surprise. "The dead have no children, Comtesse. Matthieu belongs to the vampire nation—more precisely, he belongs to me. I am his master. He is my adept, and he will serve me."

Renata had not moved. Vesta's horse paced uneasily, eying the swordpoint that Renata still held toward Vesta. "You mock him with talk of an army of the dead," Renata said. "There is no such thing. The dead are only dead." Renata took a step toward Vesta, the point of the sword moving a step closer to Vesta's leg. "You killed him, Vesta Letalia. You killed me."

Vesta's face dropped its pretense of good humor. "I killed you," she hissed. "Yes. It was a bargain. A life for a life. And I kept my bargain. But now you betray yours. Do you know the penalty for the crime of rebellion, Comtesse?" Vesta pulled her horse back a step. "Soldiers, seize this one."

The vampire soldiers behind Renata stepped forward and gripped her shoulders roughly. Renata gasped, then wheeled at blinding speed, her sword still held aloft. The sword's blade whistled, and sank into the massive right arm of the scarred vampire soldier. The other soldier, startled, released his grip on Renata.

The first soldier, his left hand now holding his almost-severed right arm onto his body, barked at his slow-witted companion. "Catch her!" he rasped. "Forget this—this wound will heal, dammit! But don't let her escape!"

It was too late however—Renata had already taken off at a vampire-swift run across the corpse-strewn battlefield. Vesta sneered down at the two soldiers standing at the hooves of her horse. "Plague vampires!" she shouted disdainfully, then wheeled the great white horse and galloped after Renata.

I had taken off running as soon as I saw Renata break free of the vampire soldiers, but I could not keep up. Even on foot, as I have said, vampires are fast. I saw that Renata was running across the field toward Matthieu, who was still riding his horse and playing his game of dismembering the dead. The thundering of Vesta's horse approached quickly behind me; I had to veer out of the path of the white horse as it overtook me and galloped after Renata.

But a small cat, even though not as swift as a Breton war-horse or a vampire in flight, is fast enough. I caught up with the three of them in a few minutes. Renata held the bridle of Matthieu's horse. Vesta's horse paced in circles, a small distance away, Vesta glowering from the saddle.

Renata was shouting—or, as best a vampire can shout. It sounded metallic, hollow, like a mortal who had lost his voice to a cold. "Release him!" she demanded. "Release Matthieu! He does not serve you either!"

"No, Comtesse," Vesta said. *"You* release Matthieu. You are the traitor to your nation!"

"No!" Renata replied. "He is my son!"

Vesta grimaced. She bent from her saddle, pulling a broken lance from the ground beside her. She spurred her horse and the animal bounded the distance between Vesta and Renata. Vesta stabbed savagely toward Renata with the lance. Renata dodged; the lance point found only empty air. Anticipating the shock of the lance striking Renata's body Vesta had shifted in her saddle, but with the empty thrust had lost her balance. Renata saw, and pulled Vesta heavily to the ground. She stood over Vesta.

"Release my son!" Renata rasped warningly. Renata raised the sword over her head.

"Matthieu!" Vesta moaned. "Defend your master!"

Renata's throat emitted a harsh grunt as she swung the sword down toward Vesta's skull. Matthieu, the black helmet still covering his face, pulled his horse close by

Renata's side and swung a mighty counterblow with his sword. Matthieu's sword blocked Renata's stroke toward Vesta. The two blades met with a reverberating crash of steel. The force knocked Renata to the ground.

Vesta regained her feet. Matthieu wheeled the horse back, and dismounted heavily from the stirrups. He pulled the bascinet off his head and ran to them, the naked blade of his sword held forward, taking up a position next to Vesta. He placed the point of his sword at Renata's throat.

Renata seemed dazed. She looked up from the ground at Matthieu's face, searching it. I heard her thoughtstreams; they also seemed to be searching, wondering at the flatness of her feeling. Wondering, what has happened to my son? To me? And also wondering, I heard, where are my tears? Why can't I cry?

"Matthieu, my son," Renata said miserably. "You do not have to serve this one as a slave."

Matthieu tightened his mouth. He looked toward Vesta. "Shall I kill her, Master Vesta?" he asked.

Vesta chuckled. "Should you kill her?" she repeated softly to herself. "No, my Sable Knight, you cannot kill her with that," Vesta said, pushing the sword away with the toe of her shoe, "any more than she could have killed our soldiers with her sword. No, we will leave her." Vesta moved back toward her white horse. "Comtesse, the vampire nation will have its justice against you. We have no need to hurry. I will consult the Council. There is a grave penalty for rebellion, Comtesse," Vesta said. "The penalty is annihilation."

Renata was hardly listening. Her eyes were on Matthieu as he drew away, grabbing the reins of his own horse and preparing to mount again.

Vesta stopped, looking down at the ground for a moment. She bent and grasped the hand of a body lying naked on the torn grass—a nobleman, presumably, since it had been stripped of armor and clothing. She noticed an ornament on one of the body's fingers that the corpse-robbers had overlooked. She pulled the object from the body's hand, and flung it at Renata. It landed close to Renata's head on the ground. Renata sat up, retrieving the object from the grass.

A red enameled ring, with a white star.

"I keep Matthieu," Vesta said, swinging herself into the saddle of the great white horse. "You may keep that. The Order of the Star. The Order of Death, would be a better name. The Companions of the Star are all around you," she said. "And yet, some of these who lie dying now will join me tonight. They will be part of my array. They will not need those rings. The ground is thick with those rings. You may keep that ring, Comtesse. Or perhaps you would like to give it to your famous brother-in-law, Captain Beaumanoir? You can ask him how he managed to survive today, eh? Why he still bears *his* ring on a living hand!" Vesta laughed, and pulled her horse about. "Matthieu, my Sable Knight. You are faithful to your master. We will become great!" She spurred her horse, and rode away toward the vampire soldiers we had left across the field. I saw that they had been joined by more—about a dozen more. Many more than we had seen the night previous. Vesta had seemingly already been at work, introducing new recruits to her nascent vampire army.

Matthieu mounted his mighty black horse, and placed the helmet back upon his head. He pulled the visor over his face, and, wordlessly, wheeled his horse and galloped after Vesta.

Renata remained sitting on the scarred earth of the battlefield. She was motionless for a long time. She stared at the enameled star ring, slipping it absently on and off of her finger. I crept up beside her, and sat. I listened as her thoughtstreams slowly calmed, the fierce rebelliousness of her fight with Vesta subsiding until they flowed again as vampire thoughtstreams—flat, black, featureless. The memory of her prior life as a mortal was fading, I knew;

she had to struggle to remember even what Matthieu had meant to her so recently. The memory would dissipate soon. But the strange, thrumming subterranean chord of mortal vibration continued to sound in the background of her thoughtstreams, and I knew that I had been right— that strange sense of a memory lurking beneath the surface had been exactly that—a memory, the memory of the powerful maternal urge to protect her son, too strong to be entirely displaced, even after death, even after transformation into the living death of a vampire.

The timeguide had brought us back to itself, I realized. I was not sure where this history would go from here. I knew that I could end the timeslide now if I wanted to— the timeguide's pathway had been completed, at least as far as Renata was concerned. And I had learned at least some of what I had come to learn. There apparently was indeed a "Sable", and it was Renata's son—Vesta herself had begun calling him her "Sable Knight." Though from what I saw of Matthieu, riding that enormous horse and playacting like a child with his sword, he certainly did not seem to be the fearsome vampire warrior that the Doctor had described. I couldn't see why Vesta and the Vampire Council would have so strong an interest in him, six hundred years in the future. Ah, but in any event, the question of where the Sable might be in that future—in the present time, that is—that was not information that this timeslide would reveal. The star ring would not act as a timeguide to lead me further along the crease in time made by Matthieu. If I wanted to do that, I would have to find some other timeguide, one bonded to Matthieu himself. That was a puzzle, and not one that I felt equipped to try to solve immediately. But at least I had learned one thing that was tangible—the Sable was not Renata herself, and it was not Lupe. Perhaps that was enough to learn for now.

But still, as I watched Renata reluctantly pull herself to her feet and begin to walk aimlessly away, it seemed to be too soon to leave this timeslide completely. I could keep the timeslide going, at least for a while, even if I might break off and go back to Forshay and my native timeframe. But I just didn't think it was right to leave Renata alone like this. I looked around me, at the hellish scene of the Mauron battlefield under the August night sky. I couldn't leave Renata here, on her own. Even a small cat would be better company than nothing. I sat on my haunches for a moment and gave each of my forepaws a quick lapping with my tongue, and then trotted away after Renata, threading my way through the black shapes of the dead.

CHAPTER NINETEEN

The summit of Forshay Mountain is actually just one promontory along a set of long ridgelines that range above Forshay village to the south and east. It is an isolated, eastern spur of the Blue Ridge that rises clifflike far to the west, like an anticipatory, rocky island rising offshore a continent, above the flat and level sea of the Piedmont plateau.

But because it rises from such flat and level land, Forshay Mountain achieves a level of drama and grandeur rather beyond what would normally be ascribed to its modest altitude. The views from the ridges are beautiful, far-off vistas from which the sharp-eyed can pick out the distant cityscape of Charlotte, off to the east, or the higher escarpments of the true mountains off to the north and the west. But in no way is Forshay Mountain really a mountain. A high ridge above flat land—that's all. Easy enough for a small cat to make its way up the slopes to the top in an hour or two.

But not so easy to find a couple of vampires and a human hostage in the moonless darkness, I thought, as my consciousness emerged from the timeslide. My eyes found their focus again, and, tired and slightly trembling, I looked around me. I had worked my way up the slopes quickly—with my cat's eyes I could penetrate the deep shadows in the tangled underbrush, and with my shortcuts I was quickly high up on the ridge. I leaped up and continued to climb the slopes. I headed for the main summit of the ridge first—what the people in Forshay call The Spire, although it looks nothing like a spire. It was just the highest point on the outcrop, a flat, naked platform of quartz and granite where the soil of the mountain had been scoured away on the north side, and trees could not grow. It was the best place to look down on Forshay village itself, far below in the valley to the north, with the distant Blue Ridge looming like thunderheads on the dark horizon beyond.

But it was deserted. The huge starry sky above the naked stone seemed to emphasize the emptiness of the space, mocking me for not finding them. I had to look elsewhere, I knew, but trying to search all along the ridgetop would take the rest of the night—too long. I sat on the bare rock to think. I could hear in my mind the occasional outcry of Lupe's frightened thoughtstreams, close by somewhere, no longer shrill so much as resigned and despairing. Perhaps because of some trick of the rock ledges, I couldn't locate the source of the thoughtstreams, however; they seemed to come from all around at once. I wished I had been able to find Renata on the climb up—I felt sure that with my cat shortcuts I had been able to move faster through the tangled woods than even a swooping vampire, but I wondered if she were able to follow Lupe's thoughtstreams in a truer direction. I listened for Renata's thoughtstreams, thinking maybe I would be able to follow those, but I could hear nothing of her. I would have to keep looking. I set out again, moving off the starlit rock of The Spire and back into the forest of the ridgeline. I would have to try every promontory on the ridge, I thought resignedly, one by one.

But a few paces into the woods, I stopped as another

thought occurred to me. There was a cliff further south below the ridgeline, that clung to the side of the mountain like a lifeboat moored to a shiphull, a place the people called the Scarp. On two sides of the narrow platform of stone and packed earth, the mountain dropped away in a sheer precipice that fell vertically for a thousand feet and more, a far sheerer and more sudden drop than anywhere else on the mountain. The Scarp was beloved of rock climbers, who would climb up and rappel down the precipice on fine sunny days with ropelines and helmets of gay, primary colors. In the quiet of midnight, however, no one came to the Scarp, except you might have occasionally seen a small cat sitting at the edge, enjoying the exhilarating feel of the cliff's thrust into unsupported space, and gazing at the broad expanse of the eastern night sky beyond the tiny lighted skyscrapers of Charlotte, miles away.

The eastern sky, I thought again.

It faced east.

The sunrise—the Scarp was a perfect place to watch the sunrise. Unblocked by the shadows of Forshay Mountain rising behind it, even though it was much lower than The Spire and the other heights of the ridgeline, the Scarp was the spot where the first rays of the rising sun fell. It was the remembrance of the Doctor's annihilation that moved my paws, now hurrying in the direction of the Scarp. Because I was sure that was where the vampires were gathering, where they had taken Lupe, where they were luring Renata. I didn't expect the Vampire Council to be original. Just lethal.

It wasn't a long run for a small cat to the Scarp—it lay just a few miles down the ridge from The Spire. I closed the distance quickly, moving through the dark foliage with hardly a rustle. I looked to the star-filled sky, wondering how many hours had elapsed. I had not kept track of the time since night had fallen at Random Farm, and of course the intervening return to the 14th century had made me lose track of the hours. Now the problem was critical, one of celestial reckoning—how long before the sun came up?

I ran along, and began to hear Lupe's terrified thoughtstreams growing more steadily now—I must be right, I must be getting closer to her. I reached the point at the ridge where the path led down the eastern slope toward the ledge of the Scarp, and as I started down I finally heard Renata's thoughtstreams—quiet, determined, grim. She was just ahead of me. I ran down the rough path, trying to catch her. I reached the verge of the clearing that gave way to the cliff, and the vault of impossibly empty, starry space beyond. I had to sit and rest—I was still tired from my timeslides in Brittany and at Random Farm, and something told me that I may need to gather my energy again very soon indeed.

"Miss Beaumanoir!" Lupe screamed, her voice half shriek and half sob. "They have me! They're *here!*" No need to read thoughtstreams to hear that. I carefully crept onto the Scarp, keeping unseen in the shadows, and looked at the scene onto which Renata had just emerged from the forest.

It was a tableau as dramatic as I could have expected from the Vampire Council. Vesta Letalia, having cast aside the tailored suit and tight hairstyle of her lawyer persona, stood before the black void beyond the ledge, with her flowing white hair and loose white tunic catching the faint starlight. The more I saw of Vesta, the more I perceived how much her bodily vanity had survived her death-transformation into a vampire. And she was, I had to admit, good-looking, in an evil demon kind of way. Beside her was Lupe, kneeling on the ground the same way that her brother had a few hours ago at Random's stone barn, her face strained and streaked with tears. The vampire assassins stood one on each side, no dark glasses this time. Their smirking eyes gleamed. Chuck raised a massive, two-handed sword of white steel, and pressed the blade against Lupe's neck.

"Different blade, now, Comtesse," he hissed at Renata. "Just to show that we're not fucking around this time."

"Be still!" Vesta commanded. Chuck kissed his lips at Renata, and then favored her with a toothy grin in the starlight.

"Let her go," Renata hissed through gritted teeth.

Vesta smiled indulgently. I could see she was loving the dramatics. "We did the research some months ago," she said, "but I think I recall that the drop from here is exactly 1,253 feet." She smiled sweetly. "The North Carolina Commerce Department has such a detailed website."

Renata's thoughtstreams were a clashing discord of alarm. She stood still on her side of the platform facing Vesta and the assassins, still as the rocks on the ledge around her. She had lowered herself into a semi-crouch, as if ready to spring, but I knew she would not with Lupe in such danger. "Let her go," Renata repeated.

Vesta straightened her spine, glaring imperiously down at Renata. "We have no desire to harm this young lady," Vesta said, "or her brother. Or did the Doctor fill your gullible mind with alarms about how the Council seeks the legendary Sable, the oh-so-powerful vampire adept that could control us all? I think you can ease your mind, Comtesse. This child and her brother aren't the fabulous Sable—they're not even vampires. And *you* are certainly not the Sable, are you, Comtesse? And yet, it is you that we want, Comtesse—it has been you that we wanted every time—in Charleston, on the farm of that pleasant Mr. Random. And now. And for the most pragmatic of reasons. We come to enforce the justice of the Council."

I heard Renata's mind struggling. "And you will release her, if I surrender to you?" she asked.

Vesta continued to glare sternly at Renata. "You always think that you are in a position to bargain, don't you Comtesse?" Vesta said. "Our aim is simple—you have been sentenced to annihilation, Comtesse—justly, I may add, for your part in aiding the treason of the so-called Doctor Movement. Your fate is sealed. There is nothing you can say to change it. But, this young lady, María Guadalupe—I think you go by Lupe, dear, do you not?" She smiled down toward the terrified girl momentarily, then cast her gleaming eyes back at Renata angrily. "We have made no promises about what might befall her if you cooperate, Comtesse. I *can* make you a promise about what happens to Lupe if you do not cooperate." She made a tiny motion with her finger.

Chuck lowered the sword to the earthen floor of the ledge. In a sudden, fluid motion Harrison grasped Lupe beneath an armpit, and gripping her by her shoulder raised her above his head, and then straightened his arm, extending it out over the chasm beyond the Scarp. The brief sound of Lupe's feet scraping the rocks of the ledge ended suddenly in a sickening silence as her feet swung free in mere air. Lupe was too terrified to scream; her eyes rolled wildly as she swayed in a nothingness of stars and blackness. I looked at Harrison grinning, like a teenage boy proud of performing a feat of strength. I saw that he had his other arm flexed, biceps rigid. He was bracing himself against Lupe's weight by grasping the end of short chain, staked into the rock of the ledge. I knew without looking that a manacle dangled from the end of the chain, beyond the tension of his grip.

"One thousand two hundred fifty-two feet," Vesta said archly. "The rocks below the cliffside are especially jagged." She smiled primly. "The website for the attraction included a specific warning for climbers."

I saw Renata tense as Lupe swung into the void beyond the ledge, Renata's mind rushing, measuring, calculating. And then, I saw her drop her gaze, resignedly. Her body sagged in defeat. She saw no escape. I knew as I listened to her mind that she would surrender to Vesta. I stretched my exhausted muscles, my mind racing. I had to do something. I couldn't think, couldn't formulate a plan—

seeing Renata so dejected was breaking my heart. I had to find a way to muster a timeslide, but simple force didn't seem to be enough, like it was in the stone barn at Random's. A saber-toothed cat just didn't seem to be helpful on this narrow ledge, with Lupe dangling above an ugly death.

Renata straightened herself nobly, and stepped forward, her arms outstretched and her wrists held together. She offered them to the assassins, but glared at Vesta with a last flash of rebellion. *"Je soumets,"* she hissed, "I will submit to you Vesta Letalia, and to your Vampire Council, but do not think you will eradicate the memory of the Doctor. Or what he stood for."

Vesta made another tiny motion with her finger, and Harrison swung Lupe back onto the ledge. Chuck pushed her back onto her knees and raised his theater-prop sword against her neck again.

"I said I submit," Renata hissed. "Release Lupe."

"First, we must secure you, Comtesse," Vesta said. Harrison had already taken one wrist and snapped the manacle in place. He pulled Renata roughly to the side, forcing her to the ground with her arms behind her, and drew another chain forward with a metallic clank against its stake driven into the rock. The manacle clicked shut on Renata's other wrist. She was pinned to the mountain.

Harrison stripped the clothes off Renata, exposing her white skin to the nighttime. He stripped her to bra and panties. "That is sufficient," Vesta said, stopping him before he went further. "We need only to ensure a complete annihilation. We need not deprive the Comtesse of her remaining modesty." She grinned at Renata. "We are, after all, civilized vampires." When Harrison stepped away, Vesta looked over the scene, satisfied. "Very well," she said. She held her hands on her hips as and surveyed her handiwork. "Yes, this goes very well indeed. I hope you appreciate the thought that went into this moment, Comtesse," she hissed to Renata. "This is an important event for you, just as it is for us. See, we found the best place to ensure that you will meet the very first rays of the sun, Comtesse, a long, open exposure to the east, so that your annihilation in the sunlight will be both swift and efficient. And with plenty of shady cover for we true, honorable members of the vampire nation to retire to, and watch your end." She glanced about her; she looked over the chasm to the east. The stars had begun to fade, and the horizon was emerging from the blackness in a dim line of celestial blue. "And just in time, it seems, Comtesse. You will not have long to wait."

Renata glared up at Vesta from the ground where she knelt, the chains pulling her wrists tightly behind her back. I could hear her thoughtstreams running fast and confused, sounding more and more like the tangled clash of contending emotions I had heard when she had still been mortal. "Let the girl go now," she hissed, her glittering vampire eyes beginning to catch the slow pale glow of the lightening sky. "You have me now. Let her go." And as she spoke, I saw her eyes—in my cat vision I could see quite clearly, though the light from the east was still so dim. I saw streaks from her eyes, streaks from those hard, vampiric eyes running down her cheeks. Tears. Renata was crying.

But Renata had come off the thanadoxicil completely now—she was entirely vampire. And, as with dreams, so with tears—say it with me—*vampires don't cry*. Another breakthrough in vampire physiology, another item to add to the growing list of exceptionalism that Renata displayed as a vampire specimen. And with no opportunity to make a careful, scientific record of what I saw. I was getting lamentably far behind in my scientific field notes. But my recordation of this new observation, like the last ones, would also have to wait.

Lupe pushed away the sword blade from her neck. She tried to get up, and get away. Chuck grabbed her arm and threw her back to the ground. "Miss Beaumanoir!" Lupe wailed.

"You ain't going anywhere, girl," Chuck said.

"You stayin' here," Harrison said.

"Right here."

Chuck raised the sword, and placed the tip of the blade at the back of Lupe's skull. "No sense letting you go, man," he said. "We been hunting all night. We're hungry, man."

"Yeah," Harrison said. "I could eat."

Vesta grinned evilly at Renata. "The nation must be fed, Comtesse," she said with satisfaction. "Or perhaps there could be a different outcome—did you think it would escape my notice that young Lupe here is another potential adept? Not so different from you, perhaps, Comtesse, once upon a time? Perhaps some greater destiny awaits Lupe after your annihilation? What do you think? The nation will have been diminished by one, with your end. Should we not replenish it by one?" Renata's mouth set firmly; she continued to weep silently.

"Perhaps we can still come to an arrangement, Comtesse," Vesta said softly. "The sun will rise soon. Then you will burn.

"But," Vesta continued, her voice now a conspiratorial whisper, "what if I agreed release you, and Miss Hernandez-Vega? Would you entertain a last chance?" Renata's eyes glanced up warily, tears clinging to the lashes. Vesta licked her lips, her breath coming faster. "You just need to give me just one thing." She leaned forward hungrily.

"Give me the Sable!" Vesta hissed. "You have the key, we *know* it! Where is it? *Where is it?"* Vesta's voice rose in frustration. *"Where is the Sable, damn you!"*

There was a crash in the underbrush above the ledge, a snapping of branches and the heavy footfall of shoes. The vampires all looked up at the sudden noise. The sound was unmistakable; there were people coming down the path from the ridgeline. And not very quietly. I listened for voices—aural or telepathic.

"God, it's dark," said Denis's voice.

"Well, go slowly," Fulda responded. "Be careful you don't fall. The ledge is just out there, somewhere."

I saw the two break from the underbrush, and stand motionless as their eyes slowly picked out the scene on the ledge in the dim blue light.

Vesta Letalia gave a slow, disbelieving laugh. "Oh, wonderful!" she said. "More company! Good evening— or maybe I should say, *good morning!*"

Denis stepped forward wonderingly, peering at her. "I saw you," he said. "You were at Random Farm. In the white car."

Vesta gave him a dazzling smile, and tossed her white hair flirtatiously. "Yes, Mr. Pearson—it *is* Mr. Pearson, isn't it?—yes, that was me. I enjoyed our drive," she said. "Did you?"

While the assassins were distracted by these newcomers, Lupe broke away. She rushed to Fulda and buried her face into Fulda's shoulder, sobbing. Chuck raised the sword threateningly.

"Leave off," Vesta commanded him. "She's not going anywhere." She smiled at the three mortals, standing uncertainly at the edge of the clearing. "No one is," she said.

All this time, I am ashamed to admit, I had suffered from a failure of imagination. The events were moving too fast, too unexpectedly, and I *was* still fatigued from the timeslides before. I was muddle-headed. I had failed to come up with an action plan. Maybe I'm getting old? Old even for a 6,000-year-old cat?

But it was at this moment that I noticed something on the ledge that I had not noticed before, something that might have been there all along, or that might have just moved itself into view as the slow creep of dawn light spread into the sky. A fallen tree trunk lying in the shadowed underbrush beyond the clearing of the ledge—

but there was something strange about it, something that had caught my peripheral vision but had not registered in my conscious mind. I stared at it full on for a moment, and as I watched, I saw it move—silently, slowly, it moved itself forward, a few inches at a time, stopping between its silent glides. Not a tree trunk, I realized—my eyes followed the length of the object in and out of the lightening shadows of the underbrush, until in the graying light they found the end of the object, and I found myself gazing into the giant eyes of a serpent's head, as broad across as a man's body. The serpent's expressionless eyes gleamed yellow like citrine gemstones; they stared unblinkingly ahead as the huge snake worked its position toward the vampire assassins. It had silently glided to within a few feet of where they stood.

I felt the serpent's eyes seek me out momentarily. A chill of fear raised my fur. I heard a clear, familiar thoughtstream speak plainly into my mind. *Be ready,* Margaret Viper's voice said. *This is going to happen fast.*

The moment seemed to hang in unearthly slowness, for a pulsebeat, another pulsebeat. I don't think I'll ever know who shouted, but it wasn't a thoughtstream signal—it was a lusty, audible, very human shout.

"Now!"

The vampires looked shocked, more at the unexpected sound than at the sudden movement from the side, and before they could react the giant serpent as thick across as a tree trunk had thrown its constrictive loops over both Harrison and Chuck, pinning their arms beneath the scaly mass and smothering their mouths and faces. The huge sword fell from Chuck's hands and with one metallic ring against the stone cliff face fell noiselessly off the Scarp into space. Vesta retreated as the snake lunged at her as well, the coils holding the vampire assassins dislodging scatterings of dirt and stones. Vesta lurched aside from the snake, seeking to flee, vampire-like, out of the half-light of the ledge and into the dark woods up the slope, but the snake's jaws opened and shut with blinding speed, clamping upon her leg and driving her face into the ground. Her white hair spread about the ledge as her arms grappled against the stones, trying to pull away. The snake dragged her back toward the cliff. I saw the giant discs of the snake's eyes catch me in their gaze for an instant again.

Hurry, Margaret signaled me. *Hurry! Time's almost gone!*

I leaped out of my hiding place in the clearing and ran toward Renata. Margaret's meaning was clear. I looked behind me. The snake's coils continued to wrestle the vampires, but they were immobilized. I saw Denis and Fulda seize the moment and rush across the ledge. Vesta, lying on her belly with the snake's jaws clasped on her legs, made a savage grab at Fulda's leg; Fulda looked down as she felt the fingers grasp at her ankle, and shrieked as she faced Vesta's furious countenance. Vesta snarled viciously with hatred, fangs extended and eyes reddened. Fulda pulled out of her grasp, and at the same moment the giant serpent, with the three vampires of the Vampire Council, slid off the edge of the precipice like a ship's hawser running overboard into the ocean. I heard no sound, no scratching against the cliff face as they fell, no thudding report below. They were gone.

Fulda glanced nervously at the long, whitening line of the eastern horizon. She had already pushed Renata to the side and yanked her leg over, exposing the long white thigh. "Denis!" she cried. "Come on, I need the box!"

Denis pulled the smooth, oblong box out of his jacket pocket. Fulda already had the first syringe in her teeth as she searched for Renata's femoral artery with the heel of her hand. The black blood jumped as she jammed the first needle in, and squeezed the plunger. "I believe you call this thanadoxicil," she said, chatting absently, avoiding the flinty stare of Renata's eyes. "Well, this is home brew, straight from Fulda's chem lab. Let's see how well it works." She handed the first syringe back to Denis, who gave her the second. "Come on, come on," she murmured to herself, looking across the ledge at the eastern horizon. It had gone from blue to white along the whole verge of the sky. Fulda pushed the second needle into Renata's leg, and the drug coursed into her body. Renata slumped forward against Fulda's shoulder unconscious, in shock as the sudden surge of thanadoxicil worked into her bloodstream and suffused her tissues. Fulda pulled out the needle, cradling Renata in one arm as she massaged the two puncture-wounds with her other hand. "You know, you should have told us," she said softly to Renata. "We would have understood. We might not have believed you at first, but we would have understood." Fulda stroked Renata's black hair and kissed the crown of her head as the knifedge of the summer sun pushed above the rim of the horizon, and the first red rays of the sun struck Renata's skin, harmlessly. I walked up and rubbed my nose against Fulda's hands, watching Renata sleep peacefully as the sunlight on her skin turned yellow and white, brightening into the cheerful summer morning. Fulda sighed, relieved.

"Denis," she said, "see if you can find her clothes. And look in my bag over by the rocks there."

"What am I looking for?" Denis asked.

Fulda smiled wearily. "I guess Margaret knew what she was talking about," Fulda said. "She told me that we should bring the medicine and the syringes, and a hacksaw. I didn't understand the hacksaw, but I brought it." Fulda lifted one of Renata's wrists, encircled with the manacles. "I'm glad I did." Fulda shifted, and let Renata lay back against the ground. "Let's get her and Lupe off this mountain."

Denis walked over, and knelt on one knee. He looked closely at Renata's sleeping face. "I still can't believe it," he said. "I mean, I know what we saw, but it's so hard to believe." He closed his eyes for a moment, rubbing them with his hand. "It could have all been a hallucination. Maybe we just jointly imagined it, and it wasn't real at all. Mass hysteria—isn't that the term?"

Fulda shook her head firmly. "No way," she said. She held up the syringe. "Nothing imaginary about it. This is chemistry, man. This is science," she said. "This is real."

Amen, I said to myself.

PART THREE

Vivid Memories of My Future

CHAPTER TWENTY

Mrs. Pearson was talking about her pronunciation of words. "No, I would never say *'sweet tater,'*" she said. "You see, it's the wrong etymology—the slang word 'tater' is a Southern white usage, not a black word. And growing up we were never allowed to use any kind of slang, anyway. My father always insisted that his children speak standard English—*English when it's English time, Geechee when it's Geechee time,'* he'd always say. Besides," she added, "we always called them 'yams,' not 'sweet potatoes'."

Fulda pushed another big forkful of the pie into her mouth, closing her eyes with pleasure as she chewed. She had already forgotten her playful attempt at a faux-Southern accent, calling the dessert Denis was handing around 'sweet tater' pie. "Well, I don't care what you call it," she said, "but it tastes heavenly."

Renata nibbled at her pie self-consciously. "It is good," she said quietly, and drank from her coffee cup.

"Maybe Mrs. Pearson could teach you to make it," Fulda said teasingly. Renata, embarrassed, would not meet her eyes.

"Me?" exclaimed Mrs. Pearson. "Oh no. I may look like a fat black mammy who can cook, but I am hopeless.

I can just about manage mac'n'cheese, and half the time I burn that. No, Denis baked this pie you're having. *He's* the cook in the family."

Fulda grinned at Renata mercilessly. "Oh, that's even better," she said.

I had been listening to Renata's thoughtstreams over the course of the evening, and had been fascinated at the odd rushes of abashment as Renata had finally discerned from the conversation that the woman Denis had visited in Charleston that weekend had been his mother. Fulda's instinct for mischief seemed to pick up the electricity in the air between Renata and Denis. She was having fun gently needling them both.

I paced around the group that was gathered at Denis's kitchen table finishing dessert. Denis had finally convinced his mother to visit Forshay for part of the summer, and Renata, Fulda and Lupe had all come out to his big house off campus for a dinner to meet her. Margaret Viper was there, too; I was glad to see her. And Denis's mother was right, he was a good cook—at least, as best I could tell from the scraps he had given the ubiquitous kitten that Renata carried to dinner in her canvas bag. A week or more had passed since the awful night up on Forshay Mountain at the Scarp, and it seemed that Forshay was once again as normal as it could be. Chief Moorland had decided not to bring any charges against Lupe, and John Random had taken up Rafael's immigration case. That was progress. I wondered, however, just how much of the story of that night Moorland and Random were truly aware of. Would they still be as helpful, I wondered, if they knew all the facts?

Indeed, the only change around Forshay College may have been Trace Cuthbert. Trace had been laid up for a couple of days after the fight at the stone barn, but seemed to have made a full recovery. He was back at Buildings and Grounds, running the tractors across the lawns of the campus. But, where once he could be depended upon to have his bronzed and muscular torso stripped to the waist on any hot day, Trace had suddenly become wary of the dangers of sunlight. Sunblock had become his obsession, and now he worked covered over in long sleeves, work gloves, sunglasses and hat. No more tanned, handsome, half-naked Trace Cuthbert. When the girls of Forshay College returned at the end of the summer, I thought, they would surely mourn the change.

The dinner party at Denis Pearson's house could have continued as it was, pleasantly and unremarkably—the most memorable events being the requisite embarrassing stories about Denis as a child that Fulda or Margaret might extract from his mother's memory. It didn't though. I heard a car pull into Denis's driveway; Denis sprang up to the front door before the visitors rang.

He preceded the guests back toward the kitchen table. "Mama, you'll never believe who it is," Denis said. "I'd like you to meet Diane Hutchinson, President of Forshay College."

President Hutchinson walked into Denis's house smilingly, every movement a camera-ready pose as if a photographer for the alumnae review might appear at any moment. I suppose she may have forgotten how to enter a room otherwise. To be fair, though, that may well simply have been the rational strategy to adopt in her position. She was dressed and coiffed as elegantly as ever; as the President went through the rituals of introduction to Mrs. Pearson, I even felt a momentary twinge of disquiet—she suddenly reminded me of the lawyerly persona of Vesta Letalia. But the feeling passed. I was put at ease by her hair—Vesta's hair, though glossy and smooth, was abruptly, shockingly white, not the gentle, honey-gold of Diane Hutchinson's.

"Denis, I'm awfully sorry to intrude like this," the President said. She turned to the man who had followed her in. "I think you all know John Random."

Random greeted the room with his wide, bearded grin.

"Renata, I'm so glad to find you here," the President continued. "It's actually you that I came to find. Margaret had mentioned that you were coming out here tonight, and... Well," she said, with a searching look. "Well, there's news. And I didn't think it could wait." She turned to Denis, still smiling, but struggling. "Denis, perhaps we could all sit your beautiful living room? What I have to say may take a little explaining."

This sounded too interesting to miss. I skittered ahead of the people as they took their coffee into the living room and found seats. President Hutchinson remained standing.

"Well, this is a little difficult," she said, her hands fluttering in unaccustomed awkwardness. "But, I suppose that everyone in this room knows about the situation involving Miss Beaumanoir." She paused. My heart skipped for a moment—had the President learned about the Vampire Council? The Doctor? About Fulda manufacturing thanadoxicil in a college research lab?

"Renata, I'm afraid we owe you an apology," President Hutchinson said. "You see, after Claude Preen recommended that your contract be terminated, Margaret here made some further inquiries about the bases for Dr. Preen's complaints. And, it is the most extraordinary thing, extraordinary..." She paused again, as if to register her disbelief. "An absolutely extraordinary series of coincidences and inexplicable mistakes—well, in my entire career I haven't seen anything like it." The group in the living room leaned in, listening rapt as the President described how, one by one, the intractable problems that Claude Preen had adduced to get Renata fired had fallen away. The University of Paris, on a second inquiry, in fact *did* have Renata's academic credentials on record— baccalaureate in 2002, doctorate 2009, both with the highest distinction. The Department of Homeland Security had, at long last, found Renata's immigration record. She was indeed a permanent resident alien, in good standing, EBI status—foreign national with extraordinary abilities in the arts, science or education. A replacement green card was already waiting for her, locked in Margaret's desk by the stairs in Everett, to go with the replacement French passport that she should have in no more than a week.

"All of which leaves this situation of the Modern European History exam, and your accommodation for Miss Hernandez-Vega," President Hutchinson said. "Well, the Board of Trustees has looked into that, and the facts surrounding Miss Hernandez-Vega's situation. And we've consulted others with knowledge of the relevant facts," she continued, with a glance at John Random. "Long story short, Renata, on balance the Board has concluded that you acted properly. It may have been better to have gone through channels, but we understand why you felt you had to make an immediate decision." The President smiled, and bent down toward where Renata sat. "The Board has concluded that the bases upon which your contract renewal was denied no longer exist, and there is no longer any reason not to renew your position at Forshay College." President Hutchinson took Renata's hand. "Renata, I hope you will agree to continue with us again next year."

Renata looked glazed, stunned. She looked from the President, to Margaret Viper. "Margaret, *you* did all this for me?" she said. "Margaret, thank you, thank you so much!"

President Hutchinson stood back up. "I hope I can take that as a yes, Renata," she said cheerfully. "I should tell you how important I personally feel it is that you continue in the history department."

Fulda laughed. "Assuming you can take another year with Claude Preen as your department chairman," she said. I found myself glancing sharply at Fulda, at the same time the President did. I could read the expression on the President's face—slight annoyance with the way certain tenured faculty regarded their privilege. Of course, I thought, Fulda did have a point.

President Hutchinson turned back to the group in the

living room, and thoughtfully bit her index finger. "Well, in fact, that's part of the story," she said. "Not really part of the *same* story, but—well, there it is. I guess there's no sense holding back this information now, since it will all come out soon enough." She stopped again, once more fighting her unaccustomed awkwardness. "Claude Preen has stepped down as chairman of the history department," she announced. "Pending an investigation into—oh, God, it makes me sick to even say this about a Forshay professor! Plagiarism. *Plagiarism,* if you can believe that!"

And Diane Hutchinson was obliged to explain about the complaint received at the *Atlanta Chronicle of Modern History* from one Kjerstin Thorstad, who contacted the editors from her new teaching post at the University of Gothenburg, and demonstrated quite fully and devastatingly that Claude Preen had appropriated entire sections of Miss Thorstad's unpublished work for his recently-published article. All without permission, or any kind of attribution or acknowledgment. It was a colossal embarrassment. The *Atlanta Chronicle* had had to issue a retraction. There was talk of a lawsuit against Preen for damages. But beyond that, however, the President declared, he has disgraced himself and, by reflection, has disgraced Forshay College.

A stunned silence lingered in the living room, as the group absorbed the import of President Hutchinson's report. Fulda broke the silence. "By any chance, Margaret," she asked, "did you have anything to do with blowing the whistle on Preen's article?"

President Hutchinson held up her hand before Margaret could respond. "Fulda, we can't go into it further," she said. "As I said, it is an ongoing investigation. Claude will be given a chance to put his case, but in the meantime he's been suspended from all his responsibilities at the College." She then turned to Margaret, and smiled. "But your question does anticipate one piece of happy news out of Dr. Preen's predicament.

Everyone," she said brightly, "I would like to announce to you all that I have asked Margaret Viper to act as interim head of the history department, effective immediately." She turned and smiled at John Random. "Margaret's academic credentials, which have only recently been brought to my attention, are more than sufficient to qualify for this role. I think we can all agree that there is no one—myself included—who has put more of her life into the success of Forshay College. And, Margaret, although over these many years you may not previously have found an opportunity to put forward your very substantial achievements, I am delighted that you have agreed to accept this post." President Hutchinson beamed. "I can't tell you how happy I am about this."

Margaret Viper rose and shook the President's hand. She grinned down at Renata, still sitting on Denis's living room couch trying to make sense of this sudden realignment of her world. "So you see, Renata dear," Margaret said, the lenses of her eyeglasses glinting, *'I'll* be your boss now. Not Dr. Preen."

Renata suddenly bustled to her feet and flung her arms around Margaret in a grateful embrace. Renata's thoughtstreams resounded with the human turmoil of emotion. I hopped silently onto a side table behind her, looking to catch Margaret's eye over Renata's shoulder.

So you did all this, Margaret? I asked into her mind.

Of course, she replied.

The University of Paris degree? The green card? Everything?

Of course, she said.

Well done, then, I said. *Brava, Margaret.*

It was nothing, she said. *One just needs to know who to call, and what to do.*

Yes, I said, *and one also needs to know* when *to call, and* when *to do.*

Ah, she said, *when—indeed!*

The mood in Denis's living room was ecstatic; hands clapped Margaret and Renata on their shoulders, multiple hugs and kisses were exchanged. Even Mrs. Pearson, though not acquainted with the College personalities and politics, beamed at the general good will.

John Random edged his way into the group, and coughed. "I have one more thing to add to the list of surprises President Hutchinson has shared with us tonight," he said loudly. The small group quieted again, finding their seats once more in Denis's living room. "Another surprise," he continued, drawing an envelope from his jacket pocket. He handed the envelope to Renata. "One that no one here has heard about yet—not even you, Diane—no one except me, and Margaret." He smiled at Margaret. "And yes, Fulda, with this one, Margaret's fingerprints are all over it."

Renata gasped as she read the letter she had extracted from the envelope. "Oh my God!" she exclaimed. "I can't believe it! Margaret—Margaret, is this really true?"

Fulda and Lupe looked expectantly at John Random. "Well, you're not going to leave us hanging, are you John?" Fulda demanded.

John laughed, and looked at Renata, still staring dazed at the letter. "I won't ask Renata to read the letter to us," he said. "She seems like she is speechless at the moment. But I'm acquainted with its contents well enough. The letter is addressed to Renata Beaumanoir from the director of the Duke University Institute of Near Eastern Culture, and contains two pieces of information. First," he declaimed, beginning to sound like a lawyer addressing a courtroom, "the letter informs Renata that the Institute would be pleased to publish her article on Constantine XI in next fall's issue of the Institute's journal."

A thrill of excitement passed through the group at this news. Even the cat on the side table sat up and took notice.

"Oh, Miss Beaumanoir!" Lupe exclaimed. "How fantastic! And Beth and Lucy at the Store will be so pleased, too!"

Renata seemed trapped between laughter and tears. She could not answer; she squeezed Lupe's arm in response, and motioned to the letter.

John Random caught the gesture. "Yes, but that's only the first point. The second is even more interesting." He paused, looking from Margaret to Renata and back again, letting the dramatic moment build. "Because," he said, "the same Institute was so impressed by Miss Beaumanoir's article that the letter also inquires whether she would be free to fill a vacancy that has just occurred in a joint fellowship underwritten by the Institute and the Turkish-American Historical Society in New York. Six months of historical and archeological research in Istanbul. A full stipend, for Miss Beaumanoir and an undergraduate research assistant of her choice."

"My goodness!" President Hutchinson exclaimed.

"Wow," said Fulda, impressed.

"Seriously?" said Denis.

"That's brilliant!" burst Mrs. Pearson.

"But," said John Random, "this requires an immediate reply. The fellowship starts in early July. Just a few weeks from now." He turned to President Hutchinson. "It would require the approval of the College. For Miss Beaumanoir's absence. And Miss Hernandez-Vega's."

Lupe looked up quickly. "Me?" she stuttered.

Random looked back at her. "Well, it is Miss Beaumanoir's choice, of course," he said, "but I happened to be provided the privilege of reading Miss Hernandez-Vega's exam essay"—he shot a look toward Margaret—"and I couldn't think of a better candidate." He turned to President Hutchinson. "Diane, I know it must seem strange to get your junior instructor back suddenly, and then just as suddenly have her request a leave for six months. But this is quite an opportunity. And, whatever damage Claude Preen may have done to the reputation of Forshay's history department, this fellowship and publication would seem to go some distance to recoup."

He smiled. "Miss Beaumanoir is, after all, working for Forshay College again. It's Forshay College that she'll be representing."

President Hutchinson smiled. "Well, this is the easiest decision I've had to make in a long time," she said. "Of course it's OK with me. I think this whole thing is remarkable. Just wonderful!" She reached out for Renata's hand once again. "Renata, we're all so very proud of you."

Fulda chuckled. "And isn't it lucky that you just now happened to get your passport straightened out?" she said. "Imagine that!"

"Yes," Margaret Viper said, "imagine that."

Margaret caught my eye again, and smiled.

Margaret, this was all you too, wasn't it? I said in her mind.

I don't know what you mean, she replied. *Renata's article is wholly a product of her own intelligence. Every word of it is hers.*

Oh, come on! I persisted. *A serendipitous vacancy in a prestigious fellowship? Am I to believe that was just luck?*

I happen to know that you don't believe in luck, Cat, any more than you believe in coincidence. Margaret smiled beatifically. *Besides, if the quality wasn't there,* she said, *all the luck in the world wouldn't help.*

Lupe looked at Renata. "Miss Beaumanoir, if you choose to take me on the fellowship, I promise I would work very hard," she said. She lowered her eyes. "It would just be so perfect," Lupe said quietly.

Renata smiled. I saw a tear escape and run down her cheek from her eyes—from Renata's soft, brown, ever-so-human eyes. "Yes," she said, smiling though her voice broke, "yes, Lupe, that would be perfect."

I sat and watched, the inevitable slight fragrance of roses lingering. I was so happy I purred. Humans are just fascinating.

CHAPTER TWENTY-ONE

I did let the timeslide in mid-14th century France continue to run for a time, although after Renata lost track of Matthieu the purposefulness of the timeslide subsided. Renata found her way back to Josselin, again walking by night and hiding in the thick banks of foliage in the Breton forests during the daytime brightness. She found the Doctor in his apothecary shop, and recognized him to be one of the living dead like herself. He took her under his guidance, as I knew he would. He even took her with him a few weeks later, when he abandoned plague-ravaged Josselin for the weeks-long oxcart journey to Paris, the Doctor's jars and bottles rattling in the cart he drove. And, most interestingly, he shared with her doses of a new tincture he had prepared, one that dispelled the vampire's terror of the day and even made it possible to walk about, unshrouded, in the light. The Doctor wanted to go to the University to study and improve his formulas. Renata proved to be a most attentive and studious pupil. No one seemed to miss them in Josselin—Father Bertrand, I believe, later described for Lady Marguerite his tender ministrations to her sister and her nephew just before the pestilence had claimed them as victims, as it had claimed her husband Cedrane Verane and their other children before. The town must have assumed that their bodies had found their way to the burning place by the river. As for the Doctor and Renata, I already knew that they were to continue in Paris for many, many years.

And so, there did not seem to be a reason not to abandon the extended timeslide entirely now. Renata still had the timeguide, her star ring—if I needed to return to that timeslide along that particular crease in time, I knew what to do. I left the Doctor and Renata to their history together and closed off the time pathway, returning to my native timeframe and once again becoming only the rather inconspicuous pet of a college teacher in a small Southern town. And I was able to catch up on my napping.

And then I found myself a few weeks later packed into a cloth and leather cat carrier for the trip to Turkey. I could, of course, have found a way to travel to Istanbul ahead of them, in my peculiar way, but I thought it would be more illuminating as a scientist—and, I admit it, more fun—to travel with them on the plane. Besides, the cat carrier was comfortable enough; not so very different from Renata's canvas bag, really, except that it had a little mesh window in the side that I could press my pink nose against, and see out of the bag. I wouldn't be allowed to travel in my usual posture, head popped out the top of the bag so I could look around—apparently, the international air transport authorities insist on travelers keeping the tops of their cat carriers zipped shut. So, the mesh porthole was a reasonable compromise, not so good for getting a full horizon view, but certainly better than no window at all.

Tickets, visas, animal quarantine regulations for small, tiger-striped cats—I didn't bother myself with any of these details, because I learned very soon after the dinner party at Denis's house that Margaret was still on the case. I was sure she would take care of everything—whether the details would be accomplished in the current timeframe or another. In fact, bolstered by her new prestige as Acting

Head of the Department of History, and by her newly-appreciated role as college fixer—and, I suspected, bankrolled by a quiet check from John Random—Margaret had coolly informed the college administration that she was going to accompany Renata and Lupe on their trip out, and spend two or three weeks in Turkey with them there. Liaison with the Institute members at the University of Istanbul, I think, was the formula she finally settled on. President Hutchinson readily agreed; even if it were just a junket, certainly Margaret Viper after all those years of service had richly earned such a consideration. I thought Margaret was just excited—like a girl whose sisters were going off to a party, the prospect was just too thrilling for Margaret not to want to go along too.

So it was that I found Margaret sitting in the seat next to me on the overnight Lufthansa flight to Munich, where we would change to the Turkish Airlines flight to Istanbul. We were in the inside seats of the wide-bodied jet, the lights darkened now and the cabin beginning to be suffused with the quiet sounds of humans drowsing. Renata had pulled my cat carrier out from under the row in front, and placed it on an empty middle seat, but through my mesh window I could see little—the tray table in front of me, above that and to the side, an illuminated screen showing a tiny jet superimposed against a map, tracking our progress. Not even halfway there. No wonder Margaret had decided to sit beside me in the quiet plane. There was plenty of time to have a nice long chat—through our thoughtstreams, of course. I couldn't see her in the seat beside me, but I could hear her mind perfectly. It simply felt good to be able to speak freely, about what I knew, about the events that had transpired, about what may lie ahead.

So, I said. *You were the snake, weren't you? On the mountain.*

Of course, she said. *It was an extinct species, but I had to find a form that was big enough for the purpose. And, a viper, of course.*

Of course.

One likes to maintain a certain stylistic consistency, doesn't one?

I couldn't help but smile to myself at this. *And is that your native form, Margaret? A snake? Or is your native form human?*

I could feel Margaret giving me her schoolmistress look of disapproval. *That is an extremely personal question to ask, Cat,* she said, *and it's none of your business. However, since you have never learned how to engage our kind in polite conversation I will overlook it this time.*

Slightly discomfited, I changed the subject. *And now,* I said, *you're traveling with Renata and Lupe to Turkey. Do you speak any Turkish?*

Of course, Margaret replied. *Perfectly.*

Did you timeslide to Turkey?

Well, she said, *I do remember the time that I spent in Turkey quite well, but I don't think I have timeslid there yet. So I expect I will soon. And that will explain the memory I have of it.*

I paused, reflecting.

So that means that your natural timeframe is somewhere in the future?

That's right, she said. *For me, I am in a timeslide now.*

I thought about this. *I shouldn't ever try to explain that to the humans,* I said, *not that you ever would. But I think they will find it all a bit confusing. The language, though—that will be handy. I don't think Renata or Lupe have any Turkish, although I think the English and French and Spanish will take them fairly far.* I stretched my paws. *Renata and Lupe must think you're able to do almost anything, by now.*

How so?

Well, the way you fixed the passports, and the green card, and the transcripts from the Sorbonne—you know.

Yes, Margaret said. *I rather enjoyed talking to the registrar at the Sorbonne. She was so intrigued to discover that had been two graduates with the same name, three hundred years apart.*

So, did Renata really get her degrees there in 1679?

Yes, Margaret said. *Well, that was the second time she attended. They didn't check further back, or they might have found records of her at the University in Paris in 1354 or thereabout. Studying under a locally famous alchemist and physician named Arcadius of Civitavecchia. Although, based on what I have gleaned of your timeslide, Cat, I am not telling you anything you don't already know.* She paused, and shifted in her seat. *You know, Cat,* she said, *you could have done all that groundwork yourself. In fact, I am a little surprised that you never undertook to take any hand in it, the whole year that Renata was at Forshay. I really don't see why you stayed so aloof.*

I thought for a moment before answering. *I consider myself a scientist, Margaret,* I replied. *In science, if the observer interferes with the experiment, then surely the results are unreliable.*

She laughed sharply—so sharply, indeed, that I thought for a moment that she must have vocalized the laugh in the conventional way. I pressed my nose against the mesh window to see if the noise had awakened any of the passengers, but I concluded that it had just been a thoughtstream—inaudible to any but me.

Observer? Science? Is that what this is to you? she demanded. *Do you really think, my dear Cat, that you can isolate yourself so perfectly? That you do not change history?*

I am an observer, I said. *I try to follow scientific method. My pleasure is the study of humans. I find humans to be of infinite interest. And so, when I study them, I try not to change their history.*

Oh, we all change history, Margaret said. *Changing or not changing isn't the trick. The trick is to retain the history. To remember it.*

I considered this.

We have the same problem that the vampires do, you know, she continued. *Time—too much time. We stand apart from it, we can slide through it, beyond it. We are both in time and detached from time. And so we are prey to the danger of not respecting time.* She paused for a moment, considering. *You could describe it by economics, Cat,* she continued. *A mortal has a tiny, finite supply of time, and thus the value of time is very dear. But an immortal has an oversupply of time—and it is too easy for us to allow the value of time to be debased. We can lose time; we can lose our memory.*

And so, you have no qualms about interfering in the history of mortal humans? I pressed.

Why should I? she answered. *If I may timeslide tomorrow and affect history yesterday, well then, it's already happened, hasn't it? It's in the past, as well as the future. Just as I am perfectly confident that in the near future I will timeslide in order to learn the highly cultured, idiomatic Turkish I already seem to know.*

None of this was news to me, but I still had questions. *But why Istanbul, Margaret?* I asked. *I know it's a beautiful city—or at least it was when I lived there fifteen hundred years ago. But it seems an arbitrary choice of destination to go to evade the Vampire Council.*

Margaret seemed to grin. *I hope you don't think that the occurrence of this trip is somehow random,* she said. *Or that the choice of Istanbul as our destination is some kind of coincidence.*

The Doctor did say something, I replied. *He said that Renata's article about Constantine XI and the fall of Constantinople tipped off Vesta. That the legends of Constantine and the Sable were the same.*

That's true enough, Margaret said. *But I'll share with you something that even the Doctor doesn't know. Something that it would be safer if our vampire friends did not fully appreciate yet.* She reached into a pocket and unfolded a piece of paper, holding it before my mesh window for me to peruse. It was an abstract from a scholarly Turkish archeological journal, summarizing a different article—this one about a recently-found cache of artifacts and documents that had been discovered in a hidden niche in the land walls outside Istanbul.

This is what the fellowship is researching, Margaret said. *And if Renata's mind is urging her toward the history of Istanbul so strongly, at just this moment, I had to wonder if this discovery was somehow related. After all, Renata is a unique vampire adept— neither of us really knows the power of her suppressed memory.*

I suddenly saw what Margaret was driving at. *And you think that these artifacts may contain something that could act as a new timeguide? To lead us to the Sable?*

You'll have to tell us that, Cat. You're the one with the bond to Renata, and through her to Matthieu.

I thought this over. *But if Vesta was aware of Renata's article, might she not know about this other article as well? And the discovery in Istanbul?*

I heard Margaret give a muffled snort of laughter. *We're not talking about scholars, Cat,* she said. *Vesta's foolish assistants found Renata's article because it was lying out in the open, on her kitchen table. I don't think the Vampire Council is keeping up with the archeological literature.*

We paused, and I thought about where all this might lead. *Aren't you taking a pretty heavy hand in all this, Margaret? I mean, all this interfering in Renata's history—is all this, all your interfering now, with Renata and Lupe, and all the rest—is this really justified? Or is it just a recreational timeslide for you, Margaret?*

She laughed again. *It's all a timeslide, Cat—as I already said. But that doesn't mean that I am flippant. I take what I am doing in this timeframe very seriously. I have been laying the groundwork for this for years, since the spring of 1970, when I first came to Forshay College. Just a few years after I had heard about the destruction of the Doctor Movement in New York by the Vampire Council. I knew, of course—I knew that Renata would come to Forshay some forty or more years later. That the Vampire Council would find her. Even that she would be accompanied by a Timeslider cat.*

I was surprised. *You knew that—all along you knew that? That you and I were both—well, that I was one of us?*

My mind could feel her smile. *That we are both Timesliders?* she asked. *Yes, of course. I knew all along that you were a Timeslider.*

You know, I said, *not to be a pedant, but we don't use that word.*

What word? she asked. *You mean 'Timeslider'?*

Yes.

Well, you just say that because you've never met another of our kind, Margaret said. *Now that we have found each other, we'll need a referent, won't we? A way to talk about another one of us. Besides,* she said, as I felt her settle back into her seat for a nap, *I quite like the word 'Timeslider'. I think it's sporty.*

I had to admit that I had never really looked at it like that. I could overlook my distaste for the word, I thought—it was worth it to now know one other person, among all the timestreams of memory, who was like me. I pawed at the cushions on the bottom of my cat carrier, preparing to take a nap myself.

Well, it'll be good to take this trip, Margaret, I said. Although I could not see her, I could tell that she had leaned her head back, eyes closed. *We can all get away from Forshay for a little while. And get away from the Vampire Council.*

Get away? Margaret said, her thoughtstreams getting sleepy. *Don't think you can relax now. Don't get too comfortable. Because we're not getting away, my dear Cat. We're going deeper.*

It was a four hour layover in the Munich airport, waiting for the Turkish Airlines connection to Istanbul. Boredom, relieved only somewhat by the minor spectacle of Renata at the bureau de change window insisting on exchanging dollars for Deutschemarks. Apparently a bit of recent European history had passed her by. Margaret gently pulled her and Lupe from the line, and gave them each some of the euros she had bought before she left. Lupe carried my cat carrier, and I watched the human traffic in the terminal swish by my mesh window, at approximately hip-pocket level. For a scientific observer of humans, it was a lovely way to travel.

We weren't going through customs yet, so we had to stay in the terminal. There was a coffee shop there, and we appropriated a table where the three women could relax and dawdle over hot coffee or chocolate, waiting for the clock to move. Lupe put my cat carrier on the table, and the three of them walked across the café to order. My mesh window faced a glass-fronted pastry case on the far wall, displaying the shop's wares: *Ausgezogene, Krapfen, Sacher Torte, Blechkuchen*.

I heard a chair scrape at the table beside me, as someone sat down. The person seemed to take his ease; although I could not see to the side of me, through my mesh window I could glimpse his long legs stretched before him and crossed at the ankles—expensive-looking, sharply creased gray trousers, fine black shoes. I looked across the room, hoping to see the man reflected in the glass of the pastry display case. The reflection was broken up by the traffic and movement in the shop, but I could make out the long dark suit, the black tie, the hat. The dark sunglasses.

The man's voice found my mind. As I recognized it, I was startled—I know I probably shouldn't have been, I probably should have been expecting the Doctor to make an appearance, but it caught me off guard. Well, a little.

Hello, Cat, the voice spoke into my mind.

Doctor! I couldn't articulate a word for several moments. *Doctor—you've become material again! I can't believe it! I wasn't sure I'd ever see you again.*

Well, you didn't expect me to stay in that mirror, did you? the Doctor said. *Yes, I have regained a corporeal presence.* He plucked at the sleeves of his expensive suit. *Not bad, don't you think?*

Very nice, I said. *Renata will be glad to see you looking so dapper and—whole. We really thought you were gone. I know Renata thinks so.*

You of all cats should understand, the Doctor said, *that the information never dies. Yes, the Vampire Council did annihilate me, or at least the body that I had inhabited at that time. But they have no respect for memory. That's why they will never understand my continuing presence.*

I was silent for a moment, trying to take it all in. It was still difficult to me to reconcile the Doctor's presence with my memory of his annihilation at Lake Marion, even though I knew he had spoken to me from the timegap in the mirror's reflection.

The Doctor spoke again, impatient at my extended silence. *Look, my friend,* he said, *I only have a few moments. It would not be good for Renata to see me just now. It's safer for her not to know that have regained my physical presence—in case the Council is still shadowing either of us. But I needed to speak with you.* He paused. *I guess I should really thank you for what you've done.*

I felt abashed. *I needed no prompting, Doctor,* I said. *Renata has become quite dear to me.*

The Doctor chuckled. *I would say in that case that perhaps the humans have taught the Timeslider something!* He regained his serious tone, and continued. *But I—we—will need your help further, I'm afraid. Both back at Forshay College as well as with Renata. You know, of course, that I transmitted information about the thanadoxicil to one of the teachers at Forshay?*

Yes, I replied, *yes, I was there.*

Well, it had to be done, given the circumstances, but that information is now out—beyond my direct control. It is in the hands of that teacher at Forshay.

Teachers, I corrected him. *There are two teachers who know about it. Denis Pearson shared the information with Fulda Myerson.*

I heard the Doctor sigh. *Yes, I suppose that was inevitable. And just as well, since Mr. Pearson didn't turn out to be a chemistry scholar after all—although I am still not sure how I made that mistake. But no matter—they have the information now. And it will now make their lives rather…complicated.*

The Doctor paused. *I'll need to call upon your special abilities from time to time. And Margaret's. If, that is, you're willing to help us.*

I thought about this. Suddenly a piece of the puzzle clicked into place. *Margaret,* I exclaimed into his mind. *She's who you meant when you talked about 'your' Timeslider, isn't she?*

Yes, of course, Cat, the Doctor replied.

And, I said, another long-puzzling question suddenly resolving itself in my mind, *she must have been the way you managed to distribute the thanadoxicil, isn't she? You got your Timeslider to do it!*

I felt the Doctor smile. *Yes again, Cat,* he said gently, *she's been my regular Santa Claus for decades now. I thought you had figured that out a long time ago.* He paused, and then renewed his original question, more urgently. *So, Cat—are you willing to help us?*

I wasn't sure exactly what he was asking for—I would certainly do anything I could to help Renata evade the Vampire Council, but I got the impression that the Doctor was talking more broadly. I glanced at his reflection in the glass case, and saw him looking about himself nervously—he was anxious to go. If I wanted to get answers to some pointed questions, now would have to be the time.

Doctor, I said through his mind, *what is this all about? I mean, just what are you trying to do?* He did not answer—I wondered if he was taken aback by the blunt question. But I brazened on. *The Doctor Movement—what is it, anyway, and why is the Vampire Council so keen to suppress it? And sending me on the timeslide to find out about the Sable—had you already known that it was Renata's son, Matthieu?*

There was a pause, and then the Doctor chuckled. *And you want your answer in twenty words or less, I suppose? Well, I can't give you all the detail before our women friends return, but let me tell you what I can.*

And so he explained—in more than twenty words, yes, but still with admirable economy. The Doctor explained that the Doctor Movement was never really intended to be a movement at all, not in any political sense anyway. The Doctor had long ago discovered what he now called thanadoxicil—it was called by many other, more poetical, more alchemical names over the centuries—but it was centuries more before he recognized the real potential of the drug. Slowly, however, he did learn what thanadoxicil could do, that it could revert vampires back into a human state, and allow them to live among the mortal humans again, as if they were mortal themselves. And it was this ability to recapture some essence of their former mortality—even artificially, impermanently, through the drug—that seemed to lead to something even grander. For the vampires who used the Doctor's thanadoxicil found that the drug had the power to give back to them a semblance of their memory, and through that to regain a shadow of their essential humanity.

It's the immortality, the Doctor said. *An immortal being might maintain its memory, but why bother? The accumulating data of unending ages is a burden. And the endlessness of available time—it makes for a static mind, a lazy mind, selfish, lethargic, incapable of strong bonds. Vesta Letalia and her allies on the Vampire Council know that. The lazy and selfish are easily dominated, and the Vampire Council slowly, over centuries, millennia, tried to arrogate to itself all authority, all power over the vampire nation, as they were pleased to call us. And the vampires, frankly, having no imagination and no better ideas, let them take that power.*

Power? I asked. *Then this is a power struggle? A civil war?*

Yes, in a way, the Doctor replied. *When I began my thanadoxicil practice in New York in 1966, I guess I was naïve—it did not occur to me what a threat the Council would perceive. I guess I was under the influence of the times. Self-exploration and all that—what the mortal humans were talking about all over New York in those days. Their own drugs, harmful, destructive drugs that they used on themselves. I thought, here was a way to help my nation, with a drug I had learned had great benefit.* He paused, and I heard him exhale loudly. *The Council hit back very hard. Almost all of the vampires who had ever tried the thanadoxicil were annihilated. And none of them were able to flee to mirrors. Renata escaped, though, as did I. I don't think there were any others. Annihilation,* he mused, *seems to be the Vampire Council's answer to everything.*

But what's changed, Doctor? What about these new events? I asked. *I never understood Charleston—why did you and Renata consent to appear before the Council at all? Why not keep hiding? Running from them? And when you said to the Council that you didn't believe in the Sable, was that true? What do you know about the Sable?*

Those are all good questions, my dear Cat, the Doctor said, *especially the last one. The fact is, I do not have any knowledge of the Sable—although I suspect that I may once have done. It's a memory, alas, that I have been able neither to retain nor to resuscitate. But I fear the answer. Vesta seems to be convinced that the Sable is real. Margaret was only able to pass along the barest sketch of your recent timeslide, Cat,* he said, *but she said that you obtained information about the Sable—information that such a thing once really existed—and that it was in fact Renata's son from her mortal life.* The Doctor paused, then asked me with urgency, but as if he feared the answer, *And is it possible that Renata's son is the great adept, the master of the vampire legion?* Despite his asking the question telepathically, the Doctor seemed breathless.

I had to give him the disappointing news. *I could not find out,* I said. *The timeguide I followed only took me so far, and the timeslide didn't follow Matthieu. But,* I continued, *he didn't seem to be very fearsome. More like a very inexperienced boy.*

But when he left you, the Doctor demanded, *did he go with Vesta? Or with others? Or alone?*

He went with Vesta, I replied. *But I learned something else that you should know, Doctor. I learned who Renata's adept master was.* I paused, wondering if giving the Doctor nothing but bad news was a kind thing to do, but I continued. I was a scientist, and the facts must be respected. *Her master was Vesta herself. Renata rebelled, even though she doesn't seem to have retained memory of that. Vesta, however, still seeks to assert a hold on her.*

I saw the reflection in glass case put his face in his hands. The Doctor was silent for a moment, and then spoke to me again. *So be it,* he said bravely. *And the information you have given me so far is of incalculable value. But,* he continued, *we must find a way to follow Matthieu. We must find if he really has become the master that Vesta believes him to be. All of our lives may depend on it.*

And how do we do that? I asked.

I could feel the Doctor give a baleful smile. *The one I might tender that question to, Cat, is...you.*

I thought of what Margaret had told me, but I pretended shock. *Me?*

Yes you. Or Margaret Viper. The Timesliders—as I understand Margaret would permit me to call you. The Doctor chuckled. *I do not have your special abilities, Cat, I am a simple vampire. Immortal, like the rest of us. But I want my memory back, Cat. When time is not valued it is not cherished. When it is not cherished, there is no memory, no history. And memory, our sense of ourselves in time, is what allows us to love that which we find in time. It's the very limitation of human time that makes it rare and precious, that makes the lives it encompasses worthy of love. I want to regain such time, Cat, because I want to regain memory. I want to regain love. And I don't want the Vampire Council—or Vesta, or any Sable—to thwart me in that.*

How does the timesliding help that?

I'm not sure, he mused. *I only know that we must find the Sable, and that the search must be made in many timeframes, many places. All over spacetime. And who else but a Timeslider could navigate that?*

The Doctor tapped the top of my cat carrier—a familiar gesture, as if he were shaking my hand, or clasping me by the shoulder. *I must leave you now, Cat,* he said. *But I think we'll see each other again soon. Istanbul,* he said thoughtfully. *I've been looking forward to getting back to Istanbul. Perhaps I shall see you on the Theodosian Walls, Cat.* I felt him smile. *Perhaps I already have.*

I did not see which way the Doctor went when he disappeared back into the airport crowds. Nor did I have much time for reflection about what he said. I did not like the idea of a vampire power struggle, or the idea that the slight, scarred-cheeked boy I had seen playing soldier on the horse at the Mauron battlefield might have become a threat to us all. Nor did I really get what he said about vampires regaining their memory. But, I did remember the changes I had noticed in Renata, just over the past weeks—the dreams, the tears. Most especially, the friendships. To see her with Lupe, you would think they were two sisters, one elder, one younger, not a teacher and her research assistant. And I had to search my own feelings, something that, as a scientist, maybe I was ill-equipped to do. But yes, I was willing to take Renata's part—I had developed that much of an attachment to her. It was unscientific, perhaps, but maybe none of this is about science in isolation. Well, in that case, perhaps a Timeslider is what Renata needs to reclaim her memory, her history. The Timesliders remember—we sometimes feel as if we are nothing but memory. Memory will never die, history will never die, as long as the Timesliders do not die. And the Timesliders will never die.

"Terminal Two, North," Lupe said as she returned to the table. "Istanbul-Atatürk Airport. We should go—the plane boards soon!" The bright excitement of exploration was in her voice. She was thrilled.

"We have plenty of time," Renata said. "But we can take the coffee to the gate and wait there, if you like."

"Yes," Margaret said, "why not?" I heard her project a quick thoughtstream into my mind. *Are you ready, Cat?*

Lupe had already grabbed the handles of the cat carrier and was walking briskly ahead. The scene outside my little mesh window swirled again with the human traffic and bustle of the airport, the happy hum of voyaging.

We were on our way.

ABOUT THE AUTHOR

Cherokee Stein Ross is the pen name of the author of *Timeslider*, and creator of the Timeslider Cat. In addition to being a competition-level ballroom dancer and former holder of the World Boxing Association welterweight championship (at least until a certain unpleasantness arose which we won't go into (she was robbed!)), the author was also youngest person ever to receive a Ph.D in both high-energy particle physics and advanced mathematics (concentration in Fourier analysis) from the Massachusetts Institute of Technology. A multi-billionaire, the author has used her vast wealth and power to accomplish innumerable unpublicized works of humanitarianism for which she expects no commendation—but let's just say that much of sub-Saharan Africa currently owes its continued existence to her. A confidential advisor to each of the last five United States presidents, if she ever gets drunk and talks to you at a party, there is a better than even chance that the CIA may be obliged to kill you.

Actually, all that is a lie—one of the benefits of a pen name is that you get to make up your own biography, and no one is the wiser. In fact, the author is a bit of a bore, including being an admitted history nerd. She is currently at work on the second Timeslider Cat novel, *The Cats of Istanbul*. She divides her time between North Carolina, New York and Boston.

www.ingramcontent.com/pod-product-compliance
Lightning Source LLC
Chambersburg PA
CBHW051320250626
47155CB00007B/2395